A MARKHAM SISTERS COLLECTION - IJKL

DIANA XARISSA

Contents

ISBN: 1986269728
ISBN -13: 978-1986269728

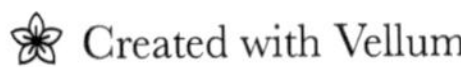

The Irwin Case

A MARKHAM SISTERS COZY MYSTERY NOVELLA

Created with Vellum

Author's Note

Welcome to the ninth Markham Sisters novella. I hope you've been having as much fun reading them as I have been having writing them. If this is the first one you've picked up, I do recommend that you read them in order, but they should stand on their own if you prefer not to do that.

The novellas begin and end with parts of Janet's letters to Bessie Cubbon, Janet's friend on the Isle of Man. You don't need to read the Isle of Man Cozy Mystery series in order to enjoy these novellas, though.

The stories are set in Derbyshire in the United Kingdom, and I do use English spelling and terms. There is a short glossary at the end of the book to help readers with some of the words I use frequently. There is also a page of notes about things that might not be familiar for readers outside of the UK. As I grew up in the US and have now been living back there for several years, I'm afraid more and more Americanisms are sneaking into my books. I do my best to eliminate them, however.

This is a work of fiction and all of the characters are fictional creations. Any resemblance that they may share with any real person, living or dead, is entirely coincidental. The sisters live in a fictional village in Derbyshire. Although some shops or businesses may bear some resemblance to real-life businesses, that is also coincidental.

I love hearing from my readers. Please get in touch if you have any comments or questions. All of my contact details are available in the back of the book.

17th April 1999

Dearest Bessie,

I can't quite believe that less than a month from today we will be arriving on the Isle of Man for a lovely holiday. Joan was reluctant to close the bed and breakfast, but I twisted her arm. As far as I'm concerned, we both need a holiday before the busy summer seasons starts. We'll probably need another one after the summer, but I'm not going to mention that to Joan yet.

Paul has gone back to London, which makes the house feel quite empty, although we have had guests nearly every weekend since Edward's visit. My darling kitten, Aggie, seems to prefer the house when it is just us, a sentiment you know I share. Still, the business seems to be doing well and Joan enjoys it, so I mustn't complain.

We had another little bit of excitement here lately, although nothing like what you've been dealing with. It all started when a very nice older couple asked if they could stay an extra night.

Chapter 1

"As we're both retired, we have the luxury of indulging ourselves," Jacob Mills told Joan. "If you're sure you don't mind, we'd really like to stay an extra night."

"I don't mind," Joan told him. "We've no one else arriving for a few days. You and Harriet are welcome to stay tonight."

"Thank you," the man beamed. "We've at least two more stately homes we want to visit. We should be able to get to them both today."

"I'm glad we can accommodate you," Joan said.

"I'll just go and tell Harriet she doesn't need to pack," the man replied. "We'll be down for breakfast in about ten minutes, if that's okay."

"It's fine," Joan replied.

The man walked out of the room. Janet got to her feet and peeked out of the kitchen doorway to make sure that he'd gone.

Joan and Janet Markham were both retired primary school-teachers. Neither had ever married, and they had planned to travel and enjoy life once they'd left work. Janet had been shocked when Joan had admitted to having had a lifelong desire to own a bed and breakfast. When the sisters had stumbled across Doveby House, a seventeenth-century manor house with its own small library, Joan had been able to persuade her sister to use their recent inheritance to purchase the place. After several months of welcoming guests, Janet still wasn't sure they'd made the right decision.

"I don't want them to stay another night," Janet said to her older sister. "You're going out tonight, which means I'll have to deal with them."

"They're a lovely couple," Joan said, beginning to assemble the ingredients she needed to make breakfast for their guests.

"They are lovely," Janet admitted. "But they talk so much. I thought I was going to fall asleep last night when they insisted on telling us every single detail of their day."

"Jacob did go on a bit, didn't he?"

"And when he finally finished, Harriet jumped in with another twenty minutes about furniture and paintings and probably other things, but I stopped listening."

Joan sighed. "I can cancel my plans for tonight if you want me to," she said. "I know the bed and breakfast is mostly my concern. I'll take care of the guests."

"You've been looking forward to tonight for weeks," Janet said. "Michael will never forgive me if I make you cancel."

"Michael understands that my work comes first."

"No, he doesn't. And as the property and the business belong to both of us, I should do my fair share of the work. You do all of the cooking and most of the cleaning. I suppose I can listen to boring guests drone on and on about their lives."

Joan gave her sister a hug. "Thank you," she said. "I really would hate to disappoint Michael, especially on such short notice."

Janet had had a few boyfriends in her youth, but Joan had never dated. Both sisters were still slightly surprised that Joan was the one who'd found a boyfriend when they'd settled into their new home. Michael Donaldson was a widower who lived in a semi-detached property across the road from Doveby House.

He was a retired chemist, and tonight he was being given some sort of award from some company with which he'd formerly done regular business. Apparently, it was rather important, and Michael was excited but nervous. He'd been delighted when he'd been told he could bring a guest. Joan had spent ages trying to work out what to wear. There was no way Janet could make her sister miss the evening.

When Jacob and Harriet came down for breakfast a few minutes later, Janet was still on her feet. "Right, well, I'll go and get the shopping done, then," she said brightly. "I hope you two have a lovely time today. I'll see you tonight."

"I forgot all about paying for the extra night," Jacob said. "Is it okay if we put it on our credit card?"

Joan looked at Janet, who sighed. Their guests didn't often pay by credit card, but the sisters had recently arranged things to allow them to more easily process card payments, just in case guests started asking. The little machine that processed the cards wasn't terribly complicated, but for some reason Joan simply couldn't get it work, at least not usually. Janet didn't have any trouble with it, so she usually handled the transactions.

"I can do that for you," Janet said, hoping she might still slip away before either Jacob or Harriet started talking.

Joan told her the amount, and Janet took the card into the library. They'd felt it was best to have the equipment in a more public area than one of the sisters' bedrooms, and the library was able to be locked, so that was where it had been installed. Janet ran the card through the machine and entered the amount. She waited patiently for the receipt to print. Nothing happened. She peered at the machine's screen.

"Card Declined," it read.

Janet frowned and sat down in the nearest chair. How was she going to tell sweet Jacob Mills that his credit card had been turned down? The man was in his seventies and a little bit hard of hearing. This was going to be uncomfortable, she thought.

Harriet and Jacob were digging into their breakfast when Janet walked back in. "I'm awfully sorry," she said. "But the card has been declined."

Harriet looked up at her and blinked several times. "But that doesn't make any sense," she said. "We've only put a few meals on it since we've been here, and I paid it off before we left home."

"I'm sorry," Janet said. "I can only tell you what the little machine said. It doesn't give any reasons."

Harriet looked at Jacob and frowned. "We'd better ring the credit card company," she said. "There must be something wrong."

"Maybe we should go home," Jacob replied. "I don't want to try to ring them from here, and I won't be able to stop worrying until we know what's going on."

"Yes, I think you're right," Harriet said sadly. "We were meant to be going home today anyway. We should go home and get this sorted."

"I'm awfully sorry," Jacob said. "I suppose we won't need the extra night after all."

"That's no problem," Joan said. "I just hope you can get everything worked out quickly and easily."

"Yes, me, too," Harriet said worriedly.

The pair seemed too upset to talk as they finished their breakfast and then headed back up to their room to pack. Janet helped her sister clear the table.

"I wonder what's wrong with their credit card," Joan said. "Are you sure you didn't do something wrong with the machine?"

"I'm quite sure," Janet replied. "The machine said 'card declined,' which I've never seen before. It didn't tell me anything more than that."

"It looks as if you'll get your quiet evening on your own tonight, then," Joan said, sounding faintly accusatory.

"I didn't want a quiet evening alone at the expense of Jacob and Harriet," Janet told her. "I just hope everything is okay with their card."

"Maybe their payment didn't process properly," Joan mused.

"Or maybe the company saw that the card was being used in Derbyshire and got worried that it had been stolen," Janet suggested.

"I hope it all works out," Joan said. "Would it be strange if I asked them to ring me and let me know?"

Janet thought about it for a minute. "I think it might be," she told her sister.

Joan nodded. "You're probably right."

A few minutes later the sisters walked the couple to the door. "I hope you enjoyed your visit," Joan said.

"Oh, we did, very much," Harriet replied. "We're hoping to come again soon, maybe in the summer. We'll ring you once we've made plans."

"We'd enjoy having you again," Joan told her.

Janet shut the door behind the pair and blew out a sigh. "The house always feels a little bit different when we have guests," she told her sister.

"You didn't complain when Edward was here," Joan remarked.

Janet flushed. "Edward is more like a friend than a guest," she said, hoping that would end the conversation about the man who'd been to stay twice. He was handsome, intelligent and more than a little mysterious. He'd told Janet that he worked for a secret government agency, and she had no reason to doubt him.

"Yes, well, I hope you'll come to enjoy having guests more, as it looks as if we're going to have a busy summer."

"At least we get a week away before we get too busy," Janet said.

"I was thinking, actually, that maybe we shouldn't go away in May," Joan told her. "I'm sure we could book guests here if we decided to stay."

"No." Janet said firmly. "I'm happy to help you run the bed and breakfast and happy to welcome guests whenever we can get them, but I'm not giving up my one week of holiday this year. We used to get six or seven weeks of holiday every summer when we were teaching. One single week isn't too much to ask."

Joan looked as if she wanted to argue, but she pressed her lips together and simply nodded.

"Anyway, I've booked our holiday cottage and asked for the cottage closest to Bessie's," Janet said. "I'm sure we're going to have a wonderful time."

"I'm sure it will be nice," Joan said a bit stiffly.

"And now I really am going to the supermarket," Janet said.

"There isn't much of a list," Joan told her. "Our next guests aren't due until Saturday, and I'm out tonight and tomorrow night as well."

"So I need to get myself something for dinner both evenings," Janet said. "And maybe a few small treats as well."

"I don't know that you need any treats," Joan said, giving her sister a sideways glance.

Janet flushed. The sisters were about the same height, but for some reason Joan always managed to remain thin, even while she cooked and baked every day. Janet, on the other hand, was curvier, even though all she did was eat what her sister had prepared.

"I'll be back for lunch," Janet promised as she found her car keys and checked that her wallet was in her handbag.

"Meeroww?" a small voice said.

"Yes, darling, the guests have gone," Janet told the kitten who was peering around the corner into the room. "You can come out and play now."

"Meerreewww," Aggie replied, leaping into the air and then bouncing her way across the floor and into the kitchen.

"I think you must be training her to dislike guests," Joan remarked.

"She liked Paul," Janet said, referring to the young man who had left recently after an extended stay. "And she liked Edward."

"As she was a gift from Edward, it's just as well that she liked him. And everyone likes Paul. He's a lovely young man."

"He is," Janet agreed. "And the house still feels rather empty without him."

A recent fire had closed the local Doveby Dale grocer's, which meant that Janet had to drive a bit further to get to the larger supermarket on the road towards Derby. Most of the time she didn't mind the extra drive, as the large shop had a better selection and better prices, but sometimes she missed the convenience of having a shop close to home.

Simon Hampton, the local shop's owner, was currently involved in a messy divorce. No one seemed to know if or when he might start rebuilding the fire-damaged structure.

It didn't take long for Janet to find everything on the shopping list. Once she'd ticked off everything that Joan had requested, she started looking for something for herself. Biscuits and ice cream were easy selections to make, but finding something for her dinner for the next two nights was more complicated.

She often chose frozen pizza when making dinner for herself, as that was something Joan didn't approve of, but she'd recently purchased a great many pizzas on sale and she was still working her way through them all. Joan tutted about it every time she opened the freezer. One of them would do nicely for dinner tomorrow, she decided as she studied the various meal options on display. Perhaps tonight she ought to treat herself to a meal out somewhere.

While Janet didn't really mind eating alone, she did feel that she had limited options if she did so. She couldn't exactly take herself to dinner at the fancy French restaurant in Doveby Dale. But there was a small café just a short distance from Doveby House. The food was always good and Janet quite liked the owners. It was perfect for a Monday night on her own.

Chapter 2

When she got back to Doveby House, Joan helped Janet put away the shopping. Janet made sure she emptied the bag with the ice cream in it. Joan didn't approve of ice cream, either, and listening to her sister complain about both ice cream and frozen pizza was more than Janet was prepared to do.

"I've just made soup and sandwiches for lunch," Joan said when they were done unpacking. "I wasn't sure what you were planning for tonight, but obviously I've going to have a large evening meal."

"I'm going to the café," Janet said.

"On your own or with friends?" Joan asked.

"On my, er, well, I'm not sure," Janet replied. She'd been planning to go on her own, but she had made a few friends in Doveby Dale now. Maybe she should ring a friend and invite her to come along.

Janet thought about it while she ate her lunch, and after they were finished and the kitchen was tidied up, she rang a friend.

"Edna? It's Janet Markham. Joan is going out tonight and I thought I might have dinner at the café. I was wondering if you'd like to join me?"

"Oh, that's terribly kind of you," Edna Green replied. The

women were both members of the Doveby Dale Ladies' Club, which was where they'd met. "I'm afraid I'm going to have to decline, though. My son and his fiancé are ringing later for a long talk about the wedding. I can't miss that."

"Another time, then," Janet said.

"I'd really like that," Edna told her.

Janet thought about trying her other friend from the club, Martha, or even one of the other women, but decided not to bother. The club was meeting again later in April; that would be soon enough to see the others.

She filled her afternoon in one of her favourite ways, curled up in the library, reading a good book. Aggie sat on her lap and purred softly while Janet enjoyed a classic Sherlock Holmes story. When Aggie decided it was time for her dinner, Janet was happy to put the book down.

"I'll finish it later," she told her kitten. "I already know what's going to happen, of course, so there's no need for you to wait for your meal."

"Ah, there you are," Joan said as Janet filled Aggie's food and water bowls. "Do you have a few minutes to help me get ready?"

"Certainly," Janet agreed, wondering what help her sister wanted.

Joan's large bedroom had its own small sitting room and en-suite bathroom. Janet followed her sister into the bathroom, where Joan had makeup spread out around the sink.

"I never wear much makeup," she said to Janet. "But tonight is important to Michael and I want to look my best. Can you help me with how to put some of this on?"

"I can," Janet said. "But I'm not sure you want to overdo it. Michael seems to care about you just the way you are. Why do you care what anyone else thinks?"

Joan shrugged. "I just want Michael to know that I made an extra effort," she said. "I know tonight is important to him."

Under Janet's careful tutoring, Joan applied a small amount of eye shadow and eyeliner. "Mascara is too messy," Joan said, studying herself in the mirror. "I always end up getting it in my eyes, and then my eyes water and it's just a big mess."

"Skip the mascara, then," Janet said. "You just need a bit of blusher on your cheeks and a nice lipstick and you'll be ready."

Joan added those things and then combed her short bob into place. "I was thinking about getting a haircut," she told Janet. "Maybe if I got my hair cut short, people would stop insisting that we look alike."

Janet grinned. Neither she nor Joan could see the resemblance, even though they both wore their hair in the same style and had the same bright blue eyes. "It's too late to get it cut for tonight," she said.

"Yes, I suppose so," Joan said. She stared at herself for a minute and then shrugged. "Michael is going to have to be happy with that," she said.

Janet helped her into the gorgeous black dress that Joan had bought for the occasion. As Joan rarely bought herself new clothes, Janet had been surprised and pleased that she'd purchased something considerably more extravagant than Janet had expected.

"You look fabulous," Janet told her after she'd zipped the dress for Joan.

"I have butterflies on top of my butterflies," Joan admitted. "Maybe I should cancel."

"You'd break Michael's heart. I'm sure he has butterflies, too. You can't possibly cancel."

"No, I know," Joan sighed. She picked up her shoes and headed for the sitting room at the front of the house. "They aren't all that bad," she told Janet, waving the shoes, "but I'm not putting them on before I have to."

Only a few minutes later, as the sisters were discussing their plans for their upcoming visit to the Isle of Man, Michael knocked on the door.

"My goodness, you look awfully handsome," Janet said as she let the man into the house.

Michael's suit had obviously been expensive and it appeared to have been custom-tailored for him. He flushed under Janet's gaze.

"I'm a nervous wreck," he admitted. "I only have to speak for five minutes, but I've rewritten my remarks at least two dozen times. Now I'm afraid I'm going to lose my notes before I give the speech." When he finished speaking, he slipped his hand into a pocket and gasped.

"You haven't left them at home, have you?" Janet asked.

Michael patted all of his pockets in turn and then sighed with relief as he found his notes in his jacket. "I put them there for safe-keeping," he muttered.

Janet laughed as Joan slipped on her shoes. "We should go," she said. "We don't want to be late."

Michael held out his arm and Joan took it with a smile. "It's going to be a wonderful evening," she said to the man.

"I hope so," Michael replied. "Oh, and you look wonderful, as well. I'm sure I forgot to say that earlier."

Janet watched as they walked down the steps and climbed into the taxi that was waiting for them at the end of the short walkway to the house. She waved to her sister as the car pulled away.

"Time to get me something to eat," she told Aggie. "You be a good girl while I'm gone."

"Meerooooww," Aggie said.

Janet went up to her room to comb her hair and add a touch of lipstick. She found her handbag and headed back down the stairs. Aggie was chasing her tail, but she stopped when she saw Janet.

"Did you think I'd left already?" Janet asked. "I'm going now."

Aggie walked to the door with her, and Janet gave her a quick scratch behind the ears before she left. The weather had been getting nicer as they worked their way into spring, but the night felt crisp and almost cold to Janet. She had been considering walking, but it was too chilly. Instead, she climbed into the car that she and Joan shared and drove the short distance to the café.

The building's small car park was less than half full when Janet arrived. She parked under the streetlight and walked into the brightly lit dining room.

"Janet, what a lovely surprise," Ted called from the middle of the room where he was taking orders. "Sit anywhere." Ted and his partner, Todd, had owned the small café for longer than Janet and Joan had owned Doveby House. They were both in their forties. Ted had ginger hair with a neat beard. He was slender, and he did all the work in the dining room. Todd, with his long dark hair always in a ponytail, mostly stayed in the kitchen. He was plump, the way that Janet thought everyone who cooked for a living should be.

"Thanks," Janet replied. She chose a table in the corner near the front of the building. Once she was seated, she looked around to see if she knew anyone else in the room. One or two people looked familiar, and Janet found herself nodding at a woman that had formerly worked at the local grocer's and another that she was sure she knew from somewhere, but she had no idea where.

"Tea? Or something else?" Ted asked a moment later.

"Oh, tea, I think," Janet said. "It's cold out there again."

"Just for tonight," Ted told her. "Then we're supposed to see a warm-up for a few days."

"That would be nice," Janet said. "I just hope it doesn't rain."

"They aren't giving rain until the weekend," Ted replied. "I'll believe that when I see it, though."

Janet laughed and then picked up her menu. Everything on it sounded good, which made making a choice difficult.

"Janet, this is Molly," Ted said a moment later, as he delivered her tea.

The young girl with Ted smiled brightly at Janet. "It's a pleasure to meet you," she said.

"Molly is going to be working here, mostly waiting tables, for the next few months or so," Ted told Janet. "She's the niece of one of Todd's friends from uni, or something like that. Anyway, we're hoping the summer will be busy enough to warrant having an extra pair of hands."

"It's nice to meet you," Janet said politely.

The girl grinned. "I was working at a pub in Liverpool, but my father thought it was a little bit rough. He suggested that I come out here and try working at a café instead."

"I can understand your father's concern," Janet said. The girl was cute and blonde and couldn't have been much over five feet tall.

If she'd been Janet's daughter, Janet wouldn't have wanted her working in a pub, either.

"Yeah, it was a little scary sometimes," the girl said. "It's much nicer here. Everyone has been incredibly sweet and no one has shouted at me yet."

"I can't imagine anyone ever shouting at you here," Janet told her.

"Anyway, can I take your order?" the girl asked.

Janet frowned. "I don't know what I want," she said with a sigh. "Everything sounds good."

"I'll be right back," Molly said. She disappeared into the kitchen, leaving Janet with Ted.

"That was odd," Janet remarked.

"Knowing Molly, she's just had an idea," Ted told her. "She's been making all sorts of little changes to the menu for customers since she's been here."

"Oh, dear," Janet said.

"No, it's good," Ted told her. "She always checks with Todd first and so far she hasn't suggested anything that was a problem for him. Our customers have never been happier."

Molly was back a minute later, while Janet and Ted were still talking. "Okay, so earlier Todd mentioned that he'd cut some of the servings of cottage pie wrong, and now he had a piece left over that was really only half a serving. I wanted to ask him if he had any other odd bits like that that he could combine to make you a meal."

"And did he?" Janet asked, intrigued by the idea.

"Yes," Molly said. "He can do you a bit of cottage pie, a small piece of fish with a few chips on the side, and half a sausage with a tiny scoop of mashed potato, if that all sounds good."

"It sounds wonderful," Janet said. "But you may find that everyone wants the same."

"I hope not," Molly laughed. "These are all odd bits that Todd wasn't sure what to do with. He'd have to start cutting up proper portions if anyone else wants the same thing."

"Which is something he could do," Ted said. "If anyone asks after they see Janet's meal, we'll make it happen," he told Molly.

"Excellent," Molly said. "So I'll tell Todd that's what you want?"

"Yes, please," Janet said.

A short time later, Todd peeked his head out of the kitchen. "I just wanted to make sure you know that you aren't getting leftover or unwanted bits of food," he told Janet. "I slice whole fish myself for the fish and chips, and we usually end up with one or two pieces that are too small to serve. I usually make them into fish pie for Ted and me."

"I hope I'm not depriving you of your dinner, then," Janet said.

"Ted hates fish pie," Todd laughed. "He's delighted. As for sausage from the bangers and mash, well, we often get odd half or three-quarter pieces from our supplier. Sometimes I put them into a sausage pie."

"Well, I'm awfully glad you had them around for me today," Janet said.

"That's because it's Monday, which means our supplier delivered today," Todd told her. "Any other day and it would have been a different story."

"Well, I'm delighted that Molly had the idea," Janet said. "She seems lovely."

"She's nice, and she's far too clever to be working in a café," Todd said. "But she can't seem to work out what she wants to do with her life. I think her father was hoping she might find inspiration here."

A buzzing noise had him on his feet before Janet could reply. "That will be something burning in the kitchen," he told Janet cheerfully. He was gone before she did more than nod.

A few moments later, Molly brought out her dinner. The plate was full to overflowing with the three meals crowded onto it.

"That doesn't look like a partial portion of anything," Janet complained as she studied the plate.

"Have you seen the full portions?" Molly asked. "Because Todd really does love to fill a plate."

Janet nodded. The girl was right. Todd always put far too much food onto every plate that went out of his kitchen. And somehow Janet always managed to eat everything she was given. Tonight she found it more of a struggle than normal, however, finally admitting defeat while leaving a few chips and her last bite of sausage.

"I just can't eat another bite," she told Molly when the girl came to clear her plate.

"Oh, that's too bad," Molly said. "Todd said to tell you that he has a half a slice of chocolate cake and half a slice of jam roly-poly. He thought you might like to put them together to make a whole pudding."

Janet's mouth began to water in spite of her very full tummy. "I can't," she protested weakly.

"Maybe he could box them up for you to take with you," Molly suggested.

Janet laughed. "Okay, you've sold me on it. If he can box them up, I'll take his half puddings off of him, as well."

Molly was back a few minutes later with a small white box. "Here you are," she said, setting the box on the table. "And I'm sorry, but here's your bill, as well."

Janet was surprised at the price of her meal. "Ted," she called the man over. "This can't be right," she complained.

Ted took the slip of paper from her and read through it. "It looks right to me," he said with a shrug.

"But you haven't charged me nearly enough for that meal," Janet argued.

"You've helped Todd clear out the kitchen," Ted told her. "None of that was saleable on its own. Todd's charged you what he paid for it, plus a small premium. It's more than fair."

"Are you sure?" Janet demanded.

"I'm positive," Ted assured her.

Janet counted out her money, adding a large tip for Ted and Molly, and then waddled out to her car with her box of puddings. Back at Doveby House, she sank down in front of the telly and slowly ate her way through the contents of the box.

Chapter 3

Joan wasn't home by midnight, so Janet gave up on waiting up for her and went up to bed. Aggie had been asleep on her lap for hours by that time, and Janet did her best to stand up without waking the kitten. Perhaps it was because her tummy was so full, but for some reason Janet struggled to get out of her chair while holding her pet.

"Yoowwwlll," Aggie said as she came awake and jumped out of Janet's arms.

"Oh, yowl to you, too," Janet said. "I'm sorry, but I simply couldn't get up without waking you."

Aggie dashed up the stairs while Janet cleared away the evidence of her snack in front of the telly. When she got to her bedroom door, Aggie was pacing back and forth in front of it. As soon as the door was opened, Aggie raced inside and jumped up onto the bed. She bounced up and down a few times on her pillow and then settled in. By the time Janet was ready to join her, the kitten was fast asleep.

For the first time that Janet could ever remember, she was up before her sister the next morning. She gave Aggie her breakfast and then tried to decide what to do next. She was perfectly capable of making herself something for breakfast, but she didn't want to upset Joan in the process. The kitchen was Joan's domain and Janet usually only used it when Joan was out with Michael. Today was something of a grey area. Joan was home, Janet had made sure of that, but it seemed Joan wasn't ready to start making breakfast.

"This is silly," Janet said to Aggie. "I'm old enough to make my own breakfast without worrying about Joan."

Aggie gave her a skeptical look as she munched her way through her own meal. Janet frowned at her and then defiantly opened the refrigerator. She pulled out eggs and bacon and then decided that she fancied an omelet. Cheese and onion were added to the small pile on the counter. A minute later, she had a frying pan sizzling with melted butter as she chopped her ingredients. While the omelet was bubbling away, she started a pot of coffee. Whatever time Joan finally surfaced, she was probably going to want coffee.

Janet was just swallowing her last bite of her impromptu breakfast, washing it down with a sip of coffee, when Joan stumbled out of her bedroom.

"Coffee?" she asked.

"I just made a fresh pot," Janet told her.

Joan stood in the doorway, staring longingly at the pot, until Janet finally got up and poured her sister a cup.

"Thank you," Joan muttered as she took the cup from Janet. She took a sip, and then after a short pause, took another longer drink. "That's better," she said as she took a deep breath.

"Do you need headache tablets?" Janet asked curiously.

"Yes, I think I do," Joan replied.

Janet pulled the bottle of tablets out of the cupboard and shook two out into her hand. She passed them to her sister, who quickly washed them down with more coffee.

"I went to bed at midnight," Janet said. "What time did you finally get in?"

"It was nearly three," Joan said. "I'm sure I've never been up that late at night before."

"I hope you were having fun."

"It was a very nice evening," Joan told her. "After the event was over, Michael was invited to go out for a few drinks with a few of his old friends. We ended up at a pub in Derby somewhere, and yes, I'll admit it, I drank too much."

Janet looked at her sister and had to bite her lip so as not to laugh. "I think I need to have a word with Michael," she said as sternly as she could. "Clearly he's a bad influence on you."

"It wasn't Michael's fault," Joan said quickly. "I just felt so, well, out of place, really. Everyone else knew one another and they kept talking about how wonderful Michael's wife had been. I didn't have anything else to do but drink and try not to cry."

"Oh, dear," Janet said. She jumped up and pulled her sister into a hug. "I am sorry," she told her.

"Michael kept trying to change the subject, but a couple of the women seemed to be almost being deliberately nasty about it," Joan said. Janet could hear repressed tears in her sister's voice. "All I wanted to do was leave, but I didn't want to spoil Michael's special evening."

Janet hugged Joan tightly again. "Michael should have told them to stop talking about her," she said angrily.

"He was talking to his friends and didn't really hear much of the conversation," Joan defended the man. "Whenever he did hear her name, he did try to shut them up, though."

"You poor thing," Janet said. "Were the women involved anyone I've met?"

"No, and you aren't likely to meet them," Joan said. "They all live in Derby with their husbands, who are all chemists, I believe. Anyway, I've written down all of their names, and if any of them ever rings to book a room, I shall turn them away."

"Good for you," Janet said. "We don't want them staying here."

A knock on the front door interrupted the conversation. Joan winced at the loud noise. Janet went to see who was at the door.

"Good morning," Robert Parsons said when Janet opened the door. "I was hoping I might have a brief word with you and Joan."

Robert was the police constable responsible for policing Doveby Dale and the neighbouring village of Little Burton. The young man took his responsibilities very seriously, and he also seemed to feel responsible for Janet and Joan. He visited frequently to check on the sisters and their guests, and both women had developed a soft spot for the good-looking and kind young man.

Janet smiled and invited the man inside. "Joan had a late night," she told him as she led him towards the kitchen. "She isn't feeling very well this morning, I'm afraid."

Joan was putting bread into the toaster when they reached the kitchen. Janet was pleased to see that some of her colour had come back, no doubt thanks to the coffee.

"Coffee?" she asked Robert. "Toast? Breakfast?"

"I'll have some coffee, thanks," Robert said. "I had breakfast about an hour ago, but if you've baked any biscuits lately, I wouldn't say no to one or two of them."

Joan nodded, and very slowly and carefully poured a cup of coffee for the man. While she was doing that, Janet piled biscuits onto a plate, which she set in front of Robert on the table.

When Joan's toast had popped, she joined Robert and Janet at the table with her dry toast and coffee. After a small nibble on her toast, she looked up at Robert.

"What can we do for you this morning?" she asked.

"I understand you had to refuse a credit card yesterday," the man said. "I was hoping you could answer a few questions about that for me."

"I don't know what I was expecting, but that wasn't it," Janet said. "I just assumed it was a glitch in our little machine or something."

"Many times, when a card gets turned down, it is simply a glitch," Robert said. "Sometimes the card company thinks it detects fraud and puts a hold on the card until they can speak to the card holder. In this case, however, it was something else."

"What?" Janet asked.

"Before we get into that, I'd like you to tell me about the guests who were involved," Robert said.

"About Jacob and Harriet Mills?" Janet asked. "Don't tell me that isn't really their name? Were they trying to use a stolen credit card? They seemed like such nice people."

Robert held up a hand. "At this point, I have no reason to believe that the couple who stayed with you were anything other than exactly who they claimed to be," he said. "But I'd like to hear what you know about them and what you thought of them before I tell you anything more."

"Let me get my notebook where I write in the bookings," Joan said. "I make notes when I speak to potential guests. I can't remember what I wrote about those two, but there might be something."

While she was gone, Janet refilled her coffee cup and topped up Robert's as well.

"Here we are," Joan said as she sat back down. "Jacob rang us about three weeks ago and asked to book for this past weekend. He and his wife wanted to tour some stately homes, he told me."

"Did he say where they were coming from?" Robert asked.

"Yes, Rugby," Joan told him.

"Did you ask him how he'd heard about Doveby House?" was the next question.

"Yes, and he told me that he and his wife had stayed here once before," Joan said. "That was over a year ago, though."

Robert nodded and made a note in his notebook. "And did he pay for the room when he booked?"

"Oh, no," Joan replied. "I don't make guests pay in advance, although I might start asking them for a deposit of some kind as we get into the summer and have to start turning away bookings. No, I told him what the rate was and that I expected payment on arrival."

"When they arrived, how did he pay?" Robert asked.

"Cash," Joan told him. "Many of our guests seem to prefer to pay in cash. I'm not sure why. We have the credit card processing machine now, but it doesn't get used much."

Robert made another note. "So what happened yesterday?"

"Jacob came down and asked if they could stay another night," Joan explained. "We don't have anyone arriving before Saturday, so

I told him they could. He gave Janet his credit card to pay for the extra night."

"And I ran it through the machine and the machine said that their card was declined," Janet added.

"And he didn't offer to try a different card?" Robert asked.

"No," Joan said. "When Janet told them that the card had been declined, Jack and Harriet decided that they needed to go home and get that problem sorted."

"I see," Robert said. "And what did you think of them?"

"They seemed like a nice couple," Joan said. "They were very, um, communicative, really. We heard all about how they met when they were only teenagers and how their parents made them wait until they were both twenty-one to marry."

"When Joan says 'communicative,' she means they talked way too much," Janet interjected. "I think I know more about their lives than I do about my best friend."

Robert smiled. "The constable who spoke with them today said something similar," he said.

"I thought they were very nice," Joan said. "They are a few years older than I am, and they've been married for over fifty years. That's a huge accomplishment."

"It is," Robert agreed. "And you had no reason to doubt anything they told you?"

"Not at all," Joan said firmly.

"Not until their credit card was refused," Janet put in.

"It doesn't seem as if that was their fault," Robert said. "Did either of them mention when or where they'd used their card while they were here?"

Janet looked at Joan and then both sisters shrugged. "Harriet said something about only charging a few meals on it since they'd made a payment," Janet said.

"And did they tell you where they'd had those meals?" Robert asked.

"I know they ate at the local café at least once," Janet said. "And they had dinner at the pub in Little Burton as well. Beyond that, I simply don't recall. And I don't know where they paid cash or where they might have used their card, either."

"They ate lunch at the café at Chatsworth the first day they were here," Joan said. "I remember Harriet was still shocked by the prices, even several hours later."

Robert made a note and then smiled at them both. "Is there anything else you can tell me about them?" he asked.

Janet shook her head. "I can't think of anything else," she said.

"Thank you for all of your help, then," Robert said. "It seems that their credit card details were stolen and their card was used to purchase some very expensive items at a shop in Leeds."

"In Leeds?" Joan repeated. "Surely no one local could have been involved, then."

"At this point, we're not ruling anything out," Robert said. "But at the moment, it seems likely that they were the victims of a group of professionals. The card details could have been stolen some weeks or even months ago, perhaps along with a great many others. I'm doing what I can to investigate, but I don't expect to be able to find anything."

"What happens to Jacob and Harriet?" Janet asked.

"The credit card company will absorb the loss," Robert told her. "They've been good customers for a great many years and the incident was clearly a complete departure from their normal spending habits. They'll have to fill out some paperwork, but they won't lose any money."

"That's good news," Janet said.

"In the meantime, if you have any other guests that have trouble with their credit cards, ring me," Robert said as he rose to his feet. "It's just remotely possible that there's a local connection to the criminals."

Janet walked Robert to the door. Joan had started to stand up, but Janet had waved her back into her seat. "You sit and rest," she said. "Let those tablets do their job."

Joan had opened her mouth to object, but no words had come out. At the door, Robert gave Janet a hug.

"Thank you for your help," he said. "Hopefully, the problem

originated in Rugby or somewhere between here and there, but as I said, let me know if you have any additional problems.

Janet nodded. "Like Joan told you, we rarely take credit cards, but we'll ring you straight away if anything else happens."

She watched the man walk down the steps and climb into his car before she pushed the door shut and locked it. Poor Joan was probably still feeling miserable. Janet wasn't in a hurry to get back to her, really.

Chapter 4

When Janet walked back into the kitchen, Joan was putting her toast plate into the dishwasher.

"Would you think badly of me if I went and laid down for an hour?" she asked Janet.

"Not at all," Janet said stoutly. "You go and rest. I hope your head feels better when you wake up."

"I'm sure it will," Joan said. "I'll be up in plenty of time to make some lunch for us both. Michael and I are meant to be going out for dinner tonight, but I'm not sure I'm going to manage that."

"It's your anniversary," Janet said. "You don't want to miss that."

"Maybe it's time to stop celebrating the monthly anniversaries of our first dinner together," Joan said tiredly. "Or maybe it's time to stop seeing one another altogether."

"You don't mean that. It's the headache talking, that's all. Get some sleep. You'll feel better in an hour or two."

Joan nodded, but she didn't look convinced. Janet watched her leave the room and then sighed. Those nasty women had really upset her sister. Janet was left wondering what they'd said about

Michael's wife that had bothered her sister so much. Asking Joan would no doubt just upset her more.

Feeling too restless to settle down with a book, Janet decided to head into the village to do some window shopping. The options within the small village were somewhat limited, but she could get a few magazines from the newsagent, at least. The sort of glossy gossip magazines that Joan frowned upon were exactly what Janet felt she needed at the moment.

The centre of Doveby Dale was only a short distance past the café where Janet had eaten the previous evening. She parked in the small car park and headed for the short parade of shops, glancing over at the police station that was visible nearby. Robert's car wasn't there, but Susan Garner's was.

Susan was Robert's civilian assistant. Among other things, the forty-something blonde was a talented knitter, and she provided the sisters with piles of beautiful blankets that they displayed in the bed and breakfast. Joan and Janet took a small commission on every sale, and Janet was reminded as she crossed the car park that Harriet Mills had purchased a blanket from them. She'd have to stop and see Susan before she headed for home, Janet decided.

The newsagent was busier than Janet had expected it to be, but she was happy to wait in a short queue to buy her magazines. Next, she visited the chemist's shop that was next door. She bought the bottle of shampoo that she'd forgotten at the supermarket the previous day, wincing only slightly at the shop's higher prices. The only other shop in the row was WTC Antiques, and Janet debated with herself about visiting.

William Chalmers was an odd mix of charm and arrogance with a dash of something slightly shady thrown in. When he'd first arrived in Doveby Dale, Janet and Joan had taken an almost instant dislike to him. Over time that had softened to something almost approaching friendship, and in the last few months William had begun to show an interest in taking his relationship with Janet even further than that. Janet wasn't quite sure how she felt about the man, although she had to admit to being flattered by the attention.

If Edward Bennett hadn't been in the picture, she probably would have let William take her out, at least once or twice.

Now she stood on the pavement in front of his shop, waffling about whether to go in or not. She'd just about decided to head back to the car when the shop's door swung open and William greeted her.

"Good morning," he said brightly. "What brings you here, and why are you simply standing outside my door?"

Janet flushed. "I was just admiring the window display," she lied, quickly trying to take in everything she could see in case he questioned her excuse.

"And where is your lovely sister today?" William asked.

"She's not feeling very well," Janet replied. "She's in bed, nursing a headache, actually."

"So you thought you'd come down and buy yourself something antique or collectable when she wouldn't have a chance to stop you," William suggested.

Janet laughed and then followed the man into the shop. It looked less cluttered than normal. "You must be doing well," she said. "I'm sure you had many more things the last time I was here."

"Paul turned into a very talented salesman," William said. "We did almost enough business to warrant my keeping him around."

Janet nodded. Paul's father had sent him to Doveby Dale after Paul had found himself in some trouble with the law. Paul had insisted that he'd only chosen his friends badly and that he was innocent of any wrongdoing. His father decided that a few months in the middle of nowhere, helping William Chalmers run his antique shop, might help put Paul back on the right track. From all accounts, the plan had worked perfectly.

"Have you had anything new that I might like?" Janet asked.

"I just received a new painting by the artist who did the one you have in your bedroom," William told her. "Come and see."

Janet followed the man through the shop to the smaller room at the back, which was set up as a small art gallery. It was there that Janet had fallen in love with the first painting, even though it had been far too expensive for her to purchase. She'd mentioned it in passing to Edward, however, and had been shocked and delighted when he'd bought it for her and had it delivered to Doveby House.

"What do you think?" William asked, gesturing towards a large canvas.

Janet studied it for several minutes before she spoke. "I would have known it was by the same man, even without the signature," she said. "But I don't like it nearly as much as I like mine."

"Why?"

Janet shook her head. "I don't know," she admitted. "But I also don't know why I like mine so much. For some reason, my painting spoke to me, but this one doesn't, I suppose."

William nodded. "For what it's worth, I don't like this very much, either. Yours had an energy about it that this one is lacking. Someone almost bought it yesterday, though."

"But they changed their minds at the last minute?"

"But their credit card didn't go through," William told her.

"Really? Did you tell Robert about it?" Janet asked.

"Robert? Do you mean Robert Parsons? Why would I involve the police?" William replied. "They were probably over their limit, or the painting would have put them over or something. I simply told them the card had been declined and they told me they'd come back once they'd sorted the problem."

"Have they been back?"

"No, of course not," William said. "Like I said, they were probably over their limit or something."

"We had a credit card declined yesterday at the bed and breakfast," Janet told him. "Robert wanted to hear all about it because it was the result of the couple having their credit card details stolen."

"Really? Well, maybe that was what happened to my couple as well," William said. "But if so, that's between them and the police. I don't think it has anything to do with me."

"Robert wanted us to ring him if we had any other trouble," Janet said. "I'm sure he'd like to hear your story as well."

"Maybe I'll ring him later," William said dismissively.

"I need to go and talk to Susan anyway. I can tell her about it and have her pass the information along to Robert, if you'd like," Janet offered.

"That would be kind of you," William said. "Perhaps I can buy you dinner to thank you?"

"That isn't necessary," Janet said.

"But I'd still like to do it," William replied. "Let me see when I'm free."

William suggested either Thursday or Friday, but Janet wasn't sure. "I'll have to ring you later today," she said. "I need to check with Joan about guests before I promise anything."

"But you will have dinner with me?" he asked.

"Yes, I will," Janet said, feeling reckless. If Joan could stay out far too late and have too much to drink, Janet felt as if she ought to at least have a nice dinner out once in a while.

She looked around the shop for a few minutes, admiring a bookshelf that she hadn't noticed before. "That would just fit in my bedroom," she said, checking the price. "Maybe Joan can get it for me for Christmas," she added when she saw how expensive the piece was.

"I can give you a better price," William said.

"I think I'd better measure the space first," Janet replied. "It might be just a tiny bit too big."

A glance at the large wall clock surprised her. "My goodness, I'm not going to have much time to talk to Susan," she said when she saw the time. "I'm meant to be home in time for lunch."

William walked her to the door and gave her a hug. "Ring me later," he said.

"I will," Janet promised.

Although the tiny police station was a short distance away, Janet decided it would be easier to walk than to move her car. Susan was just walking out of the station when she arrived.

"I was just going to collect my lunch," Susan told Janet. "They make me sandwiches at the coffee shop next door."

The small coffee shop next to the police station did excellent cakes and puddings. "I didn't realise they did more than tea, coffee and sweets," Janet said.

"Just sandwiches, really," Susan told her. "The regular girl behind the counter has a bit of a thing for Robert, so she's always happy to feed either of us."

"How does Robert feel about her?" Janet had to ask.

"You'd have to ask Robert that," Susan laughed.

"I won't keep you, then," Janet said. "Just two quick things. Our guests over the weekend bought a blanket." She reached into her handbag and pulled out the envelope where she'd put the money she'd received from Harriet.

"Oh, good," Susan exclaimed. "There's a sale on yarn at one of my favourite shops right now. I can go and stock up."

Janet laughed. "Maybe you should treat yourself to something wonderful," she suggested.

"I'd rather have more yarn," Susan told her. "But what was the other thing?"

"Robert asked me to let him know if we had any more trouble with credit cards," Janet said. "We haven't, but William Chalmers has." She told the other woman what William had told her.

"I don't know if it matters or not, but I'll tell Robert the story and he can decide whether he needs to talk to Mr. Chalmers or not," Susan said. "Thank you for sharing it with me."

"You know I always do everything I can to help the police with their investigations," Janet said. Including sticking my nose in where it doesn't belong, she added silently to herself.

She walked back to the car and headed for home. Joan is probably done making lunch and starting to worry about me, she thought. When she reached Doveby House, however, the kitchen was empty. She tapped on Joan's door and then let herself into her sister's bedroom.

"Joan? Are you okay?" she asked softly.

"Janet? What time is it?" Joan asked from her bed.

"It's nearly one o'clock," Janet replied.

"Good heavens," Joan exclaimed, sitting up and switching on the nearest lamp. "You should have woken me an hour ago. You must be starving."

"I went into Doveby Dale to do some shopping," Janet explained. "I only just got back."

Joan climbed out of bed and followed Janet into the kitchen. Together, the pair made themselves a quick lunch.

"Thank you for helping with lunch," Joan said as she dug into her meal.

"It was no problem," Janet said. "I felt bad about waking you, but I wanted to make sure you were okay."

"I'm feeling a lot better than I was this morning," Joan said. "The headache has gone and I'm not nearly as tired."

"That's good to hear," Janet replied.

"I'm still not sure about going out with Michael again tonight, though," Joan said. "I'm feeling a bit, well, uncomfortable about the whole thing."

"If you decide not to go, you'll have to explain yourself to him," Janet said. "What will you say?"

Joan frowned. "Maybe it will be easier to just go to dinner," she muttered.

Janet laughed. "Just don't tell him that that's the only reason you're there," she told her sister.

Joan managed a small smile. "I'm not sure what I'm going to tell him," she said.

While they ate, Janet told her sister about her morning, including everything that William Chalmers had told her about the credit card issue. "Of course, I told Susan the whole story when I went and paid her for the blanket that Harriet Mills bought," she added.

"And what did Susan think?" Joan asked.

"I don't know. She just said she'd tell Robert about it and let him decide what to do."

"What are you planning to do tonight?" Joan asked as they cleared the table.

"Tonight it's frozen pizza in front of the telly," Janet told her. "I'm looking forward to it."

"Then I suppose I'd better go out with Michael," Joan said. "I'd just be in your way here, urging you to eat vegetables and watch something educational."

Janet laughed. "We can't have that," she said.

"No, I suppose not."

While Joan was getting ready for her evening out, Janet rang William Chalmers. "I can do either night for dinner," she told the man. "What works best for you?"

"Let's do Friday," he suggested. "We can celebrate the weekend."

Janet agreed quickly before she could change her mind. As soon as Joan was gone, she made her pizza and found something to watch on the telly. She ate and then read her glossy magazines until she began to yawn regularly.

"I think it's time for bed," she told Aggie.

The kitten looked at her for a moment and then shrugged and headed for the stairs. Janet looked at the clock as she followed. No wonder Aggie had been surprised. It was only nine o'clock, but Janet felt as if she was struggling to keep her eyes open. For the second night in a row, she was in bed before Joan got home.

Chapter 5

The next morning Joan was busily preparing breakfast when Janet got downstairs. "What time did you get in last night?" Janet asked her.

"Oh, before ten," Joan replied. "I thought you'd still be watching mindless television, but you'd gone upstairs."

"I was tired," Janet told her. "How was your evening?"

Joan smiled at her. "It was good," she said happily.

Janet was relieved. She knew her sister really liked Michael. "Where did you go?" she asked.

"The French restaurant," Joan told her.

"Really? It's very nice, isn't it?"

"It was lovely," Joan agreed. "And Michael was very apologetic for the way I was treated on Monday evening. I do believe I'm growing rather fond of that man." Joan blushed bright red and quickly turned back to the counter where she was putting breakfast onto plates.

"I like him, and I think he's good for you," Janet told her "Just make sure he knows that I expect him to ask my permission if he decides he wants to marry you."

"Now, don't be silly," Joan said. "No one has said anything about marriage. I hardly think it's likely, not at our age."

"Why not?" Janet asked.

"Because, well, just because," Joan said, clearly getting flustered. "Breakfast is ready," she announced, changing the subject.

The pair talked about the weather and local news as they ate. Janet was just starting to clear the table when someone knocked on the front door.

"Who could that be?" Joan asked.

"Why don't I go and find out?" Janet suggested.

"Ah, good morning," the man on the doorstep said when Janet opened the door. "I was wondering if you could possibly accommodate me and my wife for two nights?"

Janet stared at him for a moment, not entirely sure how to respond. The man looked to be in his mid-forties. He had dark hair that badly needed both washing and combing. His clothes were tattered and his shoes looked as if they were falling apart.

"We're just passing through the area, you see," he added. "We're heading up to see some family in Scotland, but we thought we'd see some of the country along the way."

"Yes, well, I'm not sure if we have any rooms available," Janet said slowly. "People usually book in advance, you see."

"That's why I thought we should try first thing in the morning," the man said. "I was hoping we might get lucky. You came highly recommended, you see."

"Really? By whom?" Janet asked.

"My mate, Henry Houston. He stayed here about five years ago and said the place was wonderful."

"That would have been under the previous owner," Janet told him. "My sister and I only purchased Doveby House in the last year."

"Oh, but you're still doing bed and breakfast, right?"

"Well, yes, but I'm going to have to check with my sister about available rooms. Can you wait here a minute?" she asked.

"Sure, I'll just come in, shall I?"

"Oh, yes, of course, "Janet said, shaking her head. She was so surprised by the man and his request that she'd completely forgotten her manners. "Have a seat. I'll be right back."

She walked as quickly as she could into the kitchen. "We have a potential guest," she told Joan. "He wants a room for two nights."

"I suppose we could do that," Joan said. "Our next guests aren't due until Saturday."

"He doesn't really look as if he can afford a room," Janet said. "But he seems nice enough, I suppose."

Joan raised an eyebrow. "I'd better come and meet him," she said. "Perhaps if I tell him that he has to pay in advance, he'll change his mind."

"He said he's travelling with his wife, but I haven't seen her yet," Janet added as Joan headed towards the sitting room.

The man didn't appear to have moved from the couch by the door. When Joan entered the room, he stood up.

"I take it you're the sister who's in charge of rooms," he said. "I do hope you can accommodate us."

"I'm Joan Markham. I believe we can." She told the man the price for the room and breakfast. "I'm afraid I'll need payment in advance," she added. "We've only had one guest sneak away without paying, but that was one too many for me."

The man grinned at her. "I can understand that," he said. "The wife carries all the money. She's waiting in the car, just in case you said no." He pulled out his mobile and tapped a few keys. "That'll bring her," he said.

A minute later, there was a knock on the door. Janet opened it and smiled at the woman standing there with a large suitcase. "We're okay, then?" she asked, looking past Janet at the man behind her.

"Yeah, they can have us for two nights," the man replied. He told her the price and the woman made a face.

"That include breakfast?" she asked.

"Yes," Joan said. "Full English breakfast, unless you'd prefer something else?"

"For that money, it better be good," the woman replied as she walked into the house, dragging the suitcase behind her.

Janet thought the woman looked at least ten years older than her husband. Her clothes were in slightly better repair, but her hair also needed combing and she had a smear of her bright pink lipstick on her front teeth. She was somewhat heavier than was probably healthy for her, as well.

"As I said, I'm Joan Markham and this is my sister, Janet," Joan said.

"Oh, aye, I'm Charles Irwin and that's Carla," the man said.

Aggie wandered into the room and gave the new guests a long look.

"And that's Aggie," Janet told them. "Short for Agatha Christie."

"Who's that, then?" the woman asked.

"She's a rather well-known mystery writer," Janet said.

"Oh, I don't read much," Carla replied. "Want paying in advance, do you? Don't think we look trustworthy, eh?"

Joan smiled tightly. "I ask all of our guests to pay in advance," she said steadily. "It simplifies things."

The other woman shrugged and then pulled a large wallet out of her handbag. When she opened it, Janet nearly gasped. There were rows and rows of credit cards all along both sides.

"Should I pay cash?" Carla asked her husband.

"Yeah, that's probably easier for the women to deal with," he replied.

Carla carefully counted out the correct amount from a large pile of twenty-pound notes. She handed them to Joan, who counted them a second time.

"Thank you," Joan said. "I'll just show you to your room, then."

She handed the cash to Janet, who took it and put it into the safe in Joan's wardrobe. It would have been easier to use the safe in the library, but they were still waiting for Edward to get them the combination for that one. He was meant to be heading back to his London base in the next fortnight or so, and he'd promised to find it for them as soon as he was back.

Once Janet had done that, carefully locking her sister's bedroom door behind her, she headed back to the sitting room. Joan joined her there a moment later.

"I suppose we shouldn't complain about unexpected guests," she told Janet. "After the quiet winter we had, the extra money is welcome."

"Did you see how many credit cards they had?" Janet asked in a low voice. "You don't suppose they're involved in credit card fraud, do you?"

"No, I don't," Joan said firmly. "They seem like a perfectly ordinary couple. Anyway, if they were, surely they'd be better dressed."

Janet chuckled. "Maybe they're in disguise," she suggested.

"Maybe you've been reading too much crime fiction," Joan shot back. "We've had one credit card declined and now you're seeing card fraud everywhere."

"It does happen," Janet pointed out.

"Yes, but we've no reason to suspect Mr. and Mrs. Irwin of anything at all."

The sound of footsteps on the stairs kept Janet from replying. She and Joan both watched as the couple walked back into the room.

"It's a very nice room," Charles said. "I think we're going to like it here."

"It's nice enough," Carla sniffed. "But now we're off to explore the Dales."

"You have a key for the front door," Joan said. "Janet or I will probably be up when you get back, but if it's very late, we might not be. What time would you like your breakfast?"

The pair exchanged glances. "Oh, midday works for me," Charles said after a moment.

"Midday?" Joan echoed.

"Yes, I think that will suit us both," Carla said. "We'll see you then."

The sisters watched as the pair turned and walked out of the house.

"Midday?" Joan said again as the door shut behind them. "Who eats breakfast at midday?"

"People who like to lie in," Janet said. "Which suggests that they're planning on staying out quite late tonight, as well."

Joan sighed. "I should have told them we were fully booked," she said.

"You're terrible at lying," Janet reminded her. "I should have told them we were fully booked."

Joan shrugged. "We're committed now. At least it's only two nights."

"And I suppose we can lie in as well," Janet said. "If they aren't coming down until midday, we don't need to be up before eleven."

"I shall be getting up at my normal time, regardless," Joan told her. "You know I always do."

Janet nodded, choosing not to mention the very recent occasion when her sister had missed her normal time by many hours.

"What are you planning to do today?" Joan asked Janet before Janet could sneak away to read and play with Aggie.

"Oh, I don't know," Janet said. "Why? What needs doing?"

"I thought we might try sorting through another box or two from the carriage house," Joan said. "It would be nice to be able to clear it out, really. I'd like to see just how much space we have. We might be able to find a better use for the space than just storing old boxes in there."

Janet nodded, but she was worried. When they'd bought the house, the estate agent had suggested turning the carriage house into a small separate accommodation for additional guests. As she wasn't a huge fan of having any guests, building additional accommodation wasn't her idea of a better use of the carriage house.

"And maybe we'll find something wonderful," Joan added.

"I'll get the key and a torch," Janet said, feeling resigned. She'd managed to avoid working on the carriage house for weeks. Perhaps if they cleared out a few boxes today, Joan would forget about it for a short while again. She'd only taken a few steps when someone knocked on the door.

"Ah, good morning," the male half of the couple at the door said. "We were wondering if you might have a room available for the next two nights?"

Janet looked over at Joan, who shrugged.

"You may as well come in," Janet told the couple, who had two small suitcases at their feet.

"I'm Gary Doyle, and this is my wife, Roberta," the man said as they entered the house, each carrying a case. Gary was tall, with dark hair and eyes. He was probably in his forties, but unlike their other unexpected guests, he was impeccably dressed in what city dwellers probably thought of as "country clothes." Roberta was of a similar age and she, too, was dressed in spotlessly clean "casual" clothes. Her jewellery was tasteful but looked as if it had been expensive, and something about the couple suggested that they were quite wealthy.

"We're just passing through the area and we thought we might stop for a few days to visit some friends," Gary said.

"You have friends in Doveby Dale?" Janet asked.

"Oh, no," the man chuckled. "We have friends in Derby. But we didn't really want to stay with them. While you're a little out of the way, we thought it would be fun to experience life in a small village. That is, if you can accommodate us?"

"Two nights?" Joan asked.

"Yes, that's right," the man said.

Joan told him the amount. Gary didn't even blink.

"That's bed and breakfast?" Roberta asked.

"Yes, and I can do full English or whatever you'd prefer," Joan told her.

"Can we see the room?" was Roberta's next question.

Joan's smile faltered slightly, but she recovered quickly. "Of course you can," she said. "It hasn't been aired properly, I'm afraid, because we weren't expecting any guests today."

She led the pair up the stairs. Janet grinned as she noticed that they'd taken their cases up with them. Clearly they were hoping that they would like the room. After a moment, she followed, curious to see what the couple would think of the guest room. When they reached the top of the stairs, Joan unlocked the door to the smaller of the two guest rooms and switched on the lights. She stepped back to let the Doyles into the room.

"It's awfully small," Roberta complained.

"It's lovely and quaint," Gary said. "I think it's perfect."

"Is this the only room you have available?" Roberta asked as she walked back out of the room.

"Yes, unfortunately our other guest room is already occupied," Joan said.

"I suppose it will do," she said, her tone suggesting that she was being incredibly gracious.

"As I said, we weren't expecting you," Joan said. "Most of our guests book in advance."

"So we were fortunate that you have a room at all," Gary said. "Do we pay when we leave?"

"I do ask all guests to pay in advance," Joan told him. "It's much easier for everyone that way."

Roberta frowned, but she didn't object as Gary pulled out his wallet and counted out the correct amount.

"Here are your keys," Joan said, handing them to Gary. "The smaller one is the room key and the larger one opens the front door. If you come in late at night, Janet and I will probably be asleep when you get in. What time would you like your breakfast in the morning?"

Gary looked at Roberta. "What do you think?" he asked her.

"Oh, I don't know," she replied. "I don't want to get up too early. We don't have anywhere we have to be. Let's say nine?"

Gary nodded. "Nine sounds good," he agreed.

"Very good," Joan said.

All four of them headed back down the stairs into the sitting room.

"We're just off to see our friends, then," Gary said. "We'll see you later."

They let themselves out and Janet checked that the door was locked behind them.

"Well, we went from no guests to a full house in less than a hour," Janet said. "I hope that's all of our surprises for today."

Chapter 6

"Maybe we need to forget about the carriage house for now," Joan said.

Janet smiled. That was the sort of surprise she liked. "Okay," she said eagerly.

"What we really need is a trip to the supermarket. I hadn't planned on making breakfast for six tomorrow."

"I hadn't thought of that," Janet said. "Shall I go? Or do you want to come as well?"

Joan thought for a minute. "I'd like to come as well, but I do think one of us should stay at home. You know when we have guests, I'm always happier if one of us is home at least most of the time."

"Yes, I know," Janet said. "So do you want to go to the supermarket and I'll stay here?"

Joan shrugged. "I would like to get out, but I do hate the long drive. Maybe you should just go."

"Make me a list, please, while I run a brush through my hair," Janet told her. When Janet came back down the stairs a short time later, Joan had the list ready.

"I've added what I'd need for a chicken casserole for tonight's dinner," Joan told her. "If that doesn't sound good, you can get something else instead."

Janet thought about dinner as she drove to the supermarket. Chicken casserole did sound good, but so did a dozen other things. Too bad Joan couldn't be as accommodating as the café had been, she thought. She could only imagine the face that Joan would make if she asked her to prepare small portions of three different meals. It might be almost funny, really.

She pushed her trolley around the shop slowly, looking for things she hadn't seen before and hoping for inspiration. When she didn't find any of either, she gave up and found everything on Joan's list instead. When she finally reached the tills, the queues were long and tempers seemed short.

"We were spoiled in Doveby Dale," one woman remarked loudly. "The queues were always kept short there."

"But the prices were quite a bit higher," someone shouted.

"It was worth paying a bit more if it meant not having to stand here and watch my ice cream melt," the first woman snapped.

Janet chose what looked like the slowest-moving queue. In her experience, she always got it wrong when she tried to select the fastest-moving one, so maybe she would have some sort of reverse luck by picking the slowest. Within minutes the shop assistant behind the till had been sent on a break. Her replacement was considerably quicker, working her way through the customers in quick succession. The man in front of Janet was only buying a dozen or so items, and Janet was busily unloading her trolley when the shop assistant turned on the light over her till. Clearly, there was a problem.

Janet swallowed a sigh and kept adding things to the conveyor belt. She had fewer things left to unload than what she had already piled on the belt, so she decided that she might as well continue.

A man in a shirt and tie, presumably a manager, walked over.

"What's the problem?" he asked the girl behind the till.

"Credit card won't go through," she replied.

The man in the tie frowned. "May I see the card?" he asked the customer.

The man handed him his credit card, and the manager ran it through the computer a second time. After a moment, he shook his head.

"I'm sorry, but the card is being declined," he told the customer.

"Why?" the man demanded.

"I don't know," the manager told him. "All I know is that you'll need to pay with a different method."

"But the card is good," the customer protested.

"You'll have to take that up with your credit card company," the manager said.

The man took his card back from the manager and spun on his heel. "I'll simply do my shopping elsewhere," he said angrily.

Janet watched as he stormed out of the shop. The manager exchanged glances with the girl behind the till. "That's the second one today," he told her. "I wish I'd noticed which bank the card was from. Someone is having some problems somewhere."

He voided the transaction off the till and then took the man's shopping bags away. The girl turned to Janet and smiled.

"I hope you aren't planning on using a credit card," she said. "It seems like there's a problem with the system today."

"I'm afraid I'm going to have to," Janet said apologetically. "I never carry much cash around with me."

"Well, we'll just have to cross our fingers," the girl told her.

Janet's card went through without any difficulty, even though the total did make Janet wince slightly. Feeding unexpected guests was a costly undertaking. Maybe she should have brought some of the cash that Joan had tucked away in her safe to cover the purchase, she thought as she loaded the shopping into her boot.

She was halfway home before she thought to wonder whether she should have told the manager to ring Robert about the credit card issue. "Some help you are," she said to herself. She'd been so caught up in the moment, she hadn't even thought about Robert.

Back at Doveby House, she and Joan unpacked the shopping. "I think I'm going to ring Robert," she told Joan. "The man in front of me in the queue had his credit card declined and the manager said that he was the second today. I think Robert ought to know about it."

She rang the local station on their non-emergency number, but no one answered. "That's odd," she said to Aggie, who was chasing after one of her toys in the sitting room. "I wonder where Susan is." Perhaps the woman had just popped over to the coffee shop for a sandwich, Janet thought. She would try again later.

Joan made them lunch. "As chicken casserole is quite filling, I though we should keep things light now," she told Janet as they ate.

"What are we having for pudding tonight?" Janet asked. She'd been excited to see apples on her sister's shopping list.

"I thought as I've been out so much lately, that you might like an apple crumble tonight," Joan said.

Janet smiled widely. "I really would," Janet agreed. Apple crumble was her favourite pudding and she'd have it every night if Joan would agree.

After they'd cleared away the lunch dishes, Joan gave her a serious look. "We should each go through two boxes from the carriage house this afternoon," she suggested. "Who knows what wonderful things we might find?"

Janet frowned. She and Joan both knew that they were unlikely to find anything interesting in the boxes that had been in the carriage house for years. Maggie Appleton, the previous owner of Doveby House, had been an astute businesswoman. There was no way she'd put anything into the carriage house that had any real value.

"You know it's all just piles of papers and old books," Janet grumbled.

"I don't know any such thing," Joan told her. "I'm sure some of those boxes have been in there since before Margaret Appleton bought the house. From everything we've been told about her, I can't see her taking the time to go through them, can you?"

Janet chuckled. "From what we've heard, she was too busy getting married and divorced to dig through old boxes."

"Exactly," Joan said. "Who knows what she might have missed."

Janet sighed. She couldn't really argue any more, not when Joan was making apple crumble for pudding. "I'll go and get a torch and the keys," she said. "But only two boxes each."

"Agreed," Joan said.

They walked through the garden slowly, taking the time to enjoy the first signs of spring. "This is going to be beautiful soon," Janet said, waving an arm over the many different beds that contained flowers and shrubs. "I don't know what we would do without Stuart."

Stuart Long and his wife, Mary, lived on the other side of Michael Donaldson's semi-detached house. Stuart was a retired gardener and he looked after the extensive gardens at Doveby House in exchange for a very small salary and all the tea and biscuits he could eat. The sisters hadn't seen him much lately, as the garden didn't need much doing to it in the winter months.

"I saw Stuart yesterday," Joan said. "He told me that he'll probably be out here every day again starting next week. Mary was with him, and she wasn't very happy about his plans."

"I don't understand those two," Janet said. "They don't seem to spend much time together and they don't seem to get along very well, either."

"Mary is usually off visiting one or another of her children," Joan agreed. "Stuart seems quite happy on his own, I must say, especially when we provide him with breakfast and lunch."

Janet unlocked the door to the carriage house and pulled the cord for the single overhead light. She pushed the door open as far as it would go and made sure she had the key in her pocket before she did anything else.

"We haven't seen the ghost lately," she remarked as she switched on her torch.

"We've never seen the ghost," Joan said sharply. "Anyway, there isn't any ghost."

A sudden gust of wind blew the door shut and somehow also managed to switch off the light. Janet looked over at her sister. "I think you've made him angry," she said.

Joan rolled her eyes and then walked over to the door and pulled the light cord. The light came back on, but when Joan tried the door, it was locked.

"You have the key?" she asked Janet.

Janet patted her pocket. "I'll get it when we're ready to leave," she said. "Otherwise the ghost will just lock us in again."

Joan looked as if she wanted to argue, but she bit her tongue and then pointed to a random box. "Let's start with this one," she suggested.

Janet joined her and they pulled open the box. "Books," Janet said, feeling slightly disappointed. Thus far, the only books they'd found in the carriage house had been waterlogged nursing textbooks. She wasn't optimistic that this box would hold anything better.

"We'll take them in the house and go through them," Joan said. "It's a bit chilly out here."

Janet nodded and then flipped her torch around the space. "I'm going for this one," she said, selecting a random box that was on top of a small pile along the wall.

"What have you found?" Joan asked.

"Paperwork," Janet said sadly.

"Again, we'll have to go through it in the house," Joan said. "I'm freezing."

Janet pulled the box down and opened the one under it. No doubt the entire stack was full of the same boring papers. They might as well go through two boxes of it rather than one.

She was wrong. The second box had been carefully packed with those little packing peanuts that seem to go everywhere whenever you open a box of them.

"More papers?" Joan asked.

"No. But I'm not sure what I've found," Janet replied. She reached into the box and felt around, her fingers touching a cool and round object. Putting the torch down, she pulled it out of the box.

"What is it?" Joan wondered.

"It seems to be a glass elephant," Janet said. "I wonder if it's valuable or just cute?"

"I would suggest it isn't either," Joan told her.

Janet laughed. "But that's all that's in the box," she said. "I can put it in my room and we've cleared another box out of the carriage house."

"For that, I'd even put it in my room," Joan told her.

Janet looked at the elephant and shook her head. "No. I'll have her," she said. "I quite like her."

"You'll have to watch that Aggie doesn't knock it over," Joan warned. "It's probably quite fragile."

Janet nodded. "I'll find a safe place for her. But you have one more box to open and then we can get out of here."

Joan opened the box that she was standing closest to and sighed. "More paperwork," she said. "Maybe this wasn't such a great idea."

Janet hid a smile as she slid the elephant back into its box. "I'll take this and come back for the books," she told Joan. "Let's get out of here."

It took Janet a minute to get the door unlocked. The key didn't seem to want to turn in the lock.

"Oh, do hurry," Joan said. "I feel as if I might never get warm again."

The sisters burst out of the carriage house and into the April afternoon. The sun was already setting, but the air felt warm to them after the cold interior of the carriage house.

Neither was eager to make a second trip for their second boxes, but Janet didn't want to mention her unease and Joan simply pressed her lips together and stomped across the grass as if on a mission. Janet stood in the doorway while Joan picked up her box and then Joan did the same while Janet collected hers. Neither woman said a word, but they were both determined not to get locked inside again.

Safely back in Doveby House, Janet put the elephant in her room and grabbed a cardigan. The house was warm, but she felt chilled all the way through. Joan's chicken casserole would be the perfect evening meal, she thought as she walked back towards the kitchen.

There, Joan was sorting through piles of paper. "So far everything in this box has been from Maggie Appleton's years of ownership," she told Janet. "It's mostly old electricity and telephone bills. I'm just putting them all in a pile to put out with the rubbish."

Janet nodded and opened the box of books. She pulled them out one at a time, making note of each one.

"Anything interesting?" Joan asked.

"We have twenty-four copies of *Poems for the One I Love* by Alberta Emerson," Janet told her. "I've actually read that wrong, though, as the word 'the' is spelled 'H-T-E' on the cover. If I tell you that I think more time was spent proofreading the cover than the rest of the book, you'll know how excited I am about the find."

"Oh, dear," Joan said.

Janet opened one of the books and read the cover page. "Printed privately by Alberta Emerson, also known as Alberta Montgomery," she read. "Copyright 1937."

"I don't suppose those will be worth anything," Joan said.

"I wonder who she was," Janet said. "I've been meaning to research the history of Doveby House. Maybe she used to live here."

Joan opened her other box. After a moment, she looked up at Janet. "I think you may be right about her living here," she said. "This box seems to be full of her letters."

Chapter 7

"Letters to her or from her?" Janet asked, feeling excited.

"It appears to be both," Joan said. "And this may be her diary, as well." She held up an old and worn book. Janet could see "Alberta Montgomery" written across the front in a childish-looking loopy handwriting.

"Let me see," Janet said.

"I'm not sure we should read her diary," Joan replied. "Or her letters, for that matter."

"We need to find out who she was," Janet suggested. "She must have family that would want the letters and diaries."

"Even they won't want the books," Joan predicted.

Janet laughed. "You never know, people can be oddly sentimental about some things."

Joan went through the rest of the box. It was full of piles of letters and several diaries. "I feel weird about reading them," Joan said.

"I know, but I'm also curious," Janet said. "Let's pack them all up and put them out of the way for today. Maybe we can find out more about who she was and then decide whether to read them or not."

They repacked Joan's box and then put the books back into their box. Joan cleared a space for them in the back of her wardrobe.

"I'm not sure we've accomplished much," Joan said. "We have emptied two boxes, but we've also simply moved two from the carriage house into my wardrobe. That might be considered a step backwards, in some ways."

Janet shook her head. "You want to get the carriage house cleared out," she said. "We could simply move everything in it into the main house. That would be the fastest way to do it."

"We don't want to clutter up our lovely home with the boxes from the carriage house," Joan said. "You're just looking for ways to get around going through the boxes."

"Yes, I am," Janet agreed.

Joan shook her head. "I really think…" she began. A knock on the door interrupted her.

"Robert, what a lovely surprise," Janet said when she opened the door. She let the man in quickly, hoping that his visit would keep Joan from ever finishing her sentence.

"I can't stay long," the man warned. "I have several other people I need to talk to today."

"Come and have a cuppa," Joan suggested. "Surely you have time for that."

"Only just," Robert replied.

Joan put the kettle on while Janet filled a plate with biscuits. It wasn't long before the three were settled in around the kitchen table.

"So, what can we do for you?" Janet asked the man.

"I wanted to thank you for letting me know about the problem that William Chalmers had," Robert began. "I haven't been able to track down the gentleman who'd wanted to purchase the painting, but I'm working on it."

"Do you think his card was stolen as well?" Janet asked.

"At this point, I'm reserving judgment," Robert replied. "It just seems an awful coincidence."

"There were two declined credit cards at the supermarket this morning," Janet said. "I don't know if you know about them?"

"I don't," Robert sighed. "And I don't know if that's unusual or not, either. I'll need to ring their local constabulary and have them send someone over to talk to the manager."

"Surely it must be unusual," Janet said.

"I don't know. Since yesterday I've investigated three separate incidents like the one you reported. In one of the cases, the person's card details had been stolen and the card had been charged to its limit. In the second case, the cardholder's wife had exceeded their limit and neglected to mention it to her husband."

"Ouch," Janet said.

"Yes, rather," Robert agreed. "In the third instance, the cardholder had skipped his last two payments and the card was frozen. It seems as if there are a great many reasons why credit cards get declined, and only a small fraction of them are cause for criminal investigation."

"But Jacob and Harriet Mills did have their details stolen?" Janet asked.

"Yes, they definitely did," Robert told her. "We're still checking into their case."

"I suppose it's just as well they left when they did," Janet remarked. "We've had two new couples arrive today."

"I didn't realise you had midweek bookings this week," Robert said.

"We didn't," Joan told him. "Both couples arrived without bookings."

"Is that unusual?" Robert asked.

"Actually, it's very unusual," Joan told him. "We haven't had more than one or two other occasions where people have simply turned up on our doorstep and asked for a room. We aren't that easy to find, if you don't know that we're here."

"Did you ask either couple how they'd found you?" Robert asked.

"We should have, but no, we didn't," Joan replied.

"Charles said something about Doveby House being recommended by a friend," Janet recalled. "Apparently his friend stayed here some years ago, when Maggie Appleton was running the bed and breakfast."

"I think I might have to do some checking into him, then," Robert said. "Maggie Appleton had some interesting guests over the years."

"Interesting?" Janet asked.

"Yes, I think that's the best way to describe them," Robert said. "As far as I know, none of them ever did anything criminal, in Doveby Dale, anyway."

"It seems as if there's been something of a crime wave since we've settled here," Joan commented.

"There have been more issues lately than normal," Robert agreed. "But such things often come in odd waves. No doubt things will settle back down before too much longer."

Robert asked the women for as much information as they could provide on their new guests. Joan told him what she could.

"It isn't much," she said when she was finished. "I usually know a great deal more about our guests before they arrive."

"I wonder how the Dolyes found you," Robert said. "You might ask them tomorrow over breakfast."

"You don't think there's anything wrong with letting them stay, do you?" Janet asked anxiously.

"I've no reason to believe that they are anything other than what they seem," Robert said. "I'm just curious, that's all. They sound like the type of couple who would book themselves into somewhere posh when they go on holiday. Not that Doveby House isn't lovely, but it's not a five-star hotel in the city centre."

"No, it's definitely not that," Janet agreed.

"And we aren't all that close to Derby," Robert added. "I'm sure there must be quite a few other places to stay between here and there."

"And this time of year, it's highly unlikely that they'd all be full," Joan said.

Robert nodded. "I'd appreciate it if you'd let me know what they tell you," Robert said. "Thank you for the information about the supermarket. I hope this credit card thing is just something random."

"It sounds as if it might be," Janet said.

"Yes, so far, anyway," Robert agreed. "And with that, I'd better get going. I need to ring a lot of people this afternoon."

After Robert left, Joan got started on the chicken casserole, while Janet made a few phone calls of her own. She really wanted to find out more about Alberta Montgomery. She started with Martha Scott.

"Martha? It's Janet Markham. How are you?"

"Oh, it's good to hear from you," Martha said. "I'm fine. How are you?"

"I'm fine, too. I have a question for you, though. You grew up in Doveby Dale, didn't you?"

"I did, yes, but I left when I was eighteen and only came back recently."

"I was wondering if you knew anything about a woman named Alberta Montgomery," Janet said.

"Oh, my," Martha replied. "I haven't heard that name in years."

"So you do know who she was?"

"I do. Such a tragic story, really."

Janet felt her heart race. "Tell me the story, please."

"Why don't we have dinner together and I'll tell you then?" Martha suggested. "It's too involved to go over on the phone."

Janet thought about the chicken casserole that she could smell bubbling away in the kitchen. "I can't do tonight," she said. "What about tomorrow night?"

"That would work for me," Martha said. "I so rarely have plans."

"Where would you like to meet?"

"How about the local café? I like Todd and Ted, and I try to eat there as often as I can."

"That sounds good," Janet replied. They agreed on six o'clock.

"I'm going to ring a few people that probably know the story better than I do," Martha told Janet. "I'll find out as much as I can before tomorrow."

"Thank you," Janet said.

She put down the phone, feeling excited. "I'm going to have

dinner with Martha tomorrow," she told Joan. "She's going to tell me all about Alberta."

"How nice," Joan said. "Perhaps I'll see if Michael is free tomorrow night."

"You're welcome to join me and Martha," Janet told her. "She won't mind, and then you can hear all about Alberta, too."

"I think I'd rather spend my time with Michael, if you don't mind," Joan said. "You'll tell me all about Alberta, won't you?"

"Of course I will," Janet laughed. "And maybe I'll read her letters and diaries, too."

Joan frowned. "I'm not sure that's appropriate," she said.

"I'll talk to Martha first," Janet said. "Then we can discuss it."

"I'm going to curl up with a book for a short time," Joan said. "Dinner can look after itself for a while, and I can't think of anything else that needs doing."

Janet wasn't about to argue with her sister when she suggested something enjoyable. They both settled in the library and read until it was time for Joan to add the finishing touches to their evening meal.

"I'll call you in a few minutes," she told Janet as she left the library.

Janet nodded, her attention on her book far more than on her sister. She reached the end of the chapter and sighed. She really ought to go and help Joan with the meal. Putting the book on the nearest table, she got up and stretched before heading to the kitchen. The front door opened as she walked through the sitting room.

"Ah, I didn't expect there to be anyone in here," Charles Irwin said as he and Carla walked in.

"I was just passing through on my way to the kitchen," Janet explained.

"Well, your tea smells good, anyway," Carla said.

"Joan is a good cook," Janet told her.

"I don't suppose she could feed us as well?" Carla asked. "We've no idea where to get a meal around here."

"I'm sorry," Janet said. "But we weren't expecting guests for dinner. Joan will have only prepared enough for the two of us. I can recommend the café that's just up the road, though. They do good food at good prices."

"That sounds like what we need," Charles said.

"Yeah, sure," Carla said. "Let's just go and get something before I starve."

The pair turned and walked back out of the house, leaving the door unlocked behind them. Janet locked it before she joined Joan in the kitchen.

"Did I hear the front door?" Joan asked.

"Yes, it was just Charles and Carla, coming in to complain about being hungry," Janet said. "I sent them over to the café."

"Good," Joan replied. "I'm sure I have enough casserole for them, but I'm not in the mood to entertain guests at dinner."

"Are you okay?" Janet asked, concerned.

"Oh, I'm fine," Joan assured her. "But I'm feeling a bit cross about having unexpected guests, that's all. I much prefer when guests make proper bookings and arrive on schedule. It's bad enough I'll have to wait up for them tonight. I don't want to feed them, as well."

"Maybe they'll come home after the café and have an early night," Janet said hopefully.

"Maybe they'll come home and sit in the television lounge for hours," Joan replied.

"Perhaps we ought to consider putting televisions in the guest rooms," Janet suggested.

"As you'd be the one who would have to hear them if the guests turned them up too loud, I'll leave you to decide on that," Joan said.

Janet made a face. "You're right," she said. "No doubt they would put the volume up and then shout at one another over the noise. I think I'm happier with only having telly in the lounge down here."

"I did wonder about putting a telly in my private sitting room," Joan said. "Then you or I could watch something in there if the guests were using the telly in the lounge."

"As we both watch so much telly," Janet said.

Joan laughed. "I watch with Michael," she said. "But we watch what he likes, because I never know what else to suggest."

"I only watch telly when I'm not in the mood to read," Janet said. "And that only happens once in a rare while."

Joan served up bowls full of delicious chicken casserole, with apple crumble for pudding.

"Ice cream, as well?" Janet asked as her sister put her crumble in front of her. "What have I done to deserve this?"

"Like I said, I just feel bad that I haven't been here for the last two nights," Joan told her. "Of course, you're out tomorrow night, so maybe I shouldn't feel so guilty."

"You shouldn't feel guilty at all," Janet said. "I'm a grown adult and I can feed myself if I have to. I want you to enjoy your time with Michael, not feel guilty about it."

"I do, when I'm with him," Joan assured her. "It's only before and after that I feel bad."

"I should be happy you do," Janet said after a mouthful of crumble. "This is delicious."

Joan laughed. "I make you apple crumble even when I'm not feeling guilty," she said.

"But not with ice cream," Janet replied.

With the dishes all safely tucked into the dishwasher, Joan got the kitchen ready for breakfast the next morning. Janet was helping when they heard the front door again.

"Ah, Janice, wasn't it?" Gary Doyle asked as Janet went to investigate.

"It's Janet, but you were close," she replied.

"We're dying of starvation," Roberta told her. "Can you suggest somewhere nearby that does fast food?"

"There's a lovely little café just around the corner," Janet said. "I wouldn't call it fast food, but they are reasonably quick."

"Perfect," Gary said. "We'll go there."

They were out the door as soon as Janet gave them directions. She locked up behind them and then went to the library for her book. With both sets of guests at the local café, perhaps they would get an early night after all.

Chapter 8

In the end, Charles and Carla were back at Doveby House before seven, and Gary and Roberta returned just before eight. While both couples watched television for a short while, it seemed that no one could agree on what to watch, so both couples headed up to bed shortly after nine. Janet and Joan locked up behind them and happily took themselves off to bed as well. Aggie was already fast asleep in Janet's bed by that time.

Both sisters were up early, and they ate their breakfasts together, chatting about nothing much and enjoying the peace and quiet while their guests slept. Gary and Roberta came down for their breakfast at exactly nine o'clock.

"I feel as if I could have slept for another eight hours," Roberta told the sisters as she slid into a seat at the kitchen table. "The bed is very comfortable."

"I'm glad you like it," Joan replied. She cracked eggs and fried bacon while Janet made toast.

"We're just off to spend the day in Derby," Gary said. "We're going to meet our friends for lunch and then do some shopping. Can you suggest anywhere near here for dinner tonight? I think we'd like something nicer than the café, although the food was good there."

"There's a nice French restaurant near the centre of the village," Janet told him. "I thought the food there was excellent, and we lived in France for some time when we were younger."

"That sounds good," Roberta said. "Let's go there."

Gary nodded. "We'll need breakfast at eight tomorrow, I'm afraid," he said. "We need to get away before it gets too late."

"Eight is fine," Joan assured him as she put plates of food on the table. "I can manage earlier, if that works better for you."

"Oh, no," Roberta said with a shake of her head. "I don't want to be up by eight. I definitely don't want to be up any earlier."

Gary chuckled. "She's lazy," he told the sisters. "It's one of her better qualities."

Roberta laughed. "I don't know why I put up with you," she said to the man, her tone affectionate.

"I don't, either, but I awfully glad you do," he replied, giving her hand a squeeze.

Once they'd finished and left and the breakfast dishes were cleared away, Joan sat down at the kitchen table and sighed.

"I can't believe I have to wait for midday for our other guests," she complained.

"They'll probably be up before that," Janet said encouragingly. "They were probably exaggerating."

"I'm not sure if I should clean the Doyles' room now, or wait until later," Joan said. "The vacuum is sure to disturb Charles and Carla, isn't it?"

"If it does, you won't have to wait for midday to feed them," Janet pointed out. "It's nearly ten o'clock. They should be awake by now."

Joan nodded and then sighed again. "I can't do it," she said. "I can't bring myself to vacuum when I know they might be sleeping."

"I'll do it," Janet offered. "I have that doctor's appointment this afternoon. If you want my help with the rooms, we need to do them this morning."

"I forgot your appointment was today," Joan said. "Maybe we should get at least one room done before you leave."

It was just a regular appointment to have her eyes checked, which wouldn't take long, but Janet hadn't found anywhere nearby to have it done, so she was driving back to the same place she'd gone for years before they'd purchased Doveby House. That meant a drive of about an hour each way, which turned the whole errand into something that would take most of the afternoon.

Janet found herself creeping up the stairs, trying to be as quiet as possible on her way to help with the cleaning. Joan was behind her, also tiptoeing her way up the creaky stairs.

"This is silly," Janet whispered outside the Doyles' door. "The must be awake in there." She nodded towards the other guest room door.

"Whether they are or not, we should be quiet," Joan hissed. "Or as quiet as we can be running a vacuum cleaner."

Janet chuckled and then walked over to the small cupboard where they kept the cleaning supplies. She wheeled the vacuum into the guest room and plugged it in as Joan began running a duster over every flat surface.

"Here goes nothing," Janet muttered. She switched on the machine. It seemed louder than normal as it roared to life. While she didn't mean to, she was aware that she was working much more quickly than she usually did as she ran the vacuum over the floors in the bedroom and adjoining en-suite. When she turned the machine off, she was almost expecting to hear Charles or Carla shouting a complaint at them.

"Well, that wasn't too bad," Joan said a few minutes later as they descended the stairs. "We got through the room quickly, anyway."

"It helped that there wasn't anything out of place," Janet said. "I wonder if our other guests are keeping their room as tidy?"

"I wonder if they'll complain about the noise when they come down."

"While we're wondering things, I wonder if they'll be down before midday," Janet said, laughing.

It was actually a few minutes past twelve when the couple finally made their way down the stairs and into the kitchen.

"Ah, good morning," Charles said. "Do you have coffee?"

Joan nodded. As she was busy starting breakfast for the pair, Janet poured them each a cup of the steaming hot liquid.

"That's better," Carla said.

"Breakfast won't be long," Joan told them.

"We really should have made the effort to get up earlier," Charles said. "Let's aim for eleven tomorrow," he told Carla.

She made a face. "Must we?" she asked.

"Yes, I think so," he replied. "Otherwise we probably won't have time to see anything before we have to head north."

"Whatever," Carla said.

"Can we have breakfast at eleven tomorrow?" Charles asked Joan.

"Of course you can," Joan said. "We ask that guests check out before midday," she reminded him.

"Of course," he said. "That will work, then."

Joan put their breakfast in front of them, and the pair ate silently for several minutes.

"That was great," Charles said as he got to his feet. "I hate to run off so quickly, but we have lots to see and not many hours to see things in."

Janet heard the front door open and close just a moment later. She walked into the sitting room and watched as the couple walked down to their car. They hadn't locked the door behind them again, but then neither had the Doyles when they'd left earlier.

"Why doesn't anyone lock up behind themselves?" she asked Joan when she returned to the kitchen.

"Because they're used to staying in hotels where you don't have to?" Joan guessed.

"I suppose," Janet said. "Maybe we need to give them more specific instructions about using the door."

"Or maybe we should put a sign on it to remind them."

"Maybe."

Janet enjoyed her drive back to the area where she and Joan had lived for so many happy years while they'd both been teaching. After her appointment, she drove past the small cottage that they had shared. It looked smaller than she remembered. As she drove to Doveby House, she thought about how much better she liked their current home. Having her own en-suite was one of the best parts, but she also loved her large bedroom and, of course, the library. Perhaps having to have guests now and again was a small price to pay for living with so much luxury, she thought.

The temptation to read at least one or two of Alberta's letters before her dinner with Martha was almost unbearable. Unfortunately, Joan was opposed to the idea.

"Imagine how you'd feel in a hundred years, after you were dead, if someone read through your letters," Joan said.

"If I'm dead, I don't imagine I'll feel anything," Janet replied.

"You know what I mean."

"Yes, but really, I wouldn't mind. I've never written a letter that I'd be ashamed to have someone else read," Janet said. "Mostly they're deadly dull, all about the weather or what I had for dinner or some such thing. I'm sure Alberta's are much the same."

"Then you shouldn't mind not reading them," Joan said.

Janet sighed. "I still want to read them. You know I love history. I'm sure the letters will provide a fascinating window into life here in the nineteen-thirties."

"Maybe," Joan said grudgingly. "But they aren't ours to read. Alberta must have family somewhere. It's only proper that we pass them along to her family unread."

"I'll argue with you more later," Janet said eventually. "For now, I'm going to meet Martha and see what I can find out."

"Michael is cooking dinner for me tonight," Joan told her. "I won't be out late, though. I know we still have guests to look after."

"I won't be late, either," Janet said. "Meals at the café never take long."

She was a few minutes early when she arrived at the café. Molly found her a table in a corner.

"Should I ask Todd if he can do you three different meals again tonight?" she asked Janet.

"Oh, no, I think just one will be fine for tonight," Janet told her. She opened the menu and tried to make up her mind as she waited for her friend.

"Janet, there you are," Martha said as she crossed the room.

Janet stood up to give her friend a hug. The pair had met as members of the Doveby Dale Ladies' Club, a group that met monthly for dinner. While Janet hadn't warmed to all of the members, she had liked Martha and was glad to have found an excuse to see her again.

Martha dropped into the chair opposite Janet and beamed at her. Like Janet and Joan, Martha had never married. She's spent her working life as a nurse in York. She'd taken early retirement due to poor health, but retirement seemed to agree with her. Her grey hair was pulled back into a tight bun, and today she was wearing glasses with bright blue frames.

"How are you?" she asked Janet as she reached for a menu.

"I'm well. How are you?"

"I'm doing very well. It seems Simon Hampton has given up on tearing down my house, at least for now."

"That is good news," Janet said. Martha lived in a small house on the road that ran behind the small local grocery shop. Before the recent fire, the shop's owner had been trying to buy the houses along the street so that he could tear them down and expand.

"Is he going to rebuild?" Janet asked.

"I've no idea," Martha said. "I just know that I was told the offer he'd made on my property had been withdrawn. A few of my neighbours aren't very happy, as they were hoping to sell, but I'm delighted."

Molly came over and took orders for drinks before telling the women about the day's specials. Both women agreed that chicken Kiev was exactly what they wanted. When Molly was gone again, Janet restarted the conversation.

"So, tell me about Alberta Montgomery," she demanded.

Martha laughed. "You are eager, aren't you?"

"I'm sorry," Janet said. "But we've found letters and diaries, you see. I'm dying to read them, but Joan won't let me. She thinks we need to find the woman's family and give them all to them."

"Well, good luck with that," Martha told her. "She was the last Montgomery. There isn't anyone left."

"Oh, dear," Janet said, feeling slightly but guiltily happy to hear that. "I want to hear everything you know about her."

"It isn't much," Martha said apologetically. "I've rung around to find out more, but most people didn't remember much more than I do. You'd do better going to the Doveby Dale Historical Society, really."

"There's a historical society?" Janet asked.

"Yes, although it's really only two or three people who meet three or four times a year. I can give you the details."

"I'd appreciate that."

"Right, so Alberta Montgomery," Martha said. "I don't know how much you know about the history of Doveby House?"

"I know nothing," Janet said. "Although I'm ashamed to admit it."

"Everything I know is second- or third-hand village gossip," Martha said. "But I'll tell you what I've heard. Did you know it was built in the seventeenth century by a local farmer who'd come to think of himself as somewhat more important than he was?"

"That much I'd heard," Janet said.

"He started building it with a much grander plan, I understand, but had to scale it back as his costs kept going up."

"That sounds about right," Janet muttered.

"Yeah, nothing's changed since the seventeenth century," Martha agreed. "Anyway, when he finally finished the house, he and his wife moved in. As I understand it, they died childless, and someone from Derby bought the house. From there, I gather it changed hands quite frequently, but I don't know anything about any of the owners. I don't even know if any of them lived in the house or if they used it as a summer home or whatever."

"This is disappointing," Janet said as Molly delivered their drinks.

"Is that not what you ordered?" Molly asked. "I'm sorry."

"No, not the drinks, the story my friend was telling me," Janet quickly cleared up the misunderstanding. "The drinks are fine."

"Things got more interesting around the turn of the century," Martha told her. "Albert and Georgina Montgomery bought Doveby House and moved in. They were a young couple, newly married, with new money from his job in manufacturing. He worked in Derby and stayed there during the week, leaving his bride in Doveby Dale on her own."

"Oh, dear," Janet said.

"Actually, it seems to have worked for them," Martha said. "The only problem was that dear old Georgina didn't seem to be able to have children. It's possible that she had miscarriages or stillbirths, but nothing was ever recorded, at least as far as I know. It wasn't until 1917 that she was finally delivered of a healthy baby girl."

"Alberta?"

"Alberta."

"She and Albert must have been thrilled," Janet suggested.

"I'm sure they were," Martha agreed. "Unfortunately, they didn't exactly live happily ever after."

Molly chose that moment to deliver their food, forcing Janet to wait politely to hear the rest of the story.

Chapter 9

The first few bites of her meal almost made Janet forget about Alberta, as everything was delicious.

"This was the right choice," Martha said after a mouthful. "It's really good."

"It is," Janet agreed.

"Anyway, back to Alberta," Martha said after washing down another bite. "She grew up in Doveby House, a much doted on and rather spoiled little thing. Her mother hired a nanny for her and she was educated at home, rather than sent to the local school. The family wasn't hugely wealthy, but between Doveby House and some other property that her father owned, Alberta was certainly the most significant heiress in the area. That meant several prominent Derby area families sought her as a potential bride."

"Surely arranged marriages were a thing of the past by that time," Janet said.

"Not among the upper classes," Martha told her. "Or at least not as far as the Montgomerys were concerned. They wanted their little darling to marry into a title, you see."

"Poor little Alberta," Janet said.

"Yes, well, unfortunately for her parents, she wasn't as agreeable as they expected. They found her the younger son of a duke, who would at least make her Lady Alberta something or other, but she decided she didn't like him and refused to marry him."

"As well she should have."

"Yes, I'm sure you're right. The man in question was twenty years older than Alberta and had been married twice before. His first wife had disappeared on their honeymoon trip to India and his second had been quietly put away in an asylum after only a year of marriage. While he was titled, he wasn't much of a catch."

"What sort of parents want to tie their child to a man like that?" Janet demanded.

"Social climbing parents," Martha told her. "Remember this was over sixty years ago. Things have changed a lot since then."

Janet nodded. "But still," she said. "I feel sorry for Alberta. What happened next?"

"Young Alberta took matters into her own hands and found herself a suitor."

"Good for her," Janet said.

"Bad for her. The man was the Doveby House gardener and in no way suitable. Apparently she used to meet him in the carriage house without her parents knowing."

Janet wondered if the man in question could be the carriage house ghost. She didn't think she knew Martha well enough to tell her about the strange things that happened there. Martha might not believe in ghosts.

"This story doesn't have a happy ending, does it?" Janet asked.

Martha shook her head. "As I understand it, her parents found out about her relationship with the gardener and started keeping a closer eye on her. No one seems completely sure exactly what happened next, but the most popular version of the story is that Alberta found herself pregnant. Her parents allegedly locked her in her room."

"Again, the poor girl," Janet interjected.

Martha nodded and continued. "It's said that one night, a short while later, she looked out of her window and saw the gardener walking towards the carriage house with another woman. They say she screamed and then opened her window and tried to climb down to confront him. Apparently she got tangled up in her skirts, or maybe she was already too pregnant to try anything that ambitious. Whatever the reason, she fell to her death."

Janet felt a cold chill go down her spine. "Which room was hers?" she asked.

"The one at the top of the stairs," Martha said. "I understand it's the largest bedroom on the first floor."

Janet shivered. "Was there a full moon the night she died?"

"Oh, yes, I forgot that part. That makes it more spooky, doesn't it?"

"Every time there's a full moon, I get woken up by two screams, a few seconds apart," Janet said softly.

Martha stared at her for a minute and then nodded. "I'd heard that she still haunts Doveby House," she said.

"What happened to her parents?" Janet asked after she taken a moment to breathe deeply.

"They moved away not long after Alberta died. The local version of events says that they never settled anywhere again, but simply kept moving around, trying to escape or forget their past. The truth is probably less exciting."

"Probably," Janet agreed. "What about other family members? Joan wants to find out who the letters and things belong to."

"I don't think either Albert or Georgina had any family, at least not in the area. As I said, you should talk to the historical society. They will know a lot more than I do about all of it."

"I want to read her letters," Janet said. "And her diaries. It's a fascinating, albeit sad, story."

"You should make a book out of them," Martha suggested.

"I should," Janet agreed. "I've always wanted to write a book. I could retell the story using excerpts from the diaries and letters. Maybe I could use some of the poems from Alberta's book as well."

"Alberta's book?"

"I found a box with copies of a book of poems that Alberta had privately published in 1937," Janet explained.

"Are the poems any good?"

"I didn't even look. I just read the cover page, really. I'm going to have to sit down with them when I get home, though. I think I'm already a little obsessed with Alberta."

"I don't blame you," Martha said. "If anyone interesting had ever lived in my house, I'd be the same way. Unfortunately, the first owners were a young couple who had two children, raised them there, and then retired and moved into a retirement community. I bought the house from them."

Janet laughed. "At least you don't have ghosts," she pointed out.

"That's very true," Martha agreed.

"How is everything?" Ted asked.

"Oh, it was wonderful," Janet told him. "Probably one of the best meals I've had here."

"I'll tell Todd," he replied happily. "Chicken Kiev was another of Molly's ideas and it's selling very well."

"We sent both of the couples that are staying with us up here last night," Janet told him. "And they both enjoyed their meals."

"And we thank you for sending us the extra business," Ted said. "We're almost too busy at the moment, but I'm not complaining. After the quiet winter, we were wondering if we were going to be able to make a go of it or not. Things are definitely looking up in the last week or so, though."

"I'd hate to see you close the café," Janet said. "I'll have to start eating here more often to help keep you in business."

Ted laughed. "You know you're welcome any time," he said. "We weren't really thinking of closing, just cutting back in certain areas, really. We were going to stop taking credit cards, but as it turns out, it's a good thing we didn't. It seems as if everyone wants to pay by card these days."

"I'm going to pay with cash," Janet told him.

"Me, too," Martha said. "Only because I accidently left my credit card at home, though."

Ted cleared away their plates and talked them into pudding. Once he was gone, Martha dug a card out of her handbag.

"That's the man who's in charge of the historical society," she told Janet.

"Winifred Godfrey," she read. "He sounds like a historian."

Martha giggled. "He's very nice, but don't ring him unless you have time for a long conversation," she said. "I'm sure he'll be able to tell you more about Alberta and the Montgomery family, anyway."

Full of chicken, potatoes and sticky toffee pudding, Janet headed for home with her mind racing. She wanted to ring the man from the historical society straight away, but she thought she probably should talk to Joan first. Even more than that, she wanted to read the letters and diaries, but she knew Joan would be angry if she did so.

"The book isn't private," she argued with herself as she opened the door to Doveby House. "It was published, after all."

Privately, a little voice in her head told her. "Oh, hush," she told the little voice, startling Aggie, who was chasing shadows around the kitchen.

"Meeerreeewww?" she asked.

"Oh, nothing," Janet said. "I'm just going into Joan's room to grab a book." She pulled her keys out of her pocket and stepped towards Joan's door. Her hand hesitated on the knob. While she and Joan had never discussed it, they had an unspoken agreement that they would respect one another's privacy. Letting herself into Joan's room felt like an intrusion. Joan had said she would be home early. She really needed to wait for her sister to get her the book.

"Oh, bother," she said loudly.

Aggie looked up at her and then shook her head. Janet chuckled. "Sorry, baby," she said. "I'm just being sensible and responsible, and you know I hate doing that."

Aggie nodded and then rubbed her head against Janet's leg. Janet scooped her up and carried her into the sitting room. She sat down with a book, not the one she wanted but the best she could do, and began to read.

"I'm telling you, I didn't buy anything," Carla was saying as she and Charles walked into Doveby House a short time later.

"Well, one of us did," Charles snapped at her. "You heard what the man said, our card was declined. That means we're over our limit again. I told you the last time that happened that I was going to take your card away, didn't I? Maybe I should follow through."

"I didn't buy anything," Carla repeated herself. "I haven't bought anything other than petrol on that card in the last three months. I've been using the debit card for everything else."

"We'll see," Charles said. "I'll ring them in the morning and see who's been buying what."

"Good evening," Janet said from her chair in the corner.

"Ah, um, good evening," Charles replied. "I, um, didn't see you there."

"Yes, well, I'm sorry, but I couldn't help but overhear your conversation," Janet said. "There have been some issues in the Derby area with credit cards lately. Our last guests had their card details stolen. The thieves bought several items at a shop in Leeds before they realised it."

Charles glanced at Carla. "We'll see when I ring them tomorrow," he said.

"Why not ring them now?" Carla asked. "Someone should answer whatever time you ring."

He used his mobile to ring the number on the back of his card. While he talked, he wandered into the television room, leaving Janet and Carla in the sitting room. When he returned, his face was red.

"I suppose I owe you an apology," he told Carla. "Someone got our card details and had a shopping spree in Manchester on us."

"Manchester?" Carla repeated.

"Yeah, but they're going to send us some forms to fill out and we'll be able to get the money back," Charles said. "In the meantime, they've cancelled the card. They'll send us new ones soon."

"But what about our holiday?" Carla asked.

"We'll have to use the other card and hope it's okay," Charles said with a shrug.

Janet suggested that they might want to watch some television, with tea and biscuits, but the couple agreed that they were too upset to do so.

"We'll go up and get some sleep," Carla said. "I'm sure we'll feel better in the morning."

"Breakfast at eleven?" Janet asked, hoping that their early night might mean an earlier start the next morning.

"Yes, that sounds good," Carla replied.

Janet had only just opened her book again when the door opened a second time.

"Ring them now," Roberta said as she and Gary walked into the house. "Something must be wrong."

"I'll ring them when we get home," Gary replied. "Good evening," he added, nodding at Janet.

"Good evening," she replied. "Is everything okay?"

"Everything is fine," he told her. "We'll see you around eight."

Janet wanted to ask them if they were having credit card issues, but that seemed far too personal a question, even under the circumstances. They disappeared up to their room before Janet could work out a polite way to broach the question. Now she only had to wait up for her sister.

She could simply go to bed. Joan wouldn't forget to lock the front door or go rummaging around the kitchen for a late-night snack. But Janet was determined to get a copy of Alberta's book before she turned in for the night.

When the door opened an hour later, Janet was pacing back and forth, annoying Aggie, who was stretched out on one of the couches.

"I meant to be home hours ago," Joan said as she locked the door behind her. "But we were talking, and then we started watching a movie, and I couldn't resist watching it until the end. What time do you think the guests will get back?"

"They're all back and tucked up in bed," Janet told her.

"You weren't waiting up for me, were you? You know you don't need to do that. Michael always walks me home and makes sure I get in safely."

"I know, but I wanted to get a copy of Alberta's book, you see," Janet said. "And I didn't feel right going into your room while you were out."

"Alberta's book? Why?"

Janet told her the story as succinctly as possible.

"Interesting," was Joan's verdict. "But I still don't think we should read the letters or diaries. I suppose I can't object to you reading her book, though."

Janet followed her sister through the kitchen and into her sister's bedroom. Joan dug out the box of books and handed the top copy to Janet. "There you are, enjoy," she said.

"I'm only going to read one or two pages tonight," Janet said. "I can still have a fairly early night."

"I'm surprised both couples were back so early again," Joan said. "They both seem like the type to enjoy late nights out."

"There isn't really anywhere in Doveby Dale for a late night," Janet pointed out. "Anyway, Charles and Carla had credit card troubles, and I think that Gary and Roberta may have as well."

"Really? You'll have to tell Robert about it, assuming you haven't already."

"No, I thought I'd ring the station in the morning," Janet said. "It isn't urgent, after all."

Janet called Aggie, and the pair headed up the stairs to Janet's room. Aggie curled up on her pillow and went to sleep while Janet got ready for bed. She crawled under the duvet and propped herself up with some pillows.

"Okay, Alberta, let's see what you wanted to say so badly," she said.

The dedication page was the first surprise. It read "I blush at my boldness as I dedicate this work to Lord R." Was that a reference to the man she was meant to marry, rather than the gardener she'd fallen in love with, Janet wondered. She turned the page.

"An Ode to Love
I watch
I wait
I wonder
I love
I am invisible
I am too visible
I am sad
I am happy

Falling in love is too easy
Being in love is too difficult
The stars are out of alignment
My world is askew
Why
Why
Why

Janet looked at Aggie. "Well, I don't like it," she said. She shut the book and switched off the light. "I'll read more tomorrow," she said. "I think I need to be wide awake and in a good mood in order to appreciate Alberta's talent."

"Merrew," Aggie agreed.

Chapter 10

As Janet began to drift off to sleep, her brain began to replay various scenes from throughout the day. She recalled Charles complaining about his stolen credit card and Roberta talking about the need to ring someone. She shut her eyes tighter and rolled over. Her brain replayed Ted discussing their sudden increase in credit card payments. When she rolled over again, Aggie protested.

"I'm sorry, but I can't believe that Todd or Ted are involved in anything criminal," Janet said.

"Meeeooowww," Aggie replied.

As Janet shut her eyes again, Molly's face appeared in her head. "Molly?" she exclaimed.

"YOOOWWWWWW!" Aggie shouted.

Janet sat up and switched on the light. "Molly? But she seems so sweet," Janet said.

"Yooowwww," Aggie replied.

"Not Todd?"

"Meerow."

"Not Ted?"

"Meerroowww,"

"How about Jacob Mills?"

Aggie blinked at her and then put her head down on her paws.

Janet named a few other random people and got nothing but yawns from her pet. "Molly McDermott?" she asked.

"Yooww," Aggie replied.

Janet sat and thought about it for a minute. It made perfect sense, even if the suggestion was coming from a cat. The trouble with the credit cards started around the same time as Molly arrived. Ted had said she was the niece of a friend, or something like that. How well did anyone actually know her? Janet sighed and flopped back on her pillows. She'd ring Robert in the morning and tell him what she was thinking. He could investigate discreetly and he probably wouldn't laugh at her, at least not to her face. With that decision made, Janet snuggled back under her duvet and fell asleep.

She and Joan had their breakfast at seven. While they were eating, Janet told Joan about her late-night idea. She didn't mention Aggie's reaction to the woman's name. It would best if Joan didn't laugh at her either, she thought.

"As I've not met the girl, I can't possibly comment," Joan said. "Didn't Robert say he thought the trouble was coming from outside Doveby Dale, though?"

"Yes, but he could be wrong," Janet told her. "The thing is, both couples who are staying with us went to the café on Wednesday night, and they both had problems with their credit cards on Thursday. That seems like too much of a coincidence to me."

Joan nodded. "I suppose you may be right," she said, surprising Janet. "You go and ring Robert while I get breakfast started for our guests."

Janet was pleasantly surprised when Robert answered the phone at the police station. "I wasn't sure if you'd be there or not," she said.

"I have to spend the day in Little Burton," he told her "But I stopped in here on my way. What can I do for you?"

"Both of our guests ate at the café on Wednesday evening," Janet said. "And both of them had credit card problems yesterday. I know it could be a coincidence, but I was wondering about Molly

McDermott, the young waitress who's working at the café at the moment."

Robert was silent for a moment. Eventually he sighed deeply. "I was going to ask her to have dinner with me on her next night off," he told Janet. "She's lovely and she seems very sweet."

"Yes, and she may be," Janet said. "It's probably just me adding up two and two and getting five."

"It's an interesting theory," Robert admitted. "I'm going to have to do some digging around to see what I can find out. At the moment, we've no reason to suspect her of anything, though. Please don't repeat your idea to anyone else."

"Joan is the only one I've told," Janet assured him. "And she won't say a word to anyone."

"I'll let you know what I find out," Robert said on a sigh.

Janet disconnected, feeling guilty. She hadn't realised that Robert was interested in the young woman. Now she had to hope that she and Aggie were wrong.

Gary and Roberta were right on time. They arrived in the kitchen with their suitcases. "We're going right after we eat," Gary told them. "Thank you for your hospitality."

While Joan cooked, Janet studied the couple. There was clearly something bothering them, but she couldn't bring herself to ask them about it.

"I was wondering," Joan said in a casual tone as she served breakfast. "How did you two come to hear about Doveby House?"

Gary looked at Roberta and then at Joan. "Paul Nichols is a friend of mine," he said. "Or rather, his father is. I saw him a few days ago and he couldn't say enough good things about the time he spent here. Roberta and I had been talking about sneaking away for a few days, so we just impulsively jumped into the car and came."

"I hope Paul is doing well back in London," Janet said.

"He seems to be," Gary said. "And he seems to have grown up a great deal during his time here. His father is already giving him additional responsibilities in his company."

"That's good to hear," Joan said.

Janet walked them to the door while Joan cleared away their dishes. "Thank you for staying with us," she told them as the door.

"We had a wonderful time," Roberta said. "I think we may be back."

Janet found one of the brochures about the house that Margaret Appleton had had printed. "If you plan to come again in spring or summer, you should probably ring and book in advance," she told them. "Not only are we already getting busy, we're going away for a short while, as well."

"We'll book next time," Roberta told her. "It's quite unlike us to do anything on impulse."

Janet watched as they walked to their car and then drove away. She locked the door behind them and returned to the kitchen. Charles and Carla joined the sisters only a few minutes later.

"I know we're really early," Charles said. "But my brother has just rung and he wants me in Edinburgh today if we can manage it. If you can't do breakfast now, we understand."

"I don't," Carla snapped.

Joan and Janet exchanged glances and Janet swallowed a smile.

"Breakfast isn't a problem," Joan assured them. "Have a seat. Janet can get you some coffee while you wait."

The pair were silent while Joan cooked, and they said little while they ate beyond complimenting Joan on the food. They went back to get their bags and were gone before Joan had finished the washing-up.

"Well, that was quick," Janet said after she'd seen the pair out. "And the house is all ours again, at least until tomorrow."

"We just have to clean their rooms," Joan said.

Janet made a face. "And wash all of the bedding," she sighed. "And towels. Maybe the next time we get surprise guests, we should turn them away," she suggested.

"I was thinking, since we weren't expecting them, the money they paid is something like a bonus," Joan said. "Maybe you'd like to take half of it and buy yourself a little treat."

"I could get more than a little treat with half of that money," Janet said. "Are you sure?"

"Of course I'm sure," Joan said. "I thought I might take the other half and get myself something nice."

Janet stared at her sister. Joan never bought herself anything other than what she absolutely needed. "Like what?" she asked suspiciously.

"Oh, I don't know," Joan said airily. "I was thinking that I might like some new clothes, maybe. Everything I have is from when we were teaching, and sometimes I think it might be nice to not dress like a primary schoolteacher."

Janet nodded slowly. "I think that's a great idea," she said, wondering exactly how much impressing Michael played a part into Joan's desire to shop.

In spite of Janet's complaints, it didn't take the sisters long to get the rooms clean and tidy. The washing machine took care of the sheets and towels, and because the weather was dry, Janet hung everything outside to dry rather than using the tumble dryer that had been in place when they bought the house. She and Joan preferred to use it as little as possible, really.

The weekend was busy with two very demanding couples, both of whom preferred to stay out late and rise early. Janet stayed up one night for them and Joan took the second, but both sisters were tired and a bit grumpy by the time they'd all left on Monday morning.

"If all of our guests were like that, I'd quit," Joan said after they'd stripped the beds again.

"If all of our guests were like that, I'd move out," Janet told her.

They were carrying all of the laundry down the stairs when someone knocked.

"Oh, goodness, you get it," Joan said. "I'll take everything through to the utility room and come right back."

Janet headed for the door. She was about to open it when Joan stuck her head back in the room.

"And if anyone asks, we're fully booked for tonight," she told Janet.

Janet laughed and pulled the door open.

"Good morning," Robert greeted her.

"Good morning," she replied. "We've just been cleaning guest rooms and we could use an excuse to have tea and biscuits. Please come in."

He laughed and followed Janet into the kitchen. Joan was just emerging from the utility room as they entered.

"Just the excuse we need for a break," she greeted the man.

When they all had cups of tea and plates of biscuits in front of them, Janet grinned at the man.

"You know you're welcome to come and have tea and biscuits whenever you have the time," she said. "Was there something else you wanted today?"

Robert nodded. "You were right about Molly," he said.

"Oh, I am sorry," Janet exclaimed.

"She was stealing credit cards?" Joan asked.

"No, not stealing the cards, just the card numbers," Robert explained. "Apparently, whenever anyone used their card in the café, she'd copy the numbers and expiration date while she was putting the card through their card machine. Then she'd ring up a friend who was able to make a fake card with the number on it. Her friend would go on a shopping spree and shop until the card hit its limit. Because she had a whole network of friends around the country, she didn't think anyone would ever trace it back to her."

"She shouldn't have stolen details from both of our guests on the same night," Janet said.

"Yes, that was a mistake," Robert agreed. "You were able to spot the connection that no one else had made."

Janet thought about giving some of the credit to Aggie, but she decided that the kitten wouldn't mind if she didn't. As Aggie was upstairs, fast asleep in Janet's bed, Janet wasn't worried that she'd overhear them, either.

"I'm sorry that Molly turned out to be a criminal," Janet said as she walked Robert to the door a short while later. "Maybe you should look for a girl closer to home."

"I wish there were girls closer to home," Robert sighed. "But I can't seem to find anyone who's interested in getting involved with a lowly police constable."

"Have you ever thought about asking the girl in the coffee shop out?" Janet asked.

"Stacey?" Robert said in surprise. "I can't imagine she'd be interested."

"You might be surprised," Janet told him.

Back in the kitchen, Joan was still sitting at the table, eating biscuits.

"Are you okay?" Janet asked.

"I'm fine," Joan replied. "But I must say, I'm looking forward to our holiday next month. I think we need to get away."

Janet studied her sister for a moment. "I know those last guests were awful, but I thought you loved having the bed and breakfast."

"Mostly I do," Joan said. "And I'm sure I'll be fine once I've recovered from that lot. But we've been so busy with guests that you never told me what Alberta's poetry is like."

Janet made a face. "I never got past the first page," she admitted. "I've never been overly fond of poetry, you know. Maybe you should read some of it and see what you think."

"I will," Joan said. "Once we've finished getting the house back into order."

Janet nodded and then sighed as the washing machine announced that it was finished with a loud and high-pitched noise. "I'll get that," she told Joan. "You can tidy up in here."

Joan nodded and rose to her feet.

"And once things are settled again, I'm going to ring the man at the historical society," Janet told her. "If we can't find any of Alberta's relatives, I'm going to read her letters and diaries. I was thinking they might make a good book."

"A book?"

"Why not? They must be full of details about life in the twenties and thirties, not to mention the sensational and tragic romantic subplot. It would be a bestseller."

"I'm not sure about that," Joan said.

"Well, it might be of interest to historians, at least local ones," Janet amended.

"It might, at that," Joan said. "Let's see if we can find relatives first, though."

"Yes, dear," Janet said.

As she pulled sheets and towels from the washing machine, she started planning the book in her head. Having no idea what was in the letters or diaries, she could only plan in the most vague way. It was raining outside, so as she filled the tumble dryer, she wondered about pen names. Janet Markham didn't sound very scholarly, she thought. She'd have to give the matter more thought.

Bessie, if you have any ideas about pen names, I'd love to hear them. I've rung Winifred Godfrey, but I've only spoken to his answering machine thus far. I've left two very polite messages.

Todd and Ted were quite upset when Molly was arrested. They felt terrible when they found out that she was stealing credit card details from their customers. It doesn't seem to have hurt their business any, at least. Instead, it seems as if Doveby Dale has rallied around them. Of course, with the local grocer's still shut, more people seem to be getting meals at the café, at least once or twice a week.

I've been referring to the whole unfortunate incident as the Irwin Case, although I do feel as if I should call it the Aggie Case, really. This is the second time in a row that she's identified criminals, although I haven't told anyone else about that.

I had a lovely dinner with William Chalmers, by the way. He was at his most charming. We haven't made any further plans, but I know he will be asking again. More on that when I see you, I think.

Joan and I are both really looking forward to seeing you soon. I'll send our itinerary in my next note. In the meantime, I hope all is well with you. Be warned, I shall be spending much of our holiday trying to persuade you to return the visit.

With kindest regards,

Janet Markham (and Aggie – who is also excited about meeting you)

Glossary of Terms

- **bin** — trash can
- **biscuits** — cookies
- **booking** — reservation
- **boot** — trunk (of a car)
- **car park** — parking lot
- **chemist** — pharmacist
- **chips** — french fries
- **cuppa** — cup of tea (informal)
- **en-suite** — attached bathroom
- **fizzy drink** — carbonated beverage (pop or soda)
- **fortnight** — two weeks
- **high street** — the main shopping street in a town or village
- **holiday** — vacation
- **jumper** — sweater
- **lie in** — sleep late
- **midday** — noon
- **pavement** — sidewalk
- **petrol** — gasoline (for a car)
- **pudding** — dessert

- **puds** — puddings (informal)
- **push chair** — stroller
- **queue** — line
- **saloon car** — sedan
- **shopping trolley** — shopping cart
- **telly** — television
- **till** — checkout (in a grocery store, for example)
- **torch** — flashlight
- **uni** — university (informally)

Other Notes

In the UK, dates are written day, month, year rather than month, day, year as in the US. (May 5, 2015 would be written 5 May 2015, for example.)

In the UK, when describing property with more than one level, the lowest level (assuming there is no basement; very few UK houses have basements) is the "ground floor," and the next floor up is the "first floor" and so on. In the US, the lowest floor is usually the "first floor" and up from there.

When telling time, half six is the English equivalent of six-thirty.

A "full English breakfast" generally consists of bacon, sausage, eggs, grilled or fried tomatoes, fried potatoes, fried mushrooms and baked beans served with toast.

A semi-detached house is one that is joined to another house by a common center wall. In the US they are generally called duplexes. In the UK, the two properties would be sold individually as totally separate entities. A "terraced" house is one in a row of properties, where each unit is sold individually (usually called a row house in the US).

Acknowledgments

I'm grateful to Janice and Charlene, who keep beta reading for me for title after title. Thank you both!

Thanks to Denise, my editor, who works to correct all of the mistakes I make throughout every book. Her hard work is hugely appreciated.

And thanks to you, dear readers, who are the whole reason why I do this!

The Jackson Case

A MARKHAM SISTERS COZY MYSTERY NOVELLA

Created with Vellum

Author's Note

I hope everyone reading this is having as much fun with the Markham sisters as I am. This is the tenth novella in the series, and I have so many more plans for them. I always suggest that you read the series in order (alphabetically) as the characters and their relationships change and develop as the series continues. If you choose not to do so, each novella should be enjoyable on its own, however.

The novellas are opened and closed with sections of letters from Janet Markham to her friend Bessie Cubbon on the Isle of Man. The sisters originally appeared in *Aunt Bessie Decides* in my Isle of Man Cozy Mystery series. You do not need to read that series to enjoy this one. (By the way, the sisters will be revisiting the island in *Aunt Bessie Observes*, which will take place between this novella and the next one.)

I do use English spellings and terms as the books are set in the UK. A glossary of terms and some other notes are included at the back of the book for readers in other parts of the world. The longer I live in the US, the more likely it is that American words and spellings will sneak in. I do my best to limit those.

This is a work of fiction and all of the characters are fictional creations. Any resemblance that they may share with any real person, living or dead, is entirely coincidental. The sisters live in a fictional village in Derbyshire. Although some shops or businesses may bear some resemblance to real-life businesses, that is also coincidental.

I'm always happy to hear from my readers. All of my contact details are available in the back of the book. Please let me know your thoughts about my books (or anything else you have on your mind). I also have a newsletter that goes out once a month and provides information about upcoming releases. You can sign up for the newsletter on my website or my Facebook page.

30 April 1999

Dearest Bessie,

I'm writing this in between sorting my clothes and starting to pack. I can't believe that we will be on our way to see you in such a short time.

All of your questions about Alberta Montgomery made me smile. I, too, would like answers to them, but that's proving more difficult than anticipated.

While planning for the trip has been occupying a great deal of my time, we've had a little excitement again in Doveby Dale. It all started when our neighbour, Stuart Long, asked for a favour.

Chapter 1

"And that's that," Janet said, pushing the front door of Doveby House shut behind the second couple that had spent the weekend at the bed and breakfast. "They weren't too bad, at least."

Joan nodded. "It does seem as if we've had quite a few difficult guests lately," she said. "But both couples this weekend were quite reasonable."

"At least they didn't stay out late, and they had their breakfasts at a reasonable hour, as well."

"I am looking forward to our holiday," Joan admitted. "It will be nice to not have to worry about anyone other than myself for an entire week."

"What about me?" Janet demanded with a laugh.

"You can look after yourself," Joan told her. "And Aggie."

Janet looked at the kitten who was chasing her tail in circles and nodded. "I think I can manage that," she said.

The sisters had owned Doveby House, a seventeenth-century manor house in the village of Doveby Dale, for less than a year, and they were both still adjusting to the demands of owning a bed and breakfast. They were retired schoolteachers, who had lived together their entire lives. Janet, two years younger than Joan, had always been the more adventurous of the sisters, so she'd been shocked when Joan had suggested that they spend an unexpected inheritance on Doveby House. Janet had never known that her sister had always wanted to own a bed and breakfast, but now that they were both retired, it seemed the perfect time to make her dream come true.

"What are your plans for today?" Joan asked her sister as they walked back into the kitchen.

Janet began filling the dishwasher with the plates and cups from breakfast as she spoke. "Well, we have to get the beds stripped and the bedding washed," she said. "We don't have guests again until the weekend, do we?"

"No; at least no one has booked."

"And if anyone just turns up, we'll send them away," Janet said firmly.

"We've an expensive holiday coming up," Joan reminded her. "A little extra income wouldn't hurt."

"I thought I might try ringing Winifred Godfrey again," Janet changed the subject. "Martha thought he would be eager to talk to me about Alberta, but he never rings me back."

"Maybe he's away at the moment. How many messages have you left for the man?"

"Only three," Janet said sheepishly.

"We're both eager to learn more about Alberta, but you shouldn't pester the poor man. I'm sure he'll ring you when he has the time."

Janet nodded, but she wasn't happy about it. Besides Doveby House, their property included a small carriage house that was full of boxes. Occasionally Joan would insist that the sisters work on clearing it out. One of the boxes had been full of letters and diaries that had belonged to Alberta Montgomery, who had grown up in the house in the nineteen twenties and thirties. A second box was full of copies of a book of poetry that she'd written and had had privately published. Both sisters had read the first few poems in the book and neither had been impressed with the woman's poetic abilities. They were both fascinated by the story of her life, however.

One of Janet's friends had been able to give them the basic

outline, and Janet was eager to learn more. Poor Alberta had apparently fallen to her death from Janet's bedroom window after seeing her lover with another woman. Her parents, who were angry that Alberta was involved with an unsuitable man, had allegedly locked her in her room that night. According to the story, the moon was full the night that Alberta died. Since they'd purchased the house, Janet had been woken by screams in the night every time there was a full moon. Joan didn't believe in ghosts, but she refused to try sleeping in Janet's room during a full moon anyway.

"I need a trip to the supermarket," Joan said. "I wasn't sure if you'd want to come along?"

"I suppose I could," Janet said. Then I can make sure that we get ice cream and chocolate biscuits, she added to herself.

"Let's get the guest rooms done and then we can go."

Janet followed her sister up the stairs. They split up and each went to work in one of the two guest rooms. Bedding and towels were piled up in the hallway before Janet pulled out the vacuum and Joan began to dust. A loud buzzing noise stopped Janet just before she switched on the vacuum.

"What was that?" she asked Joan.

"Was it the buzzer on the doors to the garden?"

"It may have been," Janet replied. The house had extensive gardens, with large French doors opening into them. As the gardens were fenced, however, it was very rare for someone to arrive at those doors. Both sisters went down together to see who was there.

"Ah, ladies," Stuart Long said. "I was wondering if I could ask you for a favour?"

Stuart and his wife lived in one half of the semi-detached house across the road from Doveby House. The man was tall, with dark hair that was clearly dyed and dark eyes. He was a retired gardener who happily looked after the grounds at Doveby House in exchange for a small fee and a great deal of tea and biscuits.

"Of course you can ask," Janet said. "But I won't promise we'll say yes."

Stuart nodded. "It may not be an issue anyway," he said. "Some friends of mine and I are planning a charity event. We've actually been planning it for months; it's meant to be happening this Friday. It was going to be held in Little Burton. Unfortunately, the venue suffered from a broken pipe and the entire ground floor has over an inch of water everywhere."

"Oh, dear," Janet said.

"We're all scrambling around, trying to find a new venue," Stuart said. "I was wondering about having it at Doveby House."

"What sort of event is it?" Joan asked.

"Just wine and a charity auction," Stuart explained. He named a large and nationally known cancer charity. "We're raising money for them," he explained. "We just need a big room that will hold a hundred or so people."

Janet and Joan exchanged glances. "I'm not sure our sitting room would hold that many," she said.

"No?" Stuart said, sounding disappointed. "I couldn't recall, really. I haven't been inside the house for years."

Janet shook her head. "You know you're welcome any time," she said. "Come in now and have a look. See what you think. I'm afraid Joan is right, though, it isn't a terribly large space."

Stuart followed the sisters through the house. The sitting room was at the front. It was a large for sitting room, but perhaps not large enough for a hundred guests.

"I'm afraid you're right," he said sadly. "It isn't as large as I remembered it. We'll have to look elsewhere. Winifred was sure it would work. I wonder if he's actually ever been here."

"Winifred?" Janet asked. "Is that Winifred Godfrey?"

"Yes, do you know him?" Stuart asked.

"No, but I'm trying to meet him," Janet replied. "I understand he's an expert in local history. I want to find out more about the history of Doveby House."

"He is, or at least he thinks he is," Stuart replied. "Right now he's awfully busy with this event. I'm sure he'll be happy to talk to you once it's over, though."

"I wish we could have helped," Joan said. "We'd like to do something to give back to the community."

"You can buy tickets for the evening, once we find a venue," Stuart suggested.

"Of course," Joan said.

"And, actually, would it be a terrible imposition if we used your sitting room for a planning meeting?" he asked. "I offered to have the meeting at my house, but I'm afraid we'll be a bit cramped there."

"You're more than welcome," Joan said. "When is the meeting?"

"Tomorrow," Stuart said. "At ten."

"I'll bake some biscuits especially for you," Joan said.

"That would be wonderful," Stuart beamed.

Joan loved baking, especially for other people. Janet often thought that it wasn't quite fair that Joan was slender even though she baked sweets and treats all the time. Janet tended to be much curvier, and all she did was eat whatever Joan prepared.

"How many people should we expect?" Janet asked.

"Oh, there's, um, six of us, I think," Stuart told her. "Fred, Alvin, Winifred and I are all from the Doveby Dale and Little Burton area. Norman and Julian are from London. They're both retired fundraising consultants who are helping us out."

"Why haven't we heard anything about this before now?" Joan asked. "If the event is on Friday, shouldn't we have seen some advertising before now?"

"It was advertised some in Little Burton," Stuart said. "Simon Hampton was going to help us with that by putting up signs in his shop, but you know what happened there."

Janet nodded. A fire had recently destroyed the local grocery shop that Simon owned. It was still unclear as to whether it was going to be rebuilt or not.

"There was a problem with the printers, as well," Stuart said. "We had flyers made up, but they took longer than they were meant to. Of course, that doesn't much matter, as they all have the wrong venue on them now anyway. And we're still waiting for the tickets. It's hard to sell tickets to people when you don't actually have any tickets to give them."

"How much are tickets going to be?" Joan asked.

"A hundred pounds a person," Stuart said.

Janet covered her gasp with a cough. Joan simply raised an eyebrow. "That seems a lot," she said.

"That's what I said," Stuart told her. "Mary had a fit until I told her that we would get complimentary tickets because I'm on the committee. It is for charity, though, that's the important thing."

Joan nodded. "Yes, well, when you have a new venue sorted and you actually have tickets, let us know. Janet and I will plan on attending."

"That's very good of you," Stuart said. "We should have both of those things by tomorrow, I hope. I'm going to ring Winifred when I get home and tell him that Doveby House is out. I know Alvin had some other ideas, so, fingers crossed, we should have some answers by tomorrow."

Stuart left through the conservatory, back out into the garden. As Janet locked the French doors behind him, she shook her head. "A hundred pounds a person? That's an awful lot of money if all you get for it is wine."

"It does seem dear, but perhaps that's the going rate for such things. It isn't the sort of event that we usually attend, after all."

"No, I suppose it isn't," Janet said. "What do you suppose people wear to such things?"

Joan frowned. "I've no idea," she said. "We shall have to ask Stuart tomorrow."

"Maybe I'll ring Mary and ask her," Janet said. "She'll have a better idea than Stuart, I should imagine."

"I wonder if anyone else we know is going. Perhaps I should invite Michael to join us."

Michael Donaldson lived in the other half of the property across the road. He was a widower and a retired chemist. Joan had never had a boyfriend when she'd been younger, although Janet had had a few. Both women had been surprised when Michael had first asked Joan for dinner, but now it seemed quite natural for Joan to include the man in their plans.

"Do," Janet said. "It will be good to have at least one other person to talk with."

Joan nodded. "Maybe we'll know some of the other men on the planning committee when they come tomorrow," she said.

"None of the names sounded familiar," Janet replied. "I'm sure I don't know anyone from Little Burton. The two men from London will be strangers as well."

"Maybe the Doveby Dale Ladies' Club should attend the event," Joan suggested.

Janet made a face. She'd joined the club because both she and Joan felt that they should make an effort to be involved in their community. While it had been advertised as an active community improvement group that met regularly, it was actually a small group of women who had dinner together about once a month.

There had been some excitement a few months back when one member suggested including men in the membership, but the man in question was currently in London for an extended period and the matter hadn't been raised again. While Janet liked some of the members, others were less easy to appreciate, and she wasn't eager to spend an evening sipping wine with them. At least with dinner, she got a good meal out of the evening.

"Maybe I'll see if Edna and Martha are interested," Janet said after a moment's thought. "Perhaps they'll want to include the others, as well."

Chapter 2

With dozens of biscuits to bake, Joan really needed a trip to the supermarket. The sisters loaded bedding and towels into the washing machine and then headed out. As the local shop was still shut, it was a bit of a drive to the larger one that offered both better prices and a better selection. Janet wondered if Simon would have trouble attracting customers if he did reopen, now that everyone was getting used to the minor inconvenience of driving a bit further.

After the shopping trip, Joan made them both lunch, and then she settled in to start baking. Janet was happy to finish cleaning the guest rooms. She knew she could pop down to the kitchen for a fresh and still warm biscuit whenever she wanted one. By the time Joan was ready to make them some dinner, Janet was too full of biscuits to want anything, though.

"Maybe just something light," she finally conceded before Joan could shout at her for spoiling her appetite.

Joan frowned but didn't complain. Janet noticed that her sister didn't eat much dinner either. Perhaps Joan had been sampling her own biscuits while she'd worked.

They couldn't find anything interesting to watch on the telly, so the sisters went to their own rooms to read before bed. Janet glanced at the book that had been sitting on her nightstand for days. Perhaps Alberta's "Poems for my Love" improved as it went along, she thought. She'd only managed four pages thus far, in spite of picking the book up nearly every day. Now she settled in and forced herself to read the next dozen poems.

"I think dear Alberta was a little bit crazy," she told Aggie as she put the book back on her nightstand. "The first few poems were just not very good. They get increasingly odd as the book goes on."

"Merowwww?" Aggie replied.

"Really? You want to hear one?" Janet shook her head. "You asked for it."

She opened the book to the last poem she'd read and cleared her throat. "It's called 'To My Love,' which is what they've nearly all been called," she told Aggie. "Dewdrops, Raindrops, Peppermint drops, Candles, Lamps and Moons, Our love is the light that lights the drops that drop from forever to here."

Janet shut the book again. "I don't understand it," she told Aggie.

Aggie shook her head and shut her eyes. "Yeah, that's how I feel about it, too," Janet told her.

She picked up the romance that she was halfway through. Romance novels were a guilty pleasure, one that Joan frowned upon, but Janet didn't really mind. Joan approved only a little bit more of mysteries, with Janet finally recently getting her to read and enjoy Agatha Christie, for whom Aggie had been named. While she'd been rearranging the library, Janet had let mystery books take the best spaces near her favourite chair. Now she was wondering if she ought to rearrange the books again to add some romances to the most conveniently placed shelves.

The romance novels that had already been in the library when they'd bought the house were mostly historical romances. Those weren't Janet's favourites, but she was reading through them anyway. Now she found herself lost in Regency England as a Duke and Earl fought over the younger daughter of a lowly farmer. After an hour, she found herself sighing over the ending. "I don't think the poor girl will have lived happily ever after," she told her sleeping cat. "His family was never going to accept her, not really. She'd have been better off marrying the young man from the neighbouring farm, even if it did mean she'd have to work hard for the rest of her life."

Aggie opened one eye and then squeezed it tightly shut again. Janet laughed. "Okay, I won't bore you with the details," she said. "Let's get some sleep. Tomorrow we have a committee coming to meet in our sitting room. If I were you, I'd hide up here all morning."

Stuart was at their door at nine, looking anxious. "I never should have offered to host this meeting," he told Janet as she let him in. "I didn't sleep at all last night for worrying about today."

"It's just a meeting with friends," Janet said soothingly. "What could possibly go wrong?"

"None of them are friends of mine, exactly," Stuart said. "I just want everything to go well and for us to be able to salvage our event. We've all worked really hard to get to this point. I'd hate to see it all fall apart at the last minute."

He and Janet walked to the sitting room, where he spent half an hour arranging and rearranging the furniture. "I just don't know," he said eventually. "We usually meet at Fred's house. He has a long dining table where we can sit and meet."

"You can use the dining room, if you'd like," Janet said.

"Why didn't I think of that?" Stuart asked, shaking his head. "I knew you had a dining room, but I've never been in it," he added.

"Follow me," Janet told him.

They walked through the kitchen and into the dining room that adjoined it. A long rectangular table filled most of the space.

"This will be better," Stuart said.

"It's easier for me, too," Joan said. "I can check on you more easily from the kitchen if you're in here."

And if I'm in the kitchen, I should be able to overhear the conversation, Janet thought but didn't say. It wasn't that she was planning to eavesdrop, exactly, but she wanted to help Joan if necessary, and sound seemed to travel between the two rooms quite easily.

Joan was stacking biscuits onto plates, and Stuart stopped to admire the sweet treats as he crossed back through the kitchen.

"They look wonderful," he said. "You must let me pay you something for all of the work you've put in."

"I'm sure we aren't paying you nearly enough for the work you do in the garden," Joan replied. "Let's just assume that this makes us closer to even."

"Thank you," Stuart said. He walked back into the sitting room with Janet on his heels. In the centre of the room, he stopped and shrugged. "I don't know what to do with myself," he told Janet.

"Why don't you come in the kitchen and have a few biscuits while you wait for the others?" she suggested.

"I'm too nervous to eat," he replied. He paced around the room for several minutes while Janet watched. She nibbled on the biscuits that she'd snuck out of the kitchen as she tried to work out how to calm the poor man down. It was a few minutes before the hour when the first guest knocked.

"Shall I?" Stuart asked.

"Go ahead," Janet told him.

Stuart opened the door and greeted the man on the porch. "Fred, glad you could make it," he said. The man stepped inside.

"Janet, this is Fred Arnold," Stuart told her.

Janet offered her hand to the man, who looked exactly like a child's picture book drawing of Father Christmas. His hair was grey and he had a full beard and mustache. His blue eyes twinkled at Janet as he took her hand. "It's a great pleasure to finally meet you," he said. "I've been hearing about the beautiful and kind Markham sisters since you bought Doveby House, but I haven't been able to work out an excuse to stop to meet you."

"You should have stopped anyway. We'd have given you tea and biscuits," Janet said with a laugh.

"Biscuits?" he asked excitedly. "I don't suppose we have any for today?"

"Joan baked nearly all day yesterday," Janet told him. "Stuart, why don't you two go through to the dining room and I'll let the rest of the guests in as they arrive?"

"Are you sure you don't mind?" Stuart asked.

"Not at all," Janet assured him. "You two go and get yourselves some biscuits and I'll send everyone else through when they turn up."

The pair had only just disappeared into the kitchen when someone else knocked.

"Ah, good morning," the man said when Janet opened the door. "I'm Alvin Jackson. I'm here for the committee meeting."

"Yes, of course," Janet said. "Do come in." She stepped back to let the man into the house. He was nearly bald, and the hair that he did have had been grown long and was combed over his head to try to make it look like he had more hair than he did. As he walked past her Janet noticed that he had something of a potbelly, although he seemed to trying to hold it in as much as he could.

"I haven't been here in a few years," he told Janet. "Maggie Appleton and I were good friends, but when I started seeing my current girlfriend she didn't approve of my relationship with Maggie." He sighed. "I don't really like jealous women, but Cindy is perfect in every other way."

Having no interest whatsoever in the man's love life, Janet didn't bother to respond to his words. "The meeting is going to be held in the dining room," Janet said instead. "If you'd like to follow me?"

Janet was only just walking back into the sitting room when the next knock came. Maybe this would be Winifred, she thought, eager to finally meet the man. Instead, two strangers were standing on the porch.

"Good morning," the taller of the two said. "I do hope we're in the right place. We're looking for Stuart Long."

"You're in the right place," Janet told him. "Do come in."

The taller man was bald, although he had a large moustache. He was slender, and he was wearing a handsome suit and a fashionable pair of glasses. "I'm Norman Glover," he told Janet. "And this is my associate, Julian Snyder."

Julian was shorter and heavier, although not unattractively so. He, too, was wearing a well-made suit. He had a full head of grey hair and green eyes.

"How do you do," he said politely.

"I'm Janet Markham," she replied. "My sister and I own Doveby House."

"It's a lovely old manor house, isn't it?" Julian said. "It's a shame this room isn't a bit larger. It would be almost perfect for our event if it had a little bit more space."

"Yes, well, I'm sure you'll be able to find somewhere else that will suit," Janet said. "Everyone is in the dining room. Let me show you."

The clock in the corner of the sitting room chimed ten as Janet walked back into the room. She had been hoping to talk to Winifred about Alberta, but she didn't want to make him late for his meeting. She paced back and forth several times and then caught herself doing it. You're as bad as Stuart, she chided herself, dropping into a seat on one of the couches. She glanced through the nearest book so that she wouldn't watch the clock. When the knock finally came, she was quick to open the door, though.

"I'm late," the man in the doorway announced. "Look at that," he demanded as he walked into the house. "It's already twenty past ten. You wouldn't believe how bad the traffic was. I was stuck behind the slowest driving you'd ever want to see. I was starting to wonder if I'd ever get here."

"I'm Janet Markham," Janet told the man, who looked older than the others. Janet guessed he was somewhere in his seventies. He was short and bald, and he was scowling. "I've left a couple of messages on your answering machine. I'd like to speak to you about Alberta Montgomery," she said, assuming that the man was Winifred Godfrey. He was the only other person expected.

"Such a tragic story," he said. "Of course, I remember it like it was yesterday. She was such a beautiful woman, but quite overprotected, really. But I'm late. I'm afraid I haven't time to speak to you right now. Where is the committee meeting?"

"In the dining room," Janet said. "I can show you."

"Oh, that's quite all right," he replied. "I know my way around Doveby House. I've spent many hours in just about every room. I was very fortunate to be able to befriend many of the owners over the years."

With that, he turned on his heel and walked off towards the kitchen. Janet shook her head as he disappeared from sight.

"Don't hold your breath on befriending the current owners," she muttered softly. She hadn't liked the man at all. She followed him, stopping in the kitchen.

"Everyone that was expected is here," she told Joan.

Joan crossed over to her. "That last man was quite unpleasant," she whispered. "He stormed through the kitchen as if he thought he owned the place. He didn't even try to speak to me."

"He was upset about being late," Janet said, not sure why she was defending the man. She hadn't liked him either.

"That doesn't excuse him from having basic manners," Joan said.

"Can you hear what's being said?" Janet asked, looking towards the dining room doorway.

"Only if you stand by the kettle," Joan told her. She flushed. "I found that out because I was making them tea," she said quickly.

Janet grinned. She didn't believe that for an instant. Joan was as nosy as Janet; she was just far more embarrassed about it.

"Ah, Joan, if we could have a bit more tea?" Stuart asked as he appeared in the doorway. "We're about to start."

Janet smiled. "I'll take it through," she said, picking up the teapot that Joan had ready. She made her way around the table, pouring tea for each guest.

"I'd prefer coffee," Winifred said stiffly when she reached his place.

"Certainly," Janet said, forcing herself to keep smiling.

"We don't want to make too much work for Janet and Joan," Stuart said anxiously. "They're letting us use their home for our meeting. The tea and biscuits are a bonus."

"I can easily get coffee for Mr. Godfrey," Janet said. "And anyone else who would prefer it?"

The others all shook their heads. It only took a moment for Janet to fill a cup from the pot that Joan had made earlier. She carried it in and set it on the table in front of the local historian.

"I think we can call the meeting to order," Stuart said nervously.

"Not while there are people present who aren't committee members," Winifred snapped.

Janet flushed. "I'll get out of the way, then," she said as politely as she could manage. As she walked out of the room, Stuart tried again.

"I'll officially call the meeting to order at ten twenty-five," he said.

Chapter 3

Joan had settled in at the kitchen table, in the chair closest to the dining room.

"That isn't your normal seat," Janet teased as she went and stood by the kettle.

"I want to be close by if they need anything," Joan told her.

Janet grinned but didn't reply. She could hear the voices quite clearly from where she was standing. No doubt Joan would be able to hear them as well.

"I believe the first order of business is the relocation of the event," Stuart began.

"Yes, that is a serious problem," Julian's smooth voice replied.

"Doveby House was suggested, but as you've all seen as you came in, it simply isn't large enough," Stuart said.

"I believe I said that when it was first mentioned." Janet made a face when she recognised Winifred's voice.

"Actually, you were the one who suggested it," a cheery voice that Janet thought was Fred's replied.

"I don't believe that's correct," Winifred snapped.

"Let's not argue," Norman said firmly. "Doveby House won't do. What other options are there?"

"I've been in touch with the Little Burton Community Centre," Fred said. "They're happy to let us use the space for a small fee, but it isn't exactly elegant. It's just a big hall with basketball hoops at each end, actually."

"That won't do," Winifred said sharply. "This is a very important event and we can't have it ruined by having it somewhere ghastly like that."

"So where do you suggest?" Fred asked.

"I thought perhaps we could use the French restaurant here in Doveby Dale. It's beautiful and would set just the right tone," Winifred said.

"Have you rung to them to find out about availability?" Norman asked.

"I have," Winifred said. "Unfortunately, as it is rather short notice, they won't be able to accommodate us."

"Perhaps we should focus on actual possibilities," Julian said. "While your efforts are greatly appreciated, I'm not sure it's worth taking up time during the meeting with discussing places that won't work."

"Yeah, I mean, the list of them is considerably longer than the list of places that might," Alvin said.

"Does anyone else have any other suggestions?" Norman asked.

After a long moment, Julian spoke. "It seems that the community centre in Little Burton, no matter how unsuitable, is our only option, then."

"I'm sure we can do better," Winifred said.

"The event is on Friday," Julian pointed out. "Today is Monday, which means we have only a few days to publicise the evening and get the tickets sold. Norman and Fred have done an incredible job in securing items for the auction. Now we need to make sure we have an audience to bid on them."

"And the right sort of audience," Winifred added. "We need to invite charitable people who will give generously, not the usual sort who attend events in Doveby Dale and Little Burton."

"I think the price of the tickets will help people to understand the nature of the event," Norman said.

"We'll have to spend more money on decorating if we're going to use the community centre," Stuart said. "And I think I'll probably need some extra help. I wasn't envisioning having to do all that much, but the community centre will need a great deal of work if we're going to make it look sophisticated and elegant."

"Well, I won't be able to help," Winifred said. "I'm far too busy right now."

"I might be able to give you a hand," Fred said. "When were you planning on decorating?"

"I'll have to ring the community centre and find out when we can get access," Stuart replied. "They may have other events as late as Friday afternoon, I suppose."

"I'm afraid Julian and I will be in London until just before time for everything to start on Friday," Norman said. "I wish we could help, but I'm sure you'll do a wonderful job."

"What's the budget for decorating?" Stuart asked.

The short silence that followed had Janet and Joan exchanging glances. Poor Stuart is going to get stuck paying for everything, Janet thought to herself.

"Julian and I have brought several boxes of things that we have left over from previous events," Norman said eventually. "Why don't you go through all of that and then see what else you think you need. You'll want to take a good look at the space before you buy anything, of course."

"Where are the boxes?" Stuart asked.

"In the boot of my car," Julian replied. "We can unload them after the meeting."

"So if that's the location agreed on, we can get the tickets printed, right?" Alvin asked.

"Yes, I don't see any reason why not," Norman replied.

"I'll ring the printer as soon as we're done. I'm hoping he can do a rush order and we'll be able to have the tickets by the end of today," Alvin said.

"And you'll be able to distribute them?" Julian asked.

"Yes, I can drop them off to everyone once they're done," Alvin agreed.

"And you're each going to sell thirty-five tickets," Norman said. "That should be about the right amount of guests."

"I don't believe I can sell that many tickets," Winifred said. "I thought it was twenty-five each, anyway."

"I think thirty-five each is a better target," Norman said. "I'm sure the community centre can accommodate a few extra guests, and the more guests, the more money we can generate to help with the fight against cancer."

"As long as it's just a target," Winifred replied. "I was struggling to work out to whom I was going to sell twenty-five tickets. An extra ten is impossible."

"Oh, come now," Julian said. "You've lived in Doveby Dale for seventy-five years. You must know hundreds of people. And I'm sure they all would be delighted to be given an opportunity to help in the battle against our most deadly enemy. I'm not saying it won't be work, but it shouldn't be too difficult."

"What about the flyers?" Stuart asked. "We need them reprinted with the correct location."

"I'll talk to the printer when I order the tickets," Alvin said. "Maybe he can give us a bit of a break on the price."

"We want a phone number on the flyer. A number where people can ring for tickets," Norman said.

"We used my number on the original flyer," Winifred said.

"Yes, let's change that to mine," Norman replied. "I'd rather the calls went to my mobile than your home. The last time I rang your home number, your answering machine was full."

"People keep calling to ask about historical society matters," Winifred said. "They fill up my machine with all manner of things. I can work harder to keep the machine clear."

"You're working hard enough as it is," Norman said. "I'll handle phone orders and keep a running list. We can have those tickets at the door on the night, which means they don't even need paper tickets."

"But those sales will still count towards my twenty-five, won't they?" Winifred asked.

"I would think you would be able to sell thirty-five easily,"

Norman replied, his voice cool. "If you'd like some advice on how to do so, we can talk after the meeting."

"Was there anything else that we needed to discuss?" Stuart asked.

"I think all of the auction items are ready to go," Fred said. "I'm storing them all in my dining room, so Friday can't get here soon enough for me."

"Norman and I are working on adding one or two things to the collection," Julian said. He named an actress from one of the well-known soap operas. "We're hoping to get an autographed script from her," he said.

"And we're talking to a premier league football team about a signed ball as well," Norman added. "Which is all the more reason why we need to sell a great many tickets."

"What about the food and drink?" Fred asked. "Who was taking care of that?"

"I've been talking to Simon Hampton about donating the wine and some food," Julian said. "He's an old friend of mine. I'm sure he'll come through."

"What are we having besides wine?" Fred asked.

"Whatever Simon gives us," Julian replied. "I've asked for cheese and cracker trays, and trays of finger foods and miniature puddings. As I said, he hasn't confirmed anything yet."

"As his grocery shop is shut, where is he meant to be getting all of those things?" Stuart asked.

"He'll still have a relationship with his suppliers," Julian said dismissively. "I'm sure he'll have no trouble at all."

"If there's nothing else, I'll go and try ringing the printer," Alvin said.

"And we can unload the decorations so I can see what we have," Stuart said.

"Yes, I've a great deal to get back to as well," Winifred said.

"Don't forget that the most important thing to do now is sell tickets," Norman said as Janet heard chairs being pushed away from the table. "We need a lot of people at the auction in order to get the best possible prices for our items."

Janet moved away from the kettle, dropping into a seat across from Joan. The pair were having a lively conversation about their upcoming holiday when Alvin strolled into the room.

"Is the meeting finished?" Janet asked.

"Yes, and thank you both for your hospitality," he told them.

"You're very welcome," Joan replied.

"I'll show you out," Janet said. She rose to her feet as the rest of the committee appeared behind Alvin.

Janet walked Alvin and Fred to the door and then returned to the kitchen.

"Only if you're sure you don't mind," Stuart was saying. "It's only for a few days."

"It's fine," Joan replied. "We've been working on clearing things out, but we can take a few days off from that chore."

Janet raised an eyebrow. "Stuart is going to store the boxes of decorations in the carriage house for now," Joan explained to her. "As he said, it's only for a few days."

Janet nodded. Anything that kept her from having to sort more boxes from the carriage house was fine with her.

"Let's get the boxes out of my car, then," Norman said.

He and Stuart headed for the door with Julian and Winifred on their heels.

"I really don't think I can sell that many tickets," Winifred was saying as Janet shut the door behind them.

"I thought you wanted to talk to Winifred about Alberta," Joan said.

Janet shook her head. "I do, but he's far too busy right now. Perhaps once this event is over, he'll be more pleasant."

Joan laughed. "I hardly think so," she said.

Janet watched as Stuart and Norman moved several large boxes into the carriage house. Once they were finished, Stuart rang the buzzer on the French doors.

"Do either of you have a minute?" he asked when Janet opened the door. "I have boxes full of decorations and no idea how to decorate the space. I was hoping you might have some suggestions."

"I'll take a look," Janet said.

"Me, too," Joan added. "Although Janet is much better at such things. She used to do wonderful things with her classrooms for the holidays and for special events. I used to have her decorate my classroom as well."

The pair walked with Stuart to the carriage house. The boxes that Janet had watched him unload were all standing open in the middle of the floor. Janet couldn't help but smile as she looked at rolls of gossamer fabric, piles of coloured stars, and heaps of table covers.

"Is there a theme?" she asked.

Stuart shook his head. "We just want it to look elegant and sophisticated," he replied. "Like a fancy fundraiser you might go to in London."

Janet nodded. "There are a lot of great items here to work with," she told him. "What's the space like?"

"Like a basketball court," he replied sadly.

Janet laughed. "I'm sure you can make it look a lot better," she said.

"I don't suppose you'd like to help?" Stuart asked hopefully.

Janet thought about it for a minute. "I will," she said. "It might even be fun."

Stuart smiled. "Thank you so much," he said.

"When are you decorating?" Janet asked.

"I don't know yet," Stuart said. "But I'll let you know as soon as I do."

Janet looked at the boxes again. "When you talk to them, find out the dimensions of the room, if you can," she said. "Ideally, we'd start decorating today, but I doubt they'll be able to let us do that. At least if we have rough dimensions, I can start planning how to use what we have."

"You're the best," Stuart said, giving her a quick hug. "I'll go and ring them now. Would it help if we could see the space before Friday?"

"Yes," Janet replied.

"I'll see if I can arrange that, then, too," he said. "Oh, and one more thing," he added. "I'd appreciate it if you'd help me think of people to sell the event tickets to. I'm supposed to sell thirty-five of them, and I'm not sure where to even start."

He disappeared back to his house while Joan and Janet locked up the carriage house.

"It was kind of you to agree to help," Joan told her sister as they walked back into Doveby House.

"You can help, too," Janet said. "If we can't get into the place until Friday afternoon, we'll need all the help we can get."

"Yes, it's a big space to decorate in a very short amount of time," Joan said. "Or, at least, it looks a big space from the outside."

Janet nodded. She hadn't paid much attention to the large rectangular building that was near the centre of Little Burton, but she'd noticed it on her infrequent trips to the small village. "It does look large from the outside," she agreed. "And, well, it isn't exactly the most attractive building, is it?"

"It's rather like a large shoebox," Joan said.

Janet laughed. "It is, isn't it? I can't imagine that anyone designed it. It's really just four walls with a few windows and a door. But we shall do our best."

"In the meantime, we'll have to think about helping Stuart sell his tickets," Joan said thoughtfully. "We said we'd each buy one, and Michael is happy to come along as well, but that still leaves thirty-two tickets."

"Surely Stuart will be able to sell some of them," Janet said. "I'll ring around to the Ladies' Club membership and see if any of them are interested. I'm not sure some of them have an extra hundred pounds to spare, though. I still think it's an expensive evening."

"Yes, and one that we're being dragged into more and more," Joan said. "Let's hope we don't end up regretting that."

Chapter 4

Janet spent some time on Tuesday ringing the other women from the Doveby Dale Ladies' Club. It took some persuading on her part, but she managed to convince them all to attend the charity fundraiser. Stuart had promised to drop off any tickets that either sister sold. Janet was pleased to be able to ring him and send him to all four of the women's homes.

"I've arranged for us to have a look at the community centre tomorrow, if that works for you," Stuart told her before she disconnected. "I'll collect you at one o'clock and we can go together, if that suits."

"That's fine," Janet told him. "I'm not sure if Joan will be coming or not."

"You can let me know tomorrow," Stuart said. "I'll see you around one."

Joan had persuaded Michael to buy a ticket, and he'd rung a few of his former coworkers on Stuart's behalf as well. By the time Joan and Janet sat down to their evening meal on Tuesday, between them they'd sold ten tickets.

"At least we've sold his extra ten for him," Janet said as she swallowed a bite of steak and kidney pie.

"I was wondering if you should ask William Chalmers to buy a ticket," Joan replied.

"I did think of him," Janet admitted. "But I'm sort of avoiding him, really."

Joan nodded. "Because of Edward," she said.

Janet shrugged. Edward Bennett had been the bed and breakfast's first paying guest after the sisters bought it. He'd known Margaret Appleton, the previous owner, and he'd turned up on their doorstep claiming to have made a booking with her some time before her unexpected death. Janet had been attracted to the handsome man, even while finding his easy self-confidence and worldly sophistication somewhat worrying. Before he'd left, he'd told Janet that he worked for a secret government agency that had occasionally used Doveby House as a safe house.

Months later, Janet still wasn't sure what to believe about the man, although he'd recently spent a weekend with them. Janet had discovered that she was even more attracted to the man, which made his secretive nature incredibly frustrating. And it complicated her relationship with William Chalmers.

William had moved to Doveby Dale shortly after the sisters purchased Doveby House. Both Janet and Joan found the man disagreeable and rude on first making his acquaintance, but over time, as he'd worked on his manner, something like a friendship had developed between the three of them. Recently, however, he'd been hinting at wanting something more like a romance with Janet. She wasn't totally opposed to the idea, and if it hadn't been for Edward, she might have embraced it more enthusiastically.

"You should ask him," Joan said. "He'll feel hurt if he's left out. It's a big community event, after all."

"Maybe I should just suggest his name to Stuart," Janet said.

"Actually, Stuart should be talking to all the small business owners in Doveby Dale," Joan said. "Todd and Ted should be asked to attend, and so should that nasty man who owns the coffee shop near the police station."

Todd and Ted owned a small café near the bed and breakfast. Todd did the cooking and Ted ran the dining room, and both men were very well liked in their community. The girl who worked in the coffee shop was also well liked. The shop's owner was rarely there, and he was less popular with the residents of Doveby Dale.

"Yes, I suppose so," Janet sighed. "I hope the coffee shop man can't come. We really should find out his name," she added.

"I thought someone said he was called Robert, but I could be wrong," Joan said.

"Speaking of Robert," Janet exclaimed. "What about Robert Parsons? Do police constables go to such things?"

Joan shrugged. "I can't imagine he'd want to spend that much money for what sounds like not much in the way of entertainment," she said.

"I wonder if they'll be having any security that evening," Janet said. "I mean, it sounds as if some of the auction items might be valuable, and people might be paying with cash, mightn't they?"

"I suppose some will be. We must remember to ask Stuart about that," Joan said.

After dinner the sisters watched television for a while and then had an early night. They didn't have any guests arriving until Saturday and they were both doing what they could to enjoy having their home to themselves.

"Good afternoon," Stuart greeted the sisters when Janet opened the front door to him on Wednesday afternoon.

"Hello," his wife, Mary, said from behind him.

Janet forced herself to keep her smile in place. She wasn't overly fond of Mary. The woman spent much of her time travelling from place to place visiting her adult children. Their marriage was the second for both of them, and Janet often wondered why they stayed together when they spent so much time apart.

"Good afternoon," Joan said. "Are we ready to go?"

"Are you going?" Mary demanded.

"I thought I would," Joan replied. "I agreed to help with the decorating, after all."

"Oh, that's okay then," Mary said. "I won't bother." She turned and walked back across the street, opening the door to her home and then slamming it shut behind her.

"Is she angry about something?" Janet asked, bewildered by the woman's behaviour.

"No, not at all," Stuart said. "She was just going to come if you and I were going alone," he told Janet.

"If we were going alone? So that she could help?" Janet asked.

"Er, yes, er, I mean, sure, because it's too much work for just two people," Stuart replied.

Janet narrowed her eyes at him. "What's really going on?" she demanded.

Stuart blushed bright red. "What do you mean?" he asked.

"Stuart, we're neighbours and friends. Please tell me what's going on with Mary," Janet said.

"Her first husband wasn't exactly the faithful kind," Stuart said after an awkward pause. "She worries about me when I'm going to be anywhere alone with another woman."

Janet stared at him for a minute and then looked over at Joan. Joan looked as astonished as Janet felt. After another minute, Janet began to laugh.

"I'm sorry," she said after a deep breath. "But it's such a ridiculous notion. Perhaps she had to worry about Maggie Appleton, but I don't think I've ever given her reason to think that I'd consider having an affair with a married man, have I?"

"It isn't you," Stuart said. "It's me she doesn't trust."

Janet bit back a dozen questions. "Maybe we should go," she said instead. "Once we've seen the space, I can start planning."

The drive to Little Burton didn't take long. On the journey, Joan and Janet gave Stuart the list of names they'd come up with as possible ticket purchasers. Stuart kept nodding.

"I'll try all of them," he said as he pulled into the large car park for the community centre. "I just have to hope that Winifred hasn't beaten me to them."

The community centre was exactly what Janet had been expecting. The room was large and completely devoid of character. It was basically just a rectangle, although there was a small kitchen area tucked away in one corner.

"I suppose the caterers will be able to heat the food here," Joan said, inspecting the kitchen facilities. "I wouldn't want to try to cook in here, but I imagine it will be adequate for what they need."

"Are they planning on doing any cooking on-site?" Janet asked.

"I've no idea," Stuart said. "Julian and Norman are dealing with the food and drink. The rest of us have enough to do."

"You said it was just wine and finger foods, right?" Janet asked.

"Yes, that's right," Stuart replied.

"Will they be passed around by waiters or does the decorating plan need to include a table for food?" Janet asked. She'd pulled out a notebook and was making a rough sketch of the room.

"I don't know," Stuart said. "I'll have to ring Norman to ask. I can do that now." He pulled out his mobile phone and walked away from the sisters.

Janet was busy sketching the rough dimensions of the space. "We'll want some tables for the guests to sit at while they're drinking and eating," she said. "But we'll also need some sort of arrangement for the auction. I wonder if they're planning on using a stage, and if so, where they're getting it from and when."

Stuart was back a moment later. "He's not answering at the moment, but I've left him an urgent message."

Janet put her other questions to the man, but he wasn't able to answer any of them.

"We never really discussed any of this," he said helplessly. "We were going to use a room in a restaurant that had some things set up already.

"Maybe you can ask Norman about that as well when you speak to him," Janet suggested. "I'll just take measurements for now."

Stuart nodded and then sat down at a table and watched as Janet and Joan measured the room. He tried Norman's number a couple more times while the sisters worked.

"Mr. Long?" a voice came from near the door.

Stuart got up and crossed the room. Janet wasn't far behind him.

"Ah, you must be Mr. Grayson," Stuart said. "I was told you'd be stopping in to check on us."

"Yes, that's right," the man said. He smiled and shook hands with Stuart, who introduced Janet and Joan as well.

"But you must call me George," the man added after the introductions were complete. George was probably sixty-five, with grey hair and brown eyes. He was short, with a rounded tummy. "I'm responsible for arranging the rental of the space here. I understand you're going to be having a charity auction here on Friday evening?"

"Yes, that's right," Stuart said. "The party starts at seven. We'll want to get in as early as possible to decorate, though. We had been hoping to have the event at The Mill Restaurant. We're hoping to create a similar atmosphere in here to what they have in their private dining room."

The man raised his eyebrows. "Good luck," he said. "We have a bingo night on Thursday, but you're welcome at any time on Friday. There was meant to be a birthday party here Friday afternoon, but the child decided he wanted to go to some soft playground space instead. Normally I'd try to rebook the space, but I thought I'd let you in early instead."

"That's very kind of you," Stuart said.

"Yes, well, we will be charging you for the privilege," George said with a laugh. "We require half of the rental charge in advance and the balance on the day. I can take cash from you now, if you'd like."

Stuart looked as surprised as Janet felt. "I believe the rental is being paid for through ticket sales," he said eventually. "I'll have to talk to Norman about that, as well."

George nodded. "I do need payment by the end of the day," he said. "Otherwise, we'll cancel the event and try to rebook the space."

"The end of the day?" Stuart echoed. "I don't know if I'll hear from Norman by then."

"I hate to be the bad guy here," George said cheerfully. "But the event is only two days away."

"How much do you need today?" Janet asked.

"Fifty pounds," George said.

"Is that all?" Janet asked. "You're only charging a hundred pounds for the use of the space for the entire day?"

"We offer a discount for charitable events," George said.

Stuart opened his wallet and pulled out some notes. "I'll pay it," he said. "But I'll need a receipt to show to Norman so I can get my money back."

"Just wait here a minute and I'll get you one," George said.

He was gone less than that. "Here you are," he said, handing a slip of paper to Stuart.

"I think I've seen enough," Janet said. "Are there any ladders available?"

"Yes, there's one in the storage shed behind the building," George told her. "I can be here on Friday to let you into the shed to borrow it."

"But who will be going up the ladder?" Joan demanded.

"I suppose I can," Janet replied.

"I think that might be a job for me," Stuart argued.

"Let's worry about it on Friday," Janet said. "As long as a ladder is available, we'll work it out."

The trio headed back to Doveby Dale in silence. Stuart stared at the road, his hands tightly clenched on the steering wheel. Clearly something was bothering him. Janet didn't want to ask him what it was. Instead, she reworked her plans for the room several times, moving a makeshift stage around the place until she was happy with its location. By the time they arrived back at Doveby House, she'd added several round tables for guests and begun working out how to cover up the basketball hoops.

"I'll pick you both up at eight on Friday," Stuart told them as they got out of the car. "I can't thank you enough for your willingness to help me with this."

"It's not a problem," Janet said. While it was hard work, she was actually enjoying planning out exactly how to decorate the plain space to make it look elegant. Before she went to bed, she walked back out to the carriage house and went back through the boxes. For once the door stayed open and the lights stayed on as she worked.

"How are your plans going?" Joan asked when Janet went back into the house.

"I think I'm getting there," Janet replied. "I just hope we have enough time to decorate the whole space. It's a big room and it needs a lot of work."

"Do you think we have enough supplies to work with in the boxes that Norman gave Stuart?"

"I'm determined to make it work," Janet said. "I don't want Stuart to have to buy anything else. I'm not sure that I trust Norman and Julian to pay him back. I can see them arguing that every penny they have to give Stuart is a penny that isn't going to fight cancer."

"Well, I suppose they'd be right," Joan said.

"Yes, but poor Stuart would still be out of pocket. If they want to have a big charity event, they should have a decent budget to fund it."

"They are charging a lot for tickets," Joan admitted. "They should be using that money to pay for everything. Then whatever they raise from the auction should go to charity."

"Perhaps that is how it works," Janet said. "It all seems rather disorganised, really."

"No doubt the last-minute change of venue has thrown all of their careful plans into disarray," Joan said. "But it seems like things are slowly coming together."

"I hope so," Janet replied.

Chapter 5

Friday morning at eight, Janet wasn't feeling anything but tired. Aggie had protested loudly when Janet's alarm had gone off at half six. When Janet emerged from the shower, the kitten had fallen back to sleep.

"Enjoy," she muttered at Aggie. "I'll leave your breakfast in the kitchen. I've no idea when I'll be home to get you some lunch."

Because of Aggie, Janet and Joan had agreed that they'd take their own car to the community centre instead of riding with Stuart. If things weren't going well, only one sister would have to run home to get Aggie her lunch, and Stuart wouldn't be inconvenienced at all. Before they left, they helped Stuart pack all of the boxes of decorations into his boot.

"I'll see you there in a few minutes," Stuart said.

Janet went back inside to make sure that Aggie's water and food bowls were full before she and Joan made their way to Little Burton. They were surprised to see three cars in the car park at the community centre.

"One of them must be George's," Janet remarked as she climbed out of the car. "Maybe one of the other committee members has come to help as well."

Inside the building, she discovered she was wrong.

"Todd? Ted? What are you doing here?" she asked as she greeted the café owners. Todd's dark and unruly hair was held back in his usual ponytail. As the cook of the pair, he was slightly overweight, especially when compared with his partner, Ted, who was slender. Ted's hair and his neatly trimmed beard were both ginger.

Ted grinned at her. "Stuart came by and asked us to buy tickets for tonight," he explained. "Then he started telling us about how the three of you were going to be doing all of the decorating. When he said you were going to be up on a ladder, we offered to come and lend a hand."

Janet felt a rush of relief as she hugged the men. The two men were both probably somewhere in their forties. While she hadn't been looking forward to it, Janet had been willing to do the ladder work. She was much happier with having Todd and Ted do it, however. They were both younger and taller than Janet.

"Where do we start?" Todd asked.

"We need to unpack my boot," Stuart said.

Janet walked around the room, mentally arranging and rearranging things as the men carried in the boxes. When they were done, she turned to Stuart.

"What did Norman say about the stage?" she asked.

"He said we should do whatever we think is best," Stuart said, not meeting Janet's eyes.

"What about tables for food?" was Janet's next question.

"Again, he said he was happy for us to do whatever we liked," was the unwelcome reply.

Janet sighed. "That doesn't really help, does it?"

Stuart shrugged. "What would you suggest?" he asked Janet.

Opening her handbag, Janet pulled out several sheets of paper. "I've done three different arrangements," she told Stuart. Everyone gathered around and looked at her rough sketches.

"I think this one is the best," Joan said after a moment. "It gives them a small stage with seating around it for the auction. It also gives the caterers a long table to lay out the food on, with plenty of round tables for the guests to use while they're eating."

"I agree with Joan," Ted said. "Who is doing the food?"

Stuart sighed. "I'm not sure what's happening with that," he said. "Julian and Norman are meant to be sorting it out with Simon Hampton."

"Simon is in Portugal," Todd told them.

"Why?" Janet asked.

"He decided that he needed a holiday," Todd replied. "His company is one of our suppliers. I rang last week to ask about an issue with one of the shipments they sent. When I asked to speak to Simon directly, I was told her was away and wasn't expected back until mid-May."

"Let's get on with the decorating," Stuart said grimly. "I think we have enough to worry about without worrying about the food."

Everyone agreed on the plan that Joan liked, so it was simply a matter of making it come to life. Todd and Ted moved tables while Joan and Janet followed with chairs. Stuart worked with George on constructing a low stage out of various bits from the storage shed. Once the furniture was all in place, they began to decorate. It took every last bit of gossamer fabric to make the room feel elegant, but when they were finished, Janet was secretly incredibly pleased with herself.

"I wouldn't have believed it if I hadn't seen it myself," George told her, looking out across the tables that were all neatly covered in thick cloth covers. "It doesn't look like the same place."

"It's truly stunning," Ted said. "If we ever want to redecorate the café, I think we'll put Janet in charge of it."

"You've done quite well," Joan told her sister.

"We've one last star," Stuart said, holding up the glittery gold object. Above them, a field of stars dangled on fishing wire from the ceiling.

"Put it over the food table," Janet told him. "It's the most sparse."

"It's nearly four o'clock," Joan said. "We need to get home and get ready for tonight."

"What time does it start?" Todd asked.

"Seven," Stuart told him.

"We'll be back," Ted said. "With as much money as we can spare so that we can bid on the wonderful prizes."

"Yes, I'm meant to tell everyone that cash would be greatly appreciated tonight," Stuart said. "Julian and Norman want to be able to present one large cheque to the charity on Monday, and they won't be able to include every donation unless they're all made with cash."

"Why don't they wait a week?" Janet asked.

"They have another event next weekend in Cornwall," Stuart explained. "They'll be down there full-time as soon as they've finished the publicity for this event."

Stuart's phone buzzed as everyone headed for the door. His loud, "Pardon?" right after he'd answered made everyone stop in their tracks. After a moment he disconnected and slipped the phone back in his pocket.

"We don't have any food or drink for tonight," he said to the others, anger clearly evident in his tone.

"What happened?" Janet asked.

"Apparently, Julian talked to Simon months ago. He was meant to leave instructions before he went on his holiday, but it seems he forgot. When Norman rang today to double-check the arrangements, no one knew what he was talking about."

"So now what?" Joan asked.

"I don't know," Stuart said. "We need wine, and lots of it. And we need finger foods. People have paid a hundred pounds a person to come to this stupid thing. We can't just serve them water and expect them to bid generously on the prizes."

"Surely Norman and Julian will sort it out," Joan said. "It was their responsibility, after all."

"They're both tied up in a meeting all day for the event in Cornwall next weekend," Stuart said. "They've asked me to see what I can do."

"What can you do?" Todd asked.

"I suppose I'll have to go shopping," Stuart said miserably. "I'll ring the other committee members and tell them each to bring ten bottles of wine. Will that be enough, do you think?"

"How many committee members?" Ted asked.

"Four," Stuart told him.

"Forty bottles of wine for how many people?" was Ted's next question.

"I think there will be around a hundred," Stuart said. "I don't know how many tickets anyone else has sold, but I doubt we've sold more than that."

"Forty should be just about enough," Todd told him. "As long as the party doesn't last longer than two hours."

"That should be about right," Stuart replied. "After everyone is here, it will be all about the auction, anyway. People won't be getting drinks while that's happening. At least I hope they won't."

"What are you going to do about food?" Janet asked.

"Anyone have any ideas?" Stuart replied with a question.

"What sort of food were you planning on having?" Ted asked.

"Just finger foods and cheese and crackers and that sort of thing," Stuart told him. "I suppose I could manage a cheese and cracker tray, but that's about it."

"We could do finger foods," Todd said. "I could probably do enough for a hundred people for two hours before seven, but it will be a huge push."

"We'll pay you double what you normally charge," Stuart said. "Julian wanted Simon to donate everything, but of course we'll pay you."

"We'll only charge you for our supplies," Todd offered. "I'll donate my time and effort."

"That's very generous of you," Joan said.

"I lost my father to cancer," Todd replied. "It's a cause I'm happy to support."

"You've already lost a day's business helping out here," Janet said. "Doing the catering is above and beyond."

"We'd better get back to the café and get busy," Ted interjected. "We have a lot of cooking to do."

The pair walked out discussing exactly what they could make on such short notice.

"I need to ring the other committee members about the wine,"

Stuart said to the sisters. "I'll see you both at seven." He walked away, his phone in his hand, while Janet and Joan continued to the door.

"It doesn't seem too well organised to me," George said as he held the door open for them. "I'd have thought they'd have had all of this sorted before they started selling the tickets."

"It all seems to have been a misunderstanding," Janet said, feeling as if she needed to defend Stuart and his associates.

"Well, have fun tonight," George said. "You have done a wonderful job with the decorating, I'll give you that."

Janet glanced back at the large space and smiled. Whatever else happened, she was proud of how beautiful the room looked.

Joan had gone back to Doveby House at midday to feed Aggie, but the sisters hadn't eaten since breakfast. Food was the first thing on Janet's mind when they got back home.

"I'm starving," she announced as she pushed open the front door.

"I'm not sure if we should eat a full meal or not," Joan said. "We know there will be food tonight, after all."

Janet shook her head. "As much as I love Todd and Ted, I'm not relying on whatever they can throw together for tonight. I want a substantial amount of food and I want it now."

Joan laughed. "How about spaghetti?" she asked. "I can put that together fairly quickly, and it's lovely and filling."

"Perfect," Janet said. "I'll help if you'd like."

"I don't need help, but you can keep me company, if you don't have anything else to do," Joan suggested.

Janet sat at the small kitchen table while Joan filled a pot with water. A knock on the front door had Janet back on her feet.

"Ah, Janet, I was hoping I might have a quick word with you," Robert Parsons said in the doorway.

"Come in," Janet invited. "Joan is making us some dinner. Would you like to join us?"

"I'm afraid I don't have time," the young police constable replied. "But thank you for the invitation."

He followed Janet back into the kitchen and joined her at the table. "I just have a few quick questions for you both," he said as Joan handed him a small plate full of biscuits.

"What's happened now?" Janet asked.

"Nothing at all," Robert said with a smile. "But I've been asked to provide security for tonight and I wanted to see what you two knew about the event."

"Security?" Janet echoed.

"Apparently there are going to be some high-value items up for auction," Robert said. "And they are expecting to take in quite a bit of cash as well, I understand."

"So you'll be there to keep track of everything," Janet said.

"That's the idea," Robert replied. "I've drafted in another constable from Derby as well. Julian Glover asked for two of us."

"It's all something a mess," Janet blurted out.

"Really?" Robert asked.

"It just isn't very well organised," Janet amended herself. "The venue had to be changed at the last minute, which hasn't helped, of course, but even so, an awful lot seems to have gone wrong along the way."

"What's gone wrong?" Robert wanted to know.

"Julian and Norman were supposed to arrange for food and wine, but Stuart just found out today that there isn't anything sorted for tonight," Janet told him.

"That's a serious problem," Robert said.

"Todd and Ted have stepped in and are going to do the food," Janet said. "And Stuart is asking all of the committee members to bring wine with them."

Robert raised an eyebrow. "Do you know what was supposed to happen?"

"Julian and Norman said that they'd talked to Simon Hampton and he was going to donate the food and wine," Janet said. "But apparently he's gone on holiday and forgot to leave instructions about it with anyone."

"That's believable," Robert said. "Simon doesn't have the best reputation for supporting charities. Maybe he forgot on purpose."

Janet shrugged. "Maybe. I just hope tonight goes smoothly."

"That's one of the reasons I'm going to be there," Robert said. "To make sure everything goes to plan."

"If there is a plan," Janet muttered.

The sisters chatted with Robert for a few minutes more about the event and the committee members. He left as Joan added pasta to the boiling water. Janet showed him out and then the sisters enjoyed their dinner.

"I'm going to have a shower," Janet said after the dishes were loaded into the dishwasher. "We worked too hard this morning for me to put my fancy dress on like this."

She'd only just come out of the shower when her mobile rang.

"Janet? It's Edward," the sexy voice came down the line. "How are you?"

Janet talked while she got dressed and did her makeup. She told the man all about the fundraiser she was getting ready to attend.

"Give me all the names of the committee members again?" he asked when she'd finished.

She complied, but couldn't resist questioning him. "Why do you ask?"

"One of the names sounds familiar, but I'm not sure which one or why," he replied. "I'll let you know if I remember, but now I'd better let you go to your party."

"It was nice talking to you," Janet said.

"And you," Edward replied.

Janet disconnected the call and was halfway down the stairs when she remembered that he still hadn't given her the combination for the library safe. He'd promised to get it for her as soon as he was back in London. Maybe he wasn't there yet, though.

The safe in the library, hidden behind a small picture, was only one of a number of secrets that Doveby House held. Edward admitted to knowing the combination, but hadn't managed to open the safe on his last visit. Janet would have to make sure to ask him again the next time they spoke. For tonight, though, she had other, more pressing concerns.

Chapter 6

Joan and Janet arrived back at the Little Burton Community Centre a few minutes before seven. Joan parked in the car park and the sisters looked at the nearly empty rows around them.

"I suppose we're early," Joan said.

"I'm sure it will get busier," Janet said with more confidence than she felt.

"Maybe we should wait until someone else turns up before we go in," Joan suggested.

"I think we should get in there and get a glass of wine before they run out," Janet said. "I'd like to get something for my hundred pounds."

"You know I don't drink much or often," Joan said. "But this time I'm going to agree with you."

The sisters made their way to the door and Janet pulled. The door didn't open.

"It's locked," she said in surprise. She looked through the window and saw someone walking towards them.

"Good evening," Robert Parsons said as he opened the door. "They aren't quite ready for guests yet. I've been told to leave the door locked for another five minutes."

"Are all of the committee members here?" Janet asked.

"Yes. And Todd and Ted seem to have done a wonderful job on the food. Everything smells delicious, anyway," he told them. "Julian and Norman brought some wine, so with what the committee came up with, there should be plenty. It looks as if it's going to be a nice evening."

"I thought it would be busier," Joan remarked.

"Perhaps people are simply fashionably late," Robert suggested.

Another car pulled into the car park. "That's Michael," Joan said. She took a few steps away, greeting Michael as he emerged from his car.

"Surely you can let us in," Janet said to Robert. "We did all of the decorating, after all."

"Did you? You did a wonderful job," Robert said. "I've never seen the place looking so beautiful."

"Norman supplied everything. I just worked out where to put it," Janet told him.

"I'm going to let you three in," Robert said. "It looks as if it's going to rain and I don't want you getting wet, not when you're all dressed up."

He stood back and let the trio into the small foyer before locking the door again. "You go on through," he said. "And remind Stuart that someone from the committee is meant to be taking tickets, please."

"Do you want ours?" Janet asked.

"I don't, but they might," he replied. "Check with Stuart."

That was easier said than done, though. Michael gasped as they entered the large main room.

"This is stunning," he said. "I can't believe I'm in the Little Burton Community Centre. It looks like the ballroom of a fancy hotel."

Janet blushed. "It took a lot of hard work," she said. "Todd, Ted, Stuart, George, Joan, and I were here all day putting this together."

"Well, you did a splendid job," he told her.

"I don't see Stuart anywhere," Joan said.

Janet looked around. She could see Todd and Ted working in the kitchen along the back, but besides them, no one else was in sight.

"Where are all of the committee members?" Janet asked.

"That's a good question," Joan replied.

On a long table near the stage, the various items that were going to be auctioned were spread out. Janet decided that she'd look them over as soon as she could. She was really hoping that there wouldn't be anything there she wanted to bid on, but she knew she or Joan would probably have to buy something, under the circumstances.

Not knowing what else to do, she crossed to the kitchen. "Where is everyone else?" she asked Ted when she caught his eye.

"They're unloading Julian's car, apparently," he replied. "Julian has several cases of wine, I gather, so they all went to help."

"As it's gone seven, that seems rather foolish," Joan said. "Someone needs to be here to greet the guests."

"And tell us when to serve," Ted said. He shrugged. "I suppose we'll put food out whenever it's ready, unless someone tells us otherwise."

"I can't believe I'm cooking for a hundred people in this kitchen," Todd muttered. "Nothing will be edible."

"It all smells good," Janet said. "I'm sure it will be wonderful."

"I just hope everyone has a glass or two of wine before they eat. Maybe they won't notice the food, then," Todd said.

"Or if they do," Ted added, "maybe they won't realise who prepared it."

Janet laughed. "At the moment, we're the only guests, so you've nothing to worry about," she said.

"Julian said they were expecting a hundred and fifty people," Todd told her. "Which is considerably more than we're prepared for."

"Can we help?" Joan asked.

"There isn't any room in here for anyone else," Todd told her. "Thank you for the offer, but we'll have to manage."

The door on the far wall suddenly swung open and the

committee members began to straggle into the room, each carrying a case of wine bottles.

"No one is supposed to be in here," Winifred snapped when he spotted the sisters and Michael.

"They're fine," Stuart said quickly. "Anyway, it's ten past seven already."

"Alvin, you were going to take the first shift on the door, right?" Julian asked.

"Oh, yes, that's right," he said. "I'll collect tickets and remind everyone to bid early and often."

Julian nodded. Alvin quickly crossed the room and disappeared into the foyer. The others had stacked their boxes on one of the tables, and now Norman went to work organising the drinks.

"When do you want the food to start coming out?" Ted asked.

"Once we have a dozen or so people in here, you can bring it out as it's ready," Norman said. "If that works for you."

"That's fine," Ted said, nodding.

"Come and have a glass of wine," Norman invited the sisters and Michael. "I must congratulate you on the decorations. You've worked magic in here."

Janet blushed again as she took a glass of wine from the man. "Thank you," she murmured.

"I should have you come to Cornwall with us," he said. "We could use your magic touch in the space we're using there. I don't suppose you'd like a week's holiday in Cornwall, starting Monday?"

Janet shook her head. "We have guests coming for the weekend and one couple is staying for the week. I can't get away right now."

"If you change your mind, have Stuart ring me," Norman told her. "I'd love to work with you more."

Janet nodded and then turned away. She was flattered, but there was something she didn't like about the man. Maybe it was the way he'd left poor Stuart with the bulk of the work for tonight's event.

An hour later, the party seemed to be in full swing. Janet had chatted briefly with her friends from the Doveby Dale Ladies' Club, who all seemed to be having a good time. She'd said hello to a number of small business owners she knew from the area as well.

She was chatting with William Chalmers when Norman's voice came over the tannoy.

"We're ready to begin the auction," he announced. "If everyone could take seats, please, we'll begin."

It took the crowd about ten minutes to settle, most of the guests stopping to grab another glass of wine on their way to the seats around the stage. Janet found herself sitting between Michael and William Chalmers. Joan was on Michael's other side. The auction opened with a number of gift vouchers for local shops in the Doveby Dale and Little Burton area. When the first one went for more than twice its value, Janet decided that she was probably not going to buy anything after all.

When the auction was over, Janet was astonished at how much money had been donated. Several of the items were sold for what she considered silly prices, but no one else seemed surprised.

"I can't believe what people paid for things," she whispered to Joan as they got up from their seats.

"Me either," Joan hissed. "But Michael has been to this sort of thing before and he said it's always like this. It's for charity, you see."

"I didn't think the good people of Doveby Dale had that much money," Janet muttered.

Joan laughed. "A lot of the guests are from Little Burton," she pointed out. "And a fair few are businessmen from Derby, as well. I don't think anyone we know spent any money."

Janet thought back through the auction. Joan was right. No one they knew had purchased anything, although William had bid on a few items before their prices had skyrocketed. A large group of young people, probably in their early twenties, had stood by and watched the auction, eating and drinking throughout. Janet could only hope there was enough wine left for her to have another glass.

With the auction finished, the evening wound down very quickly. Joan walked Michael out to his car. Janet found a seat in a quiet corner and watched as people paid for their purchases and left. Todd and Ted were cleaning up in the kitchen and Stuart was busy collecting used wine glasses from around the room. After a few minutes, Janet decided to help.

"The food was fabulous," she told Todd as she carried several glasses into the kitchen. "You should be very pleased with how it went."

"It wasn't as bad as I feared," he admitted. "No one complained, anyway."

"I should think not," Janet said.

She carried in a second lot of glasses a minute later. "Where do you want these?" she asked.

"We're just stacking them into their trays and taking them back to the café to wash," Ted told her. "I'm not washing all of these by hand, that's for sure."

Janet laughed. "You should have used plastic glasses," she said.

"If we'd had any, we would have," Ted replied. "Stuart rang us at six, as we were packing up the food, to ask if we had any wine glasses. They were just lucky we did. We don't use them at the café."

"So why did you have so many?" Janet asked. She blushed as soon as the words were out of her mouth. "That's a rude question," she said. "You don't have to answer it."

Ted shook his head. "It's fine," he assured her. "Before we bought the café, we did a lot of catering. We keep talking about selling all the extras, but we haven't found the time to do that yet. Now that Todd's done this event, he'll probably want to start catering again, anyway." Ted sighed.

"You don't like catering?" Janet asked.

"I don't mind, but I like the set hours at the café," Ted said. "The problem is, we're barely breaking even at the café. A few catering jobs each month would help a lot with the bottom line."

"Maybe you'd only need to do the catering in the off-season," Janet said. "I'm sure the café will be busy during the summer."

"It's picking up," Ted acknowledged. "We'll see. I know Todd misses cooking for crowds, though. Even if we're busy, he'll still want to do an event now and then."

"Well, he's very good at it," Janet said.

"Yes, he is," Ted agreed with another sigh.

When Joan returned, she began helping with the clearing up as well. She and Janet got to work on taking down the decorations that they'd spent so much time putting up earlier. Janet couldn't help but notice that she and her sister were working much harder than any of the committee members, but she bit her tongue and carried on. Really, she was mostly helping Todd and Ted, as they were probably eager to get out of Little Burton and back home.

"Thank you both so much," Stuart said after a while. "We can help Todd and Ted. You two should go home. You've done more than your fair share of helping with this event."

"Are you sure?" Janet asked.

"I'm quite sure," Stuart said firmly. "The others from the committee can lend a hand." He leaned in close to Janet. "Goodness knows they haven't done much so far," he whispered.

"Ah, Janet, there you are," Norman said, walking up behind Stuart. "I can't thank you and your lovely sister enough for all of your hard work. And now you're tidying? You really mustn't. That's what we have a committee for, you know."

"They seemed to be busy with other things," Janet said. "I thought we would help Todd and Ted for a short while. They've worked very hard today as well."

"Yes, I understand that they have," Norman agreed. "We'll all rally around and help them get everything cleared up. You and your sister should go home and put your feet up for a few days."

"We have guests arriving in the morning," Joan said. "So there won't be any time to put our feet up, unfortunately."

Stuart walked the sisters to their car. "Thank you both again," he said. "I won't take a penny from you for the garden for the next six months."

"Don't be silly," Joan said. "You work far harder there than we did here."

Stuart shook his head. "I just know how to make it look like I work hard," he laughed. "Anyway, we can talk about it another time. Just know that I'm in your debt for now."

The sisters drove home in a companionable silence, each lost in her own thoughts. Janet was exhausted after spending nearly the entire day on her feet. She wasn't accustomed to doing that anymore, although she'd done it for years in the classroom. She could practically hear her bed calling to her as soon as they reached Doveby House.

"See you in the morning," she muttered to Joan as she headed for the stairs.

"I'll have breakfast ready at nine," Joan told her. "Then we can do the final touches on the guest rooms before our guests arrive."

"What time are they due?"

"Not until after lunch."

Janet thought about arguing for a ten o'clock breakfast, but she knew that nine was a concession on Joan's part. Joan was an early riser, no matter when she went to bed. Anyway, Janet was too tired to argue. She climbed the stairs slowly with Aggie on her heels and was asleep the second her head hit the pillow.

Their early morning breakfast was interrupted by a knock on the door.

"I do hope our guests haven't arrived early," Janet said.

She and Joan both walked to the door, just in case it was guests. It wasn't.

"You have to do something," Mary Long demanded as soon as Janet opened the door.

"Pardon?" Janet asked.

"You know Robert Parsons," Mary said. "You need to tell him that Stuart isn't involved."

"Involved in what?" Joan asked.

Mary took a deep breath. "Julian and Norman have disappeared with all of the money that was raised last night," she said. "And the police think someone local helped them get away with it."

Chapter 7

Janet stared at Mary, too stunned to speak.

"All of the money?" Joan asked.

"Apparently. They had everyone pay in cash if they could. The idea was to present a huge cheque on Monday to the charity, and Norman said they could only do that if everyone paid in cash."

"I remember Stuart saying that, but I never imagined that there was anything criminal behind it," Janet said.

"But Stuart was just as much a victim as everyone else," Mary wailed.

"Of course he was," Joan said firmly. "He put a great deal of time and effort into the evening."

"And he paid for a lot of things out of his own pocket. Norman said he'd reimburse him, but he never did."

"Oh, dear," Janet said. "I hope it wasn't too much money."

"It was more than we can comfortably afford to lose," Mary told her. "He paid for renting the space and he paid for forty bottles of wine. He also gave some money to Todd and Ted towards the cost of the food."

"Poor Stuart," Janet murmured.

"And now he's practically being accused of being involved in the theft," Mary said.

"I'm sure that's not the case," Joan said.

"He's been dragged down to the police station," Mary told her. "And he's the one who reported the problem."

"Maybe you should start at the beginning," Janet suggested.

"Why don't we sit down with some tea and biscuits," Joan said in a soothing voice.

"Yes, all right," Mary said. She followed the sisters into the kitchen and sank down in the first chair she reached. Sighing deeply, she put her head in her hands and didn't move until Joan put a teacup in front of her some minutes later.

"Here we are, then," Joan said. "Tea and biscuits."

Mary took a chocolate digestive and nibbled her way through it, with frequent sips of milky tea. When it was gone, she sat back and smiled weakly. "I needed that," she said. "I didn't get any breakfast."

"I can make you some breakfast," Joan offered.

"Oh, no, I can make do with some more biscuits," Mary said. "I'm causing enough trouble as it is."

"So what happened?" Janet asked, impatient to hear the story.

"I left the party early last night," Mary said. "I had a headache and I wasn't going to bid on anything anyway, so I didn't stay long. Stuart rang when it was over to tell me that he was going to help with the tidying and taking down all of the decorations, and that he'd be home in an hour or so. I decided not to wait up for him." She stopped and took another biscuit.

"They were still clearing up when we left," Janet told her, mostly to fill the awkward silence as the woman ate.

"So I went to bed. Stuart came in about two hours later, exhausted but happy. They'd raised much more money than they'd hoped for, mostly due to some very wealthy businessmen from Derby who were invited by Fred Arnold, I gather."

"They paid ridiculous prices for things," Joan said. "We didn't get a chance to buy anything at all."

"But those are the kind of people you want at these sorts of events," Mary said. "Stuart was just surprised that Fred knew so many people from Derby, and that they all came and spent money."

"How much money was raised?" Janet asked.

"They didn't count it all right away, but Stuart thought it was about twenty thousand pounds," Mary said.

"Wow," Janet said. "I knew things were selling for silly prices, but I didn't think they'd made that much."

"They made over a thousand pounds on ticket sales," Mary said. "Stuart said two men got into a bidding war over the signed football and that it went for several thousand pounds in the end. Apparently some people made cash donations as well, during the evening."

"They did have collection buckets scattered around the room," Janet remembered. "I glanced in one and saw quite a few twenty pound notes. People were incredibly generous."

"It was meant to be such a good cause," Joan said.

"So what happened next?" Janet asked Mary.

"When Stuart got up this morning, he rang Norman. They were supposed to be meeting to do a proper count of the money and go over the publicity for Monday. When he rang, no one answered. He tried Julian, but he didn't answer, either."

"Oh, dear," Janet said.

"Exactly. Stuart wasn't too worried yet. They'd had a late night and both men are busy with other things, so he left messages for them both and left it for half an hour. When neither man rang back, he drove over to the hotel they were using in Derby."

"They should have stayed here," Janet muttered. "We'd have kept an eye on them."

Mary nodded grimly. "That's what I said," she told Janet. "But they'd told Stuart they were staying at a big chain hotel in Derby. When Stuart got there, the hotel manager had never heard of either man. That's when Stuart rang Robert Parsons."

"But why do the police think someone local was involved?" Joan asked.

"Robert did some checking into Norman and Julian. Those aren't their real names, of course. Apparently they've done this several times before. They start by finding a small community near a big city, then they recruit someone local who can help them set up a committee to plan the event. Once it's all over, they pay their local accomplice a cut of the money before they disappear."

"So one of the committee members was in on it the whole time?" Janet asked.

"That's what Robert seems to think," Mary said.

"Who set up the committee, then?" was Janet's next question. "Surely that person is the one who's behind it all."

"Except it was Stuart who set up the committee," Mary said softly.

"Oh, dear," Janet exclaimed.

"Norman rang him up. He said he been given his name as someone who might be willing to help with a charitable fundraiser, and Stuart couldn't say no," Mary explained.

"Who gave Norman his name?" Janet asked.

"That's just it, Stuart never asked and Norman never said," Mary told her.

"Did Stuart pick the rest of the committee himself, or did he get names from Norman?" Joan wondered.

"Norman had a list with about five names on it," Mary said. "A few people turned him down, but Alvin and Winifred agreed to help. Stuart asked Fred to join as well."

"So Alvin or Winifred must be the local accomplice," Janet said.

"Or maybe the local accomplice just gave Norman the names and didn't even sit on the committee," Joan suggested.

"Surely whoever it was would have wanted to be on the committee to keep an eye on how everything was going," Janet said.

"As Robert explained it to Stuart, the local man was responsible for pushing ticket sales, especially to wealthy business owners," Mary said.

"Didn't you say that Fred sold most of the tickets to the Derby area businessmen?" Joan asked.

"Yes, but he wasn't on Norman's list," Mary said with a sigh.

"Poor Robert," Janet said. "It looks as if it's going to be a huge mess for him to untangle. I don't suppose he'll be able to track down Julian and Norman?"

"I doubt it," Mary replied. "As far as Stuart knows, they disappeared as soon as the event was over. Robert is trying to get some fingerprints from somewhere, but no one can be sure what they touched or when."

"They helped clear away the glasses, but we were all doing that. Robert can't possibly take fingerprints off of every glass," Janet mused.

"No, he's working on some of the wine bottles, the ones that Norman and Julian supplied," Mary said.

"I'm surprised you know so much about the investigation," Janet said.

Mary flushed. "Stuart came home after he rang Robert. When Robert came to talk to him, I, um, overheard a lot of their conversation."

"Stuart can't be a serious suspect if Robert told him all about the previous cases," Janet said. "He wouldn't talk about them if he thought Stuart was the accomplice."

"I hope you're right," Mary said. "After he and Stuart talked for a short while, he took Stuart down to the station. Why would he do that if he didn't think Stuart was guilty?"

"He probably just needed to get a formal statement," Joan said, patting Mary's hand. "He'll probably interview all of the committee members at the station. No matter who he thinks is behind it all, he'll want to be seen to be treating them all the same."

Mary nodded. "I suppose you're right," she said. "But it's incredibly worrying."

"Of course it is," Janet said. "But we all know Stuart didn't do anything wrong. Robert can talk to us if he has any doubts about the man."

"I'll tell Stuart," Mary said. "I just hope he gets home soon." She got to her feet. "Thank you for your kindness," she said. "I really appreciate it."

Janet walked her to the door while Joan tidied the kitchen. "Let us know if we can do anything," she told Mary. "And if you hear anything interesting."

"I'd like to hear that Julian and Norman, whatever they're really called, have been arrested," Mary said. "But I don't think that's going to happen."

"I'm sure Robert will do his best," Janet said. "I hope he finds the local accomplice quickly. I hate the thought that someone on that committee was helping to deceive us all."

Mary nodded. Janet watched as the woman walked down the steps and then across the road. Sighing deeply, Janet pushed the door shut and walked back into the kitchen. To her surprise, Joan was sitting at the table, the tea things still spread across it.

"What's wrong?" Janet asked.

"I hate that we were duped," Joan said. "And I hate that we helped those men trick our friends, as well."

Janet sat down and helped herself to a custard cream. "I can't believe we sold all of those tickets for them," she said between bites. "I thought we were helping fight cancer, not funding two con men."

"I wish I knew a way to help Robert with the investigation," Janet said.

"I imagine he'll want to talk to us at some point," Joan told her. "We were involved with the event, after all."

"So was he," Janet pointed out. "He was there, providing security so that no one stole the money before it could be stolen."

Joan nodded. "He's probably upset with himself for not suspecting anything."

"I hadn't thought of that. Poor Robert. He will be blaming himself, won't he?"

"If he does come to talk to us about it, we'll have to try to make him feel better about it," Joan said.

She got her opportunity that afternoon. Both sets of guests had arrived and then gone back out again. Janet was playing with Aggie and a ball of string when Robert knocked on their door.

"Ah, I'm glad you're home," he said when Janet let him in. "I've been running all over Doveby Dale and Little Burton trying to find people today."

"We're here," Janet said brightly. "What can we do for you?"

"If you can spare a cuppa, let's start there," the man replied.

Joan had already switched the kettle on when Janet and Robert walked into the kitchen. “How are you?” Joan asked in a concerned voice.

“A bit frustrated with myself,” the man admitted. “I should have been suspicious of those two, but I did do some checking on them and everything looked legitimate.”

“They were very clever,” Janet said.

“From what I can tell, they have the whole thing down to a system,” Robert told her as Joan set a plate of biscuits on the table. He helped himself before continuing. “I’ve found five other reports from around the country of this sort of thing. I think our Norman and Julian were responsible for three of them and they may have been involved in a fourth as well.”

“It seems a profitable enterprise,” Janet said.

“Oh, extremely,” Robert agreed. “They find a small village that’s close enough to a city where wealthy businessmen can be found, and then they find a local accomplice who wants or needs some extra cash. They get a committee together and the committee ends up doing all of the work and paying for nearly everything along the way, so the event itself is pure profit for the pair of them.”

“And you think they had a local accomplice here?” Janet asked.

“I think they must have,” Robert said. “They need local knowledge. They need to know who to put on their committee. Someone from Doveby Dale or Little Burton helped them. I don’t think I’ll be able to track down Norman and Julian, but I’m determined to work out who helped with their fraud.”

Janet frowned. “It must have been one of the committee members, mustn’t it?”

“I’m fairly sure it was,” Robert agreed. “But which one?”

“Not Stuart,” Joan said firmly.

Robert nodded. “He’s last on my list,” he told them. “And he’s only on the list because he has to be there. I know Stuart well enough to know that he’d never do something like this. But that leaves three other men. I don’t know any of them at all.”

“We don’t know them, either,” Janet said. “Although I’m trying to get to know Winifred Godfrey. That isn’t going well, though.”

“Should I ask why?” Robert asked.

Janet chuckled. "Why isn't it going well or why do I want to get to know him?" She shook her head. "He's a local historian and I'm trying to find out more about Alberta Montgomery. Unfortunately, he never rings me back when I ring him. Maybe he'll be more accessible now that the fundraiser is over."

"Surely the accomplice now has a large amount of unexplained cash," Joan said thoughtfully. "Can you search their homes or check their bank accounts?"

Robert shook his head. "All four men have offered to let me search their homes," he told her. "Which suggests to me that I'd be wasting my time. Bank records are another matter, but I doubt very much that our accomplice will put the money in the bank. He may simply use the money to fund a slightly more comfortable lifestyle for himself. It will be unnoticeable if he starts buying better quality shoes and more expensive cuts of meat using the cash he has stashed away."

"Surely whoever it was will want to buy himself something wonderful with his windfall," Janet argued. "I know I would."

"We'll be watching for that, obviously," Robert said. "But I'm really hoping to catch him before he has a chance to spend the money."

Chapter 8

The sisters told Robert everything that they knew about the committee, including what they'd overheard at the meeting that had been held at Doveby House. Then he took them through the decorating and the event itself, taking careful notes on what they told him. When they were finished, he shook his head.

"Obviously, I've rung several of my counterparts in the Cornwall area. No one knows of any upcoming charity events. I didn't really think they'd have given away their next destination, but it was worth checking," he told the women.

"So, what do you do now?" Janet asked.

"I've questioned all of the committee members once," he replied. "I shall have them back in for additional questions on Monday. I may have an associate from the Derby Fraud division sit in with me. Beyond that, I'll be keeping an eye on the four men, watching for any unusual behaviour."

"If we can help in any way, please let us know," Janet said as she walked the man to the door.

"I will do," he promised. "I would prefer it if you'd stay away from the suspects, though."

Janet shrugged. "I won't go looking for them," she told him. "But we do see Stuart quite regularly."

Robert nodded. "And I don't mind you spending time with him," he said. "As I said, he's last on my list of suspects. But please don't go looking for the others. I worry about you and your tendency to want to help."

"We have guests at the moment," Janet told him. "I won't have time to wander over to Little Burton to find anyone. If Winifred does get in touch, I promise to limit our conversation to Alberta."

"I suppose that will have to do," Robert said with a smile.

Janet watched as he walked down to his car and got inside. As the car disappeared towards the main road, Janet started to push the door shut. Movement on the other side of the street caught her eye. Stuart had emerged from his house and he was walking quickly towards her. She watched as he crossed the road and hurried up the pavement to the house.

"I thought he'd never leave," he said, slightly out of breath from the pace he'd set.

"Would you like to come in?" Janet asked.

"Yes, please," he replied, glancing behind himself nervously.

Janet stepped back to let him inside and then shut and locked the door behind them. "Come on through to the kitchen," she suggested. "We can have tea and biscuits."

Stuart followed Janet into the kitchen. Joan looked at her sister and then switched the kettle on yet again. Janet shrugged. It wasn't her fault that they'd had so many guests today.

"How are you?" Janet asked Stuart as she put the plate of biscuits in front of him.

"Terrible," he said. "And before I say anything else, I need to apologise to you both. I'm sorry that I got you involved in the fundraiser. I'm sorry you bought tickets and I'm sorry you put in so much of your time and effort to make it a special night. I never should have trusted those two. I could kick myself for being taken in and dragging so many others with me."

"You mustn't feel that way," Janet said soothingly. "They were very good at what they did."

"They were terrible at arranging things," Stuart pointed out. "They left everything to the committee, including the things they promised they would handle."

"Which was very clever of them," Janet pointed out. "You might have worried more if they'd been slick and professional, and by having the committee do everything, they didn't have to pay for anything."

"Let's not talk about that," Stuart moaned. "Mary was furious when she found out how much I'd spent on the event. Norman promised to pay me back once the dust settled, but now I'm out a lot of money."

"At least we just lost out on some of our time," Janet said.

"And the money for tickets," Stuart said.

"The event did happen, so I suppose we got what we paid for with the tickets," Janet replied. "Even if the money didn't go where it was meant to go."

"It all feels unreal," Stuart told them. "If I weren't caught in the middle of it, I wouldn't believe it. I keep thinking now of all the things that should have made me suspicious, like them asking for cash, but I was so busy planning everything that I never gave it any thought."

"I assume that keeping you all too busy to ask questions was part of the job of the local accomplice," Janet said.

"I'm not sure I believe that there was a local accomplice," Stuart replied. "I can't believe anyone else on the committee was involved in stealing that money. We worked together for over a month and they all seemed as dedicated to the project as I was."

"How well do you know them?" Janet asked.

"I've known Fred for years," Stuart told her. "He was a very successful businessman. That's why he was able to sell his tickets to the men who spent too much last night."

"Who suggested adding him to the committee?" Joan asked.

"I don't know," Stuart replied. "Norman had a list of names that he'd been given by someone. That's where he got my name. I tried everyone on his list and then added Fred as well. Someone else might have suggested him, but it might have been my idea. I simply don't recall."

"What about the others? How well do you know any of them?" was Janet's question.

"I don't know Alvin well," Stuart admitted. "I'm not terribly fond of him, either. He's retired, but he tries to act like he's twenty-five. His girlfriend probably is twenty-five. He was responsible for all of the young people at the party last night. They all ate and drank a lot and none of them bid on a single item."

"He sounds like he could use some extra money," Joan remarked.

"Maybe, but can't we all, really?" Stuart replied. "I'm not fond of the man, but I don't think he's a criminal, either."

"What about Winifred Godfrey?" Janet asked.

"Winifred? He's no criminal," Stuart laughed. "I've known him my whole life, really. He grew up in Doveby Dale, worked as an estate agent for his career, and retired as soon as he could. He'd always been interested in history, but once he was retired, he turned it into a passion. He spends most of his time in the archives in Derby, going through old papers and taking extensive notes. I can't see him having any use for extra money, really."

"Everyone can use extra money," Janet said. "Even if it's just to upgrade one's lifestyle."

Stuart shrugged. "Maybe, but Winifred seems happy enough. The local historical society is his baby. He puts hours and hours into producing their newsletter every few months, mostly writing all of the articles himself. He keep talking about putting a book together as well, but I understand that's a more expensive undertaking."

"Well, there you are," Janet said. "Maybe that's what he wanted the money for."

"Maybe," Stuart said doubtfully. "But he'd be last on my list of suspects."

"So who is first?" Joan asked.

Stuart opened his mouth and then shut it again. After a minute he took a deep breath and then blew out a long sigh. "I suppose it would have to be Alvin," he said eventually. "But I really don't believe it."

"Is it possible that the local accomplice wasn't on the committee?" Janet suggested. "Are there other people who helped with the event?"

"You and Joan," Stuart said dryly.

The women both chuckled. "But we can't have been behind it all, as we didn't even know it was happening until last Monday," Janet pointed out.

"I don't think anyone, other than the committee members, knew about it much before that," Stuart said. "I don't know if Norman and Julian really did talk to Simon about it or not, but they claimed that they spoke to him in the very early planning stages."

"I can't see Simon Hampton being involved in all of this," Joan said.

"Why not?" Stuart challenged. "I hear that he's having trouble collecting from his insurance after the fire damage, due to the circumstances. Maybe he's not as well-off as everyone seems to think."

"We can add him to the list of suspects," Janet said. "But I'm putting him at the very bottom of the list."

Stuart nodded. "It does seem far-fetched," he admitted. "But I'm grasping at straws. I hate the thought that one of the committee members was involved."

"And you can't think of anyone else who knew about the event in the early stages?" Janet asked.

"No, not really," Stuart said. "I will give the idea some more thought, though."

"Maybe they didn't use a local contact this time," Janet suggested. "That's got to be a possibility, right?"

"Where did they get my name from, then?" Stuart asked.

"That's a good question," Janet said.

"You said they had a list," Joan remarked. "Surely the accomplice was one of the men on the list."

"He must have been," Stuart said. "But I can't believe it."

"Fred was the only one not on the list, right?" Janet asked.

"Yes, that's right," Stuart replied. "There were two other names, but they both declined."

"Maybe one of them was the accomplice," Janet said excitedly.

"Don't think I didn't consider that," Stuart said. "But one of them has been on holiday in America since the end of March and the other one declined due to ill health. He's actually been moved to a care home in the last few weeks. He's not doing much more than watching telly and annoying his children, as I understand it."

"But clearly he needs money," Janet said. "Maybe he was the accomplice, but he had to drop out due to his health. Maybe that's why things fell into such disarray."

"I mentioned him to Robert," Stuart told her. "I'm sure he'll investigate, but I can't see him being involved. His health has been bad for some time now."

"At least we can add him to the list," Janet said. "Right under Simon Hampton."

"I'd put him above Simon," Stuart said. "Only because he has a more pressing need for money that could be satisfied by a much smaller amount that what I suspect Simon needs."

Janet nodded. "Maybe I should be writing all of this down," she said.

"There's little point," Joan said. "Working it all out is Robert's job, not ours. It's an interesting mental exercise, but ultimately that's all it is."

"I had a thought, though," Stuart said. "I was hoping you might be willing to help."

"With what?" Janet asked.

"I thought maybe, if we got the committee together again, we could work out who the accomplice was," Stuart said.

Janet and Joan exchanged glances. "That sounds dangerous," Janet said. "Whoever it was must be feeling guilty, and I'm sure he's afraid of being caught as well."

"That's why I thought we should get the whole group together, rather than speak to them one at a time," Stuart replied. "Surely there's safety in numbers."

"What if they were all in on it?" Joan asked.

"Surely not," Stuart said. "For one thing, I doubt Norman and Julian would want to split the proceeds that many ways."

"What makes you think they'd all want to get together?" Joan asked.

"I thought I would ring them and suggest a meeting so that we can work out what happened," Stuart said. "I thought I would tell them that I'm convinced that there wasn't any local accomplice this time and that I needed their help to prove that to the police."

"It might work," Janet said.

"But I'd really like to have the meeting here again," Stuart said. "If you don't mind. Mary is very upset and I'd hate to upset her further," he added.

"I don't mind," Janet said. She and Stuart both looked at Joan.

"I suppose it's okay," Joan said. "When were you planning to have this meeting?"

"Tomorrow? Maybe around eleven?" he suggested.

Joan nodded. "Our guests both want breakfast early, so we could do that," she said.

"Excellent," Stuart exclaimed. "I'll go and start ringing up the committee members."

"There is one condition," Joan added as Stuart got to his feet.

"Oh, what's that?" he asked.

"We need to notify Robert that the meeting is taking place," she told him.

"Oh, but I thought we could ring him after it's over," Stuart said.

"Robert specifically cautioned Janet and myself about talking to any of the suspects," Joan said. "I won't go behind his back like this. If you don't want to tell him what you're planning, I'll ring him myself."

Stuart frowned. He looked over at Janet, but she simply shook her head. Whatever her thoughts on the matter, she could tell that Joan wasn't going to be swayed.

"Okay, you can ring Robert," Stuart said. "I'll go and ring everyone else. If I don't see you between now and then, I'll be here tomorrow around half ten."

"You needn't tell the committee members that Robert will be here," Joan said as they walked the man to the door. "That's one of the reasons I offered to ring him instead of having you do it."

"They may not want to attend if they know," Stuart said. "Maybe I won't mention it."

"We'll see you tomorrow," Janet said.

As soon as the door was shut behind him, Joan headed for the phone. Susan Garner, Robert's civilian assistant at the station, was the only one in the office. Joan left a message, asking Robert to ring her back. When rang about two hours later, Janet answered the phone.

"Joan wanted to talk to me," he said.

"I'll have her pick up," Janet replied. When Joan was on the line, Janet didn't disconnect.

"I just wanted to let you know that Stuart is going to be having a committee meeting here tomorrow," Joan said. "He's hoping he can work out who the accomplice was by talking to everyone all together."

Robert sighed deeply. "Why does everyone want to play amateur detective all the time?" he muttered. "Okay, thank you for letting me know. What time is this little gathering?"

"Eleven," Joan told him.

"I'll be there at ten," Robert replied.

Chapter 9

Robert was true to his word, knocking on the door at Doveby House at exactly ten o'clock the next morning. Janet let him in, and then led him to the kitchen where Joan had the kettle on. They ate biscuits and drank tea while they talked.

"I'm still not convinced that this meeting is a good idea," Robert said.

"Stuart is very upset at the thought that someone on the committee would have helped Norman and Julian," Janet said. "He wants to have a chance to talk to everyone himself."

"I don't think the accomplice, if there was one, is dangerous," Robert said. "If I did, I wouldn't have let this go ahead."

Stuart arrived at half ten, clearly upset. "I don't want tea," he told Joan as he sank into a chair next to Robert. "I'm too worried to eat or drink anything, quite frankly. When I think back to how flattered I was when Norman rang me to ask me to be on the committee, I could scream."

"You need to calm down," Robert said. "The meeting is going to be difficult enough without you on edge."

The other man nodded and then took a long deep breath. "Okay," he said. "I'll try a cup of tea."

Joan made him his drink and everyone sat quietly while he took a few sips. "That is better," he said after a moment. "I'm sorry. The fundraiser took up a huge amount of my time and energy for the last month and I'm quite devastated with how it all turned out. I keep blaming myself for not suspecting anything."

"I didn't suspect anything, either," Robert pointed out. "And being suspicious is my job."

Janet chuckled. "They were very convincing," she said. "Remember, this was the fifth or sixth time they'd done the same thing. You weren't the only ones taken in by them."

"I suppose you're right," Stuart said. "I just feel stupid, I suppose."

"As do I," Robert told him. "I'm hoping we can work out who the accomplice was and maybe he can help us find Norman and Julian."

"Surely he won't want to betray them," Joan said.

"He might, if it means a lighter sentence for him," Robert said. "Having said that, none of the accomplices in any of the other cases were able to help. We've no reason to suppose that our accomplice will be any different."

"Julian and Norman were very careful, then," Janet said.

"Very. In all of the other cases we can tie to them, as soon as the events were over, they paid off their accomplices and disappeared. The accomplices never had any more information about the pair than what they'd told everyone. One had a special phone number for Norman, but that had been disconnected the day after the event as well."

Janet shook her head. "They really know what they're doing, don't they?"

"They do, but now that we can tie several cases together, we're doing everything we can to make their job more difficult," Robert said. "Every constabulary in the country is going to be getting a full profile on the two men and their operations. We're hoping that publicizing the cases will make it much harder for them to continue operating."

"It might work," Joan said. "If enough people see the publicity."

"As long as enough police constables see it, it should have an impact," Robert said. "If I'd seen something about it before our event, I would have asked a lot more questions, that's for sure. Small village constables usually know what's going on in their localities. They should be able to intervene if Norman and Julian try to set up shop."

By five to eleven, everyone was feeling nervous. Stuart and Robert moved into the dining room while Janet and Joan piled biscuits onto plates and boiled a fresh kettle. Alvin was the first to arrive.

"Yes, good morning," he said in a distracted tone as Janet welcomed him. He didn't say anything else, just headed straight for the dining room.

Fred was only a minute behind him. "Ah, lovely to see you again," he told Janet. "I wish these were happier circumstances, of course."

Janet walked him to the dining room and then returned to the sitting room to wait for Winifred. Joan was in place next to the kettle, ready to make hot drinks and eavesdrop.

Winifred was only a few minutes late. He answered Janet's "good morning" with a "hurumph" and then stormed off to the dining room.

"And it's lovely to see you again, too," Janet called after him. She was ninety-nine per cent certain that he couldn't hear her when she spoke, but it still made her feel better. When she walked into the kitchen, she could hear raised voices from the dining room.

"It's highly irregular," Winifred was saying. "This is a closed committee meeting, not yet another inquisition by the police. If Constable Parsons wants to talk with us, there's a place for that, and it isn't at our committee meeting."

"As some of what we have to discuss is a police matter," Stuart said, "I thought it would be helpful to have the constable with us. He's agreed to give us a short briefing on the case."

"Has he?" Winifred asked. "Has something happened, then?"

"Why don't we wait and let Constable Parsons answer that later?" Stuart asked.

"Why don't we have the constable talk first?" Winifred suggested. "Then he can go and get on with his work while we have our committee meeting."

"I'm sorry, but I'd rather wait a short while, if no one minds," Robert said. "I'm waiting for a phone call that might change what I have to tell you."

"What sort of phone call?" Winifred demanded.

"Why don't we get on with our meeting and let Constable Parsons explain everything at the end?" Stuart said. "Let's start by working out exactly how much money each of us is owed at this point."

"I never got paid for the flyers and tickets," Alvin said. "I have the receipt here."

"Thank you," Stuart said. "I paid for the hall rental, for the wine, and I gave some money to Todd and Ted for the food. They are still owed some additional funds, however."

"I didn't end up paying for anything," Fred said. "I do hope you'll be able to recover your money, at least."

"The police will have to find Norman and Julian for that to happen," Stuart said.

"Did everyone pay for everything with cash?" Alvin asked.

"I don't know," Stuart said.

"I'm sure I saw a few people writing out cheques to pay for auction items," Fred said.

"They should stop the cheques, in that case," Stuart said. "Hopefully, they've seen the news about the theft and have already done that."

"If they stop the cheques, they should give back the items they bought in the auction," Winifred said. "Otherwise they're getting them for nothing."

"Really, they should stop the first cheque and then write a second one directly to the charity," Stuart said.

"But if they write it to one of us, we can get paid back for what we spent in putting together the event," Winifred said.

"I don't have you on my list," Stuart said. "How much are you owed and for what?"

"I'm not sure I want to say," Winifred said.

"Why not?" Stuart asked.

"I paid for a few things along the way, but I had intended to tell Norman to consider it all a donation," Winifred told him.

"But we should still have an accounting of what was spent in putting the event together," Stuart argued.

"It isn't enough to worry about," Winifred replied. "I'm more interested in what we took in. How much did those two manage to steal?"

"Unfortunately, along with the money, they stole all of the paperwork from the event," Stuart said. "We don't have any idea how much they got away with."

"We should be able to work out a rough estimate," Fred suggested.

"I've tried to do that for the police," Stuart said. "I have copies of what I put together for them. I'd like you all to take a look and see what you think."

Janet looked over at Joan, who shrugged. They both knew that the numbers on the sheet Stuart was handing around were greatly inflated. He was hoping that the accomplice, on seeing the very high estimate, would get angry that he hadn't received his fair share.

"I think this seems high," Fred said. "I don't remember the auction raising that much."

Stuart named a few of the items that had sold for large sums. "Besides those, every gift voucher went for at least twice its face value, and many of the other items sold for hundreds of pounds," he pointed out.

"I'd still only put the auction at half that amount," Fred said.

"As I said, it's only an estimate," Stuart replied.

"Surely they didn't raise that much in casual donations," Winifred said.

"Actually, I'm fairly certain of those numbers," Stuart said. "I counted three of the four donation buckets myself towards the end of the evening. People were incredibly generous."

"They were indeed," Winifred said angrily.

"I believe a number of people who came intending to bid on

some of the items found themselves outbid. Several of them simply made large cash donations instead," Fred said.

"Did they, now?" Winifred asked.

"Even if we discount a portion of my estimate on the auction proceeds, it was a very successful event," Stuart said. "Imagine how wonderful it would have been to present the charity with a cheque for that sort of amount."

"I don't know that we sold that many tickets," Winifred interjected.

"I took over a hundred at the door," Alvin told him. "And I know a few people who purchased tickets and didn't bother to attend as well. I think Stuart's estimate is about right on that."

"I was sure that Norman told me we'd only sold about seventy tickets," Winifred said.

"Maybe he was hoping to hide the true amount of money that was stolen," Stuart suggested. "Like I said, they took all of the paperwork, so we can't prove any of this in court, if the men are arrested."

"Any chance of that happening any time soon?" Alvin asked.

"We are pursuing a new lead," Robert told him. "I'm sure you are all aware that in most cases the pair used a local accomplice. One of those accomplices has given us some information that is proving quite useful."

"And you think one of us was their accomplice here?" Fred asked.

"I think it's possible," Robert replied. "But they were getting better and more confident in their con. This was their most successful event yet. It wouldn't surprise me if they'd decided to stop using local assistance so that they could keep all of the money for themselves."

"That makes sense," Stuart said. "Especially since I can't see any of us being involved in something so unethical."

"That was my thought as well," Fred said. "I thoroughly enjoyed working with you all and I can't imagine that any of you would do anything criminal."

The silence that followed was interrupted by someone's mobile ringing. "Ah, that's me," Robert said. "I need to take this."

Janet rushed back to the table and sat down. She picked up a biscuit and took a bite, hoping that it looked as if she'd been sitting there the entire time. Robert barely glanced at her and Joan as he walked past, already speaking into his phone. He was back a few minutes later. The dining room had been silent during his absence.

"I'm awfully sorry, but I need to go," he announced in the doorway. "I wish I could tell you what's happening, but I can't, not yet."

"You've had a break in our case?" Stuart asked.

"I can't really comment," Robert told him. "But I'm cautiously optimistic."

With that, he turned and walked back through the kitchen. Janet walked with him to the front door.

"I'll be back in half an hour," he told Janet before he left.

When Janet got back to the kitchen, she took up her position near the kettle again. It sounded as if everyone was talking at once in the dining room.

"It's pointless to speculate," Stuart said loudly over the noise. "We'll just have to wait and see what develops. I'm just glad Robert doesn't think any of us were working with them. If he's found them, he'll be able to find out for sure fairly quickly, at least."

"You think they'll tell him if they had a local accomplice?" Winifred asked.

"Of course they will," Stuart said. "I'm sure they'll try to blame the whole thing on him, and claim they were tricked into helping, or some such thing."

"But they'll have all of the money," Alvin pointed out.

"They'll have it all stashed away somewhere," Stuart replied. "No doubt hidden in Swiss bank accounts or some such thing. They'll probably claim they didn't take anything, that it was all the accomplice's doing."

"They wouldn't do that," Winifred said sharply.

"There's no honour among thieves," Fred said in a serious voice. "Isn't that how the expression goes, anyway? I'm sure Norman and

Julian will do everything in their power to shift as much blame as possible to anyone other than themselves."

"Maybe they'll turn on each other," Alvin suggested. "Although, if they did have an accomplice here, I'd hate to be in his shoes right now."

An awkward silence followed Alvin's words. After a moment, Stuart sighed. "I don't think we'll get anything else accomplished today," he said. "Why don't we adjourn the meeting for now? We can meet again once we've learned more about why Robert had to dash away."

"I think that's an excellent idea," Winifred said. "I've an awful lot to do, you know."

Janet heard chairs being pushed away from the table. She sat back down next to Joan as Alvin walked through the kitchen.

"Thank you once again for your hospitality," he said to the sisters as he went.

Janet got to her feet to walk him to the door. Fred and Winifred were right behind Alvin. Fred nodded towards Joan, but was clearly distracted. Winifred didn't say a word; he just walked through the kitchen as quickly as he could. Janet and the others followed. Once Janet locked up the front door, she hurried back to the kitchen, where Stuart was leaning against the wall with a stunned look on his face.

"Are you okay?" Janet asked the man.

"I've been better," he replied.

Joan put the kettle on again. "You need more tea, with extra milk and sugar this time," she said.

"I can't quite believe it, but I really think Winifred helped those men steal all of that money," Stuart said as he took a seat at the kitchen table.

"From what I could hear, it sounded like that," Janet agreed.

"You should have seen his face," Stuart told her. "As soon as I started talking about Norman and Julian trying to shift the blame to their accomplice, he turned as white as a sheet. We all noticed it, although we tried to pretend we hadn't."

"We need to ring Robert," Joan pointed out as she prepared the tea.

"When he left, he said he'd be back in half an hour," Janet told her. "He should be here any minute, really."

Chapter 10

It was closer to an hour later when Robert finally turned up. Janet, Joan, and Stuart were all pacing in circles around the sitting room when he knocked on the door.

"Sorry I'm late," Robert said brightly. "I was held up by a few little things."

"It's fine," Janet said. "Just tell us what's happening."

"After your meeting broke up, Winifred came down to the station to talk to me," Robert said. "We've already released a statement to the press, so I can tell you that he's confessed to having assisted Norman and Julian with their deception."

"I knew it," Stuart exclaimed. "The look on his face when he saw the estimate of the money raised was the first hint."

"He was clearly upset, wasn't he?" Robert asked.

"Very. And he got more upset the longer the meeting went on," Stuart said.

"Have you found Norman and Julian?" Janet asked.

"Not yet, but we really do have a lead," Robert told her. "Winifred is trying to help as well, but the phone number he had for the pair has been disconnected, which isn't surprising under the circumstances."

"Did he give you any idea as to his motive?" Stuart wanted to know.

Robert shook his head. "He's trying to convince me, and probably himself, that he was mostly innocent, although that's proving difficult. I should know more in a few days, I hope."

"Surely the motive was money," Janet said.

"Probably," Robert replied. "But few things are ever entirely straightforward."

The foursome chatted about the case for a while longer, but Robert couldn't answer many of their questions.

"I'll stop back in a few days with an update," he promised. "For now, I need to get to Derby and help with the questioning."

"Winifred has been taken to Derby?" Stuart asked.

"Once he was formally arrested, he had to be taken there for processing," Robert explained. "I just stopped here on my way to tell you what I could."

Stuart didn't stay long after Robert left. "I still can't quite believe it," he told them as he got up to go. "I really didn't think anyone from our committee was involved, but I'd have almost put my name on the suspect list above Winifred's. He just isn't the type. He's been in Doveby Dale forever. I just don't understand it. I really don't."

Robert was able to offer a possible explanation a few days later. He stopped to see the sisters and found them in the garden with Stuart.

"Ah, there you are," he said as he rounded the corner of the house. "I could hear voices when I was at the front door, so I knew you were here somewhere."

"We're just planning a few changes to our garden," Janet explained. "Stuart has some wonderful ideas for ways to get even more flowers into the space."

"More flowers, more colour, more scent," Stuart said. "It's going to be even more wonderful back here."

Robert nodded. "I'm sorry to interrupt," he said. "But I'm glad you're here. I was going to stop to see you next, Stuart. This way I can talk to you all at one time."

"I think we're done out here," Stuart said. "If we're in agreement, I'll go plant shopping in the next few days and start putting things in immediately."

"I'm happy with the plans," Janet said.

"As am I," Joan agreed. "Now, how about tea and biscuits?"

"Yes, please," Janet, Stuart, and Robert all chorused.

Only a few minutes later they were all sitting around the table with their drinks and plates of sweet treats. Robert ate his way through a few biscuits before he spoke.

"Once Winifred decided to talk, we struggled to shut him up," he began. "Unfortunately, I don't think we're any closer to finding Norman or Julian, but we do know a little bit more about how they operate."

"At least you'll be able to warn other constabularies," Janet said.

"Yes, that should make a difference," Robert agreed. "And maybe the next time they try to set something like this up, they'll get caught before they manage it."

"I hope so," Stuart said. "I hate the thought that all of our hard work profited them instead of a good cause."

"It is a shame," Joan said.

"Did Winifred offer any motive for his actions?" Janet asked.

"He said he was tired of doing all the things he does and not getting any appreciation," Robert told her. "Apparently running the Doveby Dale Historical Society is hard work and he didn't feel that his work was being valued."

"So he justified stealing from a charity rather than just quit the historical society," Joan sighed.

"Yes, well, I believe he was going to do that as well," Robert told her. "He was planning to move into a retirement community in Devon, actually."

"Devon?" Janet repeated.

"That's what he said. He had a number of brochures about the place in his home. He said he'd been in Doveby Dale for his entire life and he wanted to get far away," Robert said.

"I think he's lost his mind," Stuart said. "He loves Doveby Dale and its history."

"Who will I ask about Alberta now?" Janet wondered.

"I assume someone will be taking over the historical society," Robert said.

"I suppose so, but Winifred actually knew Alberta," Janet said sadly. "I don't know that there is anyone else around who's that old."

"That was another reason that he gave for taking part in the scheme," Robert said. "He said he was old and he'd never even had as much as a parking ticket. It seems like he'd decided it was his right to do something criminal in his old age."

"Imagine if we all felt like that," Joan said. "The country would be overrun by criminal gangs of pensioners."

"I don't feel any particular need to do something criminal," Janet said. "And I certainly don't want to spend any time in prison."

"It isn't a pleasant place to be," Robert said.

They talked a while longer about Winifred and his short spell as a criminal.

"By the way, Winifred claims he was promised a third of the proceeds from the event," Robert remarked as he was getting up to leave. "Norman and Julian gave him a thousand pounds on the night of the event. He'd been stationed at the door during the auction, so he didn't know how much that raised. He was stunned by your estimate this morning."

"It was a little bit exaggerated," Stuart said. "But even so, he was cheated out of a lot of money. I can't believe he trusted them to be fair with him."

"They told him the auction raised about two thousand pounds and that seemed a lot to him, apparently. He didn't really pay any attention to the donation buckets, I gather," Robert said.

"He wasn't very good at being a criminal," Joan said.

"No, he wasn't," Robert agreed. "I'm surprised he didn't confess as soon as the crime was discovered, to be honest. I think he thought he could simply move away and pretend it never happened."

"I almost feel sorry for him," Janet said, shaking her head. "Even though he's a disagreeable man who stole from charity, he was used by Julian and Norman and then cheated by them as well."

Robert nodded. "He's a rather sad figure," he agreed. "I got no satisfaction out of arresting him."

The trio walked Robert to the door and watched as he walked to his car.

"What a strange and awful few days it's been," Stuart said. "Mary is still furious with me because of all the money I spent on the event. I've been sleeping on the couch, which is hard and lumpy, and hoping she'll go away and visit one of her children soon. Unfortunately, her oldest son's kids have chickenpox, her middle son is travelling for work at the moment, and her youngest had a huge fight with his wife and keeps threatening to come and stay with us." He sighed.

"You're always welcome to stay in one of our guest rooms when they're empty," Joan said.

"Oh, I couldn't impose like that," he replied quickly. "Especially not now, after everything that happened lately."

"Of course you could," Joan told him. "We owe you a lot for taking care of the garden. It wouldn't be an imposition, and maybe it would make Mary appreciate you more if you weren't around for a day or two."

Stuart grinned. "I may just take you up on that one day," he said. "But for today, I think I'd better go home and try to persuade my wife to forgive me. I was only trying to help a good cause. I'm sure she'll come around."

"Good luck," Janet said as the man opened the door to leave. "You'll need it," she muttered softly after he'd gone.

Joan laughed. "I hope you don't mind my inviting him to stay," she said. "But I feel bad for him, having to sleep on the couch like that."

"I didn't realise you liked Stuart that much," Janet said.

"He's been wonderful since we bought the house," Joan replied. "He keeps the gardens beautifully. Anyway, it isn't so much about liking Stuart. It's more about disliking Mary."

Janet laughed. "I don't like her either, but she won't be very happy with us if we let Stuart stay here when they're fighting."

"I know, but I don't think I care what she thinks," Joan said. "She isn't even in Doveby Dale that much."

Janet couldn't argue with that.

A week later, Janet was surprised to receive a letter in the post. She didn't recognise the handwriting on the envelope. She was even more surprised when she opened it. After she'd read it through twice, she read it aloud to Joan.

Dear Ms. Markham,

You may be aware that I am somewhat indisposed at the moment however, I know you had questions about Alberta Montgomery. I hope I can answer a few of them for you.

Alberta was a tragic figure from my childhood. We didn't have much money and we were living in one of the terraced houses on the edge of the village. The Montgomery family seemed almost like royalty to me, and their home seemed almost a castle. Alberta was an only child and to say that she was doted on would be a considerable understatement.

Her parents kept her under very close supervision at all times. She had a succession of nannies, none of whom stayed for more than a year at a time. I was told that her mother, Georgina, insisted on that so that Alberta could never become attached to any of them over her. I don't know if that's true or not.

There were all sorts of rumours about Alberta, that she was mentally unstable or that she was simple, and as she was so sheltered, the rumours seemed to grow over the years. The whole village was excited when her engagement was announced, especially as she was marrying the younger son of a duke. A step up the social ladder for the Montgomery family could only be good news for Doveby Dale.

A short while later, the rumours started again. This time people were whispering that Alberta had become involved with the gardener at Doveby House. I remember him as well. He was handsome, but common. All talk of the upcoming nuptials died down and the date kept getting pushed further and further back until we all discovered that Alberta's intended husband had married someone else altogether.

A month or so later, Alberta fell from her bedroom window and died. I've been told at least a dozen different stories about her death. People have suggested everything from suicide to murder to explain it, but the coroner ruled it an unfortunate accident. It was widely believed that she was pregnant when she died, but if she was, no mention of it was made in the official reports.

Beyond that, I don't know what else I can tell you. There have always been stories about Alberta's ghost haunting Doveby House. I've been told she screams during the full moon, but you'd be in a better position to address that than I am. I've also been told that the gardener haunts the carriage house, but I don't believe that at all.

That particular young man ended up securing a position at one of the area's stately homes. Some years later he emigrated to the US and worked for several wealthy families there. I can't imagine why he would want to haunt your carriage house. If there is a ghost in the carriage house, and I've been told several times that there is, I believe you'll have to look elsewhere to find him or her.

I hope this letter answers at least some of your questions. I wish I were at liberty to meet with you to discuss the matter further, but unfortunately, that's out of the question at the moment.

Kind regards,

Winifred Godfrey."

Janet finished reading and sat back in her chair.

"Well, I suppose that was nice of him," Joan said.

"I suppose so," Janet replied. "Nice, but odd."

"Perhaps he's bored wherever he is," Joan suggested.

"At least we know a bit more about our ghost now," Janet said. "Or rather, one of them."

"If you believe in such things," Joan replied.

"If you don't believe, you can try sleeping in my room during the next full moon," Janet suggested.

"I'm quite happy in my room," Joan told her. "Besides, we wouldn't want to confuse poor Aggie."

"Aggie gets very upset when Alberta starts shouting," Janet told her. "In fact, she gets upset before Alberta yells. Last month she woke me up by nudging my face and then huddled in my arms for several minutes before Alberta's cries."

"How very odd," Joan said, looking as if she didn't believe a word Janet was saying.

"Maybe Aggie should sleep with you during the next full moon," Janet said.

"I don't think so," Joan said. "But you can put her in one of the guest rooms. You can stay in one as well, if you'd like. Assuming we don't have guests."

"Maybe," Janet said. "For now, I'm focussed on our trip to the Isle of Man, though. There will be a full moon while we are there, and poor old Alberta will just have to shout to herself. I'm sure there aren't any ghosts in the holiday cottage on Laxey Beach, at least."

"We can agree on that," Joan said. "And on looking forward to our holiday."

I'm still hoping to meet with someone from the historical society to talk about Alberta. I'd like to be able to prove to Joan that she doesn't have any family left so that my dear sister will let me read Alberta's letters and diaries.

In the meantime, Robert hasn't yet found any trace of the men who called themselves Norman and Julian and planned the charity event scam. Winifred will be pleading guilty and probably serving a short prison sentence. I understand he's asked to serve it in a prison near Devon. I've taken to calling the entire affair "The Jackson Case" in honour of Alvin. He was my favourite suspect and I'm still slightly surprised that it was Winifred who was the local accomplice.

We will be arriving on the island on Monday the 10th of May and staying until the 16th. Joan and Aggie and I are all looking forward to the visit. See you soon.

Kind regards,

Janet Markham (and Aggie)

Glossary of Terms

- **bin** — trash can
- **biscuits** — cookies
- **booking** — reservation
- **boot** — trunk (of a car)
- **car park** — parking lot
- **chemist** — pharmacist
- **cuppa** — cup of tea (informal)
- **dear** — expensive
- **fortnight** — two weeks
- **high street** — the main shopping street in a town or village
- **holiday** — vacation
- **jumper** — sweater
- **lie in** — sleep late
- **midday** — noon
- **pavement** — sidewalk
- **pudding** — dessert
- **shopping trolley** — shopping cart
- **tannoy** — public address system

- **telly** — television
- **till** — check-out (in a grocery store, for example)
- **torch** — flashlight

Other Notes

In the UK, dates are written day, month, year rather than month, day, year as in the US. (May 5, 2015 would be written 5 May 2015, for example.)

When telling time, half six is the English equivalent of six-thirty.

A "full English breakfast" generally consists of bacon, sausage, eggs, grilled or fried tomatoes, fried potatoes, fried mushrooms and baked beans served with toast.

A semi-detached house is one that is joined to another house by a common center wall. In the US they are generally called duplexes. In the UK the two properties would be sold individually as totally separate entities. A "terraced" house is one in a row of properties, where each unit is sold individually (usually called a row house in the US).

Pensioners are men or women who have reached retirement age.

Acknowledgments

Thanks to my readers who make what I do worthwhile.

Thanks to my editor, Denise, who makes what I write readable.

Thanks to my beta readers, Janice and Charlene, who share their thoughts and improve my stories in many different ways.

The Kingston Case

A MARKHAM SISTERS COZY MYSTERY NOVELLA

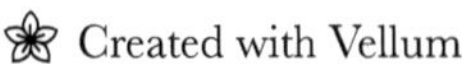
Created with Vellum

Author's Note

I seem to be moving through the alphabet very quickly with these novellas. This title is the eleventh in the series. I always recommend reading the books in order (alphabetically), but each story should be enjoyable on its own.

All of the novellas open and close with parts of Janet's letters to Bessie Cubbon on the Isle of Man. Bessie is the protagonist of my Isle of Man Cozy Mystery series, and she first met the sisters in *Aunt Bessie Decides* in that series. The sisters revisited the island in *Aunt Bessie Observes*. This is the first novella after their visit. The letters to Bessie are simply bookends for the story. You do not need to read the Bessie books in order to enjoy the novellas.

The stories are set in a fictional village in Derbyshire, so I use English spellings and terms. There is a short glossary and some other notes at the end of the book for readers outside the UK. I do apologise for any Americanisms that have snuck into the text. I've been living in the US for eight years now, so such mistakes are increasingly likely. I do my best to eliminate them.

This is a work of fiction and all of the characters are fictional creations. Any resemblance that they may share with any real person, living or dead, is entirely coincidental. Although some shops or businesses in their fictional village may bear some resemblance to real-life businesses, that is also coincidental.

I love hearing from readers. My contact details are available in the back of the book. Please let me know what you think about my books or just drop me a note to say hi. Thank you all so much for taking the time to read my stories.

26 May 1999

Dearest Bessie,

It was so nice to see you and spend some time with you earlier this month. Obviously, some of the things that happened while we were on the island were unpleasant, but I'm determined not to let myself think about them when I remember our holiday. Joan and I simply must insist that you come and visit us next. We'd love to have you in Doveby Dale.

As sad as we were to leave the Isle of Man, it was nice to get home to Doveby House. I really do love our wonderful home, even if we do have to share it with guests from time to time.

We'd only been back a few days, however, when we had a visitor who wanted us to help him solve a problem. Of course, we were eager to help. (Well, I was eager to help. Joan was less enthusiastic.)

Chapter 1

"Do you have plans for today?" Joan asked Janet over breakfast.

"I thought I would do the rest of my laundry from the holiday," Janet told her. "What with all the errands we had to do yesterday, I didn't manage to get it finished."

"I might make another trip to the supermarket," Joan said. "I know we just went yesterday, but that was really just for what we needed for a day or two. I've been making a list this morning, as it seems we're nearly out of everything."

Janet made a face. The small local grocery shop had been shut ever since it had been damaged in a fire. The next closest supermarket was a longer drive from Doveby House, the bed and breakfast the two sisters owned. While it was larger, better stocked, and less expensive than the local shop had been, it wasn't nearly as convenient, and the sisters had been trying to get into the habit of visiting it only once or twice a week.

While Janet liked going, as it gave her a chance to add things her sister wouldn't normally buy to the shopping trolley, she was still feeling tired from their travels. She really didn't want to make another trip around the shop, not after just having done so the day before. "Maybe I'll leave it to you this time," she told her elder sister.

Joan nodded. "I know we're both still tired," she said. "I should have bought more yesterday, but I didn't want to have to think about meals and cooking, really."

"We could just eat at the café today and go shopping tomorrow," Janet suggested.

This time it was Joan who made the face. She was an excellent cook who did nearly all of the cooking for the sisters and for the bed and breakfast. While they'd been on holiday, the pair had eaten in cafés or restaurants every day. Janet knew her sister wouldn't want to do the same now that they were back at home, even if Joan was still tired.

"I'll just buy what we need for a few days of simple meals," Joan said. "We have guests arriving on Friday evening, so I'll need to go shopping again on Friday anyway."

"Are we full this weekend?" Janet asked.

"Yes. We have a couple arriving on Friday night and a single woman arriving on Saturday morning," Joan told her. "Everyone is leaving on Monday morning."

"Which means a very early start on Monday," Janet said sadly.

"I'm afraid so," Joan agreed.

Their weekend guests often stayed through Monday morning, preferring to get up early on the first day of the week for their drive home rather than leaving on Sunday evening. As many of their guests hadn't come from very far away, this made perfect sense, but it did mean that the sisters had to get up very early on Mondays to make breakfast for their guests before they left for home.

"When do we start getting really busy?" Janet asked. She knew that Joan had been taking a lot of bookings for the summer months, not just for weekends but for midweek stays as well.

"June is busier than we've been, with guests every weekend and some weeknights as well," Joan told her. "July and August are busier again. I'm trying to leave a day or two each week with no guests, but that's hard to do. September is already looking busy as well, although not as bad as July and August."

Janet swallowed a sigh. She'd never wanted to own a bed and breakfast. That had been Joan's dream, although Joan had never mentioned it to her sister until recently. The pair had both worked as primary schoolteachers for their entire working lives, living together in a small cottage and sharing nearly everything from their expenses to their car. Once they'd both retired, they were planning to travel. A small and unexpected inheritance had provided them with the funds to purchase Doveby House, which Joan had spotted advertised in an estate agent's window.

They'd owned the seventeenth-century manor house for less than a year and were still learning a lot about running the business. This was their first summer taking guests regularly and Janet was already dreading it. She loved Doveby House, especially her spacious bedroom with its own en-suite, as she'd shared a single bathroom with Joan for all of her life, but she didn't enjoy having guests in the house, at least not regularly. Still, the guests helped pay their bills and had funded their recent holiday to the Isle of Man, so Janet didn't complain, at least not to Joan. What she told her kitten, Aggie, was another matter.

"We should think about whether we want to have the library open for guests or not," Janet said. The library had been one of the main reasons she'd agreed to buy Doveby House. It had come fully stocked with books, and Janet had spent months rearranging the room so every book was exactly where she wanted it. Some books had been removed, primarily old textbooks and forty-year-old travel guides. Those had been replaced on the shelves by books that the sisters had brought with them when they'd moved. In some ways Janet felt mean leaving the door to the library locked when there were guests in the house, but she also hated the thought of people moving books around on the shelves, or worse, borrowing them and not returning them.

"I think we should keep it locked," Joan said, surprising her sister. "We can always open it for any guest who asks, but I don't like the idea of people being able to wander in and out of there whenever they like."

"At least we agree on that," Janet said happily.

With the breakfast dishes stacked neatly in the dishwasher, the sisters went their separate ways. Joan headed for the supermarket that was along the road to Derby, while Janet took the stairs to her bedroom to gather up her laundry.

"Merroow," Aggie said, stretching as she stood up in Janet's bed. She slept on a pillow next to Janet's and hadn't stirred when Janet had climbed out of bed that morning.

"Oh, you are going to get out of bed today, then, are you?" Janet asked her pet.

Aggie gave her an annoyed look and then jumped down off the bed. Janet had already prepared the animal's breakfast, so she didn't need to follow her down the stairs. Once her laundry was started, Janet decided to make a phone call. The sisters had found some diaries and letters that had been written by a former resident of Doveby House. Alberta Montgomery had lived in the house in the nineteen-twenties and thirties, reportedly dying in a tragic accident when still very young. Joan didn't approve of Janet reading the woman's personal papers, so Janet was trying to find out if Alberta had any distant relatives who might want them. A box of privately published books of poetry had also been found, but having read a copy, Janet was fairly certain even the woman's relatives wouldn't want those.

Janet had been able to find out a little of Alberta's history from the man who used to run the local historical society, but he was no longer available to her. Before she and Joan had gone on their holiday, Janet had been given another name of someone who might be able to help. Now seemed the perfect time to ring Gretchen Falkirk to see what she knew. The knock on the door interrupted Janet as she was dialing.

"Ah, William," she said when she'd put the phone down and answered the door. "How nice to see you."

Janet gave her visitor an awkward hug and then stepped backwards to let him into the house. William Chalmers owned a small antiques shop in Doveby Dale. When he'd first moved to the village, both sisters had found him incredibly unpleasant, but once he'd settled in, he'd begun making an effort to fit into village life, and he and the sisters had worked their way into something like a friendship. He'd hinted several times that he might be interested in something more than just friendship with Janet, which made her slightly uncomfortable around him. Today, though, he looked worried and stressed.

"You look as if you need a cuppa," she said after she'd shut the door behind him.

His normally neatly combed grey hair was disheveled. While his dark grey suit was as beautifully cut as always, it looked to Janet as if he'd buttoned the shirt underneath it wrong.

"Oh, tea would be good," he told her. "Something stronger would be better, but I'm driving."

Janet nodded and led the man into the kitchen. He dropped heavily into the first chair he came to while Janet filled the kettle with water.

"We haven't been back long enough for Joan to bake anything," she told him. "But I have a box of shop-bought biscuits, if you'd like."

"That would be nice," William replied, sounding as if he wasn't really listening.

Janet put some biscuits on a plate and set them on the table in front of William. When the kettle boiled, she made two cups of tea, adding extra milk and sugar to William's before she set it down in front of him.

"You seem upset," she said as she joined him at the table. "Is everything okay?"

William shook his head. "I'm forgetting my manners," he said. "How was your holiday?"

Janet took a sip of tea. "It was lovely," she told him. "We were right on the beach and got quite spoiled with the view." There was no need to tell the man about the less lovely aspects of their time away, she decided.

"And did you get to spend much time with your friend?" William asked.

"We did," Janet said. "We got to see quite a lot of her, actually, and Joan and I both enjoyed her company a great deal."

"Excellent," William said. He took a sip of tea and then ate his way through several biscuits before speaking again. "I missed you," he said, nearly causing Janet to choke on a biscuit.

"Really?" she said after a moment. "I mean, I didn't expect that."

"I don't mean just on a personal level," the man said. "Although I did miss you, but I know you aren't sure about starting a relationship with me right now. All things considered, that might be good."

Janet blinked. "I don't think I understood that," she said.

William shook his head. "I'm not making sense," he told her. "I have too much on my mind."

"What's on your mind?" Janet asked.

"Two things," he replied. "For a start, you have a guest arriving on Saturday."

"We do," Janet agreed. "Joan said it was a woman on her own."

"Did Joan tell you her name?"

Janet thought for a minute. "No. We didn't discuss it, why?"

"Her name is Alice Chalmers," William said gloomily.

"A relative of yours?"

"My ex-wife."

Janet forced herself to take a long drink of her tea before she spoke. The first dozen questions that sprang into her mind were inappropriate or rude. Eventually she settled on something that she hoped was better.

"I didn't realise you'd been married," she said.

"Actually, I've been married twice," William said, looking sheepish. "My first wife and I were together for about ten years. Unfortunately, she died in a car accident during a somewhat difficult period. Alice and I met a few years later. Our relationship was always volatile, but we ended up getting married after a while. We separated the day after our first wedding anniversary. We've been divorced for many years now."

"So why is she coming to Doveby Dale?" Janet had to ask.

"She likes to see how I'm doing now and again," William said. "In the past, whenever I'm doing well, she's suggested we should try again. I'm hoping she won't like the idea of life in a small village and will just turn around and go right back to London where she belongs."

Janet bit into a chocolate digestive to keep herself from asking any of the questions that were swirling around in her head. She chewed slowly, trying to find a neutral topic to suggest once she'd swallowed. A sip of tea washed the biscuit down.

"Didn't you say you had two things to talk to me about?" she asked.

"Ah, yes, Alice's visit is just a small problem, really," William said. "The other problem seems bigger, at least to me."

"What's wrong?"

"I was hoping Joan might be here as well," William said. "I'm sure between the two of you, we can find an answer."

"An answer to what?" Janet felt as if she was losing patience.

"To who has been sending me anonymous letters," William replied.

Chapter 2

"What sort of anonymous letters?" Janet asked.

"They're well, rather threatening," William told her.

"Threatening?"

"I think that's the best way to describe them," William said.

"Did you bring them with you?" Janet asked.

"No. They're locked up in my safe at the shop," he replied. "I thought that was best in case anything happened."

"So what do they say?" Janet demanded.

"The first one said something like 'You aren't welcome here,' or words to that effect," William told her.

"How many have there been?"

"Four."

"What does Robert Parsons say?" Janet asked, wondering with their local police constable thought of the matter.

"Ah, um, that is, I, you see," William took a deep breath. "I haven't talked to Robert about it," he said eventually.

"Why not?" Janet asked in surprise.

"I hate to drag the police into this," William told her. "I like Robert, but I'm not totally comfortable with the police, really."

Janet nodded. She knew that William had spent some time in

prison for selling somewhat dodgy antiques in his former shop in London. William insisted that he'd been duped by some of the people he'd trusted to run the shop for him. Janet wasn't sure what to believe, but she could sort of understand why he might feel reluctant to consult the police over a few letters.

"What did the other three say?" she asked.

"The second one was much like the first. It said I wasn't welcome in Doveby Dale and suggested I should move back to London."

"And then?"

"The third said I should move back London or 'I'd be sorry,'" William said with a sigh.

"That's definitely threatening," Janet said. "What about the fourth?"

"It was the same as the third."

"Exactly the same?"

"The wording was the same, but the words and letters had been cut from different magazines," William told her.

"So whoever is doing this is cutting up magazines to make the words?"

William nodded. "I can even tell you where they got the words and letters for the first letter," he added, naming the country's most popular television listings guide. "I'd actually only just finished reading it and I recognised some of the words from one of the article headlines."

"Have they all come from the same magazine, then?"

"No. I haven't recognised anything in the other three notes."

Janet shook her head. "You need to ring Robert," she said.

"I thought about it, but the first one didn't seem like anything serious," William told her. "I was going to show it to you and Joan and see what you thought, but you were on holiday, so I decided I would just wait until you got back. I honestly didn't think it was anything to worry about."

"But now that you've had four, you're getting worried," Janet suggested.

"A little bit," William admitted.

"Are the envelopes done with bits cut from magazines as well?"

"No. They appear to have been printed on a standard home computer printer," William told her.

"If they have access to a computer and a printer, why not just print the actual letters as well?"

"I have no idea," William said. "It seems like it would be a lot easier than cutting and pasting things from magazines. That was one of the reasons I didn't take it all that seriously, really. It seemed like a silly prank at first."

"But now it doesn't?"

"Not as much. Not when I've been getting a new letter every day."

"You've been getting one a day?"

"The first one arrived on Thursday last week. Then I received another on Friday and another on Saturday. The fourth one was in yesterday's post. I'm not looking forward to what I'm going to get today."

"You have to ring Robert," Janet repeated herself. "Whoever is sending them could be dangerous."

"They don't seem dangerous. They seem odd and a bit silly," William told her.

"Do you have any idea who might be behind them?"

William blushed bright red. "Not at all," he said, staring down at the kitchen table.

"Who do you think is sending you the letters?" Janet pressed him.

"I don't know," William said firmly.

"But you have some idea," Janet said. A sudden thought crossed her mind. "You don't think they're from your ex-wife, do you?"

"Alice wouldn't do that," William said unconvincingly.

"But you think she might have," Janet suggested.

William shrugged. "When she decides she wants us to get back together, well, she can be a little obsessive," he told her.

"Like how?" Janet asked.

"Nothing serious, really, she just rings all the time or sends me little presents or things like that," William said. "She once tried to persuade some of my friends to talk to me on her behalf. One time she told me she'd been diagnosed with a fatal illness and just wanted to spend her dying days with me. Little things like that."

Janet stared at him, open-mouthed. "Those aren't little things," she said after a minute. "Pretending you're dying is pretty serious."

"She didn't mean to upset me," William insisted. "She was going to tell me as soon as we were back together. Anyway, she knows I won't fall for her tricks anymore. That time I insisted on seeing her doctor with her and that put an end to that."

"What would she be hoping to accomplish by threatening you?"

"She wants me to move back to London. She's made no secret of that. I used to help her around the house with odd jobs and I'm sure she misses that."

"So she's threatening you to get you to move back down south?"

"Maybe," William shrugged. "If the letters are coming from her, that is. They may not be, of course."

"Who else wants you to move out of Doveby Dale?" Janet asked.

"That's just it. I have no idea. I'd almost rather it was Alice. I can handle her. If it's someone else, well, I don't know. It's scary to think about."

"Let's ring Robert," Janet suggested.

"I don't want to get Alice into trouble," William protested. "If it is just her being Alice, then I don't want the police involved."

"But what if it isn't?"

"At least now someone else knows about the letters," William said. "If something does happen to me, the police will have a place to start."

Janet found herself staring at the man again. "If something happens to you?" she echoed. "That's a horrible thought."

William put his hand over hers. "I didn't mean to upset you," he said. "But I'm flattered that you seem to care."

"Of course I care," Janet snapped, pulling her hand away. "I'd like to think we've become friends over the past six months or so. The idea that someone might be planning to hurt you is very upsetting."

"I'm sorry. I shouldn't have burdened you with all of this. I should go to the police."

"Yes, you absolutely should," Janet nearly shouted.

"Let me see what turns up in today's post and then I'll ring Robert," William said. "Maybe he can look into things on an unofficial basis, just in case it is Alice behind it all."

"If it is Alice, you should want her arrested," Janet said. "Whoever is behind it is threatening you."

"Alice is harmless," William told her. "I almost hope it is her, although I'm sure she'll be devastated when I refuse to go back to her this time."

"I don't understand why she's coming to Doveby Dale," Janet said.

"She wants to see me and I won't visit her in London."

"Why does she want to get back together with you?"

"Every time she's in a relationship and something goes wrong, she runs back to me and begs me to take her back," William explained. "The first few times, I fell for it and we tried again, but we always end up fighting over something stupid. Eventually we both get fed up with the fighting and separate again. It was something of a vicious circle until I finally learned to simply refuse to even consider trying again."

"But she's still coming to see you here," Janet pointed out.

"Just because I stopped agreeing doesn't mean she's stopped trying," William told her. "I don't know. Just when I'm convinced she's behind the letters, I think that they're a step too far, even for her."

"So you need to make a list of your enemies," Janet suggested.

"I hope I don't have any in Doveby Dale," William said. "I know I was insufferable when I first arrived, but I'd like to think that I've made amends for my poor behaviour in those early days. I may still have a few enemies in London, but why would they want me to leave Doveby Dale? The last I knew, they were all happy that I was gone."

"What about business rivals in the area?" Janet asked.

"I don't know. I'll have to give the whole matter some thought,"

William said. "Which is ironic, because that's about all I've been able to think about for ages. I just kept thinking it was Alice, but the more we talk about it, the more I doubt that. I know Alice has behaved badly in the past, but sending anonymous and threatening letters is too much, even for her."

"Ring me when you get your post and let me know what's in it," Janet told him as the man got up to leave. "I'm going to worry about you."

"I appreciate it," William told her. "I'm hoping I'm making a big deal out of nothing, though. Maybe the notes don't really mean anything."

Janet frowned and didn't reply. The notes sounded awful and scary to her. It seemed unlikely that someone would go to the trouble of sending them if they didn't mean to scare William away.

At the door, he stopped and gave Janet a hug. "Thank you for listening to me," he told her. "I owe you dinner one night soon."

"I'd like that," Janet said. "Maybe after your former wife has gone."

"That might be best," William agreed.

Janet let him out and watched as he walked to his car in the house's small car park. She felt a horrible sense of unease about the anonymous letters. If William didn't ring Robert about them, she might just have to do it herself.

Before she pushed the door shut, she spotted Joan turning off the main road. She waited in the doorway for her sister to park and then walked down and helped her unload the car.

"The shop was far too busy for this time on a Tuesday," Joan complained as she unpacked the shopping. "Don't people have jobs to go to?"

"Surely it was mostly pensioners and young mums," Janet said. "That's who's there when I go, anyway."

"I suppose it was," Joan conceded. "But there seemed to be an awful lot of both groups today, more than normal."

"I'm sorry. I should have come and helped."

"At least you got your laundry done," Joan said.

"My laundry!" Janet exclaimed. "I forgot all about it. It's still in the washing machine."

She switched her clothes to the tumble dryer, not feeling patient enough to hang things outside to dry today. Back in the kitchen, Joan was making their lunch. They ate a light meal together that was interrupted by the phone.

"I hope you don't mind," Joan said when she'd put the phone down, "but I've invited Michael for dinner."

Michael Donaldson was the handsome widower who lived across the road from Doveby House in a small semi-detached house. While Janet had had a few boyfriends in her younger days, Joan had steadfastly refused to entertain any suitors. Both sisters had been surprised when Michael began a very slow courtship of Joan, but they were both gradually growing accustomed to the idea that Joan had acquired her first boyfriend at the age of sixty-seven.

"I never mind seeing Michael," Janet said truthfully. She liked the retired chemist a great deal, actually.

The phone rang again as they were putting the last of the dishes into the dishwasher.

"Is that Janet?" a somewhat timid voice asked when she'd answered the phone.

"It is, yes," Janet replied.

"It's Edna, Edna Green," the caller said. "I was just looking at my empty refrigerator and I can't stand the thought of driving all the way to the supermarket. I know it's terribly short notice, but are you by any chance free for dinner tonight?"

"I am," Janet said impulsively. "Where would you like to go?"

"Oh, can we just go to the café? It's affordable and friendly," Edna said.

"That sounds exactly right," Janet laughed. And it would be good to leave Joan and Michael to have a quiet dinner on their own, as well, she thought as she put the phone down.

She'd only taken a few steps away from it when it rang again. Goodness, aren't we popular today, she thought as she picked up the receiver.

"Janet? It's William."

"Oh, yes, what came in today's post, then?" Janet asked.

"It's nice to talk to you, too," William said in a teasing tone.

Janet laughed. "I'm sorry," she said. "How are you this afternoon?"

"I'm fine," William said cheerfully. "And I'm happy to tell you that I didn't get another letter today."

"Oh, that is good news," Janet said, suddenly remembering that she hadn't mentioned the letters or William's ex-wife to Joan.

"I'm sure whoever it was has grown tired of the game," William said. "I'm glad I didn't ring Robert now."

"Maybe," Janet said with less certainty. "Let's not jump to any conclusions just yet. If you don't have any more letters this week, then maybe you can forget all about it."

"And take you to dinner to celebrate," William added.

"That, too," Janet said.

The entire subject still made Janet feel quite unsettled, so she went to find her sister.

"William Chalmers visited today," she began. "His ex-wife is our guest who is arriving on Saturday."

"I did notice the surname, but she didn't mention the relationship when she booked. I wasn't about to ask," Joan said.

"And he's been getting anonymous letters," Janet said.

"Pardon?" Joan asked.

Janet repeated as much of the conversation with William as she could remember while Joan listened intently.

"I hope he's right," she said when Janet was finished. "I hope whoever was behind it has stopped."

"I still think he should ring Robert," Janet said.

"Maybe he'll get another letter tomorrow and agree to contact the police," Joan said. "Although I hope the letters have stopped."

"Me, too," Janet agreed. She turned to leave her sister and then stopped. "Oh, and I'm having dinner with Edna Green tonight. She rang just before William did."

"She rang you?" Joan asked.

"Yes."

"You didn't ring her to make plans so you could avoid Michael?"

Janet laughed. "I like Michael," she said. "But I also like Edna, and she didn't have anyone else to have dinner with tonight. I'm sure you and Michael will enjoy having the house to yourselves, as well."

"I suppose so," Joan said.

"Is everything okay with you and Michael?" Janet asked, concerned by her sister's reply.

"I haven't seen him since we've been back," Joan pointed out. "Maybe I'm just bit worried that he'll have decided he's not interested anymore."

"He rang and asked to see you tonight, didn't he?"

"Yes, but he asked if I'd make him dinner," Joan said crossly. "He said he's missed my cooking."

"That isn't very romantic," Janet frowned.

Joan sighed. "I'm sure it will be fine," she said. "I just wish you were going to be here, too."

"I can ring Edna and cancel," Janet offered.

"No. You go and have fun with your friend," Joan told her. "Michael probably won't stay long after I've fed him, anyway."

With Joan's words worrying her, Janet headed up to her room to get ready for dinner at the café.

Chapter 3

In her room, Janet rummaged through her wardrobe, looking for the perfect outfit for meeting a friend for dinner. She finally settled on a black skirt and a grey short-sleeved jumper. After a moment's hesitation, she showered again before she got dressed.

"Merrrroww?" Aggie asked as Janet combed her shoulder-length grey bob.

"I'm having dinner with a friend," Janet replied.

"Yooww!" Aggie said.

"Not a male friend, a female friend," Janet told her.

Aggie had been a surprise gift from Edward Bennett, the handsome and sophisticated man who had been their first paying guest after the sisters had bought Doveby House. He had been friends with the former owner of the house, Margaret Appleton. Before he left, after his short stay, he'd told Janet that he worked for a secret government agency that had used the bed and breakfast as a temporary safe house on occasion. Even after a recent second visit, Janet wasn't entirely sure what to believe about the man, who seemed determined to sweep her off her feet, at least when he was in the country.

The kitten stared at her for a moment and then padded away

out of the room. A moment later Janet could hear the animal bouncing down the stairs. No doubt she was going to double-check that Janet had left her dinner out for her. As if Janet would neglect her beloved pet in any way.

Janet added a touch of makeup to her bright blue eyes. She and Joan shared the same eye colour and the same hair colour and style. People often insisted that the sisters looked alike, but Janet didn't see it. Standing up, she smoothed her jumper over her curvy hips. Joan, even though she was the cook in the family, had always been slender. Janet was curvier, especially after their holiday which had been full of restaurant meals and other indulgences. Now that she was home, Janet knew she'd have to behave better. But that would have to start tomorrow, as tonight she was eating at the café up the road. You couldn't possibly be on a diet there.

"Have fun with Michael," she told Joan when she found her in the kitchen a few minutes later. "I won't be out late. It's just dinner with a friend."

"I don't know if Michael will want to watch some telly after dinner or not," Joan said, frowning. "Perhaps if he does, I'll send him home to watch on his own."

"Be nice," Janet told her. "I'm sure he missed you terribly and just didn't think to mention it when he spoke to you earlier."

"We'll see about that," Joan said grumpily.

Janet shook her head. Michael was going to be in for a long evening if Joan's mood didn't improve. When she opened the door, she startled the man in question, who was just coming up the steps at the front of the house.

"Ah, Janet, just the woman I wanted to see," he said to her. "I've brought you a little something." He handed Janet a small wrapped box.

"A present? For me?" Janet asked, feeling confused.

"I was missing your sister terribly," Michael confided. "I covered for a sick associate in Derby while you were away, and over my lunch break I did some shopping. I found several little things for Joan, and when I saw that I thought it would be perfect for you. If you don't like it, well, I don't mind what you do with it."

Janet smiled. "I'm sure I'll love it, whatever it is," she said brightly. "But for now I need to go. If it's okay with you, I'll open it later."

"Of course, that's fine," Michael assured her.

Janet went back into the house and rushed up the stairs to put the gift in her room. When she came back down, Michael was handing several similarly wrapped gifts to Joan.

"Enough already," Joan said, laughing.

"Only two more," Michael told her. "I couldn't stop thinking about you, you see," he explained. "And every time I thought about you, I seemed to stumble across something else I thought you might like. Anyway, I thought if I bought you several gifts, you'd be sure to like at least one or two of them."

"I'm sure I'll like all of them," Joan said. "I brought you a little something back from the Isle of Man as well, but only one thing."

"You did?" Michael beamed at Joan.

"I'll see you two later," Janet called as she headed out the door. She was really glad now that she'd made other plans for dinner. Seeing Joan so happy was wonderful, but she couldn't help but feel a pang of jealousy that her sister was being showered with gifts while Janet was having dinner with a female friend.

Edna was already sitting at a small table for two in the café when Janet arrived.

"I'm sorry I'm late," she greeted her friend. Edna wore her grey hair in a simple bob. Her clothes were classic and understated but had clearly been expensive. She smiled brightly at Janet.

"I was early," Edna told her. "And I didn't mind waiting."

The room was about half full and Janet looked around to see if she recognised anyone else. Aside from Ted, the co-owner of the café, she didn't see any familiar faces.

"I keep thinking I should know more people than I do," Janet said with a sigh as she picked up her menu. "We've been here for months, after all."

"I know what you mean," Edna agreed. "I didn't really know anyone in London, but you expect that in a big city. One of the reasons my husband and I wanted to move up here was so that we could live in a community where everyone knew one another, but I don't feel as if I know anyone yet."

"Except for me and other women in the Doveby Dale Ladies' Club," Janet said.

"Well, yes, there is that," Edna agreed.

Ted walked over and grinned at them. "Just the two of you tonight? Where is the rest of the club?"

"We're not meeting again for a few more weeks," Janet told him. "We only meet once a month, and only then when everyone is well."

Ted nodded. "And you don't always meet here, of course. I know some of your members like to try different places."

"It's always nice to try somewhere new," Janet said. "But I keep coming back here because you do the best comfort food."

Ted chuckled. "That's a good way to describe it," he agreed. "Todd's a genius with comfort food."

Ted was in his early forties. He had ginger hair and a neatly trimmed beard. The café dining room was his responsibility. His partner, Todd, ran the kitchen. Todd was a few years older and had dark curly hair that was always tied back in a ponytail. While Ted was slender, Todd tended to be plump, something that Janet was sure showed that he was a good cook.

"What are your specials today?" Edna asked.

"Chicken and leek pie or toad in the hole," Ted replied.

"Oh, chicken and leek pie for me," Janet said, shutting her menu without even looking at it.

"Me, too," Edna said. "That sounds wonderful."

Ted nodded. "It's really good," he told them. "I've had two helpings already and I haven't had my dinner break yet."

"You get a dinner break?" Janet asked.

Ted laughed. "Not really, but I usually grab a bite to eat around seven. That's still an hour away."

"You need more help in here," Janet said.

"We're looking for someone," Ted told her. "But after the last person we hired turned out to be, well, less than honest, we're a little worried about adding to the staff."

"We're booked up through the entire summer," Janet told him. "You'll probably get a lot busier when the tourist season starts."

"I'm sure we will," Ted agreed. "I'll just have to learn to work harder."

He collected their menus and then headed into the kitchen.

"I wonder if they'd hire me," Edna mused.

"You?" Janet repeated in surprise.

Edna chuckled. "Is that such a strange idea?" she asked.

"Well, yes," Janet told her. "I'm sure it's hard work, carrying heavy trays of food around all day, and you'd be on your feet for hours at a time as well. I hope everything is okay."

"Oh, everything is fine and I don't need the money, if that's what you mean," Edna told her. "I'm just a bit bored and feeling as if I need to do something with myself. The children are both in London. Harry's planning his wedding and never gives me a thought. Helen, well, she's busy with her career. I'm sure she never thinks of me, either. I was just thinking the other day that I might like a part-time job, that's all."

"I'm sure there are easier jobs than waiting tables," Janet said.

"Yes, I'm sure there are, as well," Edna agreed. "It would also be nice to get out of the house more and meet people, though. I do think nearly everyone in Doveby Dale eats here at least once in a while."

"You could be right about that," Janet agreed.

Ted brought their drinks. When he was gone, Janet changed the subject.

"Your son is getting married in August, isn't he?" she asked Edna.

"That's right. Keira and her mother are planning everything, and Henry is paying for it, so I'm rather out of the loop."

Janet felt sorry for her friend. She knew that Edna had been planning to move to Doveby Dale with her husband when he retired, but the man had passed away before they'd moved. As they'd already bought the house in Doveby Dale, Edna moved anyway, but Janet was sure the woman was finding it difficult being on her own for the first time in many years in a strange place where she knew no one.

"You'll be going down for the wedding, though, won't you?" Janet asked.

"Oh, yes, of course," Edna said. "I'm going down for a fortnight, actually. A week before the wedding to help them with all the last-minute things and then a week after the wedding to recover."

Janet laughed. "You'll need it," she said. "Or at least I imagine you will. Neither Joan nor I ever married, but it does seem as if weddings are incredibly complicated affairs."

"I believe Keira is keeping things simple," Edna told her. "Only one hundred and fifty guests, a sit-down dinner, and drinks and dancing afterwards."

"That's simple?" Janet gasped.

"Henry keeps insisting that it's simple," Edna said. "Then he adds on something else that Keira simply has to have." She sighed. "I really do like Keira and I think she and Henry will be very happy together, but I'm starting to worry that this wedding is going to leave Henry penniless."

"Maybe Henry should have a talk with Keira about finances before things go any further," Janet suggested.

"I mentioned that to him," Edna replied. "I think a lot of the wedding plans are coming from Keira's mother, though, and Henry is terrified of her. I'm sure it will all work out in the end."

The arrival of their food ended that discussion. Over the meal, which both women thoroughly enjoyed, they talked about the weather and the royal family as well as Janet's holiday.

"The Isle of Man sounds lovely," Edna said after they'd both ordered puddings that they knew they shouldn't have. "Maybe I shall have to holiday there one day."

"You should get the cottage next to ours the next time we go," Janet suggested. "You and Martha Scott could share, as they all have two bedrooms."

"That's an idea," Edna said. "I quite like Martha."

"We're hoping to go again in the autumn," Janet told her. "The bed and breakfast is quite busy through September, but I'm hoping we can sneak away for a few days in early October. The cottages don't shut for the season until the end of October."

"I'll have to see if I can manage it," Edna said. "Let me know how your plans develop."

Janet promised to do that as they worked their way through large slices of chocolate gateau together. By the time they'd finished their puddings, Janet was feeling full and sleepy.

"Is it too early to go home and go straight to bed?" she asked Edna as they made their way to their cars.

"I hope not," Edna said. "Because that's exactly what I have planned for the rest of my evening."

Janet laughed. "We should do this more often," she said. "Maybe without pudding, though."

"I'm not sure I want to do it again if I can't have pudding," Edna replied with a grin.

Janet drove home and let herself in, expecting to find her sister and Michael in either the kitchen or the television lounge. Instead, the house was empty, aside from Aggie, who loudly demanded more food.

"You've had your dinner," Janet told her. "Now you must wait for breakfast."

Aggie's sad expression had Janet reaching for the box of treats. "Just the one," she told the animal. "Since I had pudding, you may as well."

Janet found a note from her sister on her pillow.

"Going over to Michael's to watch telly there. He just got a new telly with a big screen."

"The things Joan will do for the man she loves," Janet told Aggie with a sigh. "She doesn't even watch telly, really. And now she's all excited about a bigger screen."

"Merow," Aggie told her.

Janet didn't go straight to bed, but she didn't stay up for very much longer, either. Curling up in bed with a good book was one of life's great pleasures. Joan wasn't home by the time Janet decided to get some sleep. Aggie had already been sleeping by her side for some time when Janet switched off the light.

Chapter 4

Joan was singing softly to herself as she made breakfast the next morning.

"I take it you had a nice evening with Michael," Janet teased from the kitchen doorway.

Joan flushed. "It was very nice, thank you," she said, a touch stiffly.

"Did he get you anything nice?" Janet asked.

Joan opened her mouth and then shut it again. After a moment, she chuckled. "He bought me so many things, it's hard to say," she told Janet. "He gave me a present for every day that I was gone, plus a couple of bonus gifts for days when he missed me even more than normal."

"That's either very romantic or a little bit weird," Janet said. "As you are the one on the receiving end, you can choose which it is."

"I think it was very sweet and romantic," Joan said firmly.

And also weird, Janet added to herself.

"He told me he got you a little something as well," Joan said.

"A box of very fancy chocolate truffles," Janet told her. "I suppose I could share them with you, if you didn't get any."

"You keep them and enjoy them," Joan told her. "It was kind of him to think of you as well."

"It was, yes," Janet agreed, feeling that little pang of jealousy again. She squashed it firmly as Joan put breakfast onto plates.

"Do you have plans for today?" Joan asked Janet as they finished eating.

"Not really," Janet said with a shrug. "I really need to ring Gretchen Falkirk, but if there is something else that needs doing, that can wait."

"I thought I might drive into Derby," Joan said. "I was thinking of having a look around the big shopping mall there."

Janet tried not to look as surprised as she felt. Neither sister was a huge fan of shopping malls. "Really? Do you need something?" she asked.

"I could do with a few more nice outfits for evenings out with Michael," Joan replied. "I think he's already seen me in everything I own."

"I'll come along," Janet said impulsively. "But only if we can have lunch there."

Joan frowned. "I wasn't planning to stay there all day," she complained.

"We have to drive over and fight with the car park," Janet said. "By the time we've done that, it will be nearly time for lunch anyway."

It didn't take much more effort to persuade Joan. Janet went back upstairs to comb her hair and touch up her makeup before they left.

"You be a good kitten," she told Aggie, who was bouncing around on Janet's bed. "I'll put some lunch out for you now, but you should wait a while before you eat it."

Aggie looked at her for a moment and then went back to bouncing.

Janet checked her appearance in the mirror. "So much for starting to eat more sensibly today," she muttered. "Another restaurant meal? You shouldn't, really." Her mirror image stuck out its tongue, making Janet laugh.

The drive into Derby was uneventful and the sisters were relieved to find the car park at the shopping mall was half empty. Janet followed her sister through a dozen or more shops while Joan tried on and rejected several different dresses.

"I just can't find exactly what I want," she told Janet when they'd walked the entire mall and purchased nothing aside from the freshly baked cookie that Janet couldn't resist.

"Maybe we should go and have lunch and then start over again," Janet suggested. "Maybe you're just too hungry to focus on what you really want."

"I know exactly what I want," Joan protested. "Something simple, elegant, and classic. Why all the shops are full of trendy dresses designed for twelve-year-old girls is beyond me."

Janet swallowed a laugh. "Come on. We'll go somewhere nice for lunch. You'll feel better after you've eaten."

Janet dragged her sister to the restaurant section of the mall. After a short debate, they agreed on a restaurant. Fortunately, it wasn't busy and they could be seated almost immediately. They ordered their food and settled back to chat.

"Janet and Joan Markham, you're far from home," a voice said at Janet's elbow.

"Owen Carter?" Janet replied as she looked at the very tall man in his late forties. He had brown hair and eyes, although his eyes were mostly hidden behind thick glasses. "But what are you doing here?"

When Michael had sold his chemist's shop to a large chain, Owen had been sent to Doveby Dale as manager. He'd fallen ill a short while later, and the sisters had visited him while he'd been in hospital. Now that he was well again, he could nearly always be found behind the counter in the shop. It was in the small parade of shops in the centre of the village, in the same row as William Chalmers's antique shop and a newsagent's. The sisters probably visited the shop at least once a week for one reason or another.

"We had a regional planning meeting here this morning," Owen explained. "Believe it or not, we're starting to think about Christmas."

"Christmas?" Janet echoed. "But it's only May."

"But it's nearly time for our buyers to start placing orders for the things we'll be stocking this Christmas." He laughed. "No pun intended, obviously."

"Who's minding the shop if you're here?" Joan asked.

"No one," Owen replied. "They actually had me close for the morning. I really must get back, really. I hate having the shop shut."

With that, the man was gone. "That was rather odd," Janet said as they watched Owen walk away.

"He's a somewhat unusual young man," Joan said.

"I can't imagine why they closed the shop just for a meeting," Janet said. "Surely Michael would have covered for him?"

"Michael had other plans for today," Joan replied, sounding slightly cross.

"What's he doing, then?" Janet asked.

"He's having lunch with his sister-in-law and his nephew," Joan said.

"His sister-in-law?"

"Yes; his wife's sister and her son," Joan clarified.

"Oh, I see," Janet said, wondering how Joan felt about the idea. Michael didn't talk about his wife very often, but from everything she knew, she believed that they'd been very happily married before the woman's untimely death. If she were Joan, she wouldn't want anyone around Michael that might remind him of his first marriage.

"They get together about once a month," Joan said.

Janet could hear tension in her sister's voice, even as she tried to sound nonchalant. "How nice for Michael," she said after a moment.

The food's arrival interrupted the uncomfortable conversation. Janet dug into the chicken with rice and vegetables, feeling relieved.

It was hard work, but Janet managed to persuade her sister to share a slice of jam roly-poly with her for pudding. Joan only ate a few bites of the sweet treat, but as far as Janet was concerned, they'd each had half.

"Now we shall start again with fresh eyes and find exactly what you want," Janet announced after they'd paid the bill and were leaving the restaurant. "Let's try that shop right where we parked. I've never been in there, but the outfits in the window are lovely."

"I'm sure it's terribly expensive," Joan hissed as they stood outside the shop in question.

"Maybe they're having a sale," Janet said optimistically.

They were having a sale, one that made their unbelievably high prices almost low enough to be considered. After a few minutes of looking, Joan found a dress she loved and a second that she quite liked.

"Try them on," the shop assistant urged her.

"I don't know," Joan replied. "I don't usually spend this much on myself."

"Try them on," Janet said. "If they don't fit or you don't like the way they look on you, then you won't feel bad if you don't buy them."

Both dresses fitted Joan's slender figure perfectly, though. "The blue one is more flattering," Janet said. "But I like both of them."

"I do, too," Joan admitted. "But I can't justify spending that much money today."

"Every second item is an additional fifty per cent off," the shop assistant told them.

"Sold," Joan said quickly.

"We should put that bag in the car before we shop any more," Janet suggested as they walked out of the shop with Joan's purchases.

"I think I've had enough for today," Joan replied. "I have two lovely new dresses that are far nicer than what I normally buy. I think we should head home before I realise how much I actually spent."

"You got both dresses for less than the regular price of either one of them, thanks to the sale," Janet pointed out.

"But I never would have paid full price for either of them," Joan said. "I never spend that sort of money on clothes."

"Perhaps you should," Janet said. "Not all the time, but once in a while, maybe you should spoil yourself."

"You don't spend that sort of money on clothes, either," Joan pointed out.

"That's because I don't generally care what I'm wearing," Janet said, laughing.

"We'll have to come back again in a few weeks and do some shopping for you," Joan told her sister as they climbed back into their car.

"I don't need anything," Janet protested. "I don't have a handsome suitor taking me out to dinner nearly every night."

"We don't go out that often," Joan replied, flushing. "And William Chalmers would take you out regularly if you'd let him."

"I don't know about that," Janet said. "And anyway, I want to see what his ex-wife is like before I agree to go anywhere with him again. She sounds a little bit scary."

"I'm not looking forward to having her as a guest," Joan replied. "If I'd known who she was, I might have told her we were fully booked."

"At least she's only staying two nights," Janet said. "It could be worse."

The drive back to Doveby Dale was uneventful. The light on their answering machine was blinking when they got home.

"You have two new messages," the machine told them. "Joan, it's Michael. Please ring me when you get home," the first message said.

Joan pushed pause on the machine so that she could use the phone. Janet went into the kitchen to see how Aggie had done with her lunch while her sister talked with Michael. She was just refilling the kitten's water bowl when Joan joined her.

"He wants me to have dinner with him and them," Joan announced.

"Them? The sister-in-law and the nephew?" Janet asked.

"Yes."

"When?"

"Tonight," Joan said anxiously.

"What did you say?"

"I said yes, because I've taken complete leave of my senses," Joan told her. "I can't have dinner with them. It will be horrible."

"It will be stressful," Janet said. "But he's been a widower for two or three years now, right? Surely they expect him to see other people?"

"I don't know what they expect," Joan said, sounding slightly teary. "I don't know anything about them, except that Michael said that they want to meet me."

"You should be flattered," Janet suggested.

"I might be if I didn't feel so unwell," Joan replied. "I'm not ready to meet them. I'm too old for this sort of thing. It's like meeting your boyfriend's parents for the first time, only worse."

"So tell him you can't make it," Janet said.

"I already told him I could. If I cancel now, he'll never believe whatever excuse I come up with."

"At least you have two lovely new dresses to chose between," Janet said brightly.

"I suppose so. You don't think they're too nice, do you? I don't want them to think that I'm trying too hard."

"They're both beautiful and perfectly appropriate," Janet said. "Wear whichever is more comfortable."

Joan sighed and began to pace back and forth across the small room. "I'm too old for this sort of thing," she repeated herself. "Why did I ever agree to have dinner with him the very first time? I should have said no that night. Think of the aggravation it would have saved me."

"And think of the fun you would have missed out on," Janet said.

Joan sighed. "I have a headache coming on. I'm going to go and lie down a while."

Janet found a book and curled up in the library to read. A few hours later, Joan was feeling somewhat better, or at least resigned to her fate.

"I'm off," she told Janet, who was still in the library. "You'll have to make yourself some dinner."

"After that gorgeous lunch, I'm not terribly hungry," Janet said. "I'll probably heat up a frozen pizza or something."

Joan looked as if she wanted to argue, but she didn't. "Don't wait up," she muttered to Janet as she turned and walked away.

Janet followed at a leisurely pace, checking that her sister had locked the front door behind herself.

"It's just us tonight," she told Aggie. "Let's make pizza and popcorn and watch mindless telly."

"Meeroowww," Aggie agreed.

Janet gave her a treat and then filled her food bowl with her dinner while she waited for the oven to preheat. She slid her pizza into the oven and then wandered back into the sitting room. The light on the answering machine was still blinking.

"We never played the second message," she told Aggie who had followed her. "It's probably just an insurance salesman, though."

It wasn't. "Janet? It's William Chalmers. Please ring me when you get this message."

Janet frowned. William sounded upset and he'd rung several hours earlier. Feeling guilty for not listening to the message when they'd first arrived home, she quickly dialed the number for William's shop. This time she got an answering machine.

"William, it's Janet," she said. "I'm sorry I didn't ring you back sooner, but we were in Derby for the day. I'm home now if you want to ring me back."

She replaced the receiver and began to pace around the sitting room. William had sounded upset when he'd rung, but that didn't mean anything was wrong, she told herself. Joan had taken the car, which meant Janet couldn't simply drive over to the antique shop to check that everything was okay. Pacing did nothing to help her nerves. She was seriously considering ringing Robert at the police station when someone knocked on the door.

"William? But whatever is wrong?" she asked when she saw the man's face.

"There were two letters in today's post," William said tightly. "And they were definitely threatening."

Chapter 5

"Come in," Janet said, stepping back to let the man into the house.

"I'm sorry that I just stopped in unannounced again," William said. "But you didn't ring me back and I didn't know what else to do."

"I did ring you back," Janet said. "About five minutes ago."

William nodded. "I should have waited at the shop for you to ring me back," he said.

"Why didn't you ring Robert?" Janet asked.

William sighed. "I knew you were going to say that. And I don't have any answer for you, except that I still think Alice might be behind it and I don't want her in trouble."

"You need to ring Robert," Janet said firmly. "Whoever is behind it, this has gone on long enough. What did today's notes say?"

A loud buzz from the kitchen sounded before William replied. He gave her a questioning look.

"My pizza," she explained. "Would you like to share it with me?"

"Are you sure you don't mind?" William asked. "I was too upset to eat much lunch, but I'm starving now."

"I'll put some garlic bread in the oven when I take the pizza out," Janet told him. "Otherwise there won't be enough food for two." Especially as she had been planning on eating the entire pizza herself, Janet thought, feeling annoyed.

"I'm imposing," William said quickly. "Why don't I come back later, after you've eaten? I'll go up to the café and grab some dinner and then come back."

Janet was very tempted to agree with the plan, but it seemed quite mean to send him away. She really didn't need the whole pizza, either, not after all she'd eaten lately. "Come and have some pizza," she said. "And tell me about the letters."

The pizza looked wonderful; the crust a lovely golden brown and the cheese perfectly melted across the top. Janet thought about telling William she'd changed her mind, but she couldn't bring herself to do it. Instead, she sliced the pizza into eight slices and set it in the centre of the table. Then she put two loaves of frozen garlic bread onto a tray and slid them into the oven.

"They'll only need about ten minutes," she told William. She handed him a plate and a fizzy drink before joining him at the table with her own drink and plate.

After a few bites, Janet felt oddly relieved to discover that the pizza wasn't nearly as good as it had looked. By the time she'd finished her first piece, she was quite happy to share the rest with William and was looking forward to the garlic bread. William ate two pieces in rapid succession before he spoke.

"I really am starving," he said apologetically. "I won't eat more than half, though."

"Eat as much as you like," Janet said, taking a second piece that was probably her last. "I like the garlic bread and I've made two loaves of it."

William nodded. "I'm hugely grateful," he said. "I didn't come here expecting dinner."

"But you were going to tell me about today's letters," Janet reminded him.

"I've put them in my safe," he told her. "But I remember exactly what they said. One was postmarked two days ago, so I assume I was meant to get it yesterday, but I didn't. That one said 'Leave Doveby Dale now. Your time is running out,'" he told her.

Janet shuddered. "That is threatening," she said. "I can't believe you didn't ring Robert immediately."

"The second one said 'Get out while you still can,'" William said.

The oven buzzed again. Janet thought about everything William had told her while she took the garlic bread out and piled it onto plates. When she sat back down, she took his hand and stared into his eyes.

"Why do you think Alice is involved in this?" she asked.

William shrugged and looked away. "It just seems like something she might do," he said. He pulled his hand away and picked up a slice of bread. Janet waited until he looked at her again before she spoke.

"There's something more specific than that," she said. "Otherwise you'd have gone to Robert by now."

William chewed silently and Janet could almost see him thinking. She crunched her way through two slices of bread before William spoke again.

"Alice has a favourite perfume. It's very distinctive. The anonymous letters all smell of that perfume," he said softly.

"Is it an unusual scent?" Janet asked. "Or can you buy it on the high street?"

"I used to buy it for her at the local chemist's shop," William replied. "I suppose that means it's readily available anywhere." He sighed. "Every time I smell it, I think of Alice, but I really don't want to think that she's behind this."

"You need to go and see Robert with the letters," Janet said firmly. "If Alice isn't behind them, you could be in real danger."

William nodded slowly. "I know you're right," he said sadly. "I just don't want to do it."

"I'll meet you at your shop tomorrow morning and go to the police with you, if you want," Janet suggested. "You can even tell Robert that talking to him was my idea. You can tell Alice that as well, if they arrest her."

William gave a forced chuckle. "I don't still love her, but she was my wife. I hate the thought of her going to prison over this."

"If it is just her idea of a good way to win you back, she probably won't go to prison," Janet said, guessing wildly.

"I hope not," William said.

When the pizza and garlic bread were all gone, Janet walked William to the door. "Thank you for everything," he said softly. "I'll see you tomorrow around nine."

Janet nodded. She reached for the door at the same time as William reached for her. The gentle kiss might have turned into something more if the door hadn't suddenly sprung open in front of the pair.

Janet jumped backwards, nearly tripping over Aggie, who had followed her out of the kitchen. William took a step in the other direction and they both looked guiltily at Joan, who was standing in the doorway.

"I didn't realise you were coming over," Joan said to William.

"Neither did Janet," William said with a chuckle. "But I needed to talk to her, so I just turned up."

"I hope everything is okay," Joan said.

"I don't know if Janet told you anything about the anonymous letters I've been receiving," William replied. "But I've had two more."

"What did Robert say when you talked to him?" Joan asked.

"I'm, um, seeing him tomorrow," William said, looking down at his shoes. "Janet is going to come with me to talk to him."

"Is she?" Joan asked. "That's good of her."

"She's been wonderful," William said quickly. "I'm truly grateful to her."

An awkward silence followed his words. Eventually Janet cleared her throat. "So I'll see you around nine," she said to William. "Good night."

"Good night," he replied. Joan was still standing in the doorway. She took a couple of steps out of the way and then shut the door behind the man.

"How was your evening?" Janet asked.

"It was, well, interesting," Joan replied. "Harriet, that's Michael's sister-in-law, was polite, but I don't think she liked me. Her son, Mike, didn't seem to want to be there at all and spent most of the evening on his mobile phone, texting other people. The important thing, I suppose, is that it made Michael happy."

"That's good news," Janet said.

"How was your evening?"

Janet shrugged. "William turned up just as my pizza finished baking, so I had to share my dinner with him," she said. "But I made some garlic bread to go with it, so we managed."

"He seemed a bit distracted when I arrived," Joan said. "No doubt he's more worried about these letters than he's willing to admit."

"He's really concerned that they're from his ex-wife, but I think he's more afraid that they aren't," Janet replied.

After giving Aggie one last treat, Janet headed to bed. She set her alarm for seven so that she would have plenty of time to get ready for her meeting with William and Robert. Just as she was drifting off to sleep, she wondered if Robert was going to be in the office or not. He split his time between Doveby Dale and Little Burton. If tomorrow was a day for him to be in Little Burton, she and William would be wasting their time. With that thought niggling at her, she managed to fall into a restless sleep.

The alarm finally put her out of her misery and angered Aggie. "Go back to sleep," Janet told the grumpy kitten. "Your breakfast will be in the kitchen whenever you want it."

Aggie gave her a satisfied smile and then put her head back down and closed her eyes tightly.

"If I got to choose, I'd come back again as my own cat," Janet told her reflection in the mirror as she got ready.

Joan had breakfast nearly ready when Janet came down the stairs.

"Oatmeal and fruit today," Joan said brightly as Janet walked into the kitchen.

Janet hesitated, thinking about going back upstairs and crawling back into bed. She didn't like oatmeal. Fruit was okay, but it was never going to replace pancakes with maple syrup as her breakfast of choice. Joan usually only made oatmeal when she was upset with Janet about something. Janet poured herself a cup of coffee while she tried to work out what she'd done to anger her sister.

"Why oatmeal today?" she asked eventually, as she couldn't come up with anything.

"We both ate a lot of rich and delicious foods on our holiday," Joan told her. "I thought we should make an effort now that we're home to eat more sensibly."

You can't get much more sensible than oatmeal, Janet thought sourly. Knowing that Joan was right didn't improve Janet's mood either. She forced herself to eat her breakfast, feeling cross with the world as she spooned up each bite. Covering the oatmeal in slices of strawberries and bananas only helped a little. "I'm meeting William at his shop at nine," she reminded Joan as they cleared the table.

"Our first guests of the weekend arrive tomorrow night," Joan said. "But you needn't worry about that. I can get their room made up and ready. Good luck with Robert."

"Thanks," Janet said. Upstairs, she combed her hair and added a touch of makeup before she headed out. The drive into the centre of Doveby Dale was a short one. The small car park for the shops was, as usual, nearly empty. Janet pulled the car into a space and looked at the short row of shops in front of her. The newsagent's was open for business, the door held open with a large rock. The chemist's shop, however, was still dark. William's shop, WTC Antiques, was also dark, but when Janet got out of her car, she could see that there were a few lights on in the very back of the building.

The door was locked, so Janet tapped on it lightly. After a moment, she saw William walking towards her.

"Thank you for coming," he told her. "We're meant to open at nine, but I won't bother until we get back from seeing Robert. It isn't as if customers are queuing up outside."

Janet smiled. She hadn't seen anyone else anywhere near the shops this morning. "I hope Robert is in today," she told William.

"He is. I rang last night and booked us an appointment," William told her. "The woman who works at the front desk at the station said we could come in at quarter past nine."

"Susan is lovely," Janet said. "And I don't know what Robert would do without her."

"We just have a few minutes to wait, then," William said. "I don't think I've added anything new to the shop since your last visit."

Janet looked around. "I've been thinking that I need a small table," she said thoughtfully. "Something to go in my bedroom, near my little desk." She'd only taken a few steps towards one of William's displays when someone knocked on the shop's door. Janet jumped and only just managed not to scream.

"Just what I need, a customer," William complained. He crossed to the door and unlocked it. "Good morning," he said politely. "I'm afraid we're opening a bit later today, due to, um, unforeseen circumstances," he told the man at the door.

"I do hope everything is okay," the man, probably in his mid-thirties, replied. Janet walked a few steps closer and studied him. He had dark brown hair that was cut in a casually floppy style that had Janet itching to suggest that he get it cut. For some inexplicable reason, he was wearing sunglasses, even though the morning was overcast. His jeans and T-shirt probably both had designer labels, Janet thought. Both were spotless and had obviously been recently ironed.

"It's fine," William replied. "Maybe you could come back later?"

"Oh, no, I'm not shopping," the man said. "I just wanted to introduce myself. I'm Jonathan Hamilton-Burke. I've just purchased the small parade of shops in Little Burton. In the coming weeks, I'll be opening my own little antique shop there."

Janet frowned as William's face fell. There had been a small craft and gift shop in Little Burton when William first opened. Janet wasn't sure how much competition the shop offered before it had closed down some months ago. Another antique shop was a different matter, however. Janet knew William was barely making ends meet now. Jonathan Hamilton-Burke might just drive him out of business.

"It's nice to meet you," William said after a long pause. "I'm William Chalmers and this is my friend, Janet Markham."

"It's lovely to meet you both," Jonathan said brightly. "I'm looking forward to getting to know everyone in Doveby Dale and Little Burton over the coming weeks and months."

"If we're lucky, we'll be too busy over the summer with tourists to get better acquainted," William said.

"Oh, I shall be hiring staff to handle the day-to-day running of the place," Jonathan said airily. "I've always fancied living up north, you see. The shop is really just a hobby."

"How fortunate for you," Janet said, trying not to sound as annoyed as she felt.

"I know, I'm a very lucky man," Jonathan laughed. "I'll be stocking my shelves with the contents of my maternal grandfather's estate. He's left me the entire thing and I've no use for ten bedrooms' worth of furniture. Not when I've bought myself a tiny five-bedroomed home."

"Well, welcome to the Doveby Dale area," Janet said, refusing to ask him how tiny a five-bedroomed home could possibly be. "I'm sure you'll be a welcome addition to the neighbourhood." The lie nearly choked Janet, but it was a social nicety that needed to be said.

"Thank you so much, Janice," Jonathan replied. "Now I must get away. I'm having lunch at Chatsworth House. The Duke of Devonshire is friends with my father, you understand."

Janet and William watched silently as the man turned and walked away. He climbed into an expensive-looking car and roared away.

"I don't really need the competition," William said softly as the car disappeared around the corner.

"Maybe he doesn't want any competition, either," Janet said. "Maybe he's been sending you the letters."

William sighed. "I'd like to believe that, but I don't think he'd bother. He's quite capable of running me out of business without any such tactics."

Janet didn't know what to say to that. After a minute, William sighed again. "Let's go and see Robert, then," he said. "This day can't possibly get any worse."

Chapter 6

"Good morning," Susan Garner greeted them when they walked into the police station a few minutes later. The station was only a short walk up the road from the shops and near a small coffee shop. "Robert is on his phone, but I'll buzz him to let him know you're here."

Once she'd done that, she and Janet chatted about nothing much while they waited. Susan was a forty-something blonde who worked as civilian front desk staff for the constabulary. Janet knew she was married and had children, but she didn't know much more about the woman. She did know that Susan loved to knit and spent much of her spare time creating beautiful blankets, jumpers, and scarves. Several of Susan's creations were carefully displayed at Doveby House where they were proving very popular with guests.

"Sorry to keep you waiting," Robert said from the doorway of his small office a moment later. "Do come in."

Janet made a face, already feeling claustrophobic in what had once been a small cottage. Robert's office was only just big enough for the three of them and William had to move his chair in order for Robert to close the door.

"You both look worried," Robert said once he'd taken a seat

behind the battered desk. "But clearly it isn't an emergency or you would have rung 999, not booked an appointment to see me."

"It's not an emergency," William agreed. "I'm not even sure it's a police matter. But Janet insisted that we come and speak to you about it anyway."

Janet bit back a sharp retort, making allowances for the man, who was under some strain. That was the only allowance she was prepared to make for him, though, she thought crossly.

"I'm glad you listened to her," Robert said. "I can spare half an hour to hear all about it. If it isn't a police matter, no harm done."

William nodded. The pause that followed was awkward. Janet finally sighed deeply and turned to William.

"If you don't tell him, I will," she said tartly, her patience just about gone.

"I've been receiving anonymous letters," William blurted out.

"I see," Robert said. "Did you bring them with you?"

William wordlessly handed the man a large envelope. Robert opened a desk drawer and pulled on gloves before he opened the envelope. The room was quiet as he shuffled through the letters and their envelopes. Eventually he looked up at William.

"You weren't sure that this was a police matter?" he asked.

William flushed. "I wasn't sure if it was serious or just someone being, well, annoying."

"I don't find these sorts of threats annoying," Robert said sternly. "They need to be taken seriously."

"I suppose," William muttered.

"Let me get some background first," Robert said. "When did you start getting the letters?"

"The first couple arrived last week," William told him.

Robert made careful note of which letter arrived on which date. "The tone seems to be getting increasingly threatening," he remarked as he went back through the letters a second time.

"I thought that as well," Janet said.

"Who do you think is sending them?" Robert asked William.

"I've no idea," William said, looking down at the floor.

Robert sighed. "You must have a suspect in mind, one that

you're trying to protect. This will be easier for both of us if you tell me who he or she is."

"I did think, at first anyway, that they might be from my former wife," William admitted. "But I can't believe that she would carry things this far."

"Why would she want you to leave Doveby Dale?" Robert asked.

"I believe she wants me to move back to London," William told him. "She often suggests that we try again with our relationship."

"But you aren't fond of the idea?"

"You could put it that way," William told Robert. "Alice is somewhat unstable. She's harmless, but I try to spend as little time with her as possible."

"Tell me about Alice," Robert invited.

"She's Alice Chalmers. She kept my name even after the divorce," William said. "What do you want to know about her?"

"Just give me some basic facts for now," Robert suggested.

"She's eleven years younger than I am," William said. "She's quite short and rather slender, which made me feel quite protective of her in the beginning. We weren't married for very long, not much more than a year."

"Can you tell me why you separated?" Robert asked.

"She, um, that is, she cheated on me," William stammered out.

"I'm sorry," Janet said quietly.

William gave her a grateful look before turning back to Robert. "Alice likes excitement and she likes to be spoiled. For a short while I enjoyed her company and her attention, but eventually she began to seem needy and demanding and I started working longer hours and avoiding her. I don't really blame her for cheating, as I wasn't around a lot, I suppose. Anyway, as soon as the divorce was final, she started ringing me and suggesting we try again. I gave our relationship a couple more tries, but eventually I gave up."

"And when did you see her last?" Robert asked.

"Just before I moved up here, I had dinner with her and told her about my plans. She wasn't best pleased, but she had a new man in her life, so she didn't complain that much," William said.

"You haven't seen her since?"

"No, although I spoke to her on the phone last week," William said. "She's coming to visit this weekend. She's booked herself a room at Doveby House."

Robert shot a quick look at Janet before returning his gaze to William. "Did you invite her to visit?"

"Not at all," William said. "She just rang and announced that she was coming. I'm sure she was disappointed with my lack of enthusiasm."

"But she's still coming?"

"Oh, yes, she won't let me stop her," William said sadly.

"And you can see her sending you anonymous letters to try to get you to move back to London?" Robert asked.

William shrugged. "I hope not," he said. "But she doesn't always consider the consequences of her actions before she acts. She's impulsive and she likes to go after the things she wants."

Robert nodded. "Is there anything specific that makes you think she might be involved in sending the letters?"

"She wears a very recognisable perfume and the letters seem to smell of it," William said quietly.

Robert nodded and made a note in his notebook. "Right, let's talk about other possible candidates for the sender," he said. "What do you think?"

"That's part of the problem," William replied. "I can't imagine why anyone else would want me out of Doveby Dale."

"Let's start with your personal life," Robert suggested. "Have you upset anyone in the village lately? Are you romantically involved with someone?"

William looked at Janet and they both blushed. Robert made another note in his notebook.

"When I first arrived in the village, I was arrogant and demanding," William said. "I didn't want anyone to know about my past, especially not that I'd been in prison, so I acted like I thought I was someone important and hoped that no one would see through my disguise. You know that didn't work out very well for me."

Janet grinned. "We like you much better now," she told the man. "Criminal record or not, you're much easier to like."

William smiled at her. "After a short while, I began to realise that I needed to change if my shop was going to succeed in this village. I'd like to think that I've become friends with several people in Doveby Dale. To the best of my knowledge, I haven't upset anyone in some months."

"And romantically?" Robert asked.

"I'm not, that is, I'm taking my time on that front," William said. "But there's only one woman I'm interested in in the village and she's sitting next to me."

Janet felt her cheeks flood with colour. She looked down at her hands and found that she'd twisted them together. When she looked up, Robert was studying her.

"Janet, are there any other men in your life who might want to get William away from you?" he asked gently.

Even as Janet was shaking her head, she couldn't help but think of Edward Bennett. Surely he was far too sophisticated to resort to something like anonymous letters to keep William away from her, she thought.

"So let's talk about the business side of things," Robert said. "Has your shop put anyone else out of business or is there a danger that it might?"

William shook his head. "One of the reasons I chose Doveby Dale was because of the lack of similar businesses in the area. The next nearest antique shop is in Derby and there's no way I'm pulling any of their business away from them."

"Tell me about the men and women locally who are your business colleagues," Robert said.

"Colleagues?" William repeated. "I suppose I would consider Owen at the chemist's shop a colleague, and Donald at the newsagent's. I do a lot of business with Stanley Moore. He has a warehouse full of antiques in Derby. Richard Kingston, who owns the coffee shop next door, might be considered a colleague as well, although he's so rarely around that I think I'd name Stacey, the poor girl who works there, before him."

"Don't forget Jonathan Hamilton-Burke," Janet said.

"That's a name I don't know," Robert said with a frown.

"He just stopped in the shop this morning," William told him. "He's opening an antique shop in Little Burton, apparently."

Robert raised his eyebrows and wrote something in his notebook. "Why did he visit your shop?" he asked when he was done writing.

"He said he wanted to introduce himself," William replied.

"Is there anything else you can tell me about him?" was Robert's next question.

"He claimed he's only opening the shop as a hobby," Janet said. "Apparently he has plenty of money, but he wants to get rid of some furniture that was his grandfather's. What better way to do that than to open your own little shop? He drives a fancy sports car that cost too much money and he needs to cut his hair."

William chuckled. "Janet has summed him up eloquently," he said.

"Whatever he's told you, he's the first person you've named who might actually have a reason for wanting you out of Doveby Dale," Robert said. "Aside from Alice, maybe."

William nodded. "It would be nice if the letters were coming from Jonathan," he said. "I wouldn't mind seeing him in prison, or at least out of Little Burton."

"I'll check him out thoroughly," Robert promised.

"He claims to be friends with the Duke of Devonshire," Janet added. "You might want to be discreet."

Robert nodded. "I can certainly do that. Next question. Do you have any enemies?" he asked William.

"I don't think so. I made full restitution to everyone who was cheated in my London shop, and the people behind that are still behind bars, as far as I know. There may be one or two former acquaintances of mine out there who wouldn't cross the road to help me, but that's a long way from sending me threatening letters. I don't think most people from my past know where I am, anyway, and for the most part they'd probably be happy that I'm up north and away from them."

"We can't immediately rule out the idea that someone from your past is simply trying to disrupt your life here," Robert said. "I'd like you to give the idea some thought. See if you can think of anyone who might be holding a grudge against you."

William nodded, frowning. "I have been thinking about that, actually," he said. "But so far I haven't come up with anyone."

"I'll want to take your fingerprints," Robert told him. "I don't imagine the crime lab will be able to do much with these letters, but I'll send them off so that they can try."

"The police have my fingerprints on file," William reminded him dryly.

"Janet, have you touched any of the letters?" Robert asked.

"No. I never even saw them before today," Janet said.

Robert asked William what time his post usually arrived. "I want to be there today when the postman turns up. I have a few questions for him and I want to see if you get another letter today," Robert told William. "I'll see you later."

William and Janet walked back through the small reception area on their way out. Janet said a warm goodbye to Susan, but William was silent. Outside, Janet put her hand on his arm.

"Are you in a hurry to get the shop opened up or do you have time for a cuppa?" she asked, nodding towards the coffee shop.

"I think I need a cuppa," William said. "No one is beating down my door, at any rate."

The street was still quiet and the car park for the shops was just as empty as it had been when Janet arrived. They walked together into the small and brightly lit coffee shop. The girl who worked behind the counter was nowhere to be seen.

"Hello?" Janet called.

"Maybe it's time to get someone else in here," a loud male voice said. There was a small door behind the counter that led to what Janet assumed was the kitchen. The voice must have come from there.

"You've no cause to get rid of me," another voice, this one female, snapped back. "I work hard. This is only the second time I've asked for time off in two years."

"And it isn't convenient," the first voice said. "I told you that you could be late today, which you were. Taking the afternoon off as well is too much."

"My mum is sick," the woman said. "I've left her home alone so that I could handle the morning and lunch crowds for you, but then I'm going back to sit with her."

"And you can stay with her for as long as you like. You won't be welcome back here," the man told her.

Janet could hear someone crying. She looked at William who shrugged. "Hello?" she called as loudly as she could, walking towards the counter.

Chapter 7

"We have customers," the male voice said harshly.

"As I no longer work here, I don't care," the other voice said.

There was a short pause before the door to the kitchen swung open and a tall and heavyset man with dark hair and eyes stomped through it. He glared at William and Janet for a moment and then sighed deeply. Janet watched as his angry expression gave way to a forced smile.

"Good morning," he said. "What can I do for you this morning?"

"Hello, Richard," William said. "We were hoping for a cuppa and a cake, if it isn't too much bother."

"Of course it's no bother," the man replied. "Sit anywhere and I'll bring everything over in a minute."

"Don't you want us to tell you which sweet we want?" Janet asked politely.

"Oh, of course, sorry. I've a lot on my mind this morning," the man said.

Janet asked for a slice of shortbread while William asked for a piece of Victoria sponge. They took seats in the corner. A moment later, the door to the kitchen swung open again. Janet recognised

Stacey, the girl who usually ran the café, as she walked out from behind the counter.

"I have all of my things," she said in a low voice to Richard. "You can send my last cheque to my home address."

"We'll see about that," Richard barked at her.

The girl opened her mouth and then snapped it shut. She turned on her heel and rushed out of the building. Janet could see tears welling up in the girl's eyes as she went.

"I'll be right back," Janet told William before she followed the girl. "Stacey," she called as soon as she was out the door.

The girl was sitting on the bench in front of the building, her face in her hands. Janet sat down beside her. When Stacey looked up, Janet handed her a tissue.

"Is your mum okay?" Janet asked.

"She had a bad fall," the girl explained. "The doctors don't think anything is seriously wrong, but she shouldn't be home alone all day. I was a late surprise. Mum is seventy-two and, well, her health isn't so good."

"I'm sorry," Janet said. "Is there anything I can do to help?"

"I don't know what," the girl said sadly. "Not unless you can find me a job that has some flexibility until Mum is well again. I really need to be bringing in some money, even if I'm not working full-time."

"The café is looking for someone," Janet told her. "Only part-time for now, but maybe with more hours as the summer gets busier with tourists."

"Really?" Stacey asked. "I hadn't heard anything."

"Ted told me himself," Janet assured her. "If I were you, I'd go and talk to him now."

"I will," the girl said. "It isn't too far to walk from here."

"If you want to wait half an hour, I'll give you a ride over," Janet offered.

"No, no, that's okay," Stacey said. "I don't mind walking. The fresh air and exercise will be good for me. I don't want Ted to see that I've been crying."

Feeling as if she'd helped a little bit, Janet went back inside. William was still waiting for their tea to arrive.

"Is Stacey okay?" he asked Janet in a whisper.

"I've sent her to Todd and Ted," Janet told him as quietly as she could. "They're looking for someone to help out for the summer, at least."

"And they're much nicer people than Richard," William said.

"Okay, tea for two and cakes as well," Richard said as he crossed the room. It took him three trips to deliver everything, and the tea was already cool by the time Janet took a sip.

"Janet Markham, I don't know if you've ever met Richard Kingston before?" William said after he'd tried his own tea and made a face.

The other man nodded at her. "You have Doveby House, right?"

"That's right," Janet agreed. "My sister and I own it."

"Nice for some," he said tartly. "I'd love to live in a big house like that."

"It's a wonderful home," Janet said. "But we have to work hard at the business to keep it going."

"Yeah, there is that," Richard conceded. "I don't think I'd like having strangers sleeping under my roof."

Janet couldn't help but nod. That was her least favourite part of her new life.

"Is everything okay here?" William asked.

"Here? Things are fine," Richard said. "The girl that sometimes helps out around here had to go, that's all. She was increasingly unreliable and I can't have that, not when I have a business to run."

"I hope you can find someone to replace her," William said. "Otherwise you'll be working awfully hard, won't you?"

"I'm not afraid of a little hard work," Richard said dismissively. "But I'm not sure how much more time or effort I'm going to put into this place."

Janet raised an eyebrow. "Oh?"

"I've been thinking about trying something else," he told her. "Maybe a card and gift shop. Or maybe I should do groceries. With the shop in the village shut now, people would probably pay handsomely for local access to milk and bread and the like."

"But we'd miss the coffee shop," William said. "It's very handy for those of us who work in the shops across the road."

"I have to do what I can do to make my living," Richard told him. "If I can make more money with less work as a grocer's, then that's what I will do."

William nodded. "It's a tempting idea," he said. "Maybe I should get out of the antique business."

"But then, when Simon Hampton rebuilds the local grocer's, you'll have to do something different again," Janet pointed out.

"So maybe I'll just stick to what I'm doing," William said with a laugh.

"You like Doveby Dale?" Richard asked.

"I like Doveby Dale a great deal," William replied.

"I'd rather live in a big city," Richard said with a sigh. "I'll never make enough money to move by selling tea and cakes, though."

"Maybe you should add more prepared food to your menu," Janet suggested.

"I can't compete with the café on the corner," Richard told her. "Those two are really good at what they do. No, I think I'll need a total change of direction if I'm going to make any real money."

The arrival of another pair of customers sent Richard back behind the counter. Janet took a bite of shortbread and then frowned at William.

"It's a bit stale," she said. "And the tea was almost cold when it arrived."

"Stacey spoiled us," William told her. "She always reheated the shortbread so you couldn't tell if it was yesterday's or not. And she always delivered piping hot tea."

"How is your cake?" Janet asked.

"It's yesterday's too," William replied. "And the custard is straight out of a tin."

"Richard won't have to worry about dealing with customers for long if he keeps up like this," Janet said.

"I wonder if he really will change the place into some sort of gift shop or something," William said. "I'll miss being able to pop over for tea, but if the tea is going to be cold anyway, maybe I won't."

They finished as much as they wanted of their snack. William insisted on paying for everything. "You were kind enough to accompany me today. It's the least I can do," he told Janet.

She only put up a token argument. At her car, she stopped and gave William a hug. "I hope Robert can work out who's sending the letters quickly," she told him. "And put a stop to them."

"I'm torn between hoping it isn't Alice because I don't want her to be in any trouble and hoping it is her because otherwise it's quite worrying."

"Ring me and keep me up to date," Janet told him.

"Don't worry, I will," William said grimly.

Back at Doveby House, Joan was nearly finished tidying the guest rooms. "Can I help?" Janet asked.

"We just need some fresh flowers for the rooms," Joan told her.

"I'll go and cut some early blooms from the garden," Janet said.

Doveby House had fairly extensive gardens, but neither sister had been blessed with a green thumb. They felt very fortunate that their neighbour across the road was a retired gardener. As the garden for his semi-detached property was tiny, Stuart Long loved spending long hours tending to the grounds at Doveby House. The sisters paid him a small stipend along with all the tea and biscuits he could eat. The arrangement seemed to suit all of them well.

When Janet went outside with her scissors, Stuart was hard at work, digging up weeds from one of the flowerbeds. "Are you planning to slice up my beautiful garden?" he demanded from his knees.

"I just need a few flowers for each of the guest rooms," Janet said. "But if you really don't want me to take any, Joan can get some from the supermarket tomorrow morning."

"I was only teasing," Stuart said. He shook his head, his dyed brown hair falling in his eyes as he did so. Brushing it away with a gloved hand he smiled at Janet. "It's your garden. You may have as many flowers as you'd like."

"As I said, I don't need many," Janet replied. "Are there any that you would suggest over the others?"

"The ones on the other side of the carriage house are actually getting quite large already," Stuart told her. "I was thinking about cutting some of them back anyway. Let's start there."

Half an hour later Janet's arms were full to nearly overflowing with beautiful flowers. "You can't even tell that we've taken anything," she marveled as she looked around.

"As I said, this section needed a trim anyway," Stuart said. "It gets quite a lot of sun. You should be able to cut flowers from here all summer long."

"That would be good," Janet said.

In the kitchen, she dug out a pair of vases and filled them with water. The flowers filled both vases easily. "I think I need another vase," she told Aggie, who was watching her with a confused look on her face. She put the third vase in the centre of the kitchen table before carrying the other two upstairs.

"Those look wonderful," Joan told her as she put the first one in the smaller of the two guest rooms, where Joan was still polishing surfaces.

"There are tons more where these came from," Janet told her. "What would we do without Stuart?"

"I hope we never find out," Joan said fervently.

With the guest rooms ready, the sisters treated themselves to an afternoon curled up in the library with books. The phone rang around four o'clock.

"It's for you," Joan told Janet after she'd answered the call. "It's William."

"Hello?" Janet said.

"I was going to ring you earlier, but Robert was here, and by the time he left, I actually had a few customers," William began.

"You've had another letter," Janet guessed.

"Yes," William sighed. "Much the same as the last. Robert opened it this time, though, and he's sent it away for fingerprinting without my even touching it."

"What did he ask the postman?" Janet wondered.

"All sorts of things about the letters," William told her. "The postman had actually noticed them, because I don't usually get much post, but he didn't think anything of it. He just assumed it was something to do with the business."

"And he didn't have any idea where they were coming from?"

"No. But he's going to keep his eyes open at the depot and see if he can spot anything," William told her.

"What else did Robert say?" Janet asked.

"He just reminded me to make a list of anyone I can think of that might be behind the letters," William told her. "But I can't think of anyone at all."

Janet set the phone down and then frowned at the receiver. The whole situation filled her with unease, but she trusted Robert to work it all out. Joan was in the kitchen, making spaghetti Bolognese and garlic bread.

"I hope you don't mind, but I invited Michael for dinner," she told Janet. "I won't be able to see him again until the guests have gone, really."

Janet nodded. She'd expected as much. When they had guests, the sisters often took turns staying in at night and staying up until their guests were all in the for evening. Even if it was Janet's turn to stay up, though, Joan didn't usually go out when there were guests at the house.

"Of course I don't mind," Janet assured her.

The trio enjoyed their meal, laughing and talking together like old friends. Once the dishes were in the dishwasher, Janet excused herself and went up to her room to give her sister and Michael some privacy. Aggie followed Janet upstairs.

"We have guests arriving tomorrow," Janet told the kitten. "You'll have to be on your best behaviour while they're here."

"Yooooww!" Aggie objected.

"Agatha Christie Markham, don't you take that attitude with me," Janet said sternly. "Our guests help pay the bills. You had a lovely holiday on the Isle of Man, didn't you? We could never have afforded that without having guests now and again."

"Merroow," Aggie said, ducking her head.

"Yes, I know, it isn't ideal," Janet said. "But so far all of the guests have loved you, so I don't know why you're complaining. You don't even have to be nice to them."

Aggie smiled at her and then jumped onto the bed and settled in on her pillow. Janet went and got ready for bed before joining the kitten in the most comfortable bed Janet had ever owned.

"At least it isn't a full moon this weekend," Janet told Aggie as she opened her latest romance novel. Aggie shivered and moved closer to Janet.

Janet's bedroom was haunted by a ghost who shouted in the night every time there was a full moon. Whenever possible, Janet and Aggie slept in one of the guest rooms on those evenings, but they couldn't do that when the guest rooms were booked. Janet was convinced that the ghost was that of Alberta Montgomery, but she couldn't prove it. Reading the woman's letters and diaries might give her a clue, but Joan was still refusing to let her do that.

Janet read for an hour before deciding to have an early night. "We can both use extra sleep before our guests arrive," she told Aggie, who was already half-asleep. When she switched off the lights, however, Janet found she couldn't sleep. It wasn't a ghost keeping Janet awake, however, it was the specter of Alice Chalmers that kept her brain whirling for most of the night.

Chapter 8

As was typical when guests were due, Joan had a dozen little jobs for Janet the next morning.

"Unless you want to do the shopping?" Joan asked after she'd handed Janet a sheet of paper with all of the chores written on it.

"I'll do the shopping," Janet said quickly. A nice long drive to the supermarket, a leisurely shop with lots of extra chocolate, and then a meandering drive home. That sounded a great deal better than tidying the sitting room and emptying the dishwasher.

"I have a list," Joan said. "Do try to stick to it."

"I'll try," Janet said. She always got everything on the list; she just added a few extra things. Joan shouldn't really complain.

"And don't take too long over it, either," Joan added. "There are lots of other things that need doing here."

"I can't control traffic," Janet pointed out, hoping there would be a lot of it. In the end, she only bought about a dozen things that weren't on the list, and she didn't dawdle as much as she might have liked, either. On her way back through Doveby Dale, she noticed the postman doing his rounds of the shops. Impulsively, she pulled into the car park and parked her car.

The postman held the door to William's shop open for her as

she approached. "Good morning," he said. "I've a large parcel for you. Is Joan at home or would you like it now?"

"Joan is home," Janet said. "We have guests arriving later today."

"I'll leave it with her, then," he said. Janet nodded and then walked into the shop. William and Robert were standing at the desk in the back corner, frowning at another plain white envelope.

"Not another one," Janet said.

"Yes, another one," William told her.

Robert was wearing gloves, and Janet found she was holding her breath as he slit the envelope open with a letter opener. He pulled the letter out and unfolded it.

"I'm running out of patience. Leave Doveby Dale now," he read aloud.

"Maybe I should just go," William muttered.

"We'll find out who's behind this," Robert told him. "I'll send this one for fingerprinting immediately."

"You didn't find any fingerprints on any of the others, except for mine," William pointed out.

"Whoever it is will make a mistake eventually," Robert said.

"If he or she doesn't kill me first," William replied gloomily.

"I'm going to make sure that doesn't happen," Robert said soothingly.

"I may just have to kill you," a voice said from the front of the shop. Everyone spun around.

"How could you send Adam Peabody to Blake?" the angry man in the doorway demanded.

"Ah, Stanley, good morning," William said. He took a few steps towards the new arrival, with Robert at his elbow. Janet followed at a more leisurely pace. She recognised the man in the doorway. Stanley Moore owned a large warehouse on the outskirts of Derby. It was crammed full of antiques. Janet had visited once with William, and she'd liked the heavyset man who was somewhere in his fifties. Now she wasn't so sure.

"Haven't I always done my best by you?" Stanley demanded.

"Of course you have," William replied. "But Mr. Peabody was

looking for such a specific item that I thought it would be best to send him to Blake. I knew for certain that he had exactly what Mr. Peabody wanted."

"Ha, what he thought he wanted, maybe," Stanley said. "He dropped over three thousand pounds with Blake on all manner of things that I could have sold him if you'd sent him to me."

"I am sorry," William said. "When I spoke to him, he insisted that he wasn't interested in anything other than an Edwardian washstand. I knew you didn't have anything in at the moment, and I'd just received Blake's new catalogue and they had several. If I'd known Mr. Peabody was looking for other items, I would have worked harder to sell him something here."

Stanley frowned and then nodded. "I suppose you're right," he said. "But I thought we had an agreement."

"We do," William said firmly. "Whenever I don't have what a customer wants, I try to source it through you or send the customer to you. This was an exceptional case. Going forward, I'll send whoever it is to you even if I know you don't have what they want, okay?"

"I don't know about that," Stanley said hesitantly. "I mean, I'm a busy man. I don't want people dropping in the warehouse every day wanting to buy things I don't have."

"That was what I thought," William said.

"That little old dear you sent me bought half a dozen things," Stanley said. "Thank you for that."

"I knew she'd be good for a big sale," William replied. "She spent quite a lot in here, but she had a long list of other things she wanted. She's just bought a house in the area and she's trying to furnish the entire thing with antiques."

"She's coming back next week to see if I got anything new in. I may have to send her to Blake, actually, as I didn't get much this week," Stanley told him.

William nodded. "Blake has a lot of inventory right now. She'll do well there."

"And he's a good guy, too," Stanley said. "I don't mind sending business his way once in a while. I was just upset to miss out on the Peabody sale."

"As am I," William told him. "He wouldn't even look around in here."

Stanley nodded. "I'd better get back to work, then." He turned to leave and then glanced back over his shoulder. "Um, sorry about the shouting," he said quickly.

He was gone before William replied. Janet blew out a breath that she felt as if she'd been holding since the man arrived.

"He's mostly noise," William told her.

"He threatened you, though," Janet pointed out. "And he's a business competitor. Maybe he's behind the letters."

"I don't think Stanley is that subtle," William said. "You saw how he gets when he's upset. He came here and shouted a bit. If he wanted to get rid of me, he'd tell me to my face, I reckon."

"You could be right," Robert said. "But he's still on the suspect list."

Janet suddenly remembered that she had shopping in the boot of her car. "I'd better go," she said. "Joan will be worrying about me."

Back at Doveby House, Janet carried the shopping into the kitchen where Joan was baking a cake. "I thought our guests might like a slice of cake to welcome them," she told Janet, not mentioning how long Janet had taken to do the shopping.

"Is this a new service we can start charging for?" Janet asked as she put the groceries away.

Joan shook her head. "I was just trying to be nice," she said. "Maybe little touches like that will make us more popular than the bed and breakfast in Little Burton."

"We're already more popular than they are, aren't we?" Janet asked.

Joan shrugged. "I had someone ring to cancel a booking for next month. She said they'd been offered a better deal in Little Burton."

"They sound like the type to order an early breakfast and then come down at eleven," Janet said. "They can make the woman in Little Burton's life miserable, rather than ours."

Joan laughed. "You may be right, but I do hate to lose business."

"You said we were going to be busy for the next three months," Janet reminded her. "An odd cancellation won't hurt."

"I suppose you're right. Oh, and the postman left a parcel for you," Joan told her.

"For me?"

"Yes, I put it on your bed."

Janet went up to her room and looked at the large box on her bed. She didn't remember ordering anything recently. Aggie watched as Janet carefully cut through the tape that sealed the box. Buried inside what seemed like a million tiny foam balls, Janet found a small ceramic rabbit. It was white, but covered with a sort of patchwork pattern that had blue flowers on it. Janet set the rabbit to one side and dug back around in the box. At the very bottom, she found a note.

"Just so that you know that I'm always thinking of you, Edward," she read to Aggie.

Aggie sniffed at the rabbit and then shrugged and jumped down off the bed. Janet found a space for it on top of one of her bookshelves and then tucked the note in a drawer. She'd wonder about it later, for now she needed to help Joan finish the tidying for their guests.

"We're locking the library, right?" Janet asked. "So it doesn't need to be tidied."

"We're locking it, but if the guests want to use it, we will let them," Joan reminded her. "It needs to be tidy."

Janet made a face. She loved her little library and she kept it spotlessly clean, but it wasn't always perfectly tidy. Sometimes she liked to leave a few books scattered around the room, books that she'd started but not finished or ones that looked interesting but that she hadn't found time to read yet. There were a few papers scattered on the desk and an empty tea mug on one of the small tables, as well. It only took Janet a minute to tidy it all away, but it made the room feel unused. She pulled a random book off a shelf and put it on one of the tables, just for aesthetics. Satisfied, she shut the door and locked it.

"William has had more letters," Janet told Joan, as they sat in the sitting room later that day waiting for their guests to arrive.

"Does he still think his ex-wife is behind them?" Joan asked.

"I think he's hoping it's her, otherwise it's quite scary," Janet replied.

"Who else could it be? Why would anyone else want William to leave Doveby Dale?"

"Robert had him make a list of business associates. Maybe someone wants to eliminate some of his or her competition. And there's a man opening a new antique shop in Little Burton, as well. Maybe he's trying to get rid of William before he even opens."

"Sending threatening letters seems an extreme way to get rid of a business rival," Joan said.

"Stanley Moore is angry with William because he sent a customer to another antique shop, rather than his," Janet offered.

"I can't see how getting rid of William would help in that case. Goodness knows where the man would have shopped if William wasn't around."

"I suppose so," Janet sighed.

A knock on the door kept them from speculating any further.

"Ah, good evening," Joan said when she opened the door. "Welcome to Doveby House," she told the couple on the doorstep.

"Thank you, thank you," the man said. The pair stepped inside, dragging their large suitcases in with them. Both of them appeared to be somewhere in their sixties. He was of average height and plump, with thinning grey hair and glasses. She was taller than he was, and her grey hair was pulled back in a tidy ponytail. They looked around the sitting room and then exchanged glances before the man spoke again.

"I'm Brock Banner and this is my wife, Helen," he said in a loud voice. "We're happy to be here."

"You're American," Janet said in surprise.

Both Banners laughed. "The accent always gives us away," Helen said. Her voice was softer than her husband's, but the accent was the same.

"We are; we are," Brock agreed. "But you mustn't hold that against us."

Janet laughed. "Of course not," she said. "But what brings you to Doveby Dale?"

"We've been travelling all across your beautiful country," Helen explained. "We started in Cornwall and we've been slowly working our way up towards Scotland. We're trying to stay in places like this rather than chain hotels and to really see the country rather than just visit the tourist sites."

"That sounds like fun," Janet said. "I'd love to do the same thing through the US."

"It would take you a good deal longer than our trip will take us," Helen said. "But we did that last year. We've done nothing but travel since Brock retired."

"How lovely," Janet said. "I wish we could travel more." As soon as the words were out of her mouth, Janet felt guilty. She and Joan had planned to travel when they'd retired, before Joan had ever mentioned wanting to buy a bed and breakfast. Janet had agreed to the purchase of Doveby House, even though she'd known that it would mean giving up on travelling. She could only hope that Joan wouldn't take the remark as a complaint about their new lifestyle.

"We've been thinking about buying ourselves a little shop or something in a village like Doveby Dale," Brock told them.

"I've always thought it would be wonderful to own a little bookstore in a small village," Helen said. "Does Doveby Dale have a bookstore?"

"No. But I wish it did," Janet replied.

"Me, I've always been more interested in antiques than books," Brock said.

"We do have an antique shop," Janet told him.

"We'll have to stop in," Helen said.

"Maybe the owner would like to sell it to us, maybe?" Brock said.

"I think William is quite happy here," Janet said. "But there is an empty space in the parade where his shop is located. A bookshop would fill it nicely."

"We'll have to see," Helen said. "Maybe we'll just keep travelling."

"Would you like some tea and cake?" Joan asked the pair.

"That would be great, just great," Brock said.

"Why don't I show you your room first?" Joan suggested.

"I'll go and put the kettle on," Janet offered.

The trio disappeared up the stairs while Janet headed to the kitchen.

"They're American," she told Aggie. "And they seem very nice, at least so far."

The Banners insisted that Joan and Janet join them for their snack. By the time they'd finished, Janet felt as if she'd known the couple for many years. She and Joan had heard all about how they'd met, their struggles with infertility, their years as foster parents, and about Brock's job in the finance industry. They'd also learned a great deal about the US as the couple told them about their travels across that vast country.

"And now we're off to explore Doveby Dale," Helen said over an hour later.

"I'm not sure there's much to explore at this hour," Joan told her. "The shops will all be shut for the night. The café and the French restaurant are probably the only things open."

"Maybe we should just have an early night, then," Helen suggested to her husband.

"Early night? An early night sounds good," he said. "I just need a short walk to work off some of that cake."

"The house has its own small grounds," Janet told him. "You're welcome to walk there. If you want to go further, there's a pavement that will take you to the main road. Just be careful, as it's quite a busy road."

"Oh, I think once or twice around the grounds will be plenty," Helen said. "We've a lot of sightseeing planned for the next two days. We need to save our energy."

"They seem very nice," Joan commented after Janet rejoined her in the kitchen once she'd opened the French doors onto the patio for the couple.

"Nice, but very, well, I mean I don't know if I know as much about you as I do about Brock and Helen," Janet said. "Some of the things they told us were rather personal, don't you think?"

"As I understand it, Americans can be like that," Joan said.

"I suppose it's just a cultural thing."

"No doubt."

The couple was back only a few minutes later. They settled into the television lounge for a while, but everyone got an early night that evening at Doveby House. Janet curled up in bed with Aggie, feeling reasonably happy with their newly arrived guests. She was still incredibly apprehensive about Alice Chalmers, but that was tomorrow's problem.

Chapter 9

The next morning was sunny and warm. Janet helped Joan get breakfast for their American guests and then, after they'd gone out for the day, gave her a hand with cleaning their room.

"You don't think they could be behind the anonymous letters, do you?" Janet asked her sister as they worked.

"I can't imagine why they would be," Joan replied. "They have the whole country to choose from if they do decide to open a shop. It isn't like they have any special reason to want to settle in Doveby Dale."

"Maybe they do but they haven't mentioned it."

Joan laughed. "We've heard their entire life story. I can't believe they left out anything."

Janet chuckled. "You may be right about that," she said.

When the chores were out of the way, Janet found herself pacing anxiously around the house. The phone startled her.

"Hello?"

"Is that Joan Markham?" a soft voice asked.

"No. I can get her for you, though," Janet offered.

"If you could, maybe you could just take a message?" the woman replied.

"Of course I can," Janet told her.

"This is Alice Chalmers. I'm booked for two nights starting today and I told Joan that I would be arriving some time around midday. I'm afraid I've become rather tangled up in something here and I'm going to be late. Please tell Joan that I won't be arriving until three or four o'clock this afternoon."

"I will do," Janet replied. "We're looking forward to your stay."

"Oh, thank you so much," the woman said.

Janet put down the phone and went to find her sister. Joan was in the kitchen, putting lunch together.

"Alice Chalmers is running late," Janet announced. "She won't be here until three or four."

Joan raised an eyebrow. "It was nice of her to let us know," she said after a moment.

"Yes. I think I might let William know as well," Janet said. "If you don't mind, I'll nip over to his shop after lunch. I'd like an update on the letters anyway, and he probably won't want to talk about that on the phone."

"You go. I'll ring your mobile if Alice arrives before you get back," Joan said.

The car park outside the shops was nearly empty, as usual. As Janet climbed out of her car, she glanced over at the coffee shop. Its car park was also mostly empty, which was less common, especially at this time of day.

William was dusting furniture when Janet walked in. The loud buzzer announced her presence and made her wince at the same time.

"Janet, how are you?" the man greeted her.

"I'm fine," she replied. "How are you?"

"Ah, well, I've been better," William said. "There was another letter this morning. Robert's sent it off to the police laboratory for all manner of tests that will reveal nothing, I'm sure."

"Think positive," Janet told him. "Maybe the culprit made a mistake this time and left a fingerprint or two on the letter."

"Maybe," William sighed. "It's all quite frustrating, and with Alice arriving today, it's too much on my mind."

"She just rang, actually, to say she's running late," Janet told him.

"When you started that, I was hoping you were going to say she wasn't coming at all," William said.

"So let's try to work out who has been sending those letters," Janet suggested. "Let's assume it isn't Alice, for the sake of this discussion."

"If it isn't Alice, I have no idea who it is," William argued. "I've been over it a dozen times with Robert. I just don't see any reason why anyone would want to chase me away from Doveby Dale."

"What does Robert say?"

"That it's probably tied to this shop in some way," William replied.

"We have a couple staying with us now that might be interested in buying a little shop like this."

"Brock and Helen Banner? They were here this morning for a short while. You can't possibly suspect them of being behind the letters. They were charming, if a bit talkative."

"Did they offer to buy the shop?"

"No," William chuckled. "Brock mentioned that having a little shop like this was one of his dreams, but Helen reminded him that travelling the world was also one of his dreams and that the two weren't compatible. I can't take them seriously as suspects."

"Okay, what about Stanley Moore?"

"If he wanted me gone, he could accomplish it easily," William said. "I buy from him and he sends customers my way. Of course, I return the favour, but he's a much bigger fish. He could undercut everything I sell and take away three-quarters of my business in short order if he wanted to. He doesn't need to send me anonymous letters to get rid of me."

"Have you told Robert all of this?"

"We talked about Stanley this morning. His outburst yesterday had Robert wondering about him, but I think he's crossed him off his list now."

"Who else is on the list?" Janet asked.

"Well, there's Jonathan Hamilton-Burke," William replied.

"He doesn't seem like the type to send anonymous letters, but I did only meet him once, briefly," Janet said thoughtfully.

"I'm inclined to agree with you. He's just playing at having a shop. I can't see him worrying about competition."

"Is that everyone?"

"Robert did mention Owen at the chemist's next door and Donald from the newsagent's, but if anything I think I'm good for their businesses. Even if only a few people stop here because of my shop, that's more foot traffic for their shops. It's bad enough we have one empty shopfront. I don't think Donald or Owen would like there to be two."

"Owen doesn't even own his shop," Janet said. "The men in suits at the corporate headquarters could decide to shut it tomorrow. I don't think he's that in love with Doveby Dale that he'd mind being moved elsewhere, either."

"He likes it here, but he's been moved fifteen times in the twenty years he's worked with the company," William told her. "He almost expects it now."

"So where does that leave us?"

"The only other suspects that Robert has mentioned are Richard and Stacey at the coffee shop."

"I hardly think you're competition for a coffee shop," Janet said. "Which reminds me, are they even open today? There was only one car in the car park, and I think it was Richard's."

"They're open, but they aren't doing very well without Stacey. Richard bakes well but he isn't very good at dealing with customers. He used to go in early in the morning and do the baking and then leave Stacey to run the place all day. That worked for everyone. Now that she's gone, he's doing it all himself and, well, it isn't good."

"Maybe he should find Stacey and beg her to come back," Janet suggested.

"I saw her last night, actually. She's working at the café and she seems to love it there. I don't think she'd come back, even if Richard begged."

"Good for her," Janet said. "I thought she'd be a good fit there."

"You were right. She and Todd and Ted seemed to be getting along well."

"Out of all of the people you've mentioned, the only one I can imagine being behind it is Richard," Janet said. "But I still can't see why he'd do it."

"I don't much like the man, but I can't see him doing something so, well, distasteful," William told her.

"Maybe it's time to go and get ourselves a coffee," Janet suggested.

"What are you planning?" William asked anxiously.

Janet chuckled. "I just thought we might drop a few hints about the letters and see how Richard reacts, that's all."

"That could be dangerous," William argued.

"They're anonymous letters, not actual death threats," Janet pointed out. "Unless today's was a death threat?"

"No. Just another 'leave or you'll be sorry' message."

"So let's go and have a cuppa. I'm not suggesting we accuse the man of anything or even talk to him directly about the letters. I just thought it might be interesting to have a loud discussion about them."

"And on the way back here we can drop in on Owen and Donald and do the same," William suggested.

Janet was pretty sure he was being sarcastic, but the idea suited her. "Yes, let's," she said.

William frowned. "I'll just get a coat," he muttered before he left the room. He locked up the shop, leaving a note on the door for customers to find him at the coffee shop if they needed him.

A man Janet didn't know was just leaving the shop as they approached.

"It's pretty grim in there," he told William and Janet. "I don't think the floors, the counters, or the tables have been cleaned since Stacey left."

Janet made a face as she followed William through the door. A glance around the room had her agreeing with the stranger's assessment. The place was a mess.

"Hello again," Richard said from behind the counter. "What do you need today?"

"William needed to get out of his shop," Janet said. "He's upset and needs tea with extra milk and sugar, and something delicious, please."

"Upset?" Richard echoed. "I hope everything is okay."

"Oh, it's fine," William said quickly. He gave Janet a look that clearly said 'be quiet,' but Janet wasn't done.

"I suppose we shouldn't really talk about police matters," she said in a loud whisper, glancing back and forth as if worried about being overheard.

"Police matters?" the man said, dropping the plate he was holding.

"Ah, we mustn't talk about this," William said loudly. "And I really shouldn't be out of the shop for long. Robert will be ringing about, well, ringing."

"Robert? The police constable?" Richard asked. "Why's he ringing you, then?"

"You'd better not," Janet said to William. "I'll have a flapjack."

"That sounds good," William said. "Make it two."

"And two milky teas?" Richard checked.

"Yes, thanks," Janet said. The pair sat down near the counter. Janet carefully folded her hands on her lap to avoid touching the top of the table. It looked sticky, and there were crumbs scattered across it as well, but it wasn't any worse than any of the other tables in the place.

They sat in silence as Richard worked behind the counter. It wasn't long before he delivered everything to their table.

"Thank you so much," Janet said. She picked up her tea and took a sip. It was lukewarm, but she wasn't about to complain. The flapjack was good, at least. She waited until Richard was back behind the counter to speak.

"Robert said he'd ring you around two, right?" she asked William.

He looked at her blankly. Janet gave him a gentle kick under the table.

"Oh, yes," he said. "Around two."

"That's when the lab was going to finish with their tests, right?"

William looked at her and then nodded slowly. "Um, yes, that's right," he muttered. As Janet tried to work how she wanted to word the next question, William took a huge bite of his flapjack. Janet nearly laughed. Obviously he didn't want to answer any more questions.

The sound of breaking crockery made Janet jump.

"Sorry, I just dropped a cup," Richard said, frowning.

And you're incredibly nervous, Janet thought. Surely this stupid plan of mine isn't working. "Are you okay?" she asked the man.

"Oh, fine," he said quickly. "I'm just a little overworked at the moment, that's all. Having to do all of the work around here myself is taking its toll. Maybe it's time to think seriously about turning the coffee shop into something else."

Janet frowned. Maybe that was the key. Maybe Richard wanted to get rid of William so that he could turn the coffee shop into an antique shop. "What would you put in here instead?" she asked.

"Oh, maybe a card and gift shop," he replied. "Something that's a lot less hard work, that's for sure."

Janet swallowed the last of her tea as her mind raced. She looked over at William, who was washing down the last of his flapjack.

"I know this has all been stressful, but at least you know Robert's close to working it all out," she said to him.

William nodded. "Shouldn't be long now," he agreed.

Janet watched as Richard fumbled with the cup he was holding. He only just managed to set it on the counter safely.

William pushed his chair back. "I'd better get back to work," he said.

"Yes, before Robert rings," Janet agreed. She stood up as well and began to walk towards the door. "Wasn't it lucky, Robert getting that fingerprint off the last letter," she said loudly as she went.

A cup crashed to the ground behind them. Janet turned around and stared at Richard. All of the colour had drained from his face.

"I think you might be unwell," she said in a concerned tone. "Can I do anything to help?"

"No; I'm fine," Richard snapped. "I may close up early, though. It isn't as if it's busy."

Janet nodded and then followed William out of the shop and back across the road.

"I don't think we need to bother Owen or Donald," she said.

"He was acting awfully guilty, wasn't he?" William asked.

"I really think my plan worked," Janet replied. "I really didn't expect it to, but I'm glad it did."

Back in William's shop, he rang Robert. Before he could tell Robert the whole story, Robert insisted on coming over.

"He's just at the station," William said. "He'll be here soon."

Janet thought the young constable must have run, as he was at the door well before she was expecting him. Both William and Janet started talking at once.

"Stop," Robert said. "I want to hear the whole story, but I can only listen to one of you at a time."

"You tell it," William said to Janet. "It was your plan."

Robert took notes and frowned a great deal while Janet was talking, but he never interrupted. "You took a huge risk doing that," he said when she'd finished. "What if he'd realised he'd given himself away and decided to get rid of both of you?"

"We were right next door to the police station," Janet pointed out. "We could have run for help if he started to get angry."

"It was still dangerous," Robert insisted. "Next time, ring me with your crazy plans before you do them."

"But you wouldn't have let me do it, and I think we've identified the culprit," Janet said.

"You may have," Robert conceded. "But I'll take it from here."

"Richard just locked up the coffee shop and put up the closed sign," William reported from where he was standing near the window.

"I'd better go and see if I can catch him," Robert said. "Although I do know where he lives, of course."

Janet watched anxiously as the man walked over to the coffee shop and knocked on the door. After a moment, Richard opened the door and spoke to him. Janet turned away when Richard stepped backwards and Robert went into the shop.

"You don't think Robert is in any danger, do you?" she asked William.

"He rang for reinforcements," William told her, nodding towards the window.

A police car pulled into the coffee shop car park and two uniformed men climbed out. Janet watched as they walked into the building. A moment later her mobile rang.

"Are you going to be back by three?" Joan asked. "I thought you might like to be here when our guest arrives."

Janet looked at the clock. It was later than she'd thought. "I'll leave now," she said.

"Let me know what happens over the road," she told William as she walked to the door.

"If I hear anything," William promised. "And good luck with Alice."

Chapter 10

When Janet got home, she told her sister all about her afternoon.

"Robert won't be very happy that you interfered in his investigation," Joan said.

"I didn't mean to," Janet replied. "I didn't really think that Richard was involved."

"You could have put yourself in danger," Joan scolded.

A knock on the door let Janet off the hook. She rushed to open it.

"Ah, good afternoon," the woman on the porch said brightly. "I'm Alice Chalmers. I have a booking."

Janet stepped back to the let the woman into the house, studying her as she did so. Alice looked younger than Janet had expected, maybe in her mid-fifties. She was petite and blonde with bright green eyes. The business-type suit she was wearing looked as if it had been expensive, and Janet recognised her shoes and handbag from photos she'd seen in a glossy magazine.

"I'm Joan Markham and this is my sister, Janet," Joan said as she stepped forward.

"It's a great pleasure to meet you both," Alice replied. "I'm sooo happy to get out of London for a short break. I know I work too hard, but I can't seem to help myself."

"Well, we both hope that you'll enjoy your stay. Let me show you to your room," Joan said.

"Do I have a kettle?" Alice asked. "I'm absolutely gasping for a cup of tea."

"You do," Joan told her.

"But why not drop off your suitcase and then join us in the kitchen for some tea and biscuits," Janet offered, eager to talk to the woman.

"That sounds delightful," Alice said.

"I'll go and put the kettle on," Janet replied.

Joan and Alice joined her in the kitchen only a few moments later.

"There's Victoria sponge if that appeals," Joan told their guest as the woman sat down.

"Oh, I can't eat anything that indulgent," the woman laughed. "Maybe just one biscuit with my tea, though."

Janet put a plate of biscuits in the centre of the table while Joan made the tea. Then the sisters sat down with their guest.

"So I have to ask," Alice began after a moment. "Do either of you know William Chalmers? He owns an antique shop here, I gather."

"We both know William," Janet said. "Doveby Dale is a small village."

"Ah, so if you've seen him lately, you probably already know that he and I were married once," Alice said.

"Yes, he did mention that," Janet told her.

"How is he?" Alice asked.

"As far as I know, he's fine," Janet replied, not wanting to bring up the anonymous letters. If William wanted the woman to know about them, he could tell her himself.

"Is he happy up here? Has he made himself some friends? Do you know if he's seeing anyone?" Alice laughed and held up a hand. "I don't mean to throw a bunch of questions at you, but I do worry about the man."

"I believe he's happy," Janet said. "And I think he has some friends. You are planning to visit him, aren't you? You can ask him yourself about such things."

"I am planning to visit him," Alice agreed. "But I'm trying to work out whether he's happy here or not before I see him."

"You want him to move back to London," Janet suggested.

Alice laughed. "Is that what he told you?" she asked. She sighed deeply. "Herbert told me not to come. He said that William would get the wrong idea, but I had to come anyway. I didn't want him to hear things second- or third-hand."

"What sort of things?" Janet asked, ignoring the look that Joan gave her. Janet knew she was asking rude questions, but she didn't care.

The woman sighed again. "This is difficult," she said. "I loved William, I truly did, but he was very, well, possessive is probably the best way to describe him. I don't know if he's truly over our relationship or not. I don't want to hurt him, you see. But, well, I don't quite know how to tell him that I'm getting married again."

"You are?" Janet blurted out. "I mean, congratulations," she added quickly.

"Thank you," Alice smiled. "Herbert is wonderful. Nothing like William, of course, although William was wonderful in his own way. Still, I decided that I needed to tell William myself, in person, before we put the announcement in the papers. Now that I'm here, though, I'm afraid I'm getting cold feet."

"I'm sure William will be happy for you," Joan said.

"Oh, I do hope so," the woman replied. "He's often hinted that we should reunite, you see, whenever I speak to him. But maybe time and distance have finally healed his broken heart. I suppose I should go and see him right away. There's no point in dragging it out, is there?

"You'll enjoy your holiday away from London more if you get the difficult part over with first," Joan said.

"Yes, I suppose you're right. Unless William takes it very badly." She sighed. "I do worry about his health, you see. He's had three heart attacks, you know."

"He has?" Janet said in surprise.

"Oh, yes, but maybe I shouldn't have mentioned it," Alice said. "Doctors do get things wrong sometimes. Perhaps he does have more than a year or two left in his heart. We can all hope."

Janet stared at the woman, not sure which question to ask next. Joan spoke before Janet could decide.

"I believe he shuts his shop for the day at five," she told Alice. "If you wanted to catch him there, you'll probably want to hurry."

"Oh, yes," Alice said, glancing at her slender gold watch. "I should go now, I suppose. Thank you for the tea and the biscuit. I'll see you later."

Janet walked her to the door, supplying her with directions to William's shop, then watched as the woman climbed into a battered old hatchback and drove away.

"I don't like her," Janet told her sister as they tidied away the tea things.

"She seemed pleasant enough," Joan replied.

"Nothing she said matches with what William told me," Janet said. "One of them must be lying."

"For your sake, I hope it's Alice," Joan said gently.

"I need to work out how I can find out the truth," Janet said. "I wish I could be a fly on the wall in William's shop right now."

"I'm afraid I can't even think of an excuse for you to go over there," Joan said. "We don't need anything from any of the shops."

"I could go and get some headache tablets or something," Janet said.

"We have several boxes of headache tablets," Joan reminded her. "Anyway, you don't want it to look as if you've just made up an excuse to check up on William."

"You're right, I don't want it to look that way. I do want to check up on William, though," Janet said with a sigh.

Janet was restless all afternoon and early evening as she wondered what was happening in William's shop. Joan made all of her favourites for dinner, including apple crumble, which distracted her slightly.

"Thank you for dinner," she said to Joan as she helped clear the table. "Everything was delicious, especially the pudding."

"I'm going to settle into the sitting room with a good book," Joan told her. "I'll wait for the guests to get home. You can go and watch some telly or something if you'd like."

"I don't know," Janet said. "There probably isn't anything on worth watching. Anyway, I'm all wound up. Maybe I should just go for a drive or something."

"And just happen to drive past the antique shop," Joan suggested. "And maybe just happen to hear a strange noise from the engine and have to stop?"

Janet shrugged. "It could happen," she said.

"Why don't you just ring William?" Joan asked. "You could tell him you wanted to know if he'd heard anything about Richard and the letters."

"I could, couldn't I?" Janet asked happily. She hadn't quite reached the phone when the front door opened.

"Ah, good evening, good evening," Brock Banner said brightly. "We've had such a lovely, lovely day, haven't we, darling?"

Helen smiled. "We have. You live in a very beautiful part of the world, you know."

Janet nodded. "We are very fortunate," she said.

"But now we've worn ourselves out completely," Helen said. "We need an hour of television and then an early night, I think." The pair wandered off to the television lounge while Janet picked up the telephone. The front door opened again behind her before she could dial.

"Good evening," Alice Chalmers said from the doorway.

Janet turned around. "You look as if you've been crying," she blurted out without thinking.

Alice flushed. "I had hoped to simply sneak in," she said in an apologetic tone. "I didn't want anyone to see me this way."

"I'm so sorry," Janet said, feeling her sister's angry glare as she walked towards Alice. "I was just surprised, that's all. I hope everything is all right?"

"I'm sure it is," Alice said in a tone that suggested she was anything but. "It's just that William took the news really badly, that's all. He, well, he said some things that were very difficult to hear."

"Oh, dear," Joan murmured.

"Of course, I'm far too in love with Herbert to go back to William, no matter what he threatens, but, well, of course I still care for William, as well. If anything were to happen to him, I'd be devastated," Alice said, wiping tears from her eyes.

"Are you saying he threatened to kill himself if you marry Herbert?" Janet asked.

"I'm hoping I simply misunderstood him," Alice said. She shook her head. "All of this upset has given me a migraine. I'm afraid I need to go straight to bed. I'll see you in the morning."

Janet watched as the other woman climbed the stairs.

"That was interesting," Joan said.

"That's one word for it," Janet snapped. She took a deep breath. "I'm sorry. I mustn't take my upset out on you. I just wish I knew what to believe."

"Ring William," Joan suggested.

"I'm not sure that's the best idea right now," Janet said.

The phone interrupted their discussion.

"Maybe that's William," Joan said as Janet reached for the receiver.

"Janet? It's Robert Parsons," the voice on the other end of the phone said.

Swallowing her disappointment, Janet replied. "Good evening. What can I do for you?"

"I'm meeting with William at nine tomorrow morning to discuss the anonymous letters. As you've been involved since the start, I thought maybe you could join us. It would save me having to repeat everything to you after I talk to William."

"I'll be there," Janet said quickly.

"Excellent. See you tomorrow."

"That's convenient," Joan said when Janet told her about the call.

"It is, rather," Janet agreed. "What time is Alice having her breakfast?"

"Eight," Joan said.

"I wonder if she'll be at the shop when I get there, then," Janet said. "Or maybe she has other plans for tomorrow."

"Time will tell," Joan said.

Alice was quiet at breakfast the next morning. Janet was too preoccupied thinking about the upcoming meeting to try to speak to her. Joan exchanged pleasantries with the woman, but beyond that the Banners kept the conversation flowing during the meal. There was just time for Janet to help Joan tidy up before she needed to leave for the meeting.

"Janet, how are you?" William asked when she walked into the antique shop a short while later.

"I'm fine," Janet replied. "How are you?" she asked as she studied his face. He didn't look at all upset.

"I'm fine," William replied. "Anxious to hear what Robert's found out and eager to see the back of Alice, but otherwise fine."

Janet chuckled, nearly convinced by his words that Alice was the one lying. Robert walked in only a moment later.

"As it happens, I can't stay long," he began. "I need to get to Little Burton to deal with a problem there, but I can let you know that Richard has confessed to being behind the anonymous letters."

"But why?" Janet asked.

"He told me that he's tired of the coffee shop and wanted to try his hand at retail," Robert replied. "As he saw it, William was his only real competition in Doveby Dale, so he decided to try to get rid of him. He says he didn't mean for the letters to sound threatening, he was just trying to suggest that William should leave. He seemed to think that William wouldn't need much of a push."

"Well, he totally misjudged me, then," William said stoutly. "I can't imagine ever leaving Doveby Dale."

"And we're glad you're here," Robert said. "I'll come back later to answer any questions you may have. I'm glad we were able to wrap this all up so quickly and easily, anyway."

He was gone before Janet muttered "you're welcome."

William laughed. "We did rather solve the case for him, didn't we?" he asked.

"I did," Janet agreed.

William laughed again. "You're right. You should get all of the credit. I owe you a huge favour."

"You can paint us another picture for the house," Janet suggested.

"I'm happy to do that anyway," William told her. "You know I love painting. My only problem is finding the time to do it. I did get some other paintings in just yesterday, though, from some other local artists. Come and see."

Janet followed the man into the small room at the back that was set up like an art gallery. They'd only just crossed the threshold when the door buzzer made its ugly noise.

"I'd better go and see who that is," William said.

Janet nodded. She'd only taken a few steps when she heard raised voices. Curious, she tiptoed back to the doorway.

"I won't do it," William said loudly.

"But what will I do without you?" a woman's voice replied. Janet recognised it as Alice's almost immediately.

"You've been without me for a long time," William said. "You only miss me when you find yourself between men."

"I'm not between men now," Alice shot back. "I'm engaged to Herbert. But when I saw you again, I realised that I can't live without you."

"Of course you can. You and Herbert will be very happy together, I'm sure. Please, Alice, just stop this. Go home and start a new life with Herbert and forget you ever knew me," William begged.

"But I still love you," Alice sobbed.

William shook his head. "You never loved me," he told her. "You love drama and excitement and feeling as if you're torn between two men who both want you. This isn't about me at all."

"That's it. I'm going back to London," Alice shouted. "You'll be sorry when something awful happens to me."

"I will," William agreed. "So please make sure it doesn't."

"You won't come back to London?" Alice asked.

"No, I won't," William replied. "I'm happy here. I have my little shop. I have a few friends. I don't need anything else."

"What about love?" Alice demanded.

"There's a woman I could easily fall in love with," William told her. "I'm just taking it slowly and carefully."

Alice glared at him for a moment and then spun on her heel and stormed out of the shop. Janet turned back around and began looking at paintings. William joined her a minute later.

"Did you sell him or her something expensive?" Janet asked.

"It was Alice, trying one more time to persuade me to move back to London," William replied. "She's left angry, which is nothing new."

"I am sorry," Janet said. "She seems very nice, really."

"I'm surprised she hasn't been telling you all sorts of lies about me," William said with a sigh.

"I haven't spent that much time with her," Janet said, stretching the truth. "Now that she's been here, surely she can appreciate why you want to stay in Doveby Dale, though."

"I hope so," William said. He crossed the room and stood in front of Janet. "Because there are some very good reasons why I can't imagine ever leaving, starting with you."

Janet blushed. She didn't stop him when he kissed her.

William and I have agreed to try to spend more time with one another, although that's going to be difficult now that summer is upon us. He will be much busier at the shop and I will be must busier at home. We're taking things very slowly. As Edward is still in the picture, at least as much or as little as always, taking it slowly with William is good for me. Having said that, aside from sending me that rabbit, I haven't heard from him since we've been back, so maybe he isn't in the picture after all.

I was very worried about the anonymous letters, so I know that I do care about William, at least somewhat. I'm still not sure I understand why Richard sent them. I saw Stacey the other day and she said that she thought he was becoming increasingly erratic in his behaviour lately. He was always difficult, but he'd become nearly impossible to work with. Maybe that helps explain things.

I've dubbed the entire episode "The Kingston Case," for obvious reasons. It wasn't until it was all over that I realised that I never asked Aggie for her opinion on the suspects. No doubt she would have identified Richard Kingston for us and saved us all some bother.

I'm not sure if I'll be able to write as often in the next few months. Joan seems to have filled our guest rooms nearly every night from now until September. Think of me, won't you?

With kindest regards,

Janet Markham (and Aggie)

Glossary of Terms

- **bin** — trash can
- **biscuits** — cookies
- **booking** — reservation
- **boot** — trunk (of a car)
- **car park** — parking lot
- **chemist** — pharmacist
- **cuppa** — cup of tea (informal)
- **en-suite** — bathroom attached to a bedroom
- **fizzy drink** — carbonated beverage (pop or soda)
- **fortnight** — two weeks
- **high street** — the main shopping street in a town or village
- **holiday** — vacation
- **jumper** — sweater
- **lie in —** sleep late
- **midday** — noon
- **pavement** — sidewalk
- **pudding** — dessert
- **shopping trolley** — shopping cart

- **telly** — television
- **till** — checkout (in a grocery store, for example)
- **torch** — flashlight

Other Notes

In the UK, dates are written day, month, year rather than month, day, year as in the US. (May 5, 2015 would be written 5 May 2015, for example.)

When telling time, half eight is the English equivalent of eight-thirty.

A semi-detached house is one that is joined to another house by a common center wall. In the US they are generally called duplexes. In the UK the two properties would be sold individually as totally separate entities. A "terraced" house is one in a row of properties, where each unit is sold individually (usually called a row house in the US).

The emergency number in the UK is 999, not 911.

Pensioners are men and women of retirement age.

Acknowledgments

Many thanks to my editor, Denise; my beta readers, Janice and Charlene, and especially to my readers who make what I do so worthwhile. I love hearing from you. Please get in touch!

The Lawley Case

A MARKHAM SISTERS COZY MYSTERY NOVELLA

Created with Vellum

Author's Note

With this, we hit an even dozen Markham Sisters novellas. I have so much more planned for the sisters, including a visit from Bessie Cubbon later this year. I always suggest reading the entire series in (alphabetical) order so that you can see how the characters change over the course of the novella, but each story should be enjoyable on its own if you choose not to read them all.

The aforementioned Bessie Cubbon is the protagonist in my Isle of Man Cozy Mystery series. Janet and Joan first appeared in *Aunt Bessie Decides*, and the sisters have remained in contact with Bessie ever since. These novellas open and close with excerpts from Janet's letters to Bessie. You do not need to read that series in order to enjoy this one.

The stories are set in the fictional village of Doveby Dale in Derbyshire. Because of the setting, I use UK English and spelling, although it is increasingly likely that American words and spellings may sneak in, as I've been living in the US for some years now. I do apologize for these errors and try to fix them when they are pointed out to me.

This is a work of fiction and all of the characters are fictional creations. Any resemblance that they may share with any real persons, living or dead, is entirely coincidental. The shops and restaurants within the story are also entirely fictional. If they resemble real businesses, that is also coincidental.

I love hearing from readers and all of my contact information is available in the back of the book. Please don't hesitate to get in touch at any time. Thank you for spending time with Janet and Joan.

23 June 1999

Dearest Bessie,

I've sat down to write to you a dozen or more times in the past month, but I never seem to get past the first sentence before I have to rush away to do something. Joan and I were expecting the summer months to be busy, but I don't think either of us truly anticipated what that meant.

This is the first day in June where we haven't had guests here and I'm delighted that we only have one couple checking in tomorrow, as well. A second couple arrives on Friday, and both couples will be here through the weekend, but thus far we actually have a day off the following week as well. It appears that we are completely booked for most of July and August.

I know that I shouldn't complain as this was always Joan's dream (even if she never bothered to tell me about it until last year), but I am rather exhausted from having to be nice to people all the time. Still, we are doing very well financially, especially as Joan has just put our rates up and that hasn't slowed down bookings in the slightest.

Besides being busy with the bed and breakfast, things have been fairly quiet in Doveby Dale of late. We did have one rather peculiar incident that all started with Stuart, our neighbour from across the road.

Chapter 1

"What time do today's guests arrive, then?" Janet asked, trying not to sound as grumpy as she felt.

"Mrs. Armstrong said that she thought they would arrive around five," Joan replied. "Any earlier and we'd struggle to have the room ready. Mr. and Mrs. Carter haven't left yet."

"I thought they asked you to have their breakfast ready for seven," Janet said. She glanced at the clock. It was half nine.

"They did, but they haven't come down yet. I was thinking about going up and vacuuming the other bedroom. Maybe that would wake them."

"Are Mr. and Mrs. Fordham out, then?"

"Yes, they had their breakfast at seven, as they'd requested. I gave them Mr. and Mrs. Carter's meals, too, so that they wouldn't go to waste."

"We should charge extra if you have to make extra food."

"We probably should. I shouldn't have started cooking until the Carters arrived in the kitchen, really, but they've been incredibly prompt every other morning, and they were insistent that they needed their breakfast ready when they got downstairs today so that they could eat quickly and get on the road back to Cornwall."

"You don't think something has happened to them, do you?"

"I certainly hope not. Maybe we should check on them."

Janet frowned. The last thing she wanted to do was bother their guests if they'd decided to lie in.

"Meeroow," Aggie said from the other side of the room.

"You think they're okay?" Janet asked.

"Mmerew," Aggie replied.

"Aggie thinks they are okay, just having a slow start," Janet told Joan.

Joan raised an eyebrow. "While I may concede that you have learned to understand Aggie when she speaks to you, I find it hard to believe that Aggie is capable of knowing whether something is wrong or not with guests behind a locked door."

"She's a very smart kitten," Janet replied. "I believe her."

Joan sighed. "We'll leave them for one more hour, but then I'm going up to check on them."

Janet shrugged. "They'll be down eventually." And while they're still up there, I don't have to wash bedding or dust and vacuum, she added to herself.

She'd been looking forward to only having one set of guests for a few days after the Carters left, until Joan had booked the Armstrongs into the empty room. While Joan had spent her years as a primary schoolteacher dreaming of owning a bed and breakfast one day, Janet, working the same job, had always looked forward to retiring and travelling the world. Now Joan was living out her dream and Janet sometimes felt stuck. She loved her sister, otherwise she never would have agreed to buy Doveby House in the first place, but the busy summer season was proving to be hard work.

The only thing that kept Janet going was the knowledge that they were tucking away a considerable profit from their little business. She knew that after the summer was over, things would be considerably quieter, and she was determined to convince her sister that they should do some travelling during those months when they would struggle to book guests.

Janet was in the seventeenth-century manor house's small

library an hour later, looking for something to read on the very full shelves, when Joan found her.

"They aren't down yet," Joan said in a worried tone.

"I'm sure they'll be down any second now," Janet told her. "Any suggestions for something different for me to read?"

"There are thousands of books in here. Just choose one at random."

"I could do that. But after all the time I spent arranging the shelves, it wouldn't be truly random."

The library had been fully stocked with books when the sisters had purchased the house. That was one of the main reasons why Janet had agreed to the purchase in the first place. Janet had spent many months working her way through the entire room, categorising and arranging the shelves exactly the way she wanted them.

"I can choose something for you if you'd prefer," Joan offered. "I still don't understand how the books are arranged. Your system doesn't make any sense to me at all."

Janet grinned. "It makes sense to me. You said I could do whatever I wanted."

"Yes, well, perhaps I was a bit hasty in that," Joan replied with a frown. "Anyway, try this one," she suggested, pulling a completely random book off the nearest shelf.

"*Gardening for Beginners*," Janet read off the cover. "I'm not sure that's exactly what I had in mind."

"Oh, dear, Ms. Markham, we are sorry," a man's voice came from the corridor outside the room.

Joan turned around. "Mr. Carter, I was just starting to worry about you," she said.

"Yes, um, well, we are sorry. I set the alarm on my phone, but, well, it seems that I turned it off and went back to sleep. It's just lucky my son rang to check on our progress towards home. He wasn't best pleased to learn that we hadn't even left Derbyshire yet," the man replied.

"Will you and your wife be wanting any breakfast, then?" Joan asked.

"I wish we could, as your cooking was one of the highlights of our stay, but sadly, we don't have time. My wife is just finishing the packing and then we'll need to be away."

"I have some cereal bars that a previous guest insisted that I buy. You're more than welcome to take a few of those with you for the drive," Joan said.

"That would be a help, actually, as we probably won't stop for lunch until late. Thank you."

Joan glanced over at Janet and then winked at her. Janet knew that Joan hated having the bars in her kitchen, but she was too frugal to throw them away. This was the perfect way to get rid of some of them. As Joan left to get the bars and show the Carters out, Janet dropped into the nearest chair.

"Gardening is the quintessential British pastime," she read from the first page of the book Joan had handed her. "It can provide hours of quiet enjoyment while making a person's surroundings more beautiful." She looked at Aggie, who was washing a paw. "I don't know. I've always thought of gardening as hard work. Maybe I'll try to catch Stuart and ask him what he thinks."

Stuart Long lived in one half of the semi-detached property across the road from Doveby House. He was a retired gardener and he spent much of his spare time looking after the rather extensive grounds around Doveby House. The sisters paid him a small amount of money for his time and then supplemented that with a continuous supply of tea, biscuits, and cakes. It was an arrangement that seemed to suit everyone.

Aggie didn't bother to reply. Instead she curled up in her bed that was in one corner of the room and went to sleep. Janet turned the page, but was immediately interrupted.

"The Carters have gone," Joan told her. "We must get their room ready for the Armstrongs."

Janet dropped the book onto the desk and followed her sister out of the room. She'd lock up the library later, once Aggie was done with her nap. The Fordhams would be out all day, anyway, and the Armstrongs weren't due until later.

Joan stripped the bed and started the laundry while Janet dusted and then vacuumed the smaller of the two guest rooms. They made up the bed with the second set of sheets and blankets, and then Joan cleaned the en-suite bathroom while Janet dusted and vacuumed the other guest room. That was a more difficult job as Mr. and Mrs. Fordham had left their things all over every surface. Janet did her best anyway.

"I'll clean the en-suite in here if you want to get some flowers for both rooms," Joan said a short while later.

"I'd rather get some lunch," Janet told her.

Joan glanced at her watch. "The morning has flown past, hasn't it? We can have a quick lunch before we finish in here, then."

It only took Joan few minutes to make sandwiches for them. Janet was quite content to let her older sister take care of the cooking and baking for both of them, although she was quite capable of looking after herself, as well. What Janet wasn't interested in doing was cooking and baking for the bed and breakfast.

As they'd lived together for their entire lives, Joan knew exactly how Janet preferred her sandwiches, anyway. "What's in this?" she demanded now as she took a bite.

"I put some spinach in both of our sandwiches," Joan told her. "It's good for you."

"But I don't want spinach in my sandwich."

"You'll barely taste it with everything else that's in there."

"But I can taste it. That's how I knew you'd done something different."

"As I said, it's good for you."

"Do I get pudding if I eat it all?"

Joan sighed. "I think you're old enough to eat healthily without having to be bribed."

"Sorry, but I don't agree. I don't like the spinach, but I'll eat it if I can have a slice of Victoria sponge when I'm done."

"How old are you again?"

Janet laughed. "I'm two years younger than you, so old enough to be retired, but not quite old enough to eat my spinach without a bribe."

Shaking her head, Joan got up and refilled her coffee cup. "You're over sixty," she pointed out as she did so.

"Yes, but nowhere near seventy," Janet replied cheerfully. "Let's not argue. As you are up, you can cut me a piece of cake."

Joan looked as if she wanted to argue, but after another sigh she unwrapped the Victoria sponge and cut off a tiny slice. She put it on a plate and then glanced at Janet. "It's come out rather thinner than I expected," she said. "I'll just cut you a slightly larger one."

Janet hid a smile as Joan cut a larger slice and handed it to her. Then Joan put the smaller slice at her own place before she rewrapped the cake. Once they'd enjoyed their cake, they went back to work.

"That's everything ready except the flowers," Joan said as they walked back down the stairs a while later. "Do you want me to get them?"

"No, I'll go," Janet replied. "I love being out in our garden. I don't spend nearly enough time out there."

"I don't either. We should make more of an effort to enjoy it."

Janet collected a pair of scissors and then headed out into the garden. For several minutes she simply stood and soaked in the glorious sights and smells of it. There seemed to be flowers everywhere, an explosion of colours and scents on all sides. She meandered along the paths that ran throughout the grounds, admiring everything as she went. She was just outside the coach house when she found the man responsible for it all.

"Stuart, everything looks fabulous," she told him.

He looked at her and then nodded. "It's doing well this year," he said. "I'm happy with most of it, anyway. There are a few persistent weed patches in one of the beds and some things aren't flowering as much as I'd like, but overall it's doing well."

"I think it's absolutely gorgeous, every inch of it. But I want a few flowers for the guest rooms. What would you suggest?"

"Let's start with the bushes that need a bit of pruning back and see how we get on," he suggested. "You may get all that you need from them."

Janet got what she needed and a great deal more by the time Stuart was finished with his pruning. "Take some home to Mary," she suggested, referring to the man's wife.

"Oh, she's off visiting her son again," Stuart said with a shrug. "She won't be back for a fortnight, at least."

A dozen questions sprang into Janet's mind, but she didn't ask any of them. Instead she thanked the man for his help.

"Always happy to help," he replied. "But do you have a minute? There's something that's been bothering me and I'm not sure if I should talk to the police about it or not."

Chapter 2

'The police?" Janet echoed. "My goodness, that sounds serious. Why don't you come inside and have a cuppa? I'll get the flowers into vases while we wait for the kettle to boil."

Stuart nodded and then followed Janet into the house. She filled the kettle and then several vases. By the time the flowers were all arranged, the kettle had boiled.

"Good afternoon," Joan said, smiling at Stuart as she walked into the kitchen. She shot her sister a questioning look.

"Ah, good afternoon," he replied. "I hope this isn't inconvenient for you. I wanted to talk to Janet about something."

"That's not a problem at all. I'll leave you two alone, then, shall I?" Joan replied.

"Oh, no need to do that. I'm happy to talk to both of you, really," Stuart said quickly.

Janet made three cups of tea and then glanced at Joan. "Maybe we could have biscuits," she said.

"I'll put some out," Joan told her. "But it is nearly time for dinner."

Janet smiled to herself as she slid into a chair. A few biscuits wouldn't spoil her dinner, and if what Stuart wanted to discuss was serious, a little bit of sugar would help.

"I hope everything is okay," Joan said in a questioning voice as she put a plate of biscuits on the table in front of Stuart.

"Everything is fine, at least I think it is," he replied. "It was just something odd that happened, that's all."

"Why don't you start at the beginning?" Janet suggested before helping herself to a custard cream.

"That's probably for the best," Stuart agreed. He ate a biscuit and drank half of his tea before he continued. "I was at the garden centre yesterday, you see. I wanted to get some new secateurs and a few other things. I was just looking around at the trees when I, well, I overheard a conversation."

"And what you heard is worrying you?" Janet asked as the man nibbled his way through another biscuit.

"Oh, yes, that's it exactly. I only heard part of the conversation, but it sounded suspicious to me." He finished his tea and picked up another biscuit.

Janet swallowed a sigh. "What was said, exactly?" she asked as Joan refilled the man's teacup.

"I'm not sure I remember the exact words, but from what I could make out, it sounded very much as if they were discussing planting, well, planting things that aren't legal in this country."

"What do you mean?" Joan asked.

"Drugs," Stuart replied. "Or rather, the plants that can be used to make certain drugs. As I said, I didn't hear the whole conversation, but that's what I believe they were discussing, anyway."

"That seems very much the sort of thing the police would want to know about," Janet said.

"Yes, I suppose so," Stuart sighed.

"Robert is a very nice man and an excellent constable," she added. "I'm not sure why you didn't go to him immediately."

Robert Parsons was the local constable charged with policing both Doveby Dale and the neighbouring village of Little Burton. He was young, but smart and kind, and Janet thought he was doing an excellent job.

"I'm sort of trying to avoid the police, especially after all that trouble a few months back. Mary is still upset with how she thinks the police treated me," Stuart admitted.

Janet nodded. Stuart hadn't been arrested or accused of any wrongdoing, but he'd been questioned extensively when money had been stolen from a charity fundraiser that he'd helped organise. "But we don't want anyone growing anything illegal in Doveby Dale," she said.

"Yes, I know, but, well, there's another reason why I didn't just ring Robert," Stuart said. He picked up another biscuit and took his time with it. As he washed it down with more tea, Janet thought about taking the tea things away from the man and demanding that he get on with the story.

"What was that other reason?" Joan asked as Stuart reached towards the biscuit plate yet again.

"I never did get a good look at the men whose voices I heard, but I saw them getting into their car a short while later. I recognised the car, you see."

"Whose car was it?" Janet asked quickly, before Stuart could start eating again.

"I don't know if you know Martin Lawley? He has a small farm on the outskirts of the village. It may even cross the border between Doveby Dale and Little Burton. It's been in his family for generations. Anyway, it was Martin's car."

"Was Martin one of the men having the conversation?" Janet asked

"Oh, no. These men were much younger, or at least they sounded much younger. Martin is probably in his late seventies. These men didn't sound anywhere near that old."

"Does Mr. Lawley have children?" Joan wondered.

"Not of his own. He has a stepson, but last I knew Nick was living and working in Manchester."

"Could one of the men have been this Nick?" was Janet's next quick question.

Stuart shrugged. "I haven't seen the man in years, and as I said, I didn't get a look at the two men who were talking in the garden centre, either, but I suppose that's one possibility."

"You should talk to Robert," Janet said.

Stuart nodded and began to eat another biscuit. Janet grabbed a custard cream and followed suit.

"You know Robert will conduct a very discreet investigation," Joan said.

"Yes, I suppose so. I just don't want to get Martin into any trouble."

"He'll be in even more trouble if his stepson starts growing drugs on his farm," Janet pointed out.

"I just wish I would have heard more of the conversation," Stuart sighed. "I may have completely misunderstood what was being said."

"As I said, Robert will be discreet, but it should be investigated, just in case," Joan said.

"I was thinking maybe I should take a ride out there," Stuart said. "It's not a very big farm. It would only take a few minutes to drive around the place and just, I don't know, see if there are any signs of anything. Martin hasn't planted anything in his fields for years. He just uses them for grazing a handful of cows and sheep. It wouldn't take long to spot any clearing or anything that might be happening."

"But it could be dangerous," Joan said. "If his stepson is planning to start growing drugs out there, he isn't going to want anyone snooping around."

"I just want to be more certain of what I heard before I go to Robert. I may have completely misinterpreted what they were discussing. Perhaps I should go and visit Martin. I owe him a visit anyway."

"I don't suppose he knew Alberta Montgomery?" Janet asked.

"He may have," Stuart said. "He's old enough to have done so, anyway."

Janet nodded. Alberta had once lived in Doveby House, and Janet was convinced that it was Alberta's ghost that screamed in the night when the moon was full. While Janet had been told the basics of Alberta's story, she was eager to find out more. An entire box filled with the woman's diaries and letters had been found in the carriage house, but Joan didn't think it was appropriate for them to read through the items in the box. Janet was eager to find any of Alberta's relatives. She was secretly hoping they might agree to let Janet read the contents of the box and maybe even write a book about their relation.

"I've been trying to reach Gretchen Falkirk, but she never answers her phone and she doesn't seem to have an answering machine," Janet said.

"Oh, she wouldn't," Stuart said. "She's not one for embracing modern technology. She's always kept to herself, but she keeps herself busy. Did you want to ask her about Alberta, then?"

"I want to ask everyone and anyone about Alberta," Janet exclaimed. "But no one seems to want to talk to me."

"You could come with me to see Martin," Stuart suggested. "We could see if his stepson is visiting and whether or not he was one of the men I overheard. I'm sure Martin wouldn't mind if we took a drive around the farm after our visit, either. We could tell him that you wanted to see it."

"Ring Robert," Joan said. "This is a police matter."

"Or maybe it isn't," Stuart replied. "It might just be me getting things muddled up. I've known Martin for a long time and I can't believe that he'd let his stepson do anything illegal on his property. I'm going to go and see Martin, whether Janet comes with me or not."

"You shouldn't go alone," Janet said quickly. "I'll come, too."

"Well, I don't approve," Joan said tightly. "You've no idea what's going on at the farm. Maybe Martin isn't even there at the moment and his stepson has taken over. You could walk into a huge drug manufacturing operation or something."

"I'm sure that isn't the case," Stuart said. "But if it will make you feel better, I'll ring Martin and ask him if we can visit. If he says no, I'll ring Robert immediately."

Joan frowned. "I suppose that's better than the pair of you just showing up on his doorstep, but I still don't like it."

"Let's see what Martin says when Stuart rings him," Janet suggested. "That may tell us everything we need to know."

"I'll just ring him now, from here, then, shall I?" Stuart asked.

Joan pressed her lips together and glared at Janet. "Use this phone," Janet suggested, gesturing towards the phone on the kitchen wall.

Stuart dialed the number from memory. Sitting at the table, Janet could just hear it ringing on the other end.

"Hello?" a man's voice said loudly.

Stuart pulled the phone away and frowned at it. "Martin? It's Stuart, Stuart Long," he after he'd returned the receiver to his ear.

"Stuart?" the other man shouted back. "What can I do for you?"

"I was just talking with the lovely sisters who now own Doveby House," Stuart replied. "We were talking about Alberta Montgomery."

"Eh? Pardon? I can't hear very well," Martin yelled.

Stuart repeated himself more loudly while Janet grabbed another biscuit. Joan frowned at her.

"Oh, Alberta, yes, what about her?" Martin said finally.

"We were wondering if you remembered her?" Stuart told him.

"Oh, aye, of course I do. She was almost royalty to us."

"Would you be willing to talk to my friends about her? Maybe we could come out and visit you at the farm?" Stuart suggested.

"Visit me? Here? Sure, I don't see why not. Bring biscuits, though. My stepson is staying with me now and he's eaten everything sweet in the house."

Stuart laughed. "We'll bring something nice for tea. How about tomorrow?"

"Tomorrow at two would work," Martin said. "As would just about any other time. I'm retired, you know. I don't do anything all day."

"We'll see you around two," Stuart replied.

"I'll be looking forward to it," the man shouted before banging the phone down in Stuart's ear.

He returned the phone to the wall and then shrugged. "He didn't seem any different, just deafer."

"That might make our conversation difficult," Janet said.

"It also means that his stepson and his associates could be discussing things right in front of the man that he knows nothing about," Joan suggested. "I still think the whole idea is dangerous."

"We'll be fine. You'll know exactly where we are. If we aren't back here by half three, you can send Robert in," Janet said. "Or maybe we should say four o'clock. I suspect I'm going to have to repeat myself a lot."

Joan shook her head. "I don't like it," she said crossly.

The doorbell saved Janet from having to reply. As Joan went to open the door, Janet let Stuart out the back way and then quickly took the vases of flowers up to the guest room. Aggie was pacing around the first floor corridor.

"I know, I know. Now that the guests are here, you want to hide in my room," Janet said. She put the flowers where they belonged and then let Aggie into her bedroom. When she heard voices on the stairs, she shut her bedroom door and stood just inside it, listening carefully to the conversation in the corridor.

"We've put you in the Montgomery Room," Joan was saying. "You have the key to your door and also to the front door of Doveby House. That way you can come and go as you please."

"It's rather small," a nasal voice that could have been male or female complained.

"I'm sorry, but it's the only room we have available at the moment. We generally take bookings several months ahead," Joan replied.

"Then it will have to do," a different voice, this one definitely female, said. "I just hope I don't get too claustrophobic in here."

"There are several large hotels near Derby if you don't think this will suit you," Joan said.

"I don't want to spend my time looking for a hotel room," the nasal voice snapped. "We'll stay here. We just won't like it."

Janet frowned. Their new arrivals didn't sound at all pleasant. She had to hope that they'd spend most of their time sightseeing or doing other things well away from Doveby House.

"As I said, this is the only room we have available," Joan said stiffly. "The en-suite is just through there."

"It's small, too," the woman complained. "But at least it's all clean. I suppose we've stayed in worse places. I just can't remember any at the moment."

"I'll be downstairs if you need anything," Joan told them. "I hope you enjoy your stay."

"Not likely," the nasal voice replied. "But we'll see."

Janet listened to her sister's footsteps as she went down the stairs. After a minute, she heard the bedroom door across the hall slam shut. She opened her door a crack and peeked out. The corridor was empty.

"You were smart to hide when you did," she told Aggie.

"Meerrowww," Aggie replied, settling into her cat bed for a rest.

Janet slipped out and locked the door behind her. Quickly making her way down the stairs, she stopped to lock the library door before she found Joan in the kitchen.

"I overheard the conversation in the corridor," she told her sister. "Our new guests sound as if they're going to be hard work."

"On the plus side, they've upset me so much that I've nearly forgotten to be cross with you about your going to meet Martin Lawley," Joan replied.

Chapter 3

Joan made shepherd's pie for dinner. They were still eating when their new guests walked into the kitchen.

"We've unpacked as best we can," the man said in his nasal whine. "There isn't very much storage space in the room, either." He was exactly what Janet had been expecting from his voice, a short, thin, unhappy-looking man in his late fifties or early sixties. He was wearing brown trousers and a brightly coloured and patterned shirt that seemed completely unlike something he would have chosen.

"I'm Janet," Janet said, ignoring his remark. She stood up and held out a hand.

He stared at her hand for a moment and then touched it with his fingertips. "I'm Malcolm Armstrong, and this is my wife, Judith," he said, nodding at the woman next to him. She was slightly taller than her husband and probably twice his weight. Her scarlet red dress was printed with what looked like tiny parrots all over it. Janet wanted to get closer to get a better look.

Judith nodded at Janet, but kept her hands in her pockets. Janet sat back down at the table and took a bite of her dinner. It was rude to eat in front of the guests, but she didn't care.

"Where can we get some dinner?" Malcolm asked. "We'd prefer something reasonably priced, but exceptional."

Wouldn't we all, Janet thought to herself. She looked over at Joan, who was frowning. Janet could guess what her sister was thinking. They could send the couple to the café up the road where the food truly was excellent, but then poor Todd and Ted, the owners, would have to deal with the unpleasant pair. She and Joan both liked Todd and Ted a great deal. Neither of them wanted to subject them to the Armstrongs.

"There are only a few restaurants in Doveby Dale," Joan said. "What sort of food do you fancy?"

"Oh, we don't want to eat in Doveby Dale," Malcolm scoffed. "We'll drive into Derby, of course. The food will be better there. Is there anywhere you can recommend?"

"We rarely go into Derby," Joan told him. "We prefer to give our business to our friends in Doveby Dale."

"Yes, well, I suppose that's more affordable for you, isn't it?" Malcolm sneered. "We'll just have to go and see what we can find."

"Good luck," Janet told them as they left the room.

Joan got up and followed behind them, no doubt to make sure that they locked the door when they left. When she came back into the kitchen, she was shaking her head.

"They didn't lock the door, did they?" Janet asked her.

"They didn't even shut it," Joan replied. "I stayed back far enough that they couldn't have known I was behind them, but they walked out of the house and went off to their car, leaving the front door wide open."

"They're terrible. If they ever ring again, make sure that you tell them that we're fully booked."

"I've already added them to my list," Joan assured her. "Monday can't get here fast enough. I've already had enough of those two."

"At least the Fordhams are nice people," Janet said. "Perhaps the Armstrongs will be out as much as the Fordhams are and we won't have to deal with them very much."

"I have to make them breakfast every morning," Joan sighed. "I wonder if they'd prefer to eat in their room. I'd rather they take their food up to their room than have to share my kitchen with them."

"Feed them in the dining room," Janet suggested. "We never use it, but they're the perfect guests for it."

"You may be right about that."

While Janet loaded the dishwasher after dinner, Joan started pulling out flour and sugar.

"What are you doing?"

"I'm just a bit upset about the Armstrongs. I'm going to bake something. That always makes me feel better."

"What will you make?" Janet asked excitedly.

"I thought I might try the American brownies from Bessie's recipe. Either that or a chocolate cake. Which would you prefer?"

"Let's try the brownies. They sound the perfect tonic to the Armstrongs."

"We have to try something," Joan muttered as she flipped through her recipe cards.

The sisters were watching television when they heard the front door open several hours later. Janet got to her feet.

"I'll go. Maybe it will just be the Fordhams."

"That means I'll have to go next time when it's sure to be the Armstrongs," Joan sighed.

When Janet walked into the sitting room a moment later, both couples were hanging up their jackets.

"Good evening," Edgar Fordham said. "We thought we'd be back hours ago, but we couldn't stop chatting to the lovely girl who works at the café."

"Stacey? She's very sweet," Janet agreed. "How was your dinner?"

"Oh, excellent," Carol Fordham replied. "You were right about that café. The food was good and the service was even better."

"Hmph, well, at least some of us had a nice evening," Malcolm Armstrong said.

"Oh, dear, that doesn't sound good," Carol replied. "Did you have a bad meal somewhere?"

"We went into Derby and found a little Italian place," Malcolm told her. "It looked nice enough from the outside and it was over half full, so we assumed it wouldn't be too bad."

"But we were badly wrong," Judith said. "The service was slow and the food was uninspired. It was nothing like what we ate when we were in Rome, nothing at all."

"They tried to tell us that they specialise in Northern Italian cuisine, but that's no excuse, is it? In the end, we refused to pay for any of it and left," Malcolm said.

"You must be hungry," Edgar suggested.

"Oh, we ate what we were given, as we were both starving," Malcolm replied. "But we didn't enjoy it."

Janet frowned. If they'd eaten the food, they should have paid for it. She and Joan always requested that guests pay in advance. She could only hope that the Armstrongs had done so. They'd find it difficult to demand any money back from Joan unless they left early, which would make Janet happy and be worth refunding them.

"As much as I'd love to curl up in your lovely television lounge, I think we need an early night," Edgar said. "We want to get to Chatsworth tomorrow."

"It's a waste of time," Judith said. "We were bored to tears there."

"We've been a dozen or more times and we always love it," Edgar told her. "To each his or her own, I suppose."

Judith shrugged. "Whatever. We should get to bed as well, I suppose. We've a lot planned for tomorrow, too."

"Really? What are you going to be doing?" Carol asked.

"Things," Judith replied. She looked over at her husband. "Are you ready to try to squeeze ourselves into that tiny little room?" she asked.

"If we must," he sighed. "I hope your claustrophobia doesn't bother you too much."

Janet stood with the Fordhams and watched the other couple as they left the room. As soon as they were gone, Edgar looked at Janet.

"Our room is larger, isn't it? Would you rather we switched rooms with them?" he asked.

"Oh, goodness, no, but thank you for offering," she replied. "You were here first and you've paid for the larger room. They only rang at the last minute and were lucky that we had a room available at all. If they truly don't like it, they don't have to stay," she said. In fact, I'd be happy to see them go, she thought.

"We won't mind. If you feel you need to move them, let us know," Carol said. "I'd hate to think that you'll be listening to them complain all weekend."

"I'm sure it will be fine," Janet lied. What she was sure of was that even if they moved the unpleasant couple into the larger room, Mr. and Mrs. Armstrong would still find things to complain about.

"Lucky you," Janet said to Joan when she walked back into the television lounge a few minutes later. "Both couples are back and tucked up for the night."

"I should have come out and helped you, then, shouldn't I?" Joan said. "I was caught up in the increasingly implausible storyline on this show, but that's no excuse."

"It wasn't a problem. Mr. and Mrs. Fordham had a lovely evening and went off to bed happily. Mr. and Mrs. Armstrong had a miserable night and went off to bed grumbling about their room again. I do hope that they paid in full in advance."

"They did, although they complained about having to do so. They're going to hate whatever I make them for breakfast, aren't they?"

"I expect so. No doubt they'll eat it all and then demand some money back from you because it wasn't what they really wanted," Janet said, repeating what Malcolm had told her about their dinner in Derby.

Joan frowned. "They won't get away with such behaviour here," she said stiffly. "I taught primary school for over forty years. I know how to deal with bullies."

Janet grinned. Tomorrow's breakfast was going to be interesting, anyway.

Aggie was fast asleep on her pillow when Janet opened her door a short while later. She got ready for bed and then crawled in carefully. When Aggie opened an eye, Janet gave her a pat. "Night night."

"Meeeoowww," Aggie said softly.

Janet was in the kitchen before Joan the next morning, something that almost never happened. She started a pot of coffee brewing and then slid slices of bread into the toaster. While she was contemplating what she wanted for her own breakfast, Joan joined her.

"You're up bright and early today," she said.

"I woke up at six feeling ready for the day. I knew if I went back to sleep, I'd regret it, so here I am," Janet explained.

"The Armstrongs asked for breakfast at seven. I don't know if I should start cooking or wait to see if they actually turn up," Joan said.

"Why not start cooking now and if they aren't done at seven, we can eat what you've made?" Janet suggested.

Joan chuckled. "You're in the mood for a full English breakfast today, then?"

"I'm always in the mood for a full English breakfast, even when it's time for lunch or dinner."

Joan nodded and began to pull out what she needed from the cupboards. "I don't know why we don't eat breakfast foods at other times of the day, or when we do, we feel odd about it. What makes scrambled eggs or pancakes right for first thing in the morning, but wrong for dinner?"

"I've no idea, but if you want to start making pancakes for dinner every week, I won't complain."

At exactly seven o'clock the kitchen door swung open. Malcolm Armstrong walked into the room.

"Is our breakfast ready, then?" he demanded.

"It is," Joan replied as she added the last slice of toast to the toast rack.

"Do you have a tray so I can take it back to our room?" he asked.

"Certainly," Joan said. She pulled a tray down and carefully loaded the plates full of food into it. By the time she added cups of coffee and orange juice to the tray, it was pretty full.

"Maybe I should help with that," Janet suggested.

"I expect one or the other of you to carry it," Malcolm snapped.

"I'm terribly sorry," Joan said. "But this is a bed and breakfast, not a fancy hotel. We don't have room service here. You're welcome to have breakfast in your room, but you'll have to carry it up there yourself. If Janet wants to take the drinks separately so that they are less likely to get spilled, you should be grateful for her help."

The man frowned. "When I pay a premium price for a place like this, I expect excellent service."

"If you think you've paid a premium price, I suggest you look at what bed and breakfast establishments charge in other parts of the country," Joan replied in a level voice.

"I don't think I like your attitude," the man said sharply.

"You're more than welcome to take your business elsewhere, then," Joan said calmly. "I'll happy refund the balance of your stay if you choose to leave."

"I'm going to talk to my wife about just that," he said, grabbing the tray and storming out of the room.

Janet waited until she heard his footsteps on the stairs before she spoke. "I really hope they leave," she said.

"I wouldn't normally agree, but in this case, I'd be happy to see the back of those two," Joan sighed.

A few minutes later Judith stuck her head into the kitchen. "We're off now. We expect our room done up with fresh bedding before we return."

"When will you be back?" Joan asked.

"Maybe in an hour, maybe this afternoon, maybe late tonight," she snapped. "We have a key for the front door, so it really isn't your business."

She was gone before Joan could reply.

"I suppose we'd better go and get their room done, then," Janet sighed. "I hope we don't disturb the Fordhams while we're doing it."

"They're meant to be coming down shortly for their breakfast. If you go and get started on the Armstrong's room, I'll get things started for the Fordhams. I'll do their room once they've finished breakfast."

Janet nodded and headed for the stairs. As she climbed them, she told herself to expect the room to be a mess, but even so she was unprepared for what greeted her in the guest room. The couple had clearly eaten breakfast in bed, as the dirty plates had been left in the middle of the bedding. A half-eaten slice of toast was sticking out from under one of the pillows and a large streak of raspberry jam ran along the top sheet. Sighing deeply, Janet began to clean.

"My goodness, I thought you'd have been done ages ago," Joan said from the room's doorway over an hour later. "They've only been here one day. How much mess could they have made?"

"It was bad," Janet said. "But I think I've taken care of the worst of it. After I found the sausage in the bottom of the wardrobe, I went back over the entire room."

"There was a sausage in the wardrobe?" Joan echoed.

Janet nodded. "I suspect they were hoping that I wouldn't notice it and that then they could claim the room wasn't cleaned properly. No doubt they'd expect some money back if that happened."

"I'm sure you've been thorough, but I think I'll go through it all again, if you don't mind," Joan said.

Half an hour later the women were satisfied.

"I really hope they decide to leave early," Janet said as she lugged all of the dirty bedding down the stairs.

"I'm tempted to give them all of their money back if they'll just go," Joan admitted. "But then I'd feel as if they'll have won."

"There is that," Janet agreed. "But I hate the thought of having to clean up after them again tomorrow."

"Tomorrow it will be my turn," Joan promised. "For now, let me make you a lovely breakfast."

Chapter 4

After breakfast, the pair quickly tidied the Fordhams' room before Janet needed to get ready for her trip out with Stuart.

"I still think this is a bad idea," Joan said as Janet waited for their neighbour to appear.

"I know you do, but I'm sure everything will be fine, and it will set Stuart's mind at rest, too. I was thinking, it's possible that the men at the garden centre just had a car that looked like his friend Martin's car. We're probably wasting our time going to see the man."

"I suppose that's one possibility," Joan replied.

"No, not possible," Stuart told Janet as he drove them through Doveby Dale. "Martin's car is a classic, mostly because he refuses to get rid of it. He does all of his own repairs and he's kept it running for decades. There probably aren't more than two or three left in the country that still run."

"Let's hope you misunderstood the men you overheard, then," Janet suggested.

"Yes, I certainly hope so. Drugs scare me."

"Me, too."

Once they'd left Doveby Dale, Stuart followed the road towards

Little Burton. After a few miles, he turned off the main road and onto a side road. Within minutes, he turned off of that road onto what looked like a dirt path.

"This isn't much of a road," Janet remarked.

"No, Martin really should have it paved or something, but it's a long way from the road to the house. He never could afford it."

They drove between some trees and then through a large clearing. Stuart slowed down.

"Nothing looks as if it's been touched for years," Janet said, looking around.

"We'll have to find an excuse to drive all the way around the farm before we leave," Stuart said. He parked in front of the small run-down farmhouse. "Here goes nothing," he muttered as he opened his door.

Stuart's knock seemed to echo around them as they waited. It felt as if they were a long way from civilization to Janet, and she was sorry she'd let Stuart talk her into coming when the door suddenly burst open. Janet jumped and let out a small scream.

"I wasn't expecting that," the man at the door shouted at her.

"I'm sorry," Janet said quickly.

"Pardon?" he replied.

"I'm sorry. You startled me when you opened the door," Janet said loudly.

"Oh, aye. I thought as much when you jumped and shrieked," the man told her. "But welcome, anyway. Come in." He turned around and began to shuffle back into the house. He was hunched over and had the weather-beaten look of a man who'd worked outside for his entire life. His grey hair was sparse and untidy and he was wearing thick glasses over his brown eyes. His clothes were clean but worn, and as Janet followed she noted that he was wearing slippers on his feet.

He led them into a cosy sitting room near the back of the small house. The couch and chairs looked comfortable but dated, with worn patches here and there. The man settled into what was clearly his chair and then waved at the couch. "Sit, sit," he shouted.

Janet sat down next to Stuart and glanced around the room. A few of the furniture pieces looked as if they might be antiques. If they were, they were probably valuable.

"So, Martin, this is Janet Markham. Janet, this is Martin Lawley," Stuart said loudly.

"It's a pleasure to meet you, Miss Markham," Martin said.

"Please, call me Janet," she replied.

He nodded. "And I'm Martin, of course. But did Stuart say you'd purchased Doveby House?"

"Yes, that's right," Janet said.

"It's a beautiful old house, Doveby House," Martin told her. "I haven't been inside it for years, of course, but I remember it fondly."

"Well, you're welcome to visit any time you'd like," Janet said. "Joan and I love having visitors."

Martin shrugged. "I don't get out much anymore. But I have something for you." He struggled to his feet and then crossed the room. When he came back, he was holding a metal candleholder that he handed to Janet.

"It's lovely," she said, studying the thick black twisted wire that held the candle. A small wooden stopper rotated along the spiral wire to lift or lower the candle as needed.

"I used to make ones like that for Doveby House when I was younger," he told her. "It was just something I did in my spare time, during the winter when I wasn't as busy with the farm."

"But you must let me pay you for it," Janet suggested.

"No, no, not at all. I have a few more lying around the place, actually. We used them all the time, and then one day we got electricity and we didn't need them anymore. I just thought that Doveby House should have at least one of them after all these years."

"Well, thank you very much," Janet said. "I will put it somewhere where it can be admired by our guests."

Martin shrugged. "They remind me of Alberta. I can almost see her standing in the doorway of Doveby House lit by candlelight. She was so beautiful, she was."

"What can you tell me about her?" Janet asked.

Martin shrugged. "She was beautiful, that much I've already said. I can't really tell you much else. Her family was the closest thing we had to royalty in Doveby Dale. They didn't speak to the lower classes."

Janet frowned. She'd been hoping for a good deal more from the man. "But I've been told she had a relationship with the gardener," she said.

"Oh, he was trouble, that man," Martin told her. "I knew that the first time I saw him. When it was all over, I thought I should have warned Mr. Montgomery about him, but I didn't expect him to chase after poor Alberta. And then, after she'd died, he simply left town. I thought he should have been arrested for something."

"Was Alberta very in love with him, do you think?" Janet asked.

"I doubt it," Martin replied. "She'd been very sheltered her whole life. I don't know if she knew what love even was, really. No, I think she was just infatuated by him and he used that to his advantage. He was able to get lots of expensive presents from her before her parents realised what was going on."

"Did he? I didn't know that."

"Oh, yes, she gave him bits of her jewellery and other things. It was said that Alberta wasn't very intelligent. I don't know if that's true or not. She had a nanny, and as I said, she was very sheltered. Bright or dumb, Will came along at just the right time."

"Will?" Janet repeated.

"Oh, that was the gardener. I can't recall his surname. He was a handsome fellow, I'll give him that. When he first came to Doveby House, I heard that he'd been sent away from one of the larger stately homes because he'd been caught in bed with the owner's wife, but like I said before, I knew he was trouble the first time I saw him."

"I've heard that Alberta was pregnant when she fell to her death," Janet said.

Martin shook his head. "I've never believed that. It was whispered at the time, of course, but I don't think it was true. I know Alberta was sneaking out to meet Will, but I don't believe things went that far, not before her parents found out what was going on and put a stop to it."

"Is it true that she saw Will with another woman the night she died?" Janet asked.

"That's how the story always went," Martin replied. "I don't know anything for sure, but it seems likely, knowing Will. He probably had a girlfriend or even two that Alberta didn't know about."

"It's such a sad story," Janet sighed.

"It is. I always think of her when I see those candleholders. Now you'll think of her as well."

Janet nodded. She already thought of Alberta every time there was a full moon. Maybe she didn't need any more reminders.

"How are things?" Stuart asked.

Martin blinked at him and then shrugged. "Things are fine, I suppose."

"You're doing okay out here on your own?" Stuart wondered.

"I was, and then my stepson turned up," Martin replied with a frown. "Now he's underfoot all day and night, him and his friends."

"I don't know that I've met him," Stuart said thoughtfully.

"You probably did when he was younger, but he hadn't been here in years before he turned up last week. His mother finally passed, and he says he wasn't sure what to do with himself after that."

"His mother was Margaret?" Stuart asked.

"No, Margaret was my first wife. We married young and she passed in childbirth. I lost the baby as well. I swore I wouldn't marry again, but then I met Bethany."

"Oh, I remember Bethany," Stuart frowned.

Martin nodded. "Everyone frowns when they remember Bethany," he said. "She wanted a father for Nick and a roof over her head, so she married me as soon as she was able to convince me that it was my idea. She was gone within a few months, chasing after some other man with more money."

"Didn't she leave her son here for a while, though?" Stuart asked.

"Aye, I kept young Nick for more than a year before she finally sent for him. I had him back again once or twice over the years, too.

I always told him he was welcome here, as long as he was willing to do his fair share of the farm work."

"And was he?" Stuart wanted to know.

"Sometimes. When he was younger, he tried hard, but I think his mother must have taught him her ways. He got lazy as he got older and then he stopped coming. I was surprised when he turned up last week, really."

"Is he staying here with you?" Janet asked.

"In his old bedroom," Martin said. "The house has three bedrooms and I've never needed more than the one. His friend, Jim, is staying in the other one."

"And how long will they be here?" was Janet's next question.

"I wish I knew. Oh, they're welcome to stay as long as they like, really, but I'm not used to having other people in the house. It's different, that's all."

Janet looked over at Stuart. She could think of a dozen other questions, but they all sounded rude when she thought about them.

"Are they helping you around the farm, then?" Stuart asked.

Good question, Janet thought.

"There's not much helping to do anymore," Martin sighed. "I've a few cows and sheep left, but they pretty much look after themselves these days. I keep saying I'm going to sell them, but I can't imagine not having some animals around the place."

Stuart nodded. "You didn't plant anything this spring?"

"Plant? Oh, no, that's too much like hard work. I haven't planted anything in years. Jasper, over across the way, he's been trying to convince me to rent him some of my land for pennies so that he can expand, but I'm still thinking about that."

"Jasper Jones? I'd have thought he has more than enough of his own land," Stuart remarked.

"That's what I told him, but he wants to try something new. I didn't really follow what he said, something about organic methods, whatever that means. I don't think it's really him that wants to do it. I think it's his son, Joseph. He's just moved back up here from the south. I understand he was involved in lots of environmental protests while he was down there. He'll be the one that wants my land."

"And you aren't interested in renting it out?" Janet wondered.

"Not to Jasper or his son, anyway," Martin laughed. "We've been neighbours for seventy-odd years and I've never liked the man. I don't mind leaving the land empty. Maybe if he offered me a lot of money, I'd change my mind, but I doubt it. I don't need money, really."

"We all need money," Stuart replied.

"I'm doing okay. I have my state pension and I put a bit away when I was younger, too. I'll have to be careful, but it should see me out," Martin told him.

"Mary and I just redid our wills for the tenth time since we've been married," Stuart said. "She keeps changing her mind on how much to leave each child."

"As I don't have children, I don't have that problem," Martin replied.

"What about Nick?" Janet asked.

Martin shrugged. "He's not really my child, but he is in my will anyway. He never seemed interested in being a farmer, so I've left the farm to my cousin in Edinburgh. Now that Nick is here and talking about trying his hand at getting the farm back up and running, I may have to reconsider that, though."

"You should wait and see if he's really serious before you make any changes," Stuart suggested.

"I won't do anything too..." the man stopped as they all heard a door slam somewhere. A moment later they could hear footsteps in the corridor.

"Martin? Where are you?" a voice called.

"We're in the sitting room," Martin shouted back.

"We?" was the reply. A moment later a dark-haired man with a beard and mustache, who was probably in his forties, strode into the room. He was wearing jeans and a T-shirt, and he stopped a few steps into the room. He stared at Stuart for a moment and then turned to look at Janet. She was starting to feel uncomfortable when he spoke again.

"Martin, I thought we agreed that you wouldn't have guests when I'm not here," he said loudly. "I don't know what you two are after, but it's time for you to leave."

"We aren't after anything," Stuart said, getting to his feet. "I've known Martin for many years. I brought my friend to meet him because she wanted to ask him about someone who used to live in Doveby Dale many years ago."

The man nodded. "I hope you understand that Martin isn't in the best health right now. Physically, he's doing okay, but mentally, well, just don't believe everything or maybe even anything he told you," he said in a whisper.

Chapter 5

"What are you whispering about," Martin demanded. "You know I can't hear you when you whisper."

"Sorry, Martin," the man said quickly. "Introduce me to your friends."

"This is Stuart Long. You'll have met him when you were younger," Martin replied. "And Janet Markham has just purchased Doveby House."

The man gave Janet a thoughtful look. "I'm sure that wouldn't have been inexpensive."

"It was surprisingly affordable," Janet replied truthfully. "The owners were eager to sell. And you are?"

"Oh, I'm Nick Berry. I'm Martin's stepson," the man said.

"I do remember you, but only slightly," Stuart said. "You've changed a lot since you were ten."

Nick chuckled, but it seemed forced. "We all get older, don't we? But what are you doing here?"

"We came to talk to Martin about Alberta Montgomery," Janet replied. "She used to live in Doveby House."

Nick shrugged. "If you say so." He glanced over at Martin and then stepped closer to Janet. "You should go now. Martin isn't well. He isn't really meant to have visitors," he said in a low voice.

"He seems perfectly fine to me," Janet replied.

"Of course, you just met him today," Nick retorted.

"I've known Martin for many years and he seems fine to me, as well," Stuart told him. "I should think you'd be happy that Martin has friends who want to visit him."

"Of course, I'm delighted," the man said sarcastically.

"Nick? I told you I have places to be," a voice shouted from the front of the house.

"I'm in the back. Give me a minute," Nick shouted.

"Who's that, then?" Martin asked.

"It's just Jim. He was waiting in the car for me," Nick told him.

"My car?" Martin demanded. "When are you going to get yours running again? I'd like my car back, you know."

"And I'd love to give it back to you," Nick replied. "I hate driving around in that ancient thing, but the garage hasn't been able to replace my brakes yet. They keep telling me they need another day. If it were safe to drive, I'd take it somewhere else."

"Hey, Nick, come on," a voice said from the doorway. "Oh, sorry. I didn't know we had guests."

Janet looked over at the man who'd just joined them. He, too, appeared to be in his forties. His hair was lighter than Nick's and cut far shorter. Sunglasses covered his eyes, even though he was indoors. Now he slid them down his nose and studied Janet over the top of them.

"They're visiting Martin," Nick said.

"Really? Why?" the man replied.

"Martin is an old friend," Stuart said. "Who are you?"

The man looked amused as he glanced over at Stuart. "I'm Nick's friend. Jim Rodgers is the name. What else do you want to know?"

Stuart looked as if he had a great many questions for the man, but Martin interrupted.

"Stop whispering, all of you," he said. "Nick, why are you here?"

Nick glanced at Jim and then sighed. "I was hoping I might borrow a few pounds," he said. "Jim and I were going to go and get some dinner somewhere, but my bank card still isn't working properly."

Martin frowned. "You've had nothing but trouble since you've been here," he said. "First your car broke down and then your bank card stopped working. Maybe you need to go back to Manchester and get everything sorted."

"I would, if the garage here would get my car repaired," Nick told him. "As it is, I'm a bit stuck. I don't think your car would get all the way to Manchester, even if you didn't mind me taking it."

"Which I most certainly do," Martin snapped. "And I haven't any more money to lend you, either. You've had over two hundred pounds off me since you've been here."

Nick flushed. "I told you, I forgot to tell the bank that I was going to be in Doveby Dale. When I tried to use the card here, they cancelled it because they thought it had been stolen. Now I'm trying to get a new card, but until I do, I don't have any access to my money."

"I suppose your good friend, Jim, is just going to have to help you, then, isn't he?" Martin said.

"He already owes me a good deal more than two hundred pounds," Jim said. "I'm running low on funds myself, now."

"Perhaps you'll have to cut your visit short," Janet suggested.

Nick looked over at Martin. "If his health was better, I might, but I'm awfully worried about him," he told Janet in a whisper.

"There's plenty of food in the kitchen," Martin said. "You two can stay home and cook something for your dinner. You don't have to eat in fancy restaurants all the time."

Nick nodded. "We'll do that, then, after we've finished running a few errands."

"What sort of errands?" Martin asked. "You've been out all day, running errands."

"Don't you worry about that," Nick replied. "We'll be on our way, and when we get back I'll cook something for all three of us." He nodded at Jim and the pair made their way out of the room.

"It was nice meeting you," Janet called after them.

Martin laughed. "It wasn't, though, was it? He can be very unpleasant, that boy. It's only because I remember the unhappy eight-year-old I once knew that I put up with it."

"You shouldn't lend him money," Stuart suggested. "You'll never it get back."

"Oh, I know, but I'm only lending him his own inheritance. He's getting one of my bank accounts, you see, and every time he asks for money, I take it out of that account," Martin laughed.

"What's wrong with his car?" Janet wondered.

"The brakes failed," Martin replied. "I know he's telling the truth on that, because I was with him when it happened. We nearly hit a stone wall, and we had to have the car towed to the garage. I'm not sure why the repair is taking so long, though."

"Maybe you should ring the garage and find out," Janet suggested. She hadn't liked the man at all, and she was highly suspicious of everything he'd told them.

"If he doesn't get the car back soon, I might just do that. I miss having my car here whenever I want to go anywhere," Martin told her. "For now, well, in some ways it's nice to have him around."

"We should go," Janet said, getting to her feet. "Thank you so much for your time. I enjoyed learning more about Alberta."

"I enjoyed talking about her and the past. It doesn't seem as if anyone is interested in what happened all those years ago. Nick isn't, anyway."

"Do you know if Alberta has any family left anywhere?" Janet asked.

Martin shook his head. "I believe her parents were both only children. There might be some distant relatives somewhere, but I've no idea where you'd even start to look for them."

Janet frowned. She really wanted to go through the box of letters and diaries that Alberta had left behind. Joan was the only obstacle. But maybe the letters themselves would hold a clue as to where to find Alberta's family. That might be an argument worth trying with Joan.

"Thank you for your time," Stuart said. "Would you mind terribly if I drove Janet all around the farm before we go? I told her a lot about it on the way over and I'm sure she'd enjoy looking around."

"I would, indeed," Janet said.

"Drive wherever you'd like," Martin told them. "There's nothing much to see now, though. As I said, I'm not planting anything and I don't have many animals left."

"It will still be interesting to see the layout," Janet told him. "I'm fascinated by everything about Doveby Dale and its history."

"Take your time and drive all the way around, then," Martin said. "From the top of the hill, you can see back across the whole farm. You may even be able to see Doveby House from up there."

"Really? I can't wait," Janet replied. She picked up the candleholder. "And thank you again for this. I'll find somewhere special to keep it back at Doveby House."

"You're very welcome. As I said, I like the idea of one of them being there," Martin said.

He led Janet and Stuart back through the farmhouse and opened the front door for them. Nick and Jim were standing near Stuart's car, talking together.

"I thought you had to be somewhere," Martin shouted at his stepson.

"We do, but we had to ring someone to check the arrangements," Nick called back.

Martin shrugged. "Always rushing off and then going nowhere," he muttered under his breath.

Janet watched as the two men climbed into the old car that was parked next to Stuart's. It didn't seem to want to start, but eventually it coughed to life. Nick drove away, giving them a bit of a wave as he pulled onto the road.

"Thanks again for everything," Stuart said to Martin. "I'm going to make a point of visiting you more often."

"You're always welcome," Martin replied. "And you are, too," he added, nodding at Janet. "It's always nice to have a pretty woman around the place."

Janet flushed and then thanked the man before following Stuart to the car. As they began to drive away, she waved to Martin, who was still standing in the farmhouse's doorway.

"That was interesting," she said after a minute.

"It was, wasn't it?" Stuart replied. "I don't like Nick and I don't trust him."

"Was he one of the men at the garden centre?"

"That's the problem. I don't think he was, but I do think Jim was one of them."

"That's odd. Maybe Nick was waiting in the car?"

"That's one possibility, I suppose. Let's see what we can find on our drive."

Stuart drove slowly along the dirt road that surrounded the farm. As far as Janet could see, there was nothing there but neglected fields. When they reached the top of a small hill, Stuart stopped the car.

"We should be able to see the whole farm from here, or most of it, anyway," he told Janet.

They climbed out of the car and Stuart pulled binoculars out of his glove box. While he took a long and slow look around, Janet tried to find Doveby House in the distance.

"I can't see anything but empty fields," she said after a minute.

"Look down there," Stuart said, handing Janet the binoculars. "Just to the left of the large tree and to the right of the farmhouse. Does that look as if someone has been preparing the ground for planting?"

Janet trained the glasses on the spot she thought Stuart was talking about. "I suppose it might," she said slowly. "But it really doesn't look all that different to the fields all around it, at least to me."

Stuart sighed. "I think you might be right. Maybe I'm just seeing what I want to see. If you look a little bit further to the left, you can see Doveby House, anyway."

Janet followed his directions and then grinned. "It is Doveby House," she exclaimed. "Although it looks really tiny from up here, even with the binoculars."

"Let's go," Stuart said. "Maybe we'll spot something on the way back down."

"There's something," Janet said a moment later. "What is that?"

A huge cloud of dust seemed to be rapidly approaching their car. Stuart pulled over to the side of the road and stopped. A moment later Nick stopped Martin's car next to him.

"What are you doing out here?" Nick demanded.

"Martin said it was okay if I drove Janet around the farm. She's interested in the history of Doveby Dale and in how this farm used to operate," Stuart replied.

"Yeah, well, I think it would be best if you left now. Martin means well, but he's not doing as well mentally as he is physically. He probably forgot what a mess these roads have become. I'd hate for your car to get damaged out here."

"The roads haven't been that bad," Stuart said. "Is Martin okay?"

"He's fine, really, he just needs some looking after. That's why I'm here," Nick told him.

"That's very kind of you," Stuart said. "We'll be on our way, then."

"You should turn around and go back the way you came," Nick said. "The road on this side isn't as good as it is on the other side."

"I'm sure we'll be fine. Turning around on such a narrow road would be difficult."

"But easier than trying to get through what's ahead. Turn around now," Nick said firmly.

"But you've just come up that way," Janet pointed out. "If you can manage in Martin's car, we should be good in this one."

"As I said, you need to turn around," Nick replied. "There's no need to argue over this. Just turn around."

Stuart looked at Janet. She shrugged. They didn't seem to have much choice but to obey, especially when Nick reversed his car so that he was blocking the road in front of them.

"Can you get turned around here?" Janet asked.

"It's going to be difficult," Stuart said. "But I don't think we have much choice."

"Why doesn't Nick want us going that way?" Janet wondered as Stuart began turning the car around.

"I don't know, but I'm determined to find out," Stuart replied.

"We need to go to the police," Janet said. "Robert can take a look around, no matter what Nick says."

"Yes, but first we have to get out of here." It took several minutes for Stuart to successfully turn the car around on the narrow road. He only just missed a small tree and a large rock. When they were finally on their way back towards the farmhouse, he glanced at Janet.

"Nick's following us," he said tightly.

"Yes, I see that," Janet replied. "I wonder where Jim is?"

She didn't have to wonder for long. As they approached the farmhouse, she noticed Jim standing near the front door.

"I wonder what they're up to," Stuart said as Nick pulled up next to the man. Jim climbed into the car and then Nick continued to follow them towards the main road.

"Where should I go from here?" Stuart asked when he and Janet finally reached the main road.

"I think we should go and see Robert immediately," Janet replied.

"I'm inclined to agree, but I'd rather not drive straight there from here, not with those two following behind."

Janet nodded. "I'd rather you didn't drive back to Doveby House, either. I know they'll find us easily enough if they want to, but I'd rather not lead them straight to our homes."

"Let's drive out to Little Burton," Stuart suggested. "Maybe Nick and Jim won't follow us."

Chapter 6

Stuart pointed the car towards Little Burton. Janet couldn't help but look back to see what Nick was doing.

"They're following us," she said with a sigh.

"Maybe they're just going the same way we are," Stuart replied. "We'll visit the shops in Little Burton. Hopefully, they'll just keep going."

There was a small parade of shops in the centre of the tiny village. Stuart pulled into the oversized car park and stopped his car. Janet tried not to be obvious about it as she watched Nick and Jim drive past them.

"I think I need a cuppa," Stuart said.

"I don't know where we can get one here," Janet frowned. "Unless you want to go over to the pub."

"If we go to the pub, I'm going to want something much stronger than tea. Maybe we could just have a short walk around the shops. That confrontation with Nick was upsetting."

Janet nodded. "I agree, but we don't want to spend too long out here. We need to get back to Doveby Dale to talk to Robert."

"I know. I just need a few minutes."

They both got out of the car. Janet found herself looking with interest at the antique shop in the centre of the row. She knew the owner of the small antique shop in Doveby Dale. William Chalmers had been arrogant and rude when she'd first met him, but he'd worked hard over the past six months or more to make friends in Doveby Dale. He's also begun hinting that he might like to be more than just friends with Janet, but they'd both agreed to take things very slowly.

Janet had been at William's shop one day recently when Jonathan Hamilton-Burke had paid him a visit. Jonathan had informed them that he was opening his own antique shop in Little Burton, news that had worried William. This was the first time Janet had been in Little Burton since, and she was surprised to see that the shop appeared to be open for business.

"I didn't realise the antique shop was already open," she told Stuart.

"I didn't realise Little Burton had an antique shop," Stuart replied. "I hope it doesn't hurt William's business."

"I met the owner. Apparently he inherited a huge house full of antiques and he's simply going to sell them all here. I suppose that means that everything he makes will be profit, doesn't it?"

"Aside from the cost of renting the shop and paying for things like electricity and whatnot."

"I understand he bought the entire building. I suppose he's planning to rent out the other spaces, but he hasn't managed that yet."

"Should we do some antique shopping, then?" Stuart asked.

"If the owner is here, I wonder if he'll remember me," Janet said.

"Ah, hello," Jonathan said from behind a long counter at the back of the large shop. "Welcome. Was there something you were looking for specifically, or are you just trying to find something that catches your eye?"

"We were just driving past and stopped on impulse," Janet told him.

The man barely glanced at her, and clearly didn't remember that he'd met her before. He looked Stuart up and down and then sighted. "If you want more information about any of the pieces, just ask." He then went back to flipping through the magazine that was on the counter in front of him.

Janet glanced at Stuart and then shrugged. When she'd first met the man, he'd told her that he was planning to hire staff to actually work in the shop. It seemed obvious that customer service was not the man's strength, but maybe whoever he'd hired had rung in sick today or something.

She turned her attention to the items on display. There were a few nice pieces, but a lot of it looked like inexpensive modern pieces rather than antiques. A lovely small table caught Janet's eye. The tag on it said "table," and nothing more. A quick check of a few other tags revealed more of the same. Across the room, she saw Stuart shaking his head.

"The tags aren't very helpful," he told Janet as they crossed paths. I thought Mary might like that bowl, but the tag simply says 'bowl,' with no description or price."

"The tags are all the same, completely useless," Janet replied. "I think I've seen enough."

"Do you think that we should ask for a few prices, just to let William know?"

Janet frowned and then glanced at Jonathan. He appeared to be reading an article in his magazine, his lips moving along with the words.

"No, let's just get out of here," she said. "William can come and see the place for himself. I'm pretty sure Jonathan won't recognise him, either."

They were back in the car before Stuart burst out laughing. "What sort of shop does the man think he's running? I can't imagine he's going to get much business with things done that way."

"It was definitely odd, but I believe he has plenty of money. I got the impression that the shop was just something he was doing for fun, so maybe he doesn't care whether it's successful or not."

"Well, unless he makes some changes, I can't see it being successful."

"There weren't very many nice things, anyway, whatever he's charging. I'd suggest that his grandfather didn't have very good taste, if everything in there truly did come from his grandfather's estate."

"Let's get back to Doveby Dale. I'm ready to talk to Robert now."

The village police station had once been a small two-room cottage. Now the front of the cottage held a desk and chair for Susan Garner, the friendly receptionist who was in her mid-forties. She worked a regular schedule at the station, while Robert moved back and forth between Doveby Dale and Little Burton during the week. As the station was usually quiet, Susan spent her spare time knitting. She was very talented, and Janet and Joan had several of the items she'd made on display in Doveby House. They were very popular with their guests, and the sisters regularly dropped off money and picked up more items from the woman.

"Good afternoon," Susan said brightly as Janet and Stuart walked into the station. "I've a nice big pile of blankets that I've just finished. I'm sure you won't want them now until autumn, though, will you?"

Janet smiled. "I'll take a few, certainly. Even in the heat of summer, the nights can have a chill, and maybe we can encourage our guests to start thinking about their Christmas shopping while they're here. Your blankets would make wonderful Christmas gifts."

"Tell that to my family," Susan laughed. "I've made so many blankets for everyone that I've been told I'm not allowed to make any more. Even my mother doesn't want any more, and she's always cold."

Janet grinned. "Our guests seem to really appreciate them. If I find they aren't selling, I'll let you know, but for now we're more than happy to keep taking them."

"And I'm more than happy for you to have them. I've no more room for anything else at home. But that isn't why you're here, is it? What can we do for you?" Susan asked.

"Is Robert available?" Janet wondered.

"He's been on the telephone all afternoon, chasing down some stolen property. I think he'll be happy to be interrupted." Susan picked up the telephone on her desk and pressed a button. A moment later the door behind her opened and Robert stuck his head out.

"Hello, hello. Come on back," he said.

Janet followed Stuart into the tiny office that always made her slightly claustrophobic. Robert settled in behind his desk while Janet and Stuart took chairs opposite him.

Constable Robert Parsons was somewhere in his twenties, with brown hair and eyes. Janet was very fond of the young man. He frequently visited the bed and breakfast to check on the sisters, although Janet wasn't sure how much his visits were motivated by the treats that Joan baked rather than anything else.

"What can I do for you today?" he asked, his pen poised over a notebook.

Stuart looked at Janet and then sighed. "I wasn't sure if we should bother you or not, but Janet thought we should," he said.

Robert looked at Janet and smiled. "Janet is usually right about such things."

Stuart nodded. "It's probably nothing, though, and I don't want to get anyone in trouble."

"I don't make it a habit of arresting people without a proper investigation," Robert told him. "Why don't you tell me the whole story and we'll go from there?"

Stuart still looked uncomfortable, but he didn't object further. "I was at the garden centre the other day and I overheard two men talking," he told the police constable. "It sounded as if they were discussing the planting and cultivating of illegal plants."

Robert made a few notes and then looked at Stuart. "What plants, exactly?" He made more notes as Stuart told him. "Can you remember their exact words?" was Robert's next question.

Stuart did his best, but Janet couldn't help but feel at his reply was somewhat vague. "I should have written it all down or something," he said at the end. "At the time I was so surprised by what I was hearing that I wasn't thinking clearly."

"Were the two men people that you know?" Robert asked.

"No, but I recognised the car they were driving," Stuart told him.

Robert raised an eyebrow. "Are you certain?"

"It was Martin Lawley's car. It's quite distinct."

"But Martin wasn't with the men?"

"He might have been waiting in the car, I suppose," Stuart replied. "I was too far away to tell."

"As far as I know, Martin lives alone," Robert said. "I'm not sure why he'd be driving two other men around the village."

"His stepson is staying with him right now. His name is Nick Berry, and he has a friend staying there as well. His name is Jim Rodgers," Stuart said.

"How do you happen to know that?" Robert wondered.

"We, ah, went and visited Martin today," Stuart replied.

"Really? Why?"

"I wanted to meet him," Janet said. "I wanted to ask him about Alberta Montgomery. He's one of the few people around who actually knew her."

"And the timing of your visit has nothing to do with what Stuart is telling me?"

Janet flushed. "Sort of," she said. "Stuart told me the whole story, and when he'd done so, I realised that Martin was probably old enough to remember Alberta. We couldn't see any harm in paying the man a short visit."

"You weren't concerned that you might be walking into some sort of illegal drug-manufacturing operation?"

"Martin would never allow such a thing on his land," Stuart said firmly. "If his stepson is growing anything, it's without Martin's knowledge."

"Was his stepson one of the men at the garden centre?"

"I don't think so, but I think his friend, Jim Rodgers was one of them," Stuart replied. "And I wouldn't be surprised to learn that Nick is involved. He and his friend were both behaving very suspiciously when we were at the farm." He told Robert about their visit and the drive they took after it.

"Again, didn't you think you might be in some danger? I'm sure I've told you before not to get involved in these things," Robert said to Janet. "Men and women who get involved in the drug trade tend to put little value on human lives."

Janet shivered. "We didn't think we were in any danger. Martin told us we were welcome, and Joan knew where we were."

"If Martin doesn't know what's happening, then he wouldn't have any reason to discourage your visit. I'm going to have to find an excuse to pay Martin a visit myself, it seems."

"I don't know if you actually need to visit," Stuart said.

"Nick chased you off the farm for one reason or another," Robert said. "I really want to find out why."

"Just don't tell Nick or his friend that we sent you," Janet said. "They already don't like us."

"Don't you worry about that. I'll find a plausible reason to visit. I'll probably wait for tomorrow, though. If I turn up only a few hours after you two left, that might make Nick suspicious."

"That's probably wise," Stuart said.

"I can start doing some investigative work from here. I'm going to find out as much as I can about Nick Berry and Jim Rodgers before I visit."

"We'll let you get started, then," Janet said, getting to her feet.

Stuart followed suit. "I hope we aren't wasting your time," he said hesitantly.

"You should always pass your concerns along to me in cases like this. If I investigate and it turns out to be nothing, I won't consider it a waste of my time, I assure you. Anyway, it's good to know that Martin has guests who are using his car." He escorted Janet and Stuart back into the outer room before saying his goodbyes.

"Here you are," Susan said, handing Janet a large box. "Four more blankets. I've put a note on the top with the prices I'd suggest for each of them. The white one is a bit more, as it was a very complicated pattern. I don't think I'll make another like it, at least not in a hurry."

Stuart insisted on carrying the box out to the car. He loaded it into his boot and then drove Janet home. At Doveby House, he carried the box inside for her as well. She only just remembered her candleholder as she climbed out of the car.

"Thank you for coming with me today," he told Janet as he set the box down on a couch.

"You're more than welcome," she replied. "I hope Robert investigates and doesn't find anything."

"I hope he doesn't find anything drug-related, but I wouldn't mind if he found something that meant that Nick and Jim left. I don't think Martin likes having them around."

"I agree that he didn't seem very happy about their visit, but I'm not sure he should be on his own, either."

"He's fine on his own," Stuart said firmly.

Janet let him out and then locked the door behind him.

"What have you brought home now?" Joan asked from behind her.

"The candleholder is from Martin Lawley. He used to make them for Alberta. The box is full of blankets from Susan."

"We could do with a few more," Joan said. "They've been very popular lately."

"I hope we don't owe Susan any money. I didn't give her any when I saw her."

"We don't. I paid her last week," Joan assured her. "But let's see what she's sent this time."

The blankets were all beautiful, especially the white one. "I've never seen such gorgeous knitting," Janet sighed as she spread the blanket out on the couch.

"That one is especially nice," Joan agreed. "I think we should try getting more for it than Susan suggested. I'm sure she must have put a lot of time and effort into it."

Janet agreed, and then the pair redid the display table at the back of the room, with the white blanket taking centre stage. Janet was amending the price list when she heard the front door open behind her.

Chapter 7

"I don't know that we want to stay for the whole weekend," Judith Armstrong said.

"Oh, dear, I'm sorry to hear that," Janet replied.

"We'll expect a full refund if we do go," Malcolm snapped.

Janet took a deep breath and then replied very carefully. "Of course, we'll refund you for any nights that you choose not to spend with us," she said. "Will you be leaving in the morning, then?"

"We haven't said we're leaving for sure," Judith replied. "We'll let you know."

Janet thought about arguing, but decided it wasn't worth it. She'd even be happy to give the unpleasant couple the full refund that Malcolm wanted if they'd just leave.

"Where would you recommend for dinner?" Malcolm asked. "I'm tired of driving around and I want to eat somewhere nearby."

Janet hesitated. The small café that was nearest to Doveby House would be perfect, but she didn't want to make Todd's and Ted's lives miserable.

"There's an excellent French restaurant near the centre of the village," she said after a moment.

Judith shook her head. "I don't like French food," she said. "Never mind. We'll find something on our own."

She turned and stomped up the stairs with Malcolm behind her. Janet briefly considered ringing the café to warn them, just in case that was where the couple ended up, but she decided against it. Todd and Ted had been in the restaurant business for a long time. No doubt they could handle difficult customers.

The door opened again a moment later. "Good afternoon," Janet greeted the Fordhams.

"Good afternoon," Carol replied. "But what do you have there?"

"We just received some new blankets from the woman who knits them," Janet explained. Carol had already expressed interest in one of the blankets. Now she took a closer look at the new arrivals.

"This is exquisite," she said, running a hand down the white one. "It must have taken ages."

"Susan is very good," Janet replied. "But she did mention that this one was very hard work."

"I have to have it," Carol said. "Unless it's crazy expensive, which it probably should be."

Janet told her the price that Joan had suggested.

"Sold!" Carol laughed. She opened her handbag and dug out her wallet. "I even have the cash, because we went to the bank this afternoon."

Janet put the money into her pocket. "When I saw that blanket, I knew it would go quickly," she told Carol. "But I didn't expect it to go that quickly."

"What do you have there?" Judith demanded.

Janet frowned. She hadn't noticed the Armstrongs coming back down the stairs.

"Isn't it gorgeous?" Carol asked, holding up her new blanket.

"If you like that sort of thing, I suppose," Judith sniffed. "I prefer unique items to mass-produced products in that way."

"That blanket was knitted by hand by a local woman," Janet said.

"Is that what she told you?" Judith asked. "Because I don't

believe it. They churn these things out in factories in China for pennies and then pass them along to unsuspecting westerners who can't tell the difference."

"I can tell the difference," Janet said. "I used to knit a great deal and I can tell the difference between machine knitting and hand knitting. I can assure you that this blanket and everything on this table was all made by hand."

Judith glanced over the table and then shook her head. "I'm not saying it isn't well done, but Malcolm and I have travelled a great deal. I've seen the factories where they make these things. You mustn't feel too foolish. Many so-called experts can be taken in by some of the better quality items."

Janet bit her tongue and counted slowly to ten in her head. Arguing with guests was never a good idea, and she really didn't want to give Malcolm and Judith any excuse for demanding their money back.

"Darling, we need to get ready for dinner," Edgar said.

Carol nodded. She gave Janet an uncertain look and then left the room with her blanket. Janet hoped that Carol's love for the blanket hadn't been diminished by Judith's comments.

"I hope I haven't upset her," Judith said with a nasty smirk.

"I'm sure she's fine," Janet lied. She went to work rearranging things on the table to fill the space that the white blanket had formerly occupied. After a moment, Judith turned and walked away.

"Let's go and try to find somewhere with edible food," she said to her husband. The pair walked out the front door, leaving it open behind them.

When Carol and Edgar came down a few minutes later, Janet was quick to reassure the woman.

"I can take you to meet Susan if you'd prefer," she offered. "Or I can give you your money back, if you're not still in love with the blanket."

"I do still love it, but I'm not sure," Carol replied. "One of my favourite things about it was that it was handmade. If it isn't, well, it simply isn't as special as I thought."

"It's definitely handmade. As I said, you can have your money back if you're unsure," Janet replied. "I've no doubt it will find another buyer almost immediately, and Susan did say she wasn't going to make any more like it because it took too much time and energy."

"Did she? I'll have to think about it," Carol said. She and Edgar left a moment later, with Carol still frowning over her decision.

Feeling angry with Judith, Janet went to find her sister. Joan was in the kitchen, making them both dinner.

"You look upset," she commented as Janet walked into the room.

Janet repeated the conversation that Joan had missed, leaving Joan shaking her head. "I do wish the Armstrongs would hurry up and leave already," she said when Janet was done. "Maybe if we offered them their money back, they'd go."

"They don't deserve their money back. In fact, they should be made to pay extra for being so difficult," Janet fumed.

"Yes, well, have some chicken and leek pie and a slice of jam roly-poly and you'll feel better."

Janet couldn't argue with her sister, and Joan was right, she did feel better after she'd eaten. Once the dinner dishes were loaded into the dishwasher, she and Joan settled down in front of the television.

"How's Michael?" Janet asked during a commercial break.

"He's fine. We'd made plans to have dinner together tonight, back when I thought we were only going to have one set of guests tonight. Once the Armstrongs arrived, I cancelled our plans."

"You should have gone anyway," Janet told her. "I can handle the guests on my own for a few hours. Anyway, they've all gone out."

"Yes, but you shouldn't have to deal with them on your own if they are here. Michael doesn't mind. Apparently there is some football match on the telly tonight."

Janet laughed. Joan had never shown any interest in men in her younger days, even while Janet had gone through several boyfriends. Both sisters had been surprised, then, when Michael Donaldson, who lived in the semi-detached house across the street, had begun to court Joan. After a shaky start, the pair had settled into a comfortable relationship, but Joan usually tried to avoid making plans with the man when the bed and breakfast was fully booked. The entire business had been Joan's idea and Janet knew that Joan felt guilty whenever she left Janet to deal with their guests.

"Anyway, I'm going to see him on Monday, after both sets of guests have gone," Joan told her. "We're going to spend the day together, touring stately homes."

"That sounds fun for you, but maybe not for Michael," Janet suggested.

"It was his idea. He suggested it. He said he thought I would need a break after having had so many guests lately, especially as we've so many more coming in the weeks ahead."

"Well, I hope you have fun," Janet said.

They watched a few old American sitcoms and then moved into the sitting room to wait for their guests to return home.

Edgar and Carol were back first.

"I've been thinking about it and I think I might not keep the blanket," Carol said. "I mean, I do like it a lot, but I don't really need any more blankets."

"That's fine," Janet assured her, mentally cursing Judith. "If you bring it back down now, I can give you your money back immediately."

Carol nodded. "I think that might be for the best," she said.

She headed up to her room while Joan went to get the money out of the small safe in her bedroom. While they were both gone, the door opened again.

"I can't imagine how you live here," Judith said as she stomped into the house. "We've yet to find anywhere with edible food or decent service."

"You didn't like the French restaurant?" Janet asked.

"We didn't go there. We thought we should simply try to the little café up the road," Judith replied.

"And you didn't like it?"

"It was dire. The food was incredibly ordinary and the waitress was stupid. In the end, we had to demand to speak to the manager," Malcolm said. "And he wasn't much better than the waitress had been."

"That is a shame. I've always had good service and very good food there," Janet said.

"In the end, the manager only took one of our meals off the bill. He said since we'd eaten everything, we mustn't have been too unhappy. I told him that we were simply starving after a most unsatisfactory lunch," Judith said.

Poor Todd, Ted, and Stacey, Janet thought. "Perhaps you'd be better off somewhere closer to Derby," she suggested.

"Perhaps. But we're too tired to think about that right now. For now, we just need to go up to our tiny little bedroom and try to sleep," Malcolm said.

Judith crossed to the table behind Janet. "It's quite chilly in our room," she said. "An extra blanket would help."

"We have more blankets upstairs. I'll walk up with you and get you one," Janet replied.

"I can just take one of these," Judith said. "I did rather like that white one, though. I don't suppose the woman who bought it changed her mind after I pointed out that it wasn't what she thought it was?"

"Even if she had, you'd have to purchase it if you wanted it in your room," Janet told her.

"How much did you charge her for it?"

Janet told her what Carol had paid for the blanket.

"That's a lot of money for what it was, but under the circumstances, if she does decide she doesn't want it, I'll buy it from you for that price," Judith said.

"I'll let you know," Janet said, determined to keep the beautiful white blanket far away from the horrible woman.

"There's no need for that," Carol said from the doorway. "I can see now that you were just saying horrible things about the blanket so that I would return it and you could snap it up. Well, I won't give you the satisfaction. I'm keeping this blanket and I'm going to love having it."

Judith stared at her for a minute and then shrugged. "As I said, it's cold in our room. That was the only reason I wanted another blanket. I would have thought, with the price we're paying for our tiny room, that we would have adequate heating."

"You can adjust the temperature in your room yourself," Joan said as she walked back into the room. "I showed you how to do that when I took you to your room."

"I don't remember that," Judith snapped.

"I can show you again now, after I've found you some more blankets," Joan offered.

"We won't need more blankets if we can adjust the temperature, will we?" Edgar said.

"Come along, then, let me show you again," Joan said. She turned and walked out of the room. After a moment, Malcolm and Judith followed.

"I'm sorry," Carol told Janet. "I let that awful woman's lies make me question my own eyes. I can see that the blanket was handmade by someone with tremendous talent. No doubt she could see that as well. I promise you I will treasure this blanket."

"It truly is lovely. I'm just glad you're going to appreciate it," Janet said.

When Joan came down a short while later, she was shaking her head. "Those two are determined to get their money back, one way or another," she said. "I checked their room again after they went out for dinner and I found that the control knob for their thermostat had been removed. I found it in the desk drawer and replaced it. No doubt they thought that when I went up with them I would find it missing and would be forced to compensate them for not having heating in their room."

Janet shook her head. "I wish I could have seen their faces when you opened the door and the knob was in place."

Joan laughed. "It just about made up for the trouble they're causing," she said. "But now I'm going to bed. I can't help but hope that they'll decide to leave tomorrow."

In her bedroom, Janet snuggled up with Aggie. "I really don't like our guests," she confided to her pet. "Edgar and Carol Fordham are lovely, but Malcolm and Judith Armstrong are terrible."

"Yooowwll," Aggie replied.

"Does that mean they're criminals?" Janet said. Aggie had been useful in the past at identifying criminals, although Janet hadn't mentioned that skill to her sister, at least not yet.

Aggie shrugged and rolled over on her side. As she began to lick her paw, Janet wondered about the men that Stuart had overheard at the garden centre.

"What about Nick Berry?" she asked.

Aggie kept licking and didn't reply.

"Okay, what about Jim Rodgers?"

"Yoooowwwlll," Aggie said.

"Martin Lawley?"

Aggie went back to her grooming.

"Martin mentioned his neighbours. What were their names?" Janet muttered. "Jasper Jones?"

Aggie switched to licking a different paw.

"What about Joseph Jones? Janet tried.

"Yooooowwwlll," Aggie said.

Janet lay back on the pillows and tried to think. If Aggie was right, the two men in the garden centre were probably Jim and Joseph. Now Janet just had to find a way to let Robert know which men he should be investigating.

Chapter 8

Janet helped Joan with breakfast the next morning, serving all of their guests in the dining room. The added distance from the Armstrongs made them slightly more bearable. They limited their complaints to the quality of the orange juice, something that Joan purchased in a carton, which was just as well. Janet wouldn't have tolerated any complaints about her sister's cooking, not when she knew how wonderful it was. Once both couples left for the day, the sisters cleaned the guest rooms.

"You start on the Fordhams' room," Joan told Janet. "It's my turn to deal with whatever the Armstrongs have left for us today."

She opened the door and Janet held her breath. "It isn't as bad as yesterday," Janet said happily. "We need to make sure they eat in the dining room every morning."

When the chores were out of the way, the pair ate a light lunch together. After that, Janet curled up in the library with a book. She quickly found that she couldn't focus, however, as she couldn't stop thinking about her conversation with Aggie the previous evening.

"I need an outing," she told Joan a short while later.

Joan was busy baking biscuits. "I have a prescription that needs collecting from the chemist's. I was going to go later, but if you're that bored, you can go and get it for me."

"I will, and maybe I'll go and see William while I'm there," Janet replied. She and the antiques dealer had agreed to take things slowly, but it had been weeks since they'd spoken. Janet couldn't help but wonder if William had found someone else or if something was wrong. She'd been unable to work up the nerve to ring him, but if she was going to be in the shop next door to his, well, it would be rude not to visit.

Janet went up to her room to get ready to go out. She ran a comb through her shoulder-length grey bob and then patted some powder on her nose. A fresh coat of lipstick finished her efforts. "You'll have to do," she told her reflection, patting a hip that was more rounded than she might have liked. Joan, even though she cooked and baked regularly, had always been slender. Janet, who rarely did either, tended to be a good deal curvier. While people always insisted that the sisters looked alike, Janet didn't agree. They did share the same hairstyle and blue eyes, but as far as Janet was concerned, that was where the resemblance ended.

"I'll be back soon," she told Joan as she collected the car keys from the kitchen drawer.

"No need to rush," Joan replied. "I'll plan dinner for six, if that suits you."

"I'm sure that will be fine, unless William asks me to have dinner with him."

"Let me know if you do make plans with William. Maybe I'll invite Michael over for your share of the roast chicken and apple crumble."

"If it's apple crumble for pudding, I'll be home," Janet laughed. "You know it's my favourite."

Joan grinned. "I thought you deserved a treat after having to deal with our guests this week."

"I do, at that, and so do you."

"It's a good thing I like apple crumble, then, isn't it?"

As Janet headed for the door, she tried to think. What was Joan's favourite pudding? Was she a terrible sister for not knowing? Joan knew hers because Joan was the one who always prepared their meals. There was no reason why Janet had to know Joan's choice, though. Joan could make her own favourite whenever she wanted it. Still feeling slightly unsettled, Janet drove into Doveby Dale and parked in the small car park for the shops.

"Ah, good afternoon," Owen Carter said from behind the counter at the chemist's shop. "How are you today?"

"I'm fine," Janet replied. She and her sister both liked the tall man who was in his late forties. He'd been sent to manage the shop when Michael Donaldson sold it to a large national chain. After dealing with some ill health, Owen was back to running the shop, and Janet couldn't remember the last time she'd been there when he hadn't been the one behind the counter. "How are you?"

"I'm very well, thank you."

"I'm here for Joan's prescription."

"Ah, yes, let me find that for you."

Janet looked around the shop for a few minutes while Owen searched through a large box. "This is a good price for tissues," she said. "I may have to buy a few boxes."

"It is a good price. We aren't carrying that brand anymore, so we're clearing them out. I have several more cases of them in the back, so I'd love it if you'd buy a few boxes."

"Can you give me a better price if I buy a whole case?" Janet asked, thinking that their guests seemed to go through an awful lot of tissues.

Owen named a price that seemed very reasonable to Janet. "Yes, please," she said.

"Here's Joan's prescription," he said. "If you can sign for it, I'll go and get your case of tissues."

Janet signed and then Owen loaded the large case into her boot for her.

"Thank you very much," she said. "I wasn't looking for tissues, but they'll definitely come in handy."

With Joan's bottle of tablets in her handbag, Janet looked over at the door to WTC Antiques. For a moment she thought about simply getting into the car and driving home. While she was arguing with herself, another car drove into the lot. Janet's heart skipped a beat when she recognised it as Martin's car. She stood very still, wishing she could make herself invisible as Nick and Jim climbed out of the car.

They ignored her and headed into the antique shop. Curiosity quickly overcame Janet's uncertainty about seeing William and she followed the pair as rapidly as she could.

"...to sell, maybe an entire household," Nick was saying as Janet walked into the shop.

William looked over at her and smiled brightly. "I'll be with you as quickly as I can," he called. William was a grey-haired man in his sixties. His suits all seemed to have been tailor-made for him, even though Janet knew that he wasn't as wealthy as he pretended to be. She also knew that he'd spent some time in prison for selling fake antiques at his shop in London. He still maintained his innocence, and Janet chose to believe him.

She nodded and began to look around. There were several new pieces scattered around the place. It wasn't her fault that the most interesting ones were closest to where William and Nick were talking.

"I'd be happy to make an appointment to come out and take a look at what you have," William told Nick. "But I'm very selective in what I purchase. If you're looking to clear an entire house, you would probably do better with Stanley Moore. He has a warehouse just outside of Derby and he'll be more willing to simply take everything off your hands."

"Maybe you could come out first and pick out the more valuable pieces," Nick suggested. "Then we could offload the rest on the warehouse guy."

"That might be an option," William said. "Let's start with an appointment for one day next week and then go from there."

Once that was set, Nick headed for the door. Jim didn't follow. "I have some coins," he told William. "Can you tell me if any of them are valuable?"

William nodded. "I'm not a coin expert, but I can probably tell you if they're anything special, at least."

Jim nodded and then pulled a handful of coins out of his pocket. William laid them out on the counter and looked at each one in turn.

"This one is worth two pounds," he said after a minute, handing the coin back to Jim. "It's a modern coin that must have been mixed up with the others."

Jim laughed. "I should be more careful, shouldn't I? I'd hate to accidently spend one of the others if it's truly valuable."

William nodded and then went back to studying the coins. "I don't think any of them are worth a fortune, but my friend the coin dealer would probably like a good look. Let me get you his details."

William walked to his desk near the back of the room. He jotted something down on a sheet of paper and then returned to where Jim was still standing. "Tell him I sent you," William said.

"Yeah, right, thanks," Jim replied. He turned and looked at Nick. "We should go."

"I'm waiting for you," Nick said.

Jim nodded and then scooped his coins off the counter. By the time he and Nick were out the door, William had crossed to Janet's side.

"I should probably start by telling you how sorry I am that I haven't been in touch," he said softly. "I've no real excuse, either, other than cold feet."

Janet flushed. "Cold feet?" she repeated.

William took her hands and waited until she looked into his eyes to reply. "Yes, cold feet. You're pretty and clever and, well, wonderful. I know we talked about taking things slowly and seeing where they went, but, well, I got scared. There, I've said it. I've always been terrible at relationships and I don't want to ruin everything. I love Doveby Dale and I want to stay here, and if I get things badly wrong with you, well, I know I'll have to go."

"So you don't want to be anything more than friends?" Janet asked.

"I don't know what I want," William told her. "That's why I haven't rung you in weeks. It's a stupid excuse and I..."

"Ah, good afternoon," a voice said from the doorway.

William dropped Janet's hands and they both looked at the man who'd just walked into the shop. He was probably in his mid-forties, with brown hair and eyes. He was wearing jeans and a grubby T-shirt, and Janet wondered what he wanted at an antique shop.

"I have a few coins I was hoping you could value for me," the man said.

"Really?" William replied. "Coins aren't my specialty, but today seems to be my day for looking at them."

"What do you mean?" the man asked, giving William a suspicious look.

"Just that you're the second person to ask me to look at coins today, that's all," William replied with a wave of his hand. "I'm sure it's just a coincidence, but I'll probably give you the same advice I gave him, which is to visit my friend in Derby who is an expert on the subject."

"Yeah, I can't get to Derby right now," the man said.

"I'm happy to take a look and give you my opinion, but I don't generally buy coins," William explained.

"Yeah, that's fine. I just want to know if I could get anything for them if I do find the time to get to Derby, that's all," the man replied.

He handed William a handful of coins and again William spread them out on the counter. This time Janet didn't have to pretend she wasn't watching.

"I can't give you an exact value on any of them, but I suggest you take them to my friend," William said after a few minutes. "These two in particular should be worth something, which isn't to say the others aren't."

The man nodded. "Are we talking hundreds of pounds or thousands of pounds?" he asked.

"Hundreds, certainly, but possibly those two could be worth as much as a thousand pounds or more each," William replied. "As I said, though, I'm not an expert."

"How about you give me five hundred pounds for the lot, then," the man suggested.

William hesitated and then shook his head. "I'm afraid I simply don't know enough about coins to be sure," he said. "I could be mistaken about what you have. Let me give you the name and number for my friend in Derby."

"Nah, that's okay," the man said. "I'll take them to Little Burton. I've heard they'll buy anything at the antique shop there."

"Really? I didn't realise the shop there was even open yet," William replied. "Good luck to you, then."

The man looked slightly surprised before he gathered up his coins and strode out of the shop.

"That was odd," William said.

"What, that you were asked to look at coins by two customers in a row?" Janet wondered.

"That was a little bit odd, but it was stranger that both men had some of the same coins, one of which I thought was rather rare. Maybe I'm confusing it with something else, though. I probably should have taken him up on his offer. There was at least a thousand pounds worth of coins there, even if I'm only right about half of them."

"Could any of them have been counterfeit?" Janet asked.

"That was what I was wondering, especially with the duplicates that the two men had. That's why I said no, actually."

"Maybe you should go and talk to Robert about them."

"I don't think a few duplicate coins are a police matter," William replied. "Anyway, I don't even know who the first man was."

"I knew the first one," Janet told him. "He's called Jim Rodgers, and he's here visiting Martin Lawley, who has a farm between Doveby Dale and Little Burton."

"The second man was Joseph Jones," William told her. "His father, Jasper, shops here from time to time. He brought Joseph in a week or so ago and introduced us."

Janet frowned. "I've heard the name before," she said. "I don't like either man. I'm glad you didn't buy the coins. I don't trust either of them."

William nodded. "But we were talking about us," he said. "Maybe we should have dinner together one night soon and really talk."

"I'd like that," Janet replied. "Do you want to set a date and time now or do you want to ring me?"

"Let's set it now, otherwise I'll chicken out."

Janet laughed and then agreed to dinner on an upcoming Saturday evening.

"Do think about talking to Robert," she said as William walked her to the door. "There's something suspicious about those two men, I'm just not sure what it is."

William shrugged. "I get a lot of odd people in here," he said. "I don't want to start bothering Robert every time."

Janet swallowed a sigh as she walked back into the car park. She couldn't very well tell William that Aggie had warned her about the men, could she?

Chapter 9

As she walked back towards her car, she noticed that Martin's car was still in the car park. A quick look around suggested that Nick and Jim weren't in the newsagent's or the chemist's. Where could they have gone? There was a small coffee shop a short distance away, but the last Janet knew, it was closed. Next door to that was the police station. Surely the men weren't there.

Janet stopped at her car and looked at the coffee shop. It was just possible that there were lights on inside it. After a moment's hesitation, she decided to investigate. The police station was right next door. What could go wrong?

A small handwritten sign was taped to the door. It read "open." Janet pushed on the door and walked inside. Her first thought was that the new owners hadn't put any effort into the place. It looked exactly the same as it had under the previous ownership, which meant tired and in need of work.

At least the tables seemed to be clean, Janet thought as she looked around the room. Only one table was occupied. Nick and Jim were sitting with the man that William had identified as Joseph Jones. In such an empty room, Janet couldn't think of any reason why she should sit next to them, even though that was what she wanted to do.

"Oh, hi," a young girl with a blonde ponytail said as she walked out of the kitchen at the back of the room. "You can sit anywhere, I suppose, although it might be easier if you sit in the same section as the others, if you don't mind."

"Not at all," Janet assured her as she selected a table next to Nick and his friends.

"We've only just opened and we've a lot more work to do, but I can get you tea or coffee and we have a few cakes on offer today," the girl told her.

"Just tea for now," Janet said.

"Sure," the girl replied. She disappeared back into the kitchen, leaving Janet alone with the three men. They ignored her and carried on with their conversation.

"…three or four more days," Joseph said.

"That long? I'd really like to get out of this place. It's so quiet, it's creepy," Jim replied.

"I'd rather do it right," Joseph replied.

"I can't go back to Manchester before then, anyway," Nick said. "I'm still waiting for my car, remember?"

"You should have had it towed to a proper garage," Jim said. "The guy here doesn't know what he's doing."

"I actually think he's good," Nick replied. "But he has to wait for the right parts. He can't stock parts for every car in the country, you know."

"I'll bet he has parts for that piece of junk you've borrowed from your father," Jim laughed.

"He probably does," Nick chuckled. "But only because my father probably has the car in that garage every other week."

"Maybe you should help your father out and total that thing. Then he could get a new car," Jim suggested.

"Nah, he loves that car. He'd never forgive me if I did anything that damaged it."

"Maybe I should total it for him, then," Jim said.

"I told you I don't want you driving it anymore," Nick said. "You weren't meant to be driving it in the first place."

"Yeah, whatever," Jim shrugged. "Can we just get everything done and get out of here?"

"I think we'll be better off with the guy in Little Burton," Joseph said. "He didn't seem to have any idea what he was doing."

"Yeah, but he also didn't have any idea of the proper value for anything," Jim said.

"I'd rather get what we can and get out of town than worry about getting a bit more money and finding the police at my door," Joseph said.

"William Chalmers isn't going to ring the police," Jim told him. "I did my research. The man spent time in prison in London for misrepresenting what he was selling in his shop there. He'll be doing his best to avoid the police, I would imagine."

"Here we are, then," the young girl was back with Janet's tea. "Are you sure you don't want to try a slice of Victoria sponge or a piece of lemon cake?"

"I'll try the Victoria sponge," Janet said, more to get the girl to go away than out of a genuine desire for cake.

The girl nodded and then moved over to the other table. "Did you gentlemen need anything else?" she asked.

"No, we're done," Nick said. He got to his feet and pulled out his wallet. He handed the girl a twenty pound note and then headed for the door, his two friends on his heels.

Janet frowned. "I don't really want that cake," she said quickly, but the girl was already gone, back into the kitchen. Janet got to her feet and walked to the café's door. She could just see through the small window as Nick and Jim got into Martin's car and drove away. She couldn't see where Joseph had gone.

"Here we are, oh, there you are," the girl laughed. "I was afraid you'd left for some reason."

"Just stretching my legs," Janet muttered. She sat down and smiled as the girl put her cake on the table. "I'll need a fork," she said after a moment.

"Oh, yes, of course," the girl said. "I will get the hang of this eventually."

Janet ate her cake and sipped her tea, trying to decide what she wanted to do next. There was nothing in what she'd overheard to suggest that the three men were involved in anything to do with drugs, but she'd heard enough to make her think that they were up to something illegal.

"I hope everything was okay," the girl said as Janet finished.

"Oh, yes, it was fine," Janet lied. The tea had been lukewarm and weak, and the cake had been dry and tasted like shop-bought rather than homemade, but Janet decided to be polite, at least for this first visit. No doubt the girl would get plenty of complaints from the good people of Doveby Dale if things didn't improve over time.

Janet paid her bill and then walked from the café to the building next door. Susan looked surprised to see her.

"You don't normally visit me twice in two days," she said.

"And I didn't even bring your money," Janet sighed. "The white blanket sold immediately. Actually, there's a story to that."

Susan looked indignant when Janet told her what Judith had said about the blanket, and then laughed when Janet finished the story.

"Fancy telling her it wasn't handmade just so that she'd not want it anymore," Susan sighed. "She doesn't sound like a very nice person."

"She isn't, but as I said, I forgot to bring your money. I'll bring it next time. I was really hoping to see Robert today."

"He's in Little Burton today," Susan said apologetically. "I should have told you that when you first arrived."

"That's okay. I wanted to tell you the story about the blanket anyway," Janet assured her.

"I can ring Robert, if it's important."

"I don't know if it's important or not. Maybe just leave him a message and ask him to ring me when he has a few minutes to talk," Janet told her. "It may be nothing at all."

"Robert trusts your instincts, though. I'm sure he'll ring you later today."

"Thanks," Janet said. She spent the drive back to Doveby House trying to work out what the three men were plotting. If all three of them were involved, of course, that meant that Aggie had missed out identifying Nick. Janet hated to think that Aggie might have made a mistake.

"You were gone for ages," Joan said when Janet walked into the kitchen.

"I'm sorry. I stopped to talk to William and then I decided to get a cuppa at the coffee shop. It has new owners, so I thought I should pay them a visit."

"I hope you didn't feel as if you had to have some cake to go with your cuppa," Joan said, giving Janet a suspicious look.

"I bought a huge case of tissues," Janet dodged the question. "Owen was selling them off."

"We do seem to go through a lot of them," Joan said.

When Janet told her the price she'd paid, Joan smiled. "That is a good price, well done."

Janet flushed. She'd left nearly all of the work that went with running the bed and breakfast to Joan and she'd never really given any thought to their expenses or profits. Maybe it was time to start taking a more active role in the business, especially as Joan didn't seem to be tiring of it. It seemed as if the bed and breakfast was going to be a part of her foreseeable future.

"Dinner in half an hour," Joan told her.

Janet nodded and then went up to her room to freshen up. "Maybe I should start doing more of the cooking, as well," she said to Aggie.

"Yooowwl," Aggie replied.

Janet laughed. It seemed Aggie didn't like that idea, anyway. "But let's talk about the men I saw today," she began, determined to get Aggie's thoughts again. Aggie blinked at her and then curled up on the bed and shut her eyes.

"You can't go to sleep on me, not now," Janet said. Before Aggie could reply, Janet's mobile phone began to ring.

"Janet, my dear, it's Edward. How are you?"

Janet sat down on the bed and tried to think of how she wanted to respond. Edward Bennett had been their first guest, turning up on their doorstep before they were ready to open for business. He'd insisted that he had a booking made with the previous owner, Margaret Appleton. During his stay, he and Janet had had a romantic dinner together, and before he'd left he'd told her about himself. If he were to be believed, he worked for a top-secret government agency that had occasionally used Doveby House as a safe house. He'd told Janet that he was interested in pursuing a relationship with her, and then disappeared for months on end.

Whenever she'd decided that he was out of her life for good, he'd ring out of the blue or send her a present in the post. Some months ago his sister had come to stay with them, and before she'd left, she'd given Aggie to Janet on Edward's behalf. The man himself had even come and spent a weekend at the house, taking Janet to dinner a few times and helping her investigate a case of arson. In spite of all of that, Janet wasn't sure how she felt about the mysterious man, and she was starting to think that she'd be better off without him in her life.

"You're not answering, which means you're angry with me," Edward sighed. "I've been in South America, dealing with, well, some issues. I sent you a little something, to let you know I was thinking of you. I hope my little bunny friend arrived safely?"

"Yes, it did. Thank you," Janet said.

"You're very welcome," Edward replied. "And I don't blame you for being cross, either. I should find a way to ring you more often. Even better, I should come and see you regularly. I keep trying and things keep coming up that get in my way."

"Perhaps you need to try harder," Janet suggested.

Edward chuckled. "I definitely need to try harder," he agreed. "But tell me what's been happening in Doveby Dale since we last spoke."

"Nothing much," Janet replied. "Although Stuart thinks we might have someone trying to cultivate drugs here."

"It's the perfect place for that sort of operation. Robert Parsons can't keep an eye on every square inch of Doveby Dale and Little Burton on his own and there are acres and acres of unused farmland. You're close enough to Derby that it would be easy to set up a distribution network. I wouldn't be surprised if Stuart is right."

Janet sighed. "What a horrible idea."

"It is, rather. I like to think of Doveby Dale as a safe oasis in an increasingly unlawful world, although you've seen more than your fair share of criminal activity since you've been there, haven't you?"

"Yes, I believe we have, although things aren't as bad here as they are on the Isle of Man. My friend Bessie keeps getting caught up in murder investigations."

"Yes, Miss Cubbon does seem to have a knack for finding dead bodies, doesn't she, although I understand you found a few yourself when you were visiting her."

"I did, and I'd rather not think about it or talk about it," Janet said quickly.

"I understand," Edward told her. "But what's raised Stuart's suspicions, and what does Robert think?"

Janet took a deep breath and then launched into a complete account of everything that had happened since Stuart had first mentioned his visit to the garden centre to her. She didn't leave out anything except for the personal remarks that had passed between her and William.

"I'm a bit worried about William Chalmers," Edward said when she was done. "He's a little too smooth and charming. I don't like him."

"He's very nice, and I like him a lot," Janet retorted.

"That's what worries me. But that's beside the point. I suggest you tell Robert everything you've told me, if you haven't already. I can imagine a few different possibilities from what you've said, and none of them are good."

"Does it sound as if it could be drug cultivation to you?"

"No, that's one thing it doesn't sound like," Edward said. "But that doesn't mean that Robert shouldn't check the farm for that as well."

"I think Robert needs more help."

"He's doing an excellent job, and he has a lot of backup in Derby if he needs it," Edward assured her. "How's Joan?"

Janet was surprised by the sudden change in subject. "She's fine. Why do you ask?"

"I want to know all about your life," he replied. "I know it doesn't seem like it, but I do care a great deal about you."

"How's your sister?"

"Ah, Margaret is fine. Still trying to change the world, and probably doing a better job than I am with it."

"The next time you talk to her, tell her I said hello."

"I will do. I might send her back up to see you and Joan again soon, actually. She could do with another holiday."

"I think we're pretty well booked through the summer, but you'd have to talk to Joan about that."

"I suspect Margaret is too busy to take any time off during the summer anyway," Edward replied. "But maybe in the autumn. Maybe we could both come and stay. I haven't spent any real time with my sister in years."

"That would be nice," Janet said, wondering if she meant it. It was bad enough only getting to see Edward once in a very rare while. She didn't really want to have to share him with his sister on one of his visits.

"And now I must go," Edward sighed. "Make sure you talk to Robert today, won't you?"

"I'll try," Janet said. She sighed when she realised that Edward had already ended the call.

"That was frustrating," she told Aggie.

"Mmerrooww," Aggie replied.

Chapter 10

A quick look at the clock showed Janet that she was dangerously close to being late for dinner. She quickly combed her hair and then washed her hands before heading down the stairs.

"I thought maybe you'd fallen asleep," Joan said.

"Edward rang."

"Really? What did he want?"

Janet shrugged. "Just to say hello, I suppose. I told him all about Stuart and the men staying with Martin Lawley, though. He thinks I need to talk to Robert about the things I overheard today."

"You were already planning to talk to Robert, weren't you?"

"Well, yes, but I thought it was interesting that he agreed."

Joan served roast chicken with vegetables, mashed potatoes, and stuffing. Janet tried to stop herself from eating too much as she didn't want to spoil her pudding. The apple crumble was every bit as delicious as she'd hoped it would be.

The sisters were just heading for the television lounge when someone knocked on the door.

"Robert, this is a surprise," Janet said as she opened the door to the young police constable.

"Susan said you want to speak to me. As I'd spent a lot of today on the telephone for various reasons, I thought maybe I could talk to you in person," he replied.

"Well, you're just in time for apple crumble," Joan said. "Come on back to the kitchen and I'll put the kettle on, as well."

Robert dropped into a chair as Joan filled the kettle. Janet sat down opposite him. "I know you said you'd check into what Nick and his friend Jim are doing at Martin's farm, but I saw both of them today and, well, I overheard some things that I thought you should know."

As Joan put a plate of crumble in front of him, Robert pulled out a notebook. "Thank you," he said to Joan. "You spoil me when I come here."

"It's only leftover crumble," Joan replied. "And tea," she added as the kettle boiled.

"Tell me about your day, then," Robert said to Janet. "Start with breakfast and go from there, please."

Janet did as he'd asked, taking him through cleaning the guest rooms and then her trip into the village. When she was done, she took a long drink of the tea Joan had given her.

"That's all very interesting," Robert said. "I'm going to have to take a closer look at all three men, I think. Jasper Jones can be a prickly character, though, so I'll have to tread carefully when it comes to his son."

"I don't think we've met Jasper," Janet said.

"You'd remember him if you had," Robert replied. "But he doesn't leave his farm very often."

Robert finished his tea and crumble and then got to his feet. "Thank you for the information. I'm going to check on a few things tonight and then follow up on the rest tomorrow. From what you've said, the men are planning to be around for a few more days, at least."

"That's certainly how it sounded today," Janet agreed.

She and Joan walked to the front door with the man. As Janet opened it to let him out, Judith, who was standing on the step outside, screamed.

"Oh, my goodness. I wasn't expecting the door to open in my

face," she gasped. "I was just waiting for Malcolm. He's parking the car."

Robert frowned at her. "You look familiar," he said.

Judith shrugged. "This is our first visit to Doveby Dale, so I doubt we've met before. I'm Judith Armstrong."

"It's nice to meet you. I'm Constable Robert Parsons," he replied.

"Constable? As in police constable?" Judith asked, glancing into the car park.

"Yes that's right. I'm in charge of the local station," Robert told her.

"But what are you doing here?" Judith asked.

"Talking to Joan and Janet. I visit them regularly. I think it's important to keep track of what's happening in the village," Robert replied.

Judith nodded. "I'm just going to go and see what's keeping Malcolm," she said. She rushed down the steps, nearly knocking Malcolm over as he was coming up the path from the car park. "I left something in the car," she said loudly as she dragged Malcolm away.

"What can you tell me about those two?" Robert asked as he watched the pair walk back to their car.

"They complain a lot," Janet said, "to the point where they manage to get their meals and things for free. They've done their best to manipulate us into refunding their stay, but we've managed to stay one step ahead of them thus far. They're deeply unpleasant people and nothing would make me happier right now than if you arrested them both and took them away."

Robert chuckled. "I get the feeling you don't like them," he said. "But I can't arrest them without cause. I am going to see what I can find out about them, though. Give me their full names and where they've come from, please?"

Joan supplied the information while Janet watched the Armstrongs. They were standing together behind their car, clearly arguing.

"Should we keep them here if they decide to leave early?" Janet asked.

"No, let them go. I'll note their plate number when I leave. I'm sure I can find them again if I need to," Robert said.

Janet nodded. He walked down the steps and headed for his car. As he got closer to the Armstrongs, they quickly dashed towards Doveby House.

"How was your day?" Janet asked brightly as the pair nearly tripped over each other in their haste to get inside.

Malcolm pushed the door shut and then leaned against it. "It was fine," he said in a clipped voice. "Just fine." He glanced at his wife. "We need to go upstairs and finish our conversation," he said.

"Yes, let's," Judith agreed. The pair scurried up the stairs, leaving Janet and Joan behind.

"That was odd," Janet said after a moment.

"It was, indeed. I'd hate to think that we're harbouring criminals."

"Me, too, but I do like the idea of them leaving early," Janet said.

"I think I might just stay in here with a book," Joan told her sister. "I think the Armstrongs might be back down soon."

Janet agreed. She went and pulled a random title from the mystery section in the library and then settled on a couch in the sitting room. Only a short while later, the Armstrongs came down the stairs with their suitcases in hand.

"As we've been saying all along, Doveby Dale simply isn't for us," Judith said. "We'll be leaving now."

"I'll refund you for the nights you won't be staying," Joan said.

"No, no, that's okay," Malcolm told her. "We don't need a refund."

Janet's jaw dropped as the couple headed for the door.

"Here are the keys," Judith said, dropping them onto the table near the door. "Thank you for everything."

They were gone before either sister could do much more than get to their feet. Janet walked to the door and watched as they threw their suitcases into their boot and drove away.

"I'm going to ring Robert and tell him that they've gone," she told Joan. "They must be wanted for something, the way they rushed out of here."

Janet had to settle for leaving a message on Robert's voice mail.

"Is it just me, or does the house feel happier now that they've gone?" Janet asked her sister after she'd put the phone down.

"I'm sure it's just you," Joan replied.

Janet made a face at her and then went back to her book feeling a good deal happier with life.

Robert paid them a visit a few days later.

"Come in and have tea and biscuits," Joan invited the man.

"I will, if you can spare them," he replied.

"You know we always have tea and biscuits for you," Joan replied.

Janet filled a plate with several different types of the homemade biscuits that Joan had been busy baking over the last few days. Joan made the tea and then they all sat down together to talk.

"I've quite a few things to tell you, actually," Robert began. "Where should I start?"

"Start with Martin Lawley's farm," Janet suggested. "Is anyone trying to grow anything illegal there?"

"No, at least not as far as we can determine. After Nick and Jim were arrested, a specialist drug squad went over the entire farm, and they didn't find any evidence of anything drug related."

"But Nick and Jim were arrested? For what?" Janet asked.

"It seems they were part of a scheme to defraud Jasper Jones of a great deal of money," Robert replied. "Jasper's son, Joseph, was behind it all, but he was using the other two men to help."

"He was planning on stealing from his own father?" Janet said, in shock.

"According to him, he was simply trying to access his inheritance a little bit early," Robert replied. "The three of them were trying to find ways to sell many of Jasper's antiques and his coin collection."

"So the coins they showed William were stolen from Jasper?" Janet asked.

"It certainly seems that way. Jasper has a huge collection that he keeps in special trays. It seems that the two men simply grabbed a few coins from each tray without having any idea what they were taking."

"What would have happened when Jasper noticed?" Janet wondered.

"It's highly unlikely that he would have, actually. The coins are kept in a safe in a first-floor bedroom. Jasper can't easily climb stairs anymore, so they probably could have cleared out the safe over time without Jasper ever realising."

"And were they going to do the same thing to Martin?" Joan asked.

"We aren't sure what their plans were. We do know that they've been working their way around the country, doing a variety of unscrupulous things to enrich themselves at the expense of other, often vulnerable people."

Janet sighed. "How can people behave in that way?"

"Most of the victims were formerly involved with Nick's mother," Robert said. "Nick has a long list of stepfathers, although we don't think most of his mother's marriages were legal ones. In one place, he and his friends managed to sell off entire rooms of antique furniture from upstairs rooms that the owner could no longer visit. In another, they helped themselves to a collection of old snuff boxes that were stored in a crawl space under the house. The owner had nearly forgotten that he had the collection. Apparently he'd inherited it from his own father and had never given it much thought. Nick, or one of his friends, found it and sold it all for a great deal of money."

"I hope you can lock them all up for the rest of their lives," Janet said.

"We may be able to do something like that, anyway," Robert chuckled. "Joseph was quite upset that Jim had pocketed a few of his father's coins. Apparently, everything they stole from Jasper was meant to go to Joseph alone since it was his father they were stealing from. Once Joseph found out that Jim had been helping himself to coins, he decided to tell us everything he knew about Jim's part in the schemes. Once Jim found out that Joseph was talking, he started doing the same. When Nick heard that the other two were talking, he gave us his version of events. We now have a long list of cases to investigate and a whole plethora of charges we can make against all three men."

"That is good news," Janet said. "I hope Martin isn't too upset about everything that's happened."

"I talked to him yesterday and he seems to be taking everything in his stride. He didn't seem terribly surprised by what I told him. I believe he was also happy to have Nick and Jim out of his house."

"I must pay him another visit," Janet said.

"Stuart said the same thing when I talked to him about everything," Robert told her.

"But what about the Armstrongs?" Janet asked. "Why did she look familiar to you and why did they rush off once they'd met you?"

Robert shrugged. "I worked out why she looked familiar later that night." He named a popular soap opera. "I'm embarrassed to admit that I watch it, but it's usually on when I get home from work at night, so I watch while I eat my dinner. Anyway, if you've ever seen it, there's a minor character who I think looks a lot like Judith Armstrong."

Janet thought for a minute. "The woman who lives next door to the loud-mouthed blonde?" she asked. "Now that you mention it, there is a resemblance."

"I'm pretty sure that's why she looked familiar to me," Robert said. "Why she and her husband rushed away after meeting me, I can't tell you."

"Maybe they were afraid that one of the local businesses complained about their behaviour," Janet said. "I know they demanded free meals just about everywhere they went. Perhaps they suddenly realised that what they were doing was bordering on fraud?" She told Robert about the sausage they'd hidden in the wardrobe and the missing thermostat knob.

He nodded. "It's one thing to complain about a bad meal and hope to get it taken off your bill, but those sorts of things are getting dangerously close to criminal. Let's hope they learned a lesson from their stay here and that they will mend their ways."

"I'm just glad they're gone. If they ever try to book again, we'll be full," Joan said firmly.

Robert ate a few more biscuits while the trio talked about people and why they treated other people so badly. When he was done, the sisters walked him to the door.

"Thank you for your help in stopping Nick and his friends," Robert said to Janet. "Jasper might not be my favourite person, but I'd hate to see him cheated by his own son."

Janet watched as Robert walked down to his car. She didn't understand how people could deliberately cheat one another, but she had a bigger worry on her mind. Why hadn't Aggie reacted to Nick's name in the same way she had to Jim's and Joseph's?

"We need to have a chat," she told Aggie a short while later.

Aggie, who was stretched out on Janet's bed, simply opened one eye and then squeezed it shut again.

I still don't know exactly what Stuart overheard at the garden centre, but at least, thanks to his (somewhat misplaced) concerns, three criminals are behind bars. As I've still not been able to reach Gretchen Falkirk, I've been back to visit Martin again. He couldn't tell me any more about Alberta, but he did share some history of Doveby Dale that was fascinating. I've taken to calling the entire thing "The Lawley Case" in his honour.

I wish I knew why Aggie got this one so wrong, but she refuses to discuss the matter. I shall be more careful, going forward, when discussing cases with her, I suppose.

We still have no idea what scared away the Armstrongs, but Joan and I are both glad they went. Joan insisted on giving some of the money that they overpaid us to Todd and Ted to cover for the meal that they managed to get for free from them. We would probably do the same for the restaurant in Derby if we had any idea which restaurant it was, but there are simply too many possibilities.

Joan and I are delighted that you are thinking of visiting us later this year. Just let us know when you are coming and we'll cancel any guests we may have scheduled. It would be especially nice if Doona could come with you. Joan and I would both enjoy seeing her again. Do let us know your plans.

All my very best wishes,

Janet and Aggie

Glossary of Terms

- **bin** — trash can
- **biscuits** — cookies
- **booking** — reservation
- **boot** — trunk (of a car)
- **car park** — parking lot
- **chemist** — pharmacist
- **chips** — French fries
- **cuppa** — cup of tea (informal)
- **fizzy drink** — carbonated beverage (pop or soda)
- **fortnight** — two weeks
- **glove box** — glove compartment
- **holiday** — vacation
- **lie in** — sleep late
- **midday** — noon
- **pavement** — sidewalk
- **pudding** — dessert
- **saloon car** — sedan
- **shopping trolley** — shopping cart
- **telly** — television

- **till** — checkout (in a grocery store, for example)
- **torch** — flashlight

Other Notes

In the UK, dates are written day, month, year rather than month, day, year as in the US. (May 5, 2015 would be written 5 May 2015, for example.)

In the UK, when describing property with more than one level, the lowest level (assuming there is no basement; very few UK houses have basements) is the "ground floor," and the next floor up is the "first floor" and so on. In the US, the lowest floor is usually the "first floor" and up from there.

When telling time, half six is the English equivalent of six-thirty.

A "full English breakfast" generally consists of bacon, sausage, eggs, grilled or fried tomatoes, fried potatoes, fried mushrooms and baked beans served with toast.

A semi-detached house is one that is joined to another house by a common center wall. In the US they are generally called duplexes. In the UK the two properties would be sold individually as totally separate entities. A "terraced" house is one in a row of properties, where each unit is sold individually (usually called a row house in the US).

Acknowledgments

Thank you, readers, for continuing on this journey with me.

Thanks to my wonderful editor, Denise, for still putting up with me even after all these books.

And thanks to my beta reading team – your help is greatly appreciated.

The Moody Case

RELEASE DATE: JUNE 15, 2018

Janet and Joan Markham are on a routine trip to the supermarket when their car gets hit from behind. When the man who hit them doesn't want to provide his name or insurance details, Janet rings her friend, Constable Robert Parsons. Robert fills out an accident report and that should be the end of that.

Meanwhile, the sisters have two single men as guests at their bed and breakfast. The guests don't appear to know one another, but they share a few peculiarities. The one that bothers Joan is that neither of them ever wants any breakfast.

While their car is being repaired, Janet borrows a sporty red coupe from the local garage. She loves driving it, but when she gets stuck in heavy traffic as the result of an accident, she's shocked to discover that one of their guests is involved. A few days later a second accident, this time involving their other guest, leaves Janet wondering if there might be something criminal going on.

Can Janet work out what's really going on? Neither guest is talking. More importantly, can Janet find a way to convince Joan to let her buy the little red car?

Also by Diana Xarissa

The Isle of Man Cozy Mystery Series

Aunt Bessie Assumes

Aunt Bessie Believes

Aunt Bessie Considers

Aunt Bessie Decides

Aunt Bessie Enjoys

Aunt Bessie Finds

Aunt Bessie Goes

Aunt Bessie's Holiday

Aunt Bessie Invites

Aunt Bessie Joins

Aunt Bessie Knows

Aunt Bessie Likes

Aunt Bessie Meets

Aunt Bessie Needs

Aunt Bessie Observes

Aunt Bessie Provides

Aunt Bessie Questions

Aunt Bessie Remembers

The Isle of Man Ghostly Cozy Mysteries

Arrivals and Arrests

Boats and Bad Guys

Cars and Cold Cases

Dogs and Danger

Encounters and Enemies

Friends and Frauds

Guests and Guilt

The Markham Sisters Cozy Mystery Novellas

The Appleton Case

The Bennett Case

The Chalmers Case

The Donaldson Case

The Ellsworth Case

The Fenton Case

The Green Case

The Hampton Case

The Irwin Case

The Jackson Case

The Kingston Case

The Lawley Case

The Moody Case

The Isle of Man Romance Series

Island Escape

Island Inheritance

Island Heritage

Island Christmas

About the Author

Diana grew up in Northwestern Pennsylvania and moved to Washington, DC after college. There she met a wonderful Englishman who was visiting the city. After a whirlwind romance, they got married and Diana moved to the Chesterfield area of Derbyshire to begin a new life with her husband. A short while later, they relocated to the Isle of Man.

After over ten years on the island, it was time for a change. With their two children in tow, Diana and her husband moved to suburbs of Buffalo, New York. Diana now spends her days writing about the island she loves.

She also writes mystery/thrillers set in the not-too-distant future as Diana X. Dunn and middle grade and YA books as D.X. Dunn.

Diana is always happy to hear from readers. You can write to her at:

Diana Xarissa Dunn
PO Box 72
Clarence, NY 14031.

Find Diana at:
www.dianaxarissa.com
diana@dianaxarissa.com

Made in the USA
Columbia, SC
30 December 2020

30052571R00213